Dear Romance Reader:

This year Avon Books is celebrating the sixth anniversary of "The Avon Romance"—six years of historical romances of the highest quality by both new and established writers. Thanks to our terrific authors, our "ribbon books" are stronger and more exciting than ever before. And thanks to you, our loyal readers, our books continue to be a spectacular success!

"The Avon Romances" are just some of the fabulous novels in Avon Books' dazzling *Year of Romance*, bringing you month after month of top-notch romantic entertainment. How wonderful it is to escape for a few hours with romances by your favorite "leading ladies"—Shirlee Busbee, Karen Robards, and Johanna Lindsey. And how satisfying it is to discover in a new writer the talent that will make her a rising star.

Every month in 1988, Avon Books' *Year of Romance*, will be special because Avon Books believes that romance—the readers, the writers, and the books—deserves it!

Sweet Reading,

Susanne Jaffe
Editor-in-Chief

Ellen Edwards
Senior Editor

WINDSONG

JUDITH E. FRENCH

AVON BOOKS ◆ NEW YORK

AVON BOOKS
A division of
The Hearst Corporation
105 Madison Avenue
New York, New York 10016

First Avon Books Printing: December 1988

For my very special friends
in R.W.A.
who make it all possible—
thank you

Prologue

Connemara, Ireland
May 10, 1743

Rolling clouds covered the moon, plunging the rocky path into inky blackness. Instinctively, Linna O'Neill slowed her step, feeling her way with callused bare feet and beginning to hum a tune to hold back her shapeless fears of what loomed behind her in the darkness. The sound of her own voice was worse than the silence, and she broke off in mid-syllable, mentally chiding herself for her foolishness.

From somewhere far off, a dog howled, and she shivered, clutching her thin, bruised arms against her chest. A howling dog was bad luck, maybe even a sign that someone had died. She licked her dry lips and tried to whistle, but nothing came out. She had forgotten the basket; that was bad luck enough for one night. Gill would whop her certain if he found out. She would have to run back tomorrow and fetch it. It was too late now; she'd already come two-thirds of the way from Maggie O'Shaughnessy's cottage, and her knee hurt from where she'd slid and struck a rock coming down the hill.

1

Not that she minded carrying the eggs and the honey to the old woman. Maggie had always been good to her, even offering her a bit of the precious sweet on fresh-baked bread. Blessed Mary in heaven! She'd never tasted anything so wonderful. She could have eaten the whole loaf without a crumb left over for the chickens. That and the buttermilk Maggie had insisted she drink with the bread were all she'd had since breakfast. She'd missed the evening meal and there'd been nothing for any of them at noon. Damn Gill Flynn for his pinching ways! Most days, her stepfather took his nooning in the castle kitchen. Little he cared if they went hungry, even Mam—and her growing large with child again.

A sharp rock sliced the center of Linna's big toe and she winced in pain, sinking down to cradle her foot in her hands. Gingerly, she touched the cut, feeling the sticky wetness that oozed between her fingers. It smarted something awful, but she wouldn't give in to tears. She'd be eleven on her next Saint's Day, too big to cry over a little hurt like a baby. Her stepfather had given her lumps far worse than this and hard words to wash them down with, too.

The loud crack of gunshots echoed across the valley and the pain of her injury was forgotten as she leaped to her feet and raced for an outcrop of rocks that provided the nearest shelter. Another shot rang out as she scrambled up the ridge and threw herself facedown behind a boulder, heart pounding. She lay there almost too frightened to breathe for a long time, and then just as she gathered the courage to rise, she heard the unmistakable sound of a galloping horse.

Cautiously, Linna peered around the boulder to see

a lone rider silhouetted against the dark shadows of the ridge by a ghostly sliver of moonlight. Was the man wearing a uniform? "Old Scat take him if he's a soldier," she swore under her breath. The English soldiers had brought nothing but pain and sorrow to Ireland since the time of Oliver Cromwell. She'd seen men hanged with her own eyes, and had felt the blow of an English fist when she didn't get out of the road fast enough. If the rider was English, she hoped he'd fall and break his Sassenach neck!

As if in answer to her prayer, the horse stumbled and the rider pitched over the animal's neck to fall full-length on the ground. "Holy Mary, forgive me," Linna cried, clapping a hand over her mouth. Another shiver passed through her. The man lay without moving. Was it murder she'd done? Would her soul go to hell for wishing a man to his death?

The horse slowed and then stopped, looking back at the man on the ground. The animal was breathing hard; foam dripped from his mouth and his dark sides were streaked with sweat. "Poor thing," Linna murmured. "You've been run near to death." She strained her eyes to see the man. If he was dead, he couldn't hurt her. The horse was frightened. "Whoa," Linna called softly. "Whoa. Don't be afraid."

Nervously, Linna chewed her lip. Suppose the man wasn't a Sassenach? The horseman could have been anyone, even Sir Edmond. What if it was someone running away from the English soldiers? Trembling, Linna crept from her hiding place. It could do no harm to go and see if he was dead. If he was alive, and he wasn't an enemy soldier, maybe she could do something to help him.

The horse raised his head and whinnied at her. Linna froze, every muscle tensed to flee. There was no sound but the heavy breathing of the animal and the ever-present whisper of the Connemara wind. Step by step, she made her way closer to the prone body on the ground until at last she stood over him.

"Sir," she ventured timidly. He wore no uniform. His clothes were those of a gentleman, his leather boots worth more than a cottier would see from a year's labor in the fields. "Sir, are you dead?" She spoke in Gaelic; her English was none too good, although she could make do in a pinch. The man was bareheaded and his crow-black hair was cut longer than that of the soldiers she had seen. Linna bent and touched his shoulder, drawing back with a gasp when she found the rich cloth wet with blood. She struggled to roll him over onto his back.

"By Our Lady!" she swore softly. The stranger was a young man with a face as smooth and unlined as an angel. "You be little more than a lad yourself." Linna caught her breath as the fickle moonlight showed a ragged hole in his shoulder. "You've been shot." Relief flooded through her. If he was dead, it was none of her doing. She laid her hand on his lips and was rewarded with a faint hint of breath. "And not even dead at all," she assured herself.

She supposed the thing to do was to run home and tell her stepfather. He'd go to the bailiff and someone would come and fetch the wounded man. But that someone would likely be the soldiers, and if he wasn't a soldier, God strike her dead if he wasn't running from them.

Rapparees hid in the hills and harried the English soldiers, stealing their horses and supplies and burning their camps. Men whose land and homes had been confiscated by English justice had nothing more to lose. Most Irishmen would help them if they could, pretending to know nothing, secretly glad to see someone getting the best of the bastard English.

Was this man a rapparee? He'd get short shrift from Sir Edmond if he was. The lord, Sir Edmond Beatty, was Irish, but his family had betrayed their religion, and their people had become more English than the English. There'd be no sympathy from him for an outlaw. He'd be turned over to the soldiers quicker than you could say a Hail Mary.

Linna looked from the horse to the man, unsure what to do. She didn't know how to stop a man from bleeding to death, or how to help him escape, but there were people who did. Maggie O'Shaughnessy would know. People said her son Stephen was with the rapparees. If Linna could just hide the stranger someplace until she could talk to Maggie . . .

Linna's eyes widened as she spied a flintlock pistol lying on the ground. Even a child knew it was illegal for an Irishman to carry a weapon. Gingerly, she picked it up and held the gun at arm's length. If he was English, she was in a lot of trouble, but if he was Irish . . . Her throat tightened. She wouldn't be the first child to hang in Connemara. If the soldiers caught them, they'd both swing from a gibbet and birds would peck the flesh from their bones.

The remains of a hanged man still dangled from a tree at the crossroads. The sight had given her nightmares until Father Joseph had assured her the dead man's soul was safe in heaven. "Pray for him, but don't let it bring you terror, little Mary Aislinn." Father Joseph was the only one who ever called her by her whole name, and it always made her feel grown up and important.

It was Father Joseph who had told her that her name was the same as that of Sir Edmond's daughter, and that it was an old and proud name in Ireland. ''Brave and noble women have borne that name, Mary Aislinn. Be faithful and obedient and it may bring you God's blessing.''

So far the name had brought her nothing but taunts. There were many who thought it too fine by far for Finola O'Neill's bastard daughter, and the first of these were her stepfather, Gill, and his son Sean. When Gill was in his cups, it made sense to find a dark corner to hide in, or even better to take refuge behind the cow. Gill was none too steady on his feet when he was drunk and too lazy to chase her down when he wasn't. Sean, at fifteen and fair on to be a giant when he reached his full growth, was far worse. Liquor only made Sean more dangerous. He'd hated her ever since she was a babe; why she couldn't fathom. And Father Joseph or not, she hated Sean back with a passion greater than anything else in her life.

Linna pushed at the prone figure again with her bare foot. Was she willing to risk a beating or worse to help him? Father Joseph's advice sounded good when he gave it, but being obedient had never saved her any bruises that she knew of. She tugged at the sticky end of a pigtail. Who or what was she to be obedient to? Her stepfather? The authorities? The Church?

Linna chewed the inside of her bottom lip. *Brave and noble women . . . ,* Father Joseph had said. It would be a brave thing to help a wounded rapparee, wouldn't it? It might even make her a heroine, like Saint Edana in the stories. A chilling thought knifed through her. Saints usually died a horrible, bloody death. Linna sighed; she didn't think she wanted to die painfully just yet, not even for the promise of heaven above.

The man groaned and Linna jumped back. Moonlight played across his pain-etched features as his eyelids flickered open. "Help me," he murmured, struggling to raise himself on one elbow. "Or if you cannot . . . fetch me my pistol so that I can give Georgie's boys a warm welcome when they come for me."

Linna dropped to her knees as her eyes met his. The young rapparee's voice was hoarse and strained, but it touched a chord within her. She caught his big hand in her small chapped one and squeezed it tight. "I'll help ye," she promised fiercely. "As God is my witness, the Sassenach shall not have ye!"

Chapter 1

*Accept the things
to which fate binds
you. And love the
people with whom
fate brings you
together, but do so
with all your heart.*

—Marcus Aurelius

*Connemara, Ireland
December 1753*

"I won't marry him! I won't!"

Linna shuddered as her half sister's anguished screams echoed down the gray stone corridors and marble staircase of Mount Beatty. The heavy door crashed open and the draft caught the pale yellow candle flame, nearly plunging the damp, shadowy chamber into darkness. Linna's needlework tumbled to the floor as she sprang to her feet and gave a deep curtsy. "My lady."

"Go to her, Linna," Lady Maeve ordered. "You're

8

the only one who can calm her when she's in such a state. If she doesn't stop her hysterics, she'll have another . . ." She trailed off, unwilling to admit, even to Linna, that her only daughter was subject to attacks of the falling sickness.

"I'll do what I can, my lady," Linna said, hastily gathering up the tangled length of lace. "I tried to get her to eat a little oat porridge with milk, but she'd have none of it."

Lady Maeve went to the open stone hearth and held out her thin fingers to the fire. "This place is as cold as the grave," she complained. After a quarter century in Connemara she still missed the gentle breezes of Killarney. She turned abruptly back toward Linna. "Stop staring at me with those calf eyes! This marriage is not of my making. You, above all, should know that. Do you think if I had any choice I'd break my vow to the Holy Mother? Send a sickly girl to the wilderness of the American Colonies to wed a wanted man?"

"No, my lady," Linna replied softly. Her eyes smarted with unshed tears. No use to cry over what couldn't be helped. Ten years of life in the manor house hadn't wiped away the hard lessons of her childhood. Still, the unfairness of it all tore at her insides. Mary Aislinn wanted so desperately to give her life to God. She had planned on entering a convent since they were children.

Selfishness battled with genuine concern for her gently born half sister. It was Mary Aislinn who had found Linna—a ragged, half-wild urchin—and taken pity on her. Although it would be years before Mary Aislinn realized that she and Linna had the same father, Mary Aislinn had brought her to Lady Maeve and demanded that her mother let Linna stay in the big house as a servant-companion. Linna knew what her life would have been if she'd stayed in the village; she owed Mary Aislinn a debt that could never be repaid.

Still . . . Try as she might, Linna couldn't stifle a ripple of inner joy. If Mary Aislinn didn't enter the convent, she wouldn't have to, either. They would go to the Maryland Colony together. Even life among the savages was better than being walled up in a prison of stone, or—Linna swallowed hard—returning to her stepfather's cottage as another unwanted mouth to feed.

"Her father has signed the betrothal agreement," Lady Maeve said flatly. "Even now the bridegroom dismounts in the courtyard. You must convince her to be reasonable." She straightened her shoulders, knotting her hands together. "Sir Edmond will be furious if there's a scene in front of Master Desmond."

Linna's dark eyes widened in astonishment. "Pardon me, my lady, but I thought she was marrying—"

"He's using another name, but Mary Aislinn is marrying a Desmond. Say nothing unless you'd witness a hanging instead of a wedding. There's still a price on Rory Desmond's life, and I cannot see for the life of me why Sir Edmond insisted on his coming to Mount Beatty for the ceremony." The older woman drew her lips into a hard line. Lady Maeve was fond of Linna, despite her birth, and usually of a kind nature. The drawn features and shrill tone were evidence of her unhappiness and fear for her daughter's future. "If you didn't know the true identity of the bridegroom," Lady Maeve continued bitterly, "you're the only one on the manor. It's common knowledge in the kitchen. My husband's man has a loose tongue. Were he *my* servant, I'd have had him whipped from the county long ago."

"I knew of a Rory Desmond once," Linna dared. "A long time ago." The rapparee she had rescued that dark night bore the name Rory Desmond.

"What is that romantic ditty they sing in the bailey? 'The Brave Young Rapparee.' How does it go?" Lady Maeve mimicked.

> *"They shot him down on the cold, cold ground,*
> *That brave young rapparee.*
> *They shot him down on the cold, cold ground,*
> *And the stones they wept to see."*

Linna nodded, her eyes on the floor. "Aye, my lady," she admitted. She knew the tune well and it had often brought tears to her eyes.

Lady Maeve sniffed haughtily. "The hero of the song and our Colonial bridegroom are one and the same. But clear your head of romantic nonsense. Truth is somewhat harsher. We will be lucky if he isn't foul-mannered and hunchbacked." She sighed loudly. "Now go at once and prepare Mary Aislinn to welcome Master Desmond. I will go down to greet him and make excuses for her delay."

"Yes, my lady." Linna curtsied again and hurried from the room. If she knew Mary Aislinn, it would take more than urging to get her to go down and meet her husband-to-be. It would take four strong guardsmen and a thick cloth to gag her. Mild-mannered she might be, but once her head was set on a thing, wild horses couldn't tear her from it.

The empty hallway was unlit and she had no candle,

but Linna knew the way by heart. She shared none of the superstitions that kept the maids in terror of this passageway after dark. If ghosts walked Mount Beatty, they had no power to harm the living. What troubled Linna was the man in the courtyard claiming to be Rory Desmond.

On impulse she gathered her heavy skirts and darted down a narrow corridor and into an empty chamber. Pushing open a casement window and ignoring the blast of bone-chilling wind, Linna leaned out as far as she could, peering into the swirling mists below. Bobbing torches showed little but the milling forms of men and stamping horses. Whinnies and shouts drifted upward, distorted by the thick mist. Linna shivered as she slid from the wide sill and pulled the window shut. It was impossible to distinguish familiar faces and voices from those of the strangers.

Feeling foolish, Linna retraced her steps, making her way through the darkness to the main corridor and then continuing down a flight of stairs to Mary Aislinn's chambers. She heard her half sister's sobbing through the paneled door.

Mary Aislinn's bedchamber was warm, heated by a roaring fire and insulated from the chill by wall hangings and thick carpets. A small maid bobbed a halfhearted curtsy and scurried out of the room. Linna paused and looked around, never ceasing to be astonished at the waste of so many beeswax candles burning at once. "Mary, what are we to do with you?" she demanded.

Her half sister crouched in the center of her poster bed with her knees drawn up and her long red hair—the exact coppery-gold shade as Linna's—strewn about her shoulders and face like a mantle. Mary's green eyes were swollen and red with weeping, her nose was running, and her cheeks bore long scratches from her own nails. "I . . . I won't do it," Mary wailed. Even her voice was hoarse and distorted from her tantrum. "You promised me you'd think of something. You promised!" she accused. "I can't marry him. I'd rather die!"

"Atcch, Mary," Linna soothed, coming to the bed and sitting on the edge of it. "Calm yourself, do. Would you bring on one of your spells? You know how terrible you feel afterward." She placed a hand on Mary's shoulder. "Father Joseph—"

"I don't care what Father Joseph says! I don't care if I do have a spell. I wish I would, right in front of him. He'd not want me to wife then, would he?" She threw herself backward against the heaped pillows and covered her face with her beringed hands. Linna saw that Mary's nails were bitten off raggedly, something she had not done in years.

"How do you know that this is not God's will?"

"It's not! It can't be. The Blessed Virgin came to me in a dream and told me to serve her. You know that! This is naught but Papa's doing. He thinks to turn me from my faith by this marriage, but I won't go through with it."

"Your lady mother says the contract is signed. You cannot defy Sir Edmond."

"Can't I?" Mary raised her head, revealing an unnatural fierceness in her bloodshot eyes. "They'll have to drag me bound and kicking to the altar. What can he do to me? Beat me? Lock me in the dungeon?" Her face took on a feral cunning. "With my poor health, do you think Papa could bear it as long as I?" She shook her head. "Thomas may be his favorite, but he cares for me. I know he does! He'd not be the cause of my death.''

Linna ignored the truth of her statement. ''Lady Maeve says that his name is really Rory Desmond. If he is the man I once knew, he's handsome beyond belief, Mary. And a great hero of the people.'' She struggled to keep her tone light as an inner voice protested, *It can't be him. Not now—not after so long.* Rory Desmond—the man of her dreams—was naught but a fairy tale, a foolish young girl's fantasy.

''Rebel or Sassenach, it's all the same to me,'' Mary Aislinn said. ''I'll be the bride of Christ or no bride at all.''

For more than an hour Linna pleaded futilely with her to at least go down and meet her intended, but Mary remained stubbornly insistent that she would not even speak to him. She reluctantly allowed Linna to brush the tangles from her hair, braid it, and wrap the braids around her head in a coronet. Nothing could be done for the swollen eyes and tearstained face other than to apply cold water. Mary Aislinn refused to allow Linna to dust her face with fine powder or to add color to her cheeks.

''You look like a corpse,'' Linna said.

''So much the better. If Father comes to drag me from my chambers, it will give him second thought.'' Mary picked up the tiny silver-framed hand mirror and pouted into it. ''You know I care nothing for my looks. You're the vain one. A holy sister must be concerned with inner beauty, not with—'' A knock on the door brought them both upright.

Linna caught her breath and glanced toward the doorway with trepidation, then sighed with relief as Mab's familiar features materialized out of the gloom of the corridor. "Mab," she cried. " 'Tis only you. We thought it might be—"

"The master?" Mab grunted her disapproval of the whole affair as she closed the door firmly behind her and hurried to the bed. "And well for the pair of ye it isn't!" She pursed her lips and folded her arms over her chest. "What can ye be thinking of?" she demanded. "To make Master Des—" A wave of purple crossed the pocked face. "Your bridegroom stood in the great hall like an unwelcome visitor," she finished.

Mab had been Mary Aislinn's nurse and Lady Maeve's before that. Now that her charge was too old for a nurse, she acted as maid and chaperon. But her former position gave her privileges that only death would take from her. Mab had no awe of her young mistress and would chastise her when she saw fit. "For shame, Mary!" She turned accusing eyes on Linna. "And ye, child. Did ye not try to sway her from this stubborn willfulness?"

Linna dropped her eyes. Mab was not truly angry with her. She knew Mary Aislinn's tempers as well as any.

"I won't meet him, and I won't marry! They can't force me," Mary repeated. "Father—"

"The master is not here, thank the Blessed Mother," Mab snapped. "There was a fire on his Yorkshire estate and he stayed to note the damage. Your lady mother was forced to deal with your betrothed alone. And the Colonial's some put out. I can tell ye."

"What did Mother say to him?" Mary bit her thumbnail.

"She told him ye were ill. He's gone to his room, pleading fatigue, but a swaddled babe could see his anger. Ye're beginning your marriage on the wrong note, me girl. A new husband must be cosseted. He expects shy smiles and blushing obedience."

"He's not my husband."

"Have you seen him, Mab?" Linna asked. "Is he a big man with hair like a crow's wing? Is he handsome?"

"Hush, Linna. What talk is that? Show some respect for your new master," Mab said. "Have I not taught ye better?"

Linna murmured a subdued reply. Mab was as upset by the turmoil as they all were. Linna had no wish to trouble her further. Mab had been good to her since she came to live at Mount Beatty, making certain that she received fair treatment from the servants and never failing to open her strong arms when Linna needed comfort. Mab had made no bones of the affection she felt for Linna, an affection she couldn't always manage for Mary Aislinn.

"He is lodged in the green room," Mab continued. "And Lady Maeve has retired for the night. In the morning, she expects ye to greet him proper and to apologize for your being sick tonight."

"My head hurts," Mary Aislinn complained.

"Will you stay with her, Mab?" Linna asked, feigning a yawn. "It's been a long day and—"

"Go along with ye. Of course I'll stay with her. Ye need your sleep, too. But"—Mab frowned—"the mistress has asked that ye take your breakfast in the kitchen, Linna. To avoid unpleasant questions."

"But Linna always dines with us," Mary protested.

"It doesn't matter," Linna soothed. "Sleep well, Mary. And you too, Mab." Averting her eyes, she hurried from the chamber. She would not wait until morning to see this Rory Desmond. She would see him tonight. If he was an impostor, she would expose him before Lady Maeve and if he wasn't . . . Her breath caught in her throat and she quickened her step down the darkened hallway. *If it is my Rory Desmond* . . . "No," she murmured and shook her head. She would not worry yet. If it was true, something would come to her—it always did.

The great case clock on the stair landing had struck eleven when Linna scratched apprehensively on the green room door. This section of the manor was cold and damp; by daylight one could see the stones weep moisture. 'Twas said that it was ancient before Cromwell set foot on Irish soil, that holy monks had once trod these stones. Linna had never believed in ghosts, but sometimes she felt an unexplained presence and found it oddly comforting.

Her trembling was not from the bitterness of the Connemara winter, but rather an exhilaration for the ploy she was about to attempt. If she were found out, Lady Maeve would be furious. As for her father, Sir Edmond . . . Linna pushed him from her mind. The master was far away in Yorkshire in England. No matter how angry Lady Maeve had become with Linna for her wayward adventures in the past, she had always sheltered her from the master's disapproval. Linna hoped this would be no exception. Boldly, she knocked and was rewarded by a man's irritated reply.

"Aye? What is it?"

Linna pushed open the door and shuffled head down into the dimly lit room with her bundle of peat for the fire. From Mab's room, she had borrowed a patched skirt and a large white apron. Wooden clogs covered her feet and she had pulled several pairs of homespun stockings over her legs to thicken them and keep the shoes from sliding off. A great cap covered her hair and hung down over her neck and ears, the limp ruffle lying flat against the cook's woolen shawl that usually hung by the kitchen door.

The shawl had once been thick and warm, the strands of wool closely knit, the very color of the coarse sand that pooled between the rocks on the isles of Aran. But that had been three generations ago and the shawl was fit now only for a kitchen wench to wrap about her shoulders when she ventured out to throw slops. Still, the ragged garment was ample enough to cover Linna's arms and the great hump of a feather pillow she had stuffed between her shoulder blades.

Linna had smeared her face and hands with soot. A great streak of goose grease and ashes marred one cheek, and she had hung Bridget's charm of garlic and herbs about her neck, knowing the strong smell would make the Colonial keep his distance.

"There's fuel here aplenty, old woman. Go about your business and leave me in peace."

She continued across the room as though she had not heard him, dragging one foot as she walked and taking care to keep bent over so that the candlelight would not reveal her features. In the village was a woman born deaf who had never learned to speak as others did. It was her monotone mumble that Linna affected, answering the man with an incomprehensible string of garble and waving in the general direction of the stone hearth.

"Begone, I say." The command was firm but not harsh and spoken in a low, rich timbre.

The voice was deeper than she remembered, and Linna was certain she had never heard anyone with such an accent. The tang of Connemara rang true in the Colonial's speech, but it was tempered by a soft, lazy slur. Dumbly, she shook her head and pointed once more to the fire.

"Ah, go on with ye then," he said. "But be quick about it. I'd have some sleep this night."

Linna dropped her bundle of peat before the hearth and lowered herself stiffly to her knees. Every summer there were mummers at the Tinkers' Fair, and she and Mary Aislinn had delighted in their playacting. One man especially had the knack of making himself into an old woman, a fat priest, or even a soldier, using only a bit of cloth and a horsehair wig. She and Mary Aislinn had often imitated the tinker, giving their own performances for a laughing Mab and whatever maid could be snatched from her duties to act as audience. Now, that skill for mimicry was put to good use as Linna employed every part of her body and every cautious movement to become the old deaf woman.

The Colonial turned his back and for the first time, Linna dared to raise her eyes from the floor. Through lowered lashes she peered warily in his direction. Shining black leather boots reached almost to his knees, and above that a band of white stocking gave way to sky-blue breeches filled by muscular thighs. Linna caught her breath. The man was undressing!

She was no stranger to a man's naked body. No girl-child could live nine to a one-room cottage and fail to see more than she should. Linna had witnessed her stepfather and her stepbrother in the altogether time and time again. But neither of them had ever looked like this.

The Colonial's tight-fitting breeches seemed molded to the curves of his hips and buttocks, nipping in to encompass a waist surprisingly narrow in a man so big. Above the breeches, he wore nothing.

Unknowingly, Linna licked at her dry upper lip with the tip of her tongue. A delicious warmth crept up through her midsection as she stared at her sister's betrothed. She had never seen a man so beautiful or so clean. Sinew and muscle rippled beneath the broad expanse of bronzed back and well-built shoulders. Linna's eyes widened in admiration as he turned to lay his shirt across a chair and she caught a glimpse of the brawny bulge of one upper arm.

The back of his sturdy neck was almost hidden by a queue of thick dark hair. Linna swallowed hard. Not only did the Colonial wear his own hair, rather than a wig, but his hair was as clean and shiny as . . . as a crow's wing. Was this really Rory Desmond? Could it be?

She remembered him as a big man, but surely not this big. She had dragged him a long way to hide him in the rocks. Linna had been strong, even as a child, her muscles used to hard work and heavy lifting. But surely she would have remembered such rock-hard thews. And—she dropped her gaze a few inches—the Rory Desmond she knew had had no scar running down his back. This scar was old and long healed, four pale ribbons of white against the man's tanned skin. Something or someone had hurt him badly. She shuddered to think of the pain he must have suffered with such an injury.

Without warning, the man turned toward her, and for a long heartbeat, Linna clamped her dirty hands over her mouth and stared into his face. He was older than the young rapparee she had tended; his countenance was stamped with the mark of one who had witnessed much of life. His skin was tanned and his features weathered, but the wide brown eyes beneath those craggy brows were the same. He was her Rory Desmond—she would pledge her immortal soul on it!

Her staring caught his attention and he glanced down at her. She dropped her head and fumbled with the pile of fuel. "What's wrong with ye, old woman?" he demanded. "Ye look as though ye've seen a banshee."

Linna mumbled something, groaned, and covered her face with her hands. Still grumbling nonsense, she rose and hobbled toward the door.

"Wait," Desmond called. "There's a question I would have answered. The young mistress, Mary Aislinn, is she—"

Ignoring him as though the room were empty, Linna continued through the open doorway and shuffled into the corridor.

Exasperated, he followed her to the door and watched as she made her way into the gloomy darkness. "Like as not you're a specter yourself," he said wryly.

Linna stifled a chuckle, hardly daring to breathe until she had turned down one narrow hallway and then another, twisting and turning through the great stone house until she was certain he couldn't be following her. An idea flickered to life in the back of her mind, an idea so preposterous that it caused a tingling in her fingers and toes and made her struggle for breath.

Folding her arms over her chest, she leaned back against the wall and sank down to the stone floor. Holy Mother in heaven! Did she dare to suggest such a thing? Did she dare to go through with it if they agreed?

The cold stone bit into her back and she raised a damp hand to her cheek. She was certain that the sisters at the convent would be kind to her if she went to France with Mary Aislinn. Her days would be filled with hard work, and prayer, and peace. She would never have to worry about going hungry again or being beaten. There would be no more hiding from *gentlemen* who thought any serving wench was fair game for their lewd pleasures.

But if she followed Mary into the convent, she would be giving up the world as surely as if she had become a member of the enclosed order herself. There would be no more headlong gallops across rocky fields on horseback and no more climbing trees to reach the shiniest apple on the top branch. She'd never again throw off her clothes to splash naked in Galway Bay or rise at dawn to walk barefoot through the woods.

Resolutely, she got to her feet and retraced her path to Mab's room. Taking off the grotesque costume, she scrubbed away the soot and smell with cold water and lye soap, then donned her own garments. Without bothering to light a candle, she hurried, heart in her throat, back to Mary Aislinn's chambers.

She swung open the door to see Lady Maeve in her dressing gown beside Mary's bed. "My lady!" Linna cried, dropping a quick curtsy.

Mary Aislinn sat up and sniffed. Obviously, she had been creating another disturbance, but Linna didn't believe she'd had a spell. Her face had none of the ashen cast it took on after her fits.

"Where were you?" Mary demanded. "Mab went to get you and you weren't in your room." She stuck out her lower lip in the way that Linna always thought made her look like a sheep. "I need you, Linna."

Linna took a deep breath and came toward Lady Maeve. "My lady," she began firmly. "My lady, I think I have the solution to Mary Aislinn's problem.''

''Yes?'' Lady Maeve said sternly. ''What is it?''

For a second, Linna caught Mab's glance of warning, but it was too late for caution. ''My lady, Mary Aislinn. The Colonial, Desmond, has not seen either of us. Sir Edmond is in Yorkshire. If I take Mary's place, she would be free to follow her heart's desire to serve God. Let me pretend to be Mary Aislinn and marry Rory Desmond instead. If we leave immediately for the Colonies and she goes to France before the master returns, who will be the wiser?''

Chapter 2

"Saint Joseph protect us!" Mab's lined face turned as white as her cap. "The girl's overwrought, m'lady," the serving woman cried as she edged between Linna and her mistress. "She meant no disrespect, did ye, Linna?"

Mary Aislinn's mouth hung open, her eyes wide with astonishment. "Y-you?" she stuttered as she found her voice. "You marry Rory Desmond?"

Linna sank to her knees before Lady Maeve and looked up into her face. "All these years, my lady, it has been a source of laughter in the courtyard that I should have the same name and hair as Mary Aislinn."

Linna was treading carefully here. Lady Maeve knew as well as she did that Sir Edmond had fathered her on a chambermaid, and that the girl had given her the same name as Lady Maeve's daughter out of spite. Linna could see her mistress's delicate cheeks taking on a rosy hue. If Lady Maeve flew into a rage before she could find the right words to convince her, she would receive a whipping instead of a husband.

"Please, my lady," Linna murmured. "If you would just hear me out." She must use logic if she was to convince Lady Maeve. Her heart's argument that she had cherished the memory of the handsome young rapparee, that she had gone over and over every word they had ever spoken to each other, that she had idolized him with all the passion of a lonely, unloved child, would hold no weight with her mistress. Reason and Lady Maeve's maternal instinct to protect her daughter might sway her.

"You?" Mary Aislinn repeated. "You take my place?" she scrambled to the edge of the bed and thrust out her bare feet for Mab to enclose in fur slippers. "How could you? It would be a grave sin, wouldn't it? To do such a thing?"

"Could it be coincidence, Lady Maeve, that you brought me to Mount Beatty, that you permitted me to serve as companion to Mary Aislinn and share her lessons?" The last was less than a whole truth and Linna hoped Lady Maeve would not point it out to her.

No one had intended that Linna learn algebra, or French, or horsemanship, and certainly not better than Mary Aislinn. And Lady Maeve must have been confused when such poignant notes were emitted from the harp when Mary Aislinn was supposed to be practicing, yet her daughter could not play a simple melody for guests. "You have felt, my lady—we have all felt Mary's calling for the Church. Could it be that this was what was meant to be?"

Lady Maeve's pale eyes bored into Linna's. "Do you realize what you are suggesting? That we betray not only this Colonial but the master of Mount Beatty as well."

"She meant no harm," Mab soothed. "Hush, Linna. No more of this wild talk of ye taking—"

"No!" Mary Aislinn said. "I want to hear more." She laid her hand on Linna's wrist. "He is a Protestant.

What of your own soul? 'Twould be a sin to marry out of the faith.''

''Aye,'' Linna answered softly, feigning a meekness she did not feel. ''A sin. But with the mark of bastardy already staining my soul, wouldn't it be less a sin than if you made this marriage? And wouldn't I acquire some measure of forgiveness by making the sacrifice so that you could serve Our Lord?''

Mab made a clicking sound with her tongue, and Linna bit the inside of her cheek to keep from giggling. Mab had seen through her as usual. Mab knew that she was not offering to take Mary's place to protect her half sister, but for some scheme of her own. Linna dropped her eyes to the floor. If she laughed, the jig was up.

''I have always thought it was a strange thing,'' Mab observed, ''that they should bear the same name.''

Linna glanced at Mab from the corner of her eye. Lady Maeve was as superstitious as the cook, and she had made no secret of her fears. Mary Aislinn had come after several stillborn children, and was so weak and sickly that Lady Maeve had despaired of the infant's life. She had promised Mary Aislinn to the Church if she lived. The lady had told Sir Edmond that to break that sacred pledge would bring a curse down upon Mary's head.

Linna hesitated, then plunged ahead with an outright lie. ''I went to see the Colonial for myself, so that I could tell Mary Aislinn whether he was of a kindly appearance or not, and I was coming back through the haunted corridor—the Monk's Walk.''

''You saw a ghost?'' Mary Aislinn cried.

''Oh, no! I saw nothing . . . but I did feel something . . . something cold.''

"The walls are cold," Lady Maeve said.

"No, my lady, this was not the walls. Nor anything of this earth. I felt a presence, and inside my head a voice spoke."

Mab crossed herself. "Holy Mother forgive her," she whispered.

"And? What did you hear?" Lady Maeve demanded.

"It was the voice of an old man, so soft I could barely make it out, and spoken in the old language, my lady. He said, 'She must go to France and you must go west across the sea.' "

"Were you frightened?" Mary asked. "What did you say?"

"I didn't say anything. I ran to find your lady mother." Another lie. Linna was piling one upon another, but there was no other choice. "I went to your room, Lady Maeve, but you weren't there. Then I came here. The thought came to me as I ran—that I must take Mary's place. What else could it mean?"

"Let her, Mother," Mary Aislinn said. "If we wait until Father comes, he'll force me into this marriage and I'll die, I know I will."

"Are you certain you know what this would mean, Linna?" the mistress demanded. "You will leave Connemara for a strange land, never to return again. You will have to deceive your husband all your life."

"If it means that Mary Aislinn can enter the convent, I will do anything," Linna declared with passion.

"There will be no turning back," Lady Maeve said. "Mary Aislinn, you would have to leave at once by coach for Shannon. There, your Uncle John would see you safely to France and the sanctuary of the convent. I paid your dowry to the Church from my own estates last year when it became evident you wished with all your heart to join a holy order, and your father knows nothing of it. But do you realize it may be many years before we meet again? Are you brave enough to do this alone?''

"I am." Mary Aislinn's chin firmed. "It was meant to be. I cannot turn my back on my calling."

"But Linna was to go with you. You still must have a servant. Perhaps Mab—"

"Begging yer pardon, m'lady," Mab interrupted, "but 'twould be better for me to go along with Linna. No one else could be trusted to keep the secret. Katie is a good and pious colleen, and she is younger and stronger than I am. Let her go with the young mistress. The Colonial would never believe ye would let your daughter go without a serving woman."

"You'd leave your home to go to the Colonies?" Mary said. "You, Mab?"

"Who better, m'lady? I am a widow with no children. My mother has passed on to her reward and my old father lives comfortably by my brother's hearth. It is my place to go. I have been a member of this household for so long, I can advise Linna on how to play the part of a gentlewoman."

Lady Maeve sank into a chair and stared down at her cradled palms. "What tale can we give Desmond, to have him leave in haste with Linna?"

Linna rose and moved closer to the fire. "I have thought of a plan, my lady. If it works, we will be gone before first light."

The swirling mists had given way to a steady, driving rain as Linna, garbed now in her sister's fur-trimmed dressing gown, knocked once more at the Colonial's bedroom door. "Desmond," she called urgently. "Desmond, wake up."

The door swung open and Linna jumped back as a candle was thrust into her face.

"What do you want?"

Linna's voice caught in her throat as she spied the gleam of steel in the strange man's hand. This was not Rory Desmond! Dark he was, with heavy black brows and a cruel face. Ebony hair hung below his shoulders and his eyes were oddly slanted.

"Who is it, Ty?" Desmond's voice came from the direction of the bed. "Wait! I'm putting something on."

Linna took a step back into the clammy darkness of the corridor, unable to take her eyes off the knife-wielding guardian of the bedchamber.

"Who are you? What do you want?" the buckskin-clad apparition repeated.

Linna's hand was trembling so that she couldn't hold her own candle upright. Moistening her thumb and forefinger on the tip of her tongue, she pinched out the wavering flame. Every instinct told her to run, to forget this mad scheme and retreat to the safety of her own chamber. Her knees were weak and her mouth tasted of old copper. Still, a stubborn will held her firm until Desmond's suspicious face appeared beside the wild man.

"Well? What is it?" Rory demanded. "Do ye never sleep in this godforsaken house?"

"If . . . if you are Desmond, I must speak with you," she managed. "Alone."

Rory stepped past his companion and looked up and

down the hall. "There's nothing ye can't say in front of Ty." The Colonial wore only breeches and boots. Once again, Linna was dangerously close to that naked chest and those massive shoulders that would do justice to a blacksmith. "What time is it?" He took her arm roughly and pulled her into the room. "Well, speak up, girl. Ye've no need to fear us. What is it ye want of me?"

Linna shook off his hand. " 'Tis you I've come to speak with and you alone," she said firmly. "If you would hear what I have to say, you'll put your watchdog out. If not, I'll be on my way." She crossed her arms over her breasts and waited for what seemed like an eternity. The only sounds in the room were the rain and the wind beating against the windowpanes and the hiss and snap of the fire on the hearth.

Then the silence was broken by a low chuckle from the watchdog. Making no more noise than a shadow, he set the candlestick on a table, picked up a Brown Bess rifle, and stepped out into the hall, closing the door behind him.

"What . . . who is he?" Linna asked softly.

"Tyburn Griffith, half Lenni-Lenape and half Welshman. Probably the best hand-to-hand fighting man east of the Monongahela, except for me, of course." Desmond grinned. "Now, what can I do for ye that would not trouble my conscience or your confessor?"

"You can show more respect for your betrothed!" she lashed out. "I've heard many things of you, Rory Desmond, but the one thing they failed to tell me was that you were a boasting fool!"

Desmond's eyes narrowed and he stepped back, taking in the richness of her gown and the ring on her hand for the first time. He seized her hand and lifted it to see the heavy gold betrothal ring. "You're Mary Aislinn?"

"I am," she replied. That part at least was no lie. "And I have come here in good faith to save your neck from an English rope."

Desmond flushed. "Your pardon, mistress." He grabbed for a shirt over a chair and turned his back as he pulled it over his head. "Considering my earlier reception, you cannot blame me for failing to recognize the bride-to-be." He turned back and fixed her with a steady, soul-stripping gaze. "Now, what talk is this of English ropes?"

Linna exhaled sharply. "We have no time for games, sir. You have been betrayed! Even now, an informant has ridden for the British troops."

Strong hands closed around her upper arms. "By God, woman, if your father—"

"My father has nothing to do with it. You were a fool to set foot in Connemara. Men are starving here. Do you think they would hesitate to turn you in for British gold? What is one more dead rapparee?"

His fingers bit into her flesh and he pulled her so close she could feel his breath on her cheeks. "And you? What part have you in this?"

Storm clouds swirled behind his eyes. The sheer power of the man was terrifying, yet she forced her eyes to meet his gaze and hold it. "You were my father's choice, not mine," she answered boldly. "But we are betrothed. My place is with you. I have come here to warn you, and to tell you that you must flee now—tonight!"

"And you?" His breath was sweet, his voice strangely calm to belong to those eyes, those coiled muscles. "What of you, little Mary?"

"Linna," she insisted. "I am called Linna. And I will come with you, if you still want me."

"And our wedding? Have you an honest cleric hidden beneath your dressing gown?"

"That, sir, I was not able to manage," she flung back. "But if you will give me your word as a gentleman that we will be wed as soon as one can be found, I will entrust my honor to you and flee with you this night."

Slowly he released her. "How do I know I can trust you?"

"You don't." The cold of the floors had seeped up through her thin slippers and turned her feet to ice. She began to shiver and moved closer to the fireplace.

He followed her, catching her chin in his big hand and gently turning her face up to his. "Why didn't you come down to meet me earlier?"

"I-I was afraid," she lied.

"Of me . . . or of being caught in the trap?"

"Fool!" She caught up the poker and jabbed viciously at the fire. "Earlier there was no trap. My maid came to me and told me."

"Did she also tell you who the traitor was?"

"Yes."

"Who then?"

"Tom. A groom. Does it matter who he is? He has gone for the soldiers, I tell you."

"And I am to believe you rose from your bed and came at once to warn me." Desmond's deep voice was neither believing nor disbelieving.

"No." She caught a stray spark and extinguished it with the poker. "I went at once to Lady— to my mother. She told me to come to you."

"Your mother told you to offer to run off into the

night with a wanted man?" He chuckled softly. "Why didn't she send a servant?"

Linna dropped the poker. "She told me to come because it wasn't safe to trust a servant. If you are captured, you may bring all our house down around us. The penalty for aiding enemies of the Crown is death." Linna's mouth was dry and her heart was beating so hard she was certain Desmond could hear it. "My mother didn't tell me to go with you. That was my idea. If you don't want me . . ." She shrugged. "We will help you escape anyway. A coach is being readied. If you can reach the bay, we can get a fisherman to take you out to meet a smuggling ship. For a price, they will take you anywhere."

Desmond's brow creased with suspicion. "These arrangements seem to have been made quickly enough. How can I be certain it's just not a plan to rid yourself of an unwelcome guest?"

"The arrangements are standing ones. Protestant house or not, we are still Irish here. There are items which come and go without the heavy burden of English taxes. Have you been so long from Connemara that you do not remember?" Linna started for the door. "It is plain you do not want me, Colonial. So be it. I wish you safe journey back to your wilderness."

"If your mother gives her approval, I will take you," he said suddenly. "She would not willingly let you walk into a trap. Take me to her—Linna, is it?"

"Yes." She nodded solemnly. "She will come here as soon as she has sent a man ahead to wake the fisherman."

"I thought you said none of the servants could be trusted?"

"For all your trust of me, you might as well be

Sassenach yourself," she cried. "I said there was no servant she could send to you. If you do not believe your betrothed, would you have heeded a maid or potboy?"

"If we flee the English soldiers, I will have no trunks, and boxes, and bridal furniture. What of your dowry?"

"My maid, Mab, I will not travel without. But she is strong and as like to toss an Englishman as you. I will bring one trunk. My mother can send the rest of my belongings by ship. As for the dowry you so obviously need, you can wait here for it and the soldiers, or you can trust to my father's honor as he must trust to yours."

"How do I know I will get it?"

"How do I know you will truly wed me?"

Rory laughed. "You strike a hard bargain for a colleen." He held out his hand to her.

She shook her head. " 'Tis not the custom, Master Desmond. Rather, we should share a kiss of peace."

"Aye, that can be managed too." He pulled her into his arms and pressed his warm lips to hers in a gentle, exploring kiss. Linna's arms went around his neck and for long seconds, she kissed him back.

At last, she pushed him away and brought her fingertips to brush her still-tingling lips. "You have much to learn of manners, Colonial," she said softly. "But I believe I have much to learn of kissing."

Chapter 3

The horses' iron-clad hooves clattered and slipped on the wet paving stones as the carriage lurched out of the torchlit courtyard, through the massive gates, and out onto the main road that led to Galway. Rain beat against the roof and sides of the coach, nearly drowning the crack of the whip and shout of the driver.

Linna, Mab, and Linna's single leather trunk were crowded into one seat and the Colonial sat facing them, a Brown Bess across his lap and two loaded pistols on the seat beside him. Desmond's half-Indian companion rode beside the coachman in the drenching rain.

"Nice weather for a drive," Rory observed wryly. "Any more rain and the ship could have come to Mount Beatty for us."

Linna forced a wooden smile at the Colonial's attempt at black humor. She would take no easy breath until they were safe aboard the smuggler's vessel and clear of Irish waters. Until then, there were a hundred things that could go wrong. They could meet Sir Edmond on the road, or the coach could lose a wheel or break an axle. They could be stopped by a routine British patrol, or Lady Maeve could change her mind and send armed retainers after them.

Linna slipped her hand into the pocket of her heavy
woolen cloak and fingered her rosary. Her lips moved
in silent prayer. For all her pious declarations that she
was making this sacrifice for Mary Aislinn, the truth
was it was for herself. She was deceiving the dark
stranger across from her, and to enter the holy state
of matrimony under such conditions must be a mortal
sin.

The single lantern at her feet only succeeded in
making the darkness around them blacker. She could
not even make out Desmond's face, just the vague
outline of his features as he pushed aside the window
panel and peered out into the stormy night.

For all his light banter, Desmond was clearly concerned for their safety. The armed servants that rode
behind the coach on horseback would protect against
highwaymen and other low sorts; they would offer no
protection against soldiers.

Mab had uttered no sound of complaint. That in
itself was unnerving. Linna had not expected Mab's
offer to accompany her to the Colonies, but she was
grateful for it. Of all the women at Mount Beatty, she
was closest to Mab. In the strangeness of the new land,
Mab's sharp tongue and sound advice would be a comfort and a blessing.

Their leave-taking had been so hurried that there
had been little time for goodbyes. It had been impossible to go to her stepfather's cottage and bid farewell
to her half sisters and half brothers, even if she had
dared. Her own mother was dead and in her grave two
years this past Michaelmas Day. Linna would miss the
little ones, but an ocean was not enough to put between
her and her stepfather or her stepbrother, Sean.

The coach hit a hole in the road, slamming Mab and the trunk against Linna, and Linna fell forward on her knees almost into Rory's lap. She caught the corner of her lip on the stock of the rifle and her chin on the Colonial's knee. The lantern tipped over, extinguishing the candle and plunging the interior of the coach into blackness.

"Oooh!" Linna's sudden stop was followed almost immediately by the pain of Mab's knee striking her in the ribs. "Ouch."

"Are ye hurt?"

In the midst of confusion and the smart of Linna's bleeding lip, strong hands closed on her waist and pulled her upright.

"Linna?"

Mumbling protests that she was fine, she struggled to get her feet under her in the rocking coach, stepped on a petticoat, and fell into Rory's lap a second time. In her efforts to catch her balance, one hand caught him in a delicate spot and he gasped in pain. The strain was too much on Linna's nerves, and she began to giggle. Rory's low curse became a chuckle until they were breathless with laughter.

"By God, woman! With you along, I need no English soldiers to finish me off. Do ye mean to make a gelding of me before the wedding?" In his efforts to right her, Rory's hand slipped into her cloak and accidentally brushed the curve of her breast.

Linna stiffened and jumped back.

"Beg pardon, my lady," he said hastily. "I meant no offense."

Mab's offended sniff from the far corner of the coach made clear her opinion of the episode.

"And none taken," Linna murmured. Shivers

passed up her spine and threatened to set her teeth to chattering. The Blessed Mother alone knew how her face could be so hot and her body so cold. She'd been grabbed before by men, fore and aft, but no man's hand had ever caused such unnerving sensations. She felt as if she'd been struck by lightning. Even now, the breast he'd touched felt achy and swollen. The heat had spread from her face to the center of a woman's temptation, and lustful thoughts were bobbing up in the back of her mind like seals on the surface of the salt sea.

Would her husband-to-be think her brazen? She drew herself up and tightly wrapped her cloak around her. Had she touched what she'd thought she'd touched? Saint Patrick in heaven! She'd not only touched it, she'd mauled it. It had been an accident, but then she'd compounded her error by laughing at his misery.

The physical part of marriage was something she'd reconciled herself to accept. A woman's duty to her husband was to give him children and to provide for his sexual needs. No one had ever told her that a woman might have those same desires. Either her education had been sadly lacking or she was a brazen hussy, because the kiss she'd shared with Rory and now his intimate touch had made her eager for her wifely duties.

"I would not have you think . . ." Linna began lamely. "I did not mean to . . ." What was wrong with her tongue that she could not form the simplest apology?

"What did you say?" Rory leaned forward and rested his hand on her knee.

"Oh!" He did think her a trollop. What should she

do? Ignore his hand, or give him a great clout beside the ear?

Rory swore beneath his breath and removed his hand from Linna's knee. Why in God's name had he let his mother choose an innocent maid for his wife? By custom, betrothed was as good as married. A widow would have thought as little of his hand on her knee as a fly on the roast beef. The kiss the bold wench had given him earlier had made him hope she might not be as prudish as most of her kind. "There is nothing so saintly as an Irish virgin," his father used to say. Rory thought that virgins were vastly overrated, although, until now he could honestly say he had only made love to one.

He had loved his shy little first wife as truly as any man can. She was a picture bride, fair-haired and blue-eyed with skin like rose-tinted silk. She'd been only sixteen when they'd wed, and it had taken him four long weeks to consummate their marriage. Gentle Rachel. She had never taken to bed sport. It had been a disappointment to him, but the only one. Soft-spoken and laughing Rachel. They'd never had an argument; she'd never questioned or nagged him. Rachel had died last winter, as quietly as she had lived, fading away in a matter of hours from childbed fever.

The familiar pain of that memory knifed through him, and Rory turned again to stare out into the rain. He'd wanted no woman after Rachel's death. It had been months before he'd finally gone to a tavern in Annapolis and spent his passion on a willing barmaid. From time to time, he had repeated the performance, but there had been no woman who really caught his fancy until now.

Only a fool would have carried away his betrothed on this mad flight through the night. Why didn't he have the sense to go alone? Arrangements could have been made for Linna to come to Maryland later. He'd tried to convince himself that by bringing her along he assured himself there was no treachery. Rory smiled grimly. Like hell! He'd brought her along because there was something about her that excited him, something in those eyes that promised a spirit to match his own.

Linna was fair of face and form, fairer than any unseen bridegroom had a right to expect. If her red-gold hair tumbled about her face like a dairymaid's, and her dimples seemed too merry for a lady, they could not truly be called faults. The generous sprinkling of freckles over her shapely nose was appealing; her somewhat pointed chin and firm mouth might or might not be evidence of a stubborn nature. He had decided the first time he'd stared into Linna's chestnut-brown eyes with flecks of green that they reminded him of the rocky fields of Connemara. Yes, she was a fair maid, and at twenty, if she didn't take the pox or lose her figure from having too many children too fast, she'd have those looks for many years to come. But it was not her beauty or her bosom and hips that had convinced him he could not leave without her.

What that elusive something was, he couldn't say. Her courage had impressed him, the fact that she was willing to leave clothes and baggage, Mother and kin behind and flee with him into the night. What other woman would do such a thing for a man she'd known for the space of a few heartbeats?

Linna had shown a toughness, an honesty that called

to him. He wanted her—in his arms, and in his bed, not for an hour, but for a lifetime. He wanted her as suddenly and fiercely as he'd never wanted another woman. Not even Rachel.

Rory exhaled sharply and turned back to look at Linna, only a shadowy form in the darkness. He could make out nothing of her face or eyes, but he knew she was watching him. The devil take the British soldiers! If it were not for the dour maid in the far corner, he would have taken Linna in his arms and made love to her here and now. He would have had her!

"Sir."

Rory was pulled from his reverie by her softly lilting voice. "Aye, my lady." The throbbing, incandescent heat in his groin intensified and he shifted on the seat, imagining what it might be like to cup her bare breast in his hand. He swallowed hard. She'd not known to moisten her lips before kissing—he would teach her that.

"I'm wondering . . ."

"Aye?" There was a clean smell about her that he could not place. It permeated the strong odors of horse and wet wool and wood, making the space around her uniquely her own.

"What am I to-to call you?"

"Colonial would not be appropriate, would it? Especially since you'll soon be a Colonial yourself." He eased his hand onto her knee again.

Mab stifled a cough and pulled her shawl up over her head.

"I think not!" Linna replied, pushing his hand aside.

Rory's hand captured hers and held it fast. The hard surface of the gold betrothal ring on Linna's finger cut into his palm and he gloried in the symbolism. She belonged to him! "Do you find fault with my given name?" he asked hoarsely.

"No."

"Then call me Rory." His fingers stroked her wrist and he felt her tremble. "You're cold, colleen. Shall I come over and warm you?"

"It is not seemly," she protested.

"To be warm, or to use my Christian—" A warning shout from the driver's box snapped him upright.

"A band of riders coming fast behind us!" Ty yelled.

"Can you shoot a pistol?" Rory demanded.

Numbing fear coursed through Linna's veins. It couldn't be soldiers! It couldn't! She'd lied about the informer. It had to be Sir Edmond or Lady Maeve's men. "No," she stammered.

"Can you load one? In the dark?" Her silence was answer enough and he swore a foul oath. "Foolish question, right?" He learned across the coach and swung open the door on the far side. "I hope you think quick, or we both may hang." Suddenly, he grabbed the front of Mab's shawl. "Betray me, woman, and you'll be the first to die," he warned. Before she could answer, he was gone out the door.

A musket shot rang out and then another. Linna clung to the edge of the seat in terror.

"Soldiers, mistress," an outrider called, pulling his horse up beside the coach. "Do we stop or keep going?"

Linna leaned against the opening and shouted, "How many men in the box?"

"What?"

"How many men?"

"Two."

"Tell the coachman to stop. But tell the stranger to play dumb. He must not speak!"

Another shot, and then the first of the troop of riders was coming even with the coach. .

"Stop!" Linna screamed. "Stop the coach!"

The coach gradually slowed then rocked to a sliding stop and the door was flung open.

"Out! In the name of King George!" a gruff voice commanded in English. "Come out or be dragged!"

Slowly, Linna appeared in the doorway and offered her hand to the soldier. "You needn't shout, sir," she reprimanded. "There's only myself and my maid. Do we look like desperate characters?"

A fine misty rain fell against her face as Linna stepped down into the ankle-deep mud followed closely by Mab. A dozen English soldiers surrounded the coach. Linna noticed that her servants had already dismounted, and the coachman and Ty were climbing down from the box. Rory Desmond was nowhere to be seen.

"State your name and business," a young officer ordered.

"Rather, sir, I believe you should state your name and business," Linna said coldly. "By what right do you stop me on the king's highway? Have you a warrant?"

"I do, indeed. For one Rory Desmond."

"And do I look like Rory Desmond, whoever he may be? Or perhaps this is the gentleman you seek." She indicated Mab. "Your fugitive is not here, sir, and I deeply resent that you have cost me a pair of new shoes. These are ruined!''

"What of these men?'' the officer asked. "Is he any of these?''

A gray-haired soldier reined his horse close to look into Ty's face and then that of the driver. "No, sir.''

"Are you certain, McMann?''

"Positive, sir. I'd know him, even after all this time. The bastard put a ball through my chest.''

"I am Sir Edmond Beatty's daughter,'' Linna said. "And I am on my way to Shannon to visit my uncle. Is there any law against that?''

"Search the coach again,'' the officer said. "Check under the seats and in the boot. Turn out those trunks and we'll see what's in them.''

"Don't you dare!'' Linna threatened. "I'll not have my things—''

A corporal opened the first trunk and spilled feminine garments into the mud. "Nothing here, sir.''

"My gowns!'' Linna screamed. The second trunk, containing Rory's belongings, teetered on the edge of the coach. "Don't stop there,'' Linna insisted furiously. "Ruin everything else, too. Expose my underthings to your common soldiers.''

"Nor here,'' called the man from the boot.

"My apologies, Mistress Beatty,'' the officer said. "You may continue your journey.''

"I'll have your name and rank, sir,'' Linna stormed, trying not to look at the unopened trunk. "Your superiors shall hear of this. My father—'' Her protests were lost in the mill of horses' feet as the soldiers mounted and rode off down the road.

"Have ye lost what wits ye ever had?'' Mab cried. "Stop yer caterwauling and get back in the coach, girl. Ye'll get us all killed.''

Ty caught her about the waist and lifted her into the coach. A servant gathered the muddy clothing, stuffed it back into her trunk, and heaved it through the open door. The driver climbed into the box and cracked his whip over the horses, and the coach began to roll forward.

"Saint Bridget protect us," Mab muttered. "What have I got myself into?"

"Where is he?" Linna asked. "If he jumped out on the road, why didn't the soldiers see him? And how will he ever catch up with us?"

As if in answer to her questions, the far door swung open and a muddy apparition appeared in the doorway. Mab screamed and struck out at it. Linna began to laugh.

"Stop your cackling, woman, or you'll ride where I did," Rory threatened. He dropped onto the seat and began to pull off his mud-caked shirt.

"Where were you?" Linna asked. "They searched the coach. I saw them. How did you—"

"They didn't look under the damned coach, did they?"

"Under the coach?" she repeated dumbly.

"It's not a ride I'd recommend," he conceded. "But I like it better than the rope . . . although I've not tried that."

"But the coach was moving. What did you hold on to?" Linna asked.

"Damned little, I can tell you." Rory leaned close to her and placed a muddy hand on her arm. "Where did you learn to be such a consummate liar? I had no idea my bride-to-be had such talent."

"Lucky for you I have a ready tongue in my head. If they'd opened your chest, what then?"

"Any more complaints from you and they'd have locked you up as a public scold."

A crude phrase in Gaelic slipped from Linna's lips.

"Linna!" Mab gasped. "For shame!"

"What did you say?" Rory demanded.

Linna clasped her hands over her mouth. "I didn't mean—" she began.

Rory chuckled. "For that you shall pay a forfeit, my girl." He dragged her struggling into his lap and placed a lingering kiss on her surprised mouth.

Linna drew in a long, shuddering breath as Rory's lips brushed her throat and earlobe. Her pulse quickened as rills of sweet aching coursed through her veins. Her mouth met his again and the tip of his tongue touched hers. Rory groaned deep in his throat as he wound a single tendril of her damp hair around his finger.

"Mayhap I should ride in the box with the driver," Mab said, breaking the spell.

Linna stiffened and pulled free, her breathing ragged. What was there about this man that affected her so? "I'm sorry," she murmured.

"Nay," Rory answered softly, "there's naught to be sorry about, so long as it's only me you kiss like that. We've a long sea journey ahead of us, sweet colleen. And I've much to teach ye about being a wife."

Linna slid back on the opposite seat. "But I am not your wife yet," she protested.

"We are betrothed," he assured her. "In the eyes of God and man, it is the same."

Betrothed, yes, but not to me—to another. "No. Not the same. We must be wed by a man of God."

"And so we shall, as soon as possible. Have I not given you my word on it?"

"And I give you my word, Rory Desmond. I will not share your bed until I share your name."

"We shall see about that," he promised. "It's a long way to Maryland."

"Then I'd advise you to find us a priest before we set foot on board ship," she lashed back. "For I'm no slattern that can be had for a few pretty words. I'll not risk my immortal soul for any man . . . not even you."

Chapter 4

Linna grasped the side of the swaying coach and peered out through the driving rain as the vehicle skidded sideways on the rocky slope and came to an abrupt halt. A horse whinnied, and the coachman cracked his whip, shouting above the wind. The coach lurched and settled at an ominous angle. Linna could see nothing but rain. An inky blackness enveloped the coach and its three occupants in a spectral realm of wind and water.

Rory opened the door on the far side and leaned out. "Where are we?" he demanded.

The coachman's face loomed in the doorway. "Less than a mile from the village, sir. You'll have to go on horseback the rest of the way—or on foot. The wheel's sunk to the axle, and it may be cracked."

"Ty?" Rory called.

"Yep," came the deep reply. "We'll go no farther with this thing. And by the looks o' the trail ahead, we'd best go the rest of the way on foot."

"Steep?"

"Aye, and rocks the size of yer head. A horse could break a leg easy in the dark."

"We'll walk then." Rory turned to Linna. "You heard him. Are ye game to try it, or will ye sit here and wait for morning? It's not too late to change your mind about coming with me."

Linna's answer was to pull the hood of her cloak up over her head and open the door on her side. She slid down onto the wet stones and braced herself against the coach, trying to get her bearings. Grumbling, Mab followed. Linna ignored her, concentrating on the direction of the wind and the slope of the road. She had been to the fishing village before, but years ago and in broad daylight. Satisfied that the wind was coming off the bay, she turned into it, lowered her face, and began to walk along the rough track.

Rory caught her arm. "Do ye know where you're going?"

"I think so. The road should bend sharply to the left. When it does, the banks on either side will protect us from some of the wind."

"How far to the village?" he shouted, leaning close to her. Even so, the wind distorted his voice and carried off part of his words.

"I'm not sure. A mile, maybe two."

"I can put you on a horse and lead it if you want," he offered. "We're using the coach horses to carry the trunks."

"No." She shook her head. "The path narrows, and there's a steep drop-off before we reach the village. It will take longer to walk, but we should get there in one piece."

"Lead on then, colleen."

The mile seemed like ten as Linna's woolen cape became soaked. Her leather shoes slipped on the stones and grew leaden with mud. Once, she pitched forward and would have fallen on her face if not for Rory's strong grip on her arm. When at last the faint glow of light from a cottage pierced the blackness, Linna felt like cheering.

Rory pounded at the door, and it was opened by a tall, thin man with a dour face. Reluctantly, the man stood back, allowing them to file into the single-room structure. Linna crossed to the fire and threw off the sodden cloak, holding out her hands to the blessed warmth.

The cottage had no true fireplace in the English sense; the peat fire burned on a stone hearth with a smoke hole above in the roof. Linna inhaled the heady fragrance of the peat. Someone had told her that there were no peat bogs in America, that trees were so numerous that they were burned as fuel in poor men's houses. She was not certain she believed the tale, or even wanted to. The smell of peat and the sight of blue smoke rising above the cottages were as much a part of home as the moors of purple heather and the gray stone walls that lined the rocky fields.

"You've come on a fool's errand," the man said in Gaelic. "No one will row you out to the ship in this weather."

Linna gazed around the room. A red-faced woman and two children crouched together on a pallet in the far corner. The woman flushed and looked away as Linna's eyes met hers. She's afraid, Linna thought. And who can blame her?

"I was told you would do it for the right price," Rory insisted. "We must reach the ship before she sails."

"The devil take you," the fisherman swore. "Who will fill my old woman's belly if I lose my boat?"

"Offer to buy his boat," Linna said in English.

Rory's brow furrowed with concern. "I'll not risk your life. If he thinks the weather too dangerous to—"

"Take this," Linna called in Gaelic as she pulled a coin from the folds of her garment and tossed it to the fisherman. "You can buy two boats with that—and hire a boy to help you lift your nets."

The woman's eyes brightened at the flash of gold. "Go on, Shane, take them," she urged. "The damage is already done. If the Sassenach find them here, they'll hang us all."

For a long minute her husband stared at the gold coin, weighing it in his hand. "All right. But we must go now. And if we all drown out there"—he motioned toward the bay with his chin "—the fault is none of mine."

The fisherman led the way out into the rain and down to the beach. A second taciturn man appeared from the darkness, and together the two pushed a dory into the surf. Linna grasped Mab's hand and squeezed it tight as she stared at the turbulent water. Before Linna could protest, Rory grasped her about the waist and swung her into the boat. Quickly, he and Ty settled the trunks into the spaces between the wooden seats, then Rory came to sit beside her. Shunning Ty's help, Mab waded into the ankle-deep waves and climbed in at the stern.

"Ready?" Shane called. His companion grunted a reply, and they shoved the boat out into the surf, then scrambled in to settle themselves at the oars.

Rory leaned close and caught Linna's hand. "Courage, girl,'' he said. ''They know the sea. We'll make it.''

If the walk from the coach to the village had been unpleasant, it was nothing compared to the ordeal in the open, pitching boat. It seemed to Linna that the two men rowed for hours in the rain and tossing waves while Mab retched and moaned in the stern of the dory. Linna's own stomach was none too steady, and her hands and feet were numb with cold. With every wave, water sloshed over the bow, soaking her face and gown. Her eyes stung from the salt, and her teeth chattered. It was impossible to stop shivering. Against her will, tears began to slip down her cheeks, and she bit the inside of her cheek to keep from crying out with fear.

Rory Desmond was a silent figure beside her, withdrawn and brooding, staring out into the stormy abyss beyond the bow of the fragile craft. Only once did he clamp a powerful arm around her shoulder as the dory smashed into a huge wave, then dove sickeningly into the trough.

Too frightened even to pray, Linna shut her eyes and buried her face in his sodden cloak as the boat quivered in the grasp of the waves, then slowly righted itself and picked up the familiar rhythm. Her heart slowed and Rory's arm fell away. Unconsciously, she stiffened, forcing back the doubts that rose to torment her. What madness had possessed her to leave Beatty Hall and come with this stranger? Where was the man she remembered—the teasing rapparee who had laughed in the face of danger?

Finally, when it seemed her endurance had reached its limits, the murky outline of a ship materialized out of the gloom. Shane shouted and a lantern appeared on the deck. Invisible hands swung it back and forth. The two fishermen rowed the dory around to the leeward side of the sailing ship, then called out in unison, and a ghostly apparition appeared at the ship's rail to toss a line.

"State your business," a hard voice called in Gaelic, "or prepare to meet your maker." Suddenly the rail bristled with armed men.

"Four paying passengers for France," Shane answered in the same tongue.

"Who are ye?"

" 'Tis Shane O'Flaherty, you great boob. I see you standin' there, Connor Burke. Are you sayin' you don't know your own cousin?"

"Have ye seen the color of their coin?"

Shane laughed. "I have, Connor Burke. And it's yellow as bog butter."

"Come aboard then, passengers, and welcome," Torchlight flared, and a Jacob's ladder tumbled over the side of the ship.

The dory banged against the side of the larger vessel with every wave, then swung away, leaving an impossible expanse of dark water between Linna and the fragile-looking rope and wood ladder. Mother of God! Surely they didn't expect them to climb that. She'd fall and be crushed between the dory and the ship.

Rory slipped an arm around her shoulder and shouted above the rain, "You must wait until the man on the ship gives the order, then grab on and climb. Don't hesitate and don't look down. Can you do it?"

Too frightened to speak, Linna nodded, but when she tried to stand, her legs buckled under her. Her fingers felt as though they were made of wood.

"We've two ladies on board," Shane called to the ship. "Can ye lower a rope?"

"And a sedan chair, too?" Connor returned sarcastically. A minute or two passed and then a coil of rope dropped into the dory. Connor Burke leaned over the rail. "Tie that round 'er ladyship's middle and we'll haul her aboard like a great fish."

Rory swore under his breath and looked back at Ty. "You go aboard first," he said.

The half-breed grinned wolfishly. "Jest what I was thinkin', Rory." He patted the oilskin-wrapped musket that lay across his lap. " 'Twould be better to have a friendly face to greet ye on deck."

"Leave the musket with me," Rory said. "The powder's too wet to fire. Ye've Jenny, haven't ye?"

Puzzled, Linna watched Ty stand and pull a twelve-inch hunting knife from a sheath at his waist and clamp it between his teeth. Keeping his balance in the pitching boat, he moved to the center seat and stepped up on it.

"We're sending a man up the ladder," Shane shouted in Gaelic. "The waves have a pattern," he explained to Rory. "The fifth one is the highest. Tell your man to grab the ladder and climb on that one. Connor! Man comin' aboard!"

Rory counted aloud, and on the fifth wave Ty jumped. He was not more than halfway up the Jacob's ladder when his foot slipped. For seconds, Ty tried to cling to the slippery rung with one hand, then a sudden gust of wind tore him away. Mab screamed as he fell into the black void between the ship and the dory and vanished beneath the turbulent water.

"Mother of God," Linna whispered.

The dory slammed against the hull of the larger ship

so hard that Rory was thrown to his knees. "Ty!" he screamed into the wind. "Ty!"

"The sea has claimed him," Shane said in his own tongue.

" 'Tis God's will." The second fisherman hastily crossed himself.

Linna looked away, then cried out as Ty's head bobbed to the surface on the far side of the boat. "Rory! Look!"

"There!" Rory shouted. "Your oar, man! Give him your oar!"

The fisherman in the stern leaned out as far as he could and Ty grasped the end of the oar. Rory dropped his cloak and dove into the water. Between them, they pulled Ty, sputtering and gasping for breath, into the boat. Shane offered Rory a strong hand as he climbed over the side.

"Ty?" Rory demanded, slapping him on the back. "Are ye all right?"

Ty leaned over the side and vomited up great gouts of water. Weakly, he raised his head. "I lost Jenny," he rasped.

Rory threw back his head and roared. "Better the knife than you, old friend. I'll buy ye another when we reach France."

"None like Jenny," Ty grumbled. "With a notch for every Iroquois scalp."

"The captain says ye must board now or not at all," called a distorted voice from the ship. "We kin wait no longer."

" 'Tis too dangerous," Shane advised. "Come back with us to the village and we'll try again with another ship tomorrow night." He laid a hand on Rory's shoulder. "We'll hide ye from the Sassenach, I swear it."

"Nay, Shane," Rory answered. "We've put ye in enough danger. We'll board now. It's away from Connemara I'll be by sunrise."

"Away ye may be," Shane said, "but the question is, my lord, do ye go to France or to a watery hell?"

"Linna?" Rory turned cold eyes on her. "Are you with me?"

Too frightened to speak, she nodded. For better or worse she would follow this man. There was nothing behind her in Ireland, and even a chance at a new life in America was something to reach for.

"Aye, we're agreed then. Are ye game to try it again, Ty?" Rory demanded.

The big man grunted in assent and took his position in the center of the boat. Fearfully, Linna watched as the men counted the waves and Ty leaped for a hold on the Jacob's ladder. This time, he made the climb safely, pulling himself over the rail of the ship and waving to the others. "Nothin' to it," he yelled back.

Rory turned to Mab. "You next, woman." She crawled forward in the dory, and he knotted the rope around her middle. A man on the ship signaled and they began to pull her up.

When Mab was safely aboard, suffering no more than a few bruises and the loss of her dignity, Rory looked at Linna. "Well, colleen, which shall it be, the rope or the ladder?"

She hesitated for only a heartbeat. "The ladder. I'll not be knocked about like a barrel of salt pork."

Rory laughed. "I thought I saw a bit of fire in those dark eyes." He reached down to slice off a length of the rope. "But I've no wish to lose you into the sea. Ye may not be as lucky as Ty." He knotted the rope securely about the first trunk and steadied it as Ty pulled it aboard, then they repeated the same motions with Linna's trunk.

When the rope was dropped again, Rory turned his back to Linna. "Give me your wrists," he ordered. She obeyed without thinking, and he crossed her hands and tied them in front of his neck, then fastened his cloak around them. "I'll do the climbing for us both," he explained, securing the musket to one shoulder with the rope.

"God go with ye," Shane murmured.

Rory braced himself on the seat as the fisherman began to count. On the fifth wave, he jumped. Linna gasped as they swayed against the side of the ship. If Rory fell, they'd never be able to swim tied together— they'd go straight to the bottom.

Ty's face loomed above them. "Climb, ye black-haired son o' Satan!" he yelled.

Rock-hard thews rippled beneath Rory's wet shirt as he pulled them hand over hand up the swaying ladder. Linna laid her face against his back in the darkness and murmured a silent prayer. The sound of Rory's boots hitting the wooden deck was the sweetest song she'd ever heard. Someone fumbled with the cloak and cut the rope at her wrists.

Linna swayed against Rory and looked down at the dory pulling away.

"Safe voyage," Shane bid them in Gaelic.

"And the same to you," Linna whispered. Rory's arm went around her waist and caught her.

"You're none too steady on your feet, girl," he said, sweeping her up into his arms. "Show me the way to the captain's cabin," he ordered the nearest sailor. "My wife needs to get warm and dry before she comes down with lung fever."

"I can walk," Linna protested.

Rory didn't bother to reply as he carried her across the deck. He ducked his head and descended several steps to enter a small cabin lit by a single lantern. Crossing the room, he laid her on the narrow bunk and shouted for Mab.

Vaguely, Linna was aware of a stranger's voice. Rory answered him roughly, then the conversation was cut off as both men left the cabin, closing the door behind them. Mab began to strip off Linna's wet clothing. Linna tried to help, but her fingers refused to bend.

"Fash, girl, you're all ice," Mab fussed. "Into bed with ye." She pulled off Linna's shoes and stockings, then tucked her under the covers.

"You're as wet as I am," Linna said. The warmth of the woolen blankets and the heaviness of her eyelids seemed to drag her down into soft blackness. Against her will, she fell into a deep, dreamless sleep.

Linna woke in total darkness to the sound of a human scream. Stunned with fear, she sat bolt upright as the cabin door banged open and two figures burst into the room. A flintlock roared and the intruders slammed the door and shot the iron bolt. Linna bit down on her hand and retreated to the far corner of the bunk.

"Linna! Mab! On your feet! Be quick!"

Relief flooded through her at the sound of Rory's voice. "What is it?" she cried. "What's wrong?"

"Be it you for certain, sir?" Mab asked, striking a light. The spark caught and lantern light illuminated the cabin. Mab rose from her spot on the floor, a cutlass dangling from her hand. "No offense meant to ye, Master Desmond, but I thought—"

"You thought right, Mab. Dress as quick as you can, both of you."

"Why?" Linna demanded. "Is it the British? Have they caught up with us?"

"Do as I say," he commanded roughly.

Heat rose in Linna's cheeks and she pulled the woolen blanket higher around her naked body. "With you and him in the room?"

"Do as I say! I'm in no mood to—"

Linna's scream cut off his words as she threw herself from the bunk and backed against the wall, pointing to the tiny rain-streaked window. "A man," she stammered. "There was a man's face there."

Rory moved to the window. "He's gone now. In any case, it's too small for anyone to come through."

"But not too small to shoot through—either way," Ty said.

"Aye." Rory dropped to his knees and opened his sea chest. He began to dig through the contents, pausing for an instant to glare up at Linna. "Didn't I tell you to get dressed?" Without waiting for a reply, he tossed an oilcloth sack to his companion. "That powder should be dry enough to fire." Quickly, he pulled a bundle from the chest and unwrapped a flintlock pistol. His eyes watched the door as his hands began to load the weapon.

Mab glanced from Rory to Linna's ashen face. With a sigh, she threw open Linna's trunk and pulled out a shift and a plain woolen gown. Stockings and serviceable shoes followed. "Have the decency to look away," Mab snapped at Ty.

The hawk-faced man hastily turned his back and faced the door. "No disrespect meant, missus," he mumbled. "I was watchin' that window to see if our weasel would come back."

Mab made a screen with the blanket as Linna pulled the shift and dress over her head, then dropped to the floor to tug on the stockings. "Please tell me what's happening," Linna said. A cold chill ran through her and her teeth began to chatter. "If not the Sassenach, then who?"

"The captain thought to make more on our passage than we bargained for," Rory said bitterly.

Ty chuckled softly. "He planned on feedin' us to the fish."

"Holy Mary," Mab whispered as she wrapped the blanket around Linna's shoulders.

"I heard a scream," Linna said.

Ty turned back and grinned. "That was the captain."

Rory stuck the loaded pistol in his belt and began a systematic search of the cabin. "I'm afraid we have a bit of trouble on our hands."

"What happened?" Linna repeated.

Rory threw back a Turkey-red carpet and gave a satisfied sound. "Here's what we need, Ty—the captain's personal arsenal." The hinged floorboards swung open to reveal a cache of muskets, pistols, and cutlasses.

Ty said something in a foreign tongue and Rory answered in the same language. It was unlike anything Linna had ever heard. "It seems to me this is more of a pirate vessel than an honest smuggler's ship," Rory added in Gaelic.

"Is the captain trying to murder us?" Linna asked.

"Not anymore," Rory said. "He tried to run me through with a cutlass."

''Why won't he try again?'' Mab asked suspiciously.

''Ty tossed him overboard.''

''You killed the ship's captain?'' Linna whispered.

Ty shrugged. ''How was I to know the bastard couldn't swim?''

Chapter 5

The storm seemed to weaken with the coming of dawn. As the first rays of iridescent violet-rose broke through the clouds, the gusting wind slackened, calming the white-capped waves that had tossed the ship so violently through the night. From the small window, Linna watched the Atlantic turn from dull black to a shimmering blue-green and heard the cries of hungry sea gulls circling above.

In the last hours before sunrise the ship's crew had made no attempt to assault the captain's cabin. The four inhabitants had waited, listening for the slightest sound that an attack was imminent, but all had been quiet.

"They're probably too busy trying to keep the damned ship from sinkin'," Ty had offered. "We can wait until they've weathered the blow."

The thought that the crew would wait to seek their revenge was hardly comforting to Linna. She knew they were greatly outnumbered. She and Mab could only be considered liabilities. "If I had known that shooting guns was a required skill for a Colonial's wife, I would have made it a priority in my training," she informed Rory wryly. "It seems my education is greatly lacking."

"I'll teach you when we reach Maryland. I wouldn't say being a good shot is a prerequisite, but there's no doubt it would have come in handy on this journey." Rory's taut face showed the strain of the sleepless night as he paced the small chamber.

"How many of them you reckon to be out there?" Ty asked lazily. He cradled the captain's silver-handled cutlass he'd taken from Mab, polishing the lengthy steel blade with his shirt tail. "I'd feel better about this scrap if I hadn't lost Jenny."

Linna toyed with her portion of cheese. There had been wine and brandy aplenty in the cabin, but the only food was a wheel of cheese and a half loaf of stale bread. Mab had divided it, giving the two men a double portion.

"Eat," she urged Linna. "God only knows when ye'll eat again. Dip the bread in the wine, it will go down easier."

Woodenly, Linna obeyed. Logic told her that Mab's advice was sound, but fear closed her throat and made even the delicious cheese taste like mud in her mouth. "Do all women in the Colonies shoot?" she asked softly.

"Nay, girl," Ty replied. "Rachel could not shoot or ride a horse."

"Rachel?"

Rory's features hardened as he glared at Ty. "My wife."

Linna heard Mab's gasp of astonishment, and her mouth went suddenly dry. "Your wife? I don't understand."

"Didn't Lady Maeve tell you?" Rory's voice was flat and emotionless. "I recently lost a wife to childbed fever. I am a widower with a child."

"A child?"

"Yes, an infant daughter, Anne. Do you find that a problem, madam?" he asked coldly.

"No, of course not," Linna stammered. "I just . . . I didn't know. No one told me. I'm sorry for your loss."

Ty unfolded his long legs and stood up. "Pay no attention to him, girl. He loved his Rachel dearly, and he's not been the same since her death." He fixed Rory with an intense gaze. "Do ye mean to blame her for Rachel's passin'?"

Rory flushed. "No, 'tis not your fault, Linna. I didn't mean to speak so. 'Twas just surprise that your lady mother didn't—"

A loud pounding at the door cut him off. Rory motioned the women to get down, and he and Ty took positions on either side of the cabin door, weapons ready.

"You in there!" a man called in Gaelic.

"Shall I unlock the door and give them a taste of hot lead?" Ty asked.

Rory shook his head. "What can we do for ye?" he called back in the same tongue.

"We want to talk."

"Talk away," Rory answered.

"Not this way. Unbolt the door. I'll come in unarmed, if you gi' me your word I'll not be harmed."

"Don't open the door," Mab insisted, moving closer to Linna. "It's a trick and we'll all be murdered."

"We have the muskets," Rory said.

"I thought ye might," the man replied.

"What's he sayin'?" Ty demanded. "Don't he speak the king's English?"

"Have ye a name?" Rory motioned to Linna and shoved a loaded pistol into her shaking hands. "Get back behind the table and pull the trigger if I tell you," he whispered.

"Connor Burke," the man answered loudly.

"Are ye shriven, Connor Burke?" Rory returned to his place by the door.

"Who wants to know?"

"Rory Desmond."

There was silence from the far side of the door. Linna crouched in the corner beside Mab; the older woman was murmuring the rosary under her breath. Linna drew in a long, ragged breath and held the heavy flintlock out in front of her.

"Rory Desmond, is it?" came the faintly amused voice from the passageway. "Do ye know of the mountains called the Twelve Pins, Rory Desmond?"

"I do."

"I heard tell of a man by the name of Rory Desmond, but he's long dead, no doubt."

"And the Connor Burke I heard of was nigh hanged at Lough Ree by the Sassenach," Rory countered.

"By the sacred wounds of Christ, if ye be that rapparee, what color horse were ye riding that day?"

"Red as the Sassenach blood we spilled," Rory said.

"Open the door, Rory Desmond. Ye'll get no harm from me or mine this day," Connor cried.

Ty shook his head. "Whatever ye're perlaberin' about, don't be forgettin' one of them has a gun."

"How many guns do ye have, Connor Burke?" Rory called. "And you're wasting your time to lie. You nearly blew my head off last night."

"I'm that sorry about it, Rory Desmond. 'Twas a case of mistaken identity. We mistook you two fer the blackguards what threw the captain, Finn Shaughnessy, into Galway Bay."

"Sorry covers no spilled milk. Throw the musket overboard and throw it where we can see from the window," Rory ordered.

"Damnation! Ye'd beggar a man. Do ye know the price of a French musket?"

"Over the side with it."

"Ye're a hard man with no pity for a poor seafaring brother."

"So I've been told." Rory turned his head and looked at Linna, motioning to the single window. She watched until she saw a musket tumble into the sea, then nodded.

Cautiously, Ty opened the door and Connor Burke stepped slowly into the cabin, his hands in the air. Ty slammed the door again and bolted it. The man was no taller than Linna, with carrot-red hair and bright blue eyes, and he moved with the swinging gait of a seaman.

"Move over there," Rory ordered. "Slow."

The Irishman grinned boyishly. "Can I be lowerin' me hands, Rory Desmond? I've come to do ye no harm, I swear on me mother's grave."

Rory stuck his pistol in his belt and waved grandly toward a chair. "Mab, some wine for the gentleman. Is it Captain Burke, by any chance?"

Connor grinned wider, exposing a gold-capped tooth. "You're a man wi' the sight and that's fer certain." He nodded to Linna. "Apologies, mistress. A sight of sins I've committed with these two hands, for which I'll burn in hell I've no doubt, but harmin' a woman is not among 'em.''

"Attempted murder of my betro—'' Linna corrected herself smoothly, "Of my husband is not doing me harm? And holding us prisoner in this cabin for hours?''

"No, mistress,'' Connor protested. "You've the wrong of it. The door was locked from the inside, not the out. And fer the rest . . .'' He spread his hands palm up on the table. "I've sins enough of me own without takin' on those of Finn Shaughnessy. 'Twas a black deed he conceived, and he's paid the price. I had no part of it.''

"This is not the time for accusations and recriminations,'' Rory admonished with a twinkle in his eye. "Captain Burke has come peaceably to settle our dilemma, is that not so, Captain Burke?''

"Aye, I have.'' Mab slammed a cup of brandy on the table and Connor lifted it in salute to Linna and drained it in a single swallow. "With profit to us all,'' he added.

Ty leaned against the cabin wall, the musket cradled lightly in his arms, and gazed menacingly into the Irishman's face. "If he looks crossways,'' Ty warned, "I'll blow him to kingdom come.''

"I don't understand all yer companion says,'' Connor said, "but his meaning is clear.'' He held out the empty cup for Mab to refill. "What do ye want?''

"A safe ship for the Colonies or a safe port. We'll pay the amount agreed upon, no more, no less.''

Connor Burke shook his head. "Nay, I cannot agree. I've not made much use of the life ye saved at Lough Ree, but I value it just the same. I'll find a ship for you and yours, Rory Desmond, and ye can keep your gold. Besides''—he arched a pale eyebrow and chuckled— "ye've already given me this sloop.''

"And the rest of the crew," Rory said shrewdly, "will they go along with you?"

"They will, indeed, unless they want to join Finn Shaughnessy at the bottom of the sea." Grinning, he stood and offered Rory his gnarled hand. "I'll see the lot of ye safe on yer way to America," he promised, "or old Scat can have my soul without a fight."

Despite Linna's doubts, Connor Burke kept his word. Two days later, the sloop hailed the *Betty Jane*, a brigantine flying a Dutch flag and captained and crewed by New Englanders. The *Betty Jane* had taken on cargo in Amsterdam and was bound for Philadelphia. Although the ship had poor facilities for passengers, the captain was glad to accept their gold and take them aboard, no questions asked.

"The *Betty Jane*'s been known to change flags depending on what waters she sails," Connor Burke said as they prepared to transfer from the sloop to the brigantine, "but Cabbot's an honest man and a good captain. A winter crossing of the Atlantic is never an easy row to hoe, but I'm bettin' ye'll make it alive and kicking."

Linna thought secretly that Connor Burke's risk was a great deal less than their own, since it was their lives and not his that would be lost if the *Betty Jane* sank on the way to Philadelphia, but she held her tongue and allowed Rory to assist her down the Jacob's ladder into the longboat. The sea air was cold and crisp, but the ocean was as calm as a mill pond. The sailors bent their backs to man the oars, and the longboat glided effortlessly across the blue-green water to the waiting ship.

This time Linna and Mab were able to climb the ladder unassisted. Rory lifted her over the railing, and

Linna glanced about curiously as the trunks were brought aboard. To her relief, the *Betty Jane* was much larger than the smuggling vessel and spotlessly clean. Captain Cabbot and his first officer, John Slaybough, stepped forward to greet them politely in oddly accented if correct English. The captain was a tall, middle-aged man with iron-gray hair and a slight limp, a much more reassuring captain than Connor Burke.

"We've little room for passengers, as I told you before," Captain Cabbot explained to Rory. "The ladies must share a cabin, your man can bunk in the fo'c'sle with the crew, and you'll squeeze in with Mr. Slaybough." He threw up a hand, and Linna noticed with shock that it was missing two fingers. "If that arrangement's not agreeable to you, you're only wasting your breath to say so. We've no more room. Take it or leave it."

"We'll take it and gladly," Rory agreed.

"Good." The captain nodded to Linna. "I'll do what I can to make your voyage a pleasant one, Mistress Desmond. I must insist that you and your maid keep to your cabin unless you are accompanied by your husband or Mr. Slaybough or myself. I've a good crew and I mean to keep them that way. You're safe below decks anyway. This weather won't last, and I'll not be responsible for having you washed away." He glanced at his first officer. "You can have Jeremy show the ladies to their cabin."

"Yes, sir," Slaybough answered. "Jeremy!"

"Sir." A stocky mulatto boy of about twelve years of age appeared beside Mab.

Linna looked hesitantly at Rory.

"Go on with the boy," he said. "Ty can bring your trunk down, and you can settle in."

With one last look at the cloudless blue sky overhead, Linna followed the cabin boy through an open door and down a narrow passageway to a cramped, bare cubicle. Mab shook her head and muttered under her breath as the boy struck a light and lit a single foul-smelling candle. He stuck the candle into a brass and wood lantern and hung it from a hook overhead, then hastily backed out of the room and hurried away.

"Mother of God," Linna murmured. The cabin was worse than she had expected. Two narrow bunks, stacked one upon another, filled nearly half of the windowless room. A wooden shelf ran along the space not occupied by the door on the opposite side. One end wall held brass hooks above a space just wide enough for a sea chest, and the other was taken up by a crude built-in cupboard. The only piece of furniture in the room was a three-legged pine stool.

Mab grunted and opened the single door at the bottom of the cupboard. It contained a covered bucket. "Our necessary," she said gloomily. Behind the double doors, the top half of the cabinet was empty except for two tin cups, two battered pewter porringers, and three chipped china plates.

Linna warily felt the mattress on the top bunk. "I think it's stuffed with straw," she ventured. Several clean woolen blankets were stacked on the bottom bunk along with two lumpy pillows.

"Here's yer trunk and yer woman's sack," Ty called from the open doorway. Linna flattened against the bunks as the big man stepped into the room and slid the trunk against the wall. "Pretty snug quarters, I'd say," he observed. "But they're a lot better than what I'll be gettin' in the fo'c'sle." He unslung a leather water bottle from around his neck and hung it on a hook, then tossed Mab her bundle. "Captain says he looks for a fast crossin'. Six weeks if we're lucky."

"And if we're not?" Mab asked.

"Eight weeks, ten. Hell, I don't know. Sometimes three months or more. Winter's usually faster than a summer voyage—but rougher, o' course."

"Thank you, Ty, for bringing the things," Linna said weakly. Six weeks? How could she bear being shut up in this dark hole for six weeks?

"No trouble." He backed out the door. "Captain says yer to take supper in his cabin wi' him and Rory. Jest the lady," he added, suddenly remembering Mab. He turned an amused gaze on her. "Wouldn't feel too bad about being left out if I was you. New Englanders ain't much for company to my way o' thinkin'. Bible thumpers all of 'em. Time they get done prayin' over the food, it's plumb cold."

"Thank you, Ty," Mab said firmly, closing the door. She pursed her lips and glanced at Linna. "That one's more savage than Welsh, if ye ask me, and a Welshman's the closest thing to a wild man I know of. Ye'd best keep him in his place, Li— Miss Linna, or ye'll have trouble, I'm warning ye."

Linna sank onto the bunk and hugged her arms tightly against her chest. "What have we let ourselves in for, Mab?"

"Whatever it is, we'll face it. There's no going back, girl."

"I know, Mab," Linna whispered, "and that's what frightens me."

The first days of the voyage aboard the *Betty Jane* fell into a pattern. Linna and Mab took a simple meal alone in the cabin in late morning, and about noon

Rory would come to escort them onto the deck for an hour's exercise and fresh air. The afternoons were spent in the cabin, and usually Linna was invited to take supper with Rory, the captain, and Mr. Slaybough in the captain's cabin. After the meal, if the weather was decent, Linna walked with Rory and Captain Cabbot a few times around the deck before returning to the cabin for the night.

The monotony of the hours in the tiny cabin was almost more than Linna could bear. Her only chance to be with Rory was in the company of either Mab or the captain, and they'd had no opportunity for private speech since they'd been aboard the *Betty Jane*.

Lying on her straw mattress, staring at the boards of Mab's bunk overhead, Linna tried to understand the man she had committed her future to. In the coach, on the ride from Mount Beatty to the fishing village, Rory had seemed a charming, roguish companion. There had been no doubt from their kisses—and the way he had looked at her—that he'd found her attractive in a sexual way. Rory's intense male virility had been frightening, yet it drew her to him in ways she had never thought possible.

On the smuggling vessel, she had seen glimpses of the bold rapparee she remembered from her childhood. Rory had shown courage and intelligence in the face of danger. He'd been protective of her, but he'd not touched her or even looked at her as though she was his wife-to-be. And now, since they'd boarded the *Betty Jane*, he'd been a distant stranger, coolly polite and solicitous for her welfare without extending any genuine affection.

Was she a fool to hope that marriage to Rory Desmond might bring love? Did any man and wife find that intangible substance the poets wrote of—outside the gossamer boundaries of a fairy tale? Had she created a man in her dreams that no flesh and blood man could emulate?

The candle flickered and went out, leaving Linna in darkness. Mab's snores blended with the creaking of wood and the sigh of waves against the hull. Linna wound a bit of woolen blanket around her finger as she had done in childhood and rubbed it against her cheek. The blanket smelled of salt and tar and was faintly damp, but it was as clean as every corner of the *Betty Jane*. I feel empty, she thought. There were no tears; the ragged child she'd once been had learned the futility of tears. "Damn you, Rory Desmond," she whispered into the shapeless pillow. "I want to love you, and you won't let me."

A faint scratching noise caught Linna's attention. She caught her breath and listened. Was that a rat? The scratching came again, and she sat up. She'd seen no rodent droppings in the cabins or passageways, but she assumed every ship must have them. "Rats, ugh." Linna hated them. A shiver passed through her. What if it was in the room? Was it worse to lie here or to get out of the bunk and strike a light? Suppose she stepped on the rat in the darkness? Yet, if she stayed in bed, it might run over her face when she was asleep.

Fear made her bold, and Linna leaped up and fumbled with the flint and steel on the shelf beside the lantern. On the fifth try she got a spark. Her searching fingers found the spare candle and she lit it, quickly moving the light about to be certain no rat lurked in the corners.

A squeak behind her startled her so that she jumped and almost dropped the candle. It came from the other

side of the door, she was certain of it. Trembling,
Linna raised the latch and swung open the door. To
her surprise and delight, the intruder was a huge orange
cat with a black spot over one eye and a missing ear.

"Hello there," Linna said. "Will you come in?"

With the lordly air of a proprietor, the cat strolled
leisurely into the cabin and hopped up on Linna's bunk.
Linna closed and locked the door, stuck the candle in
the lamp, and moved it to the stool. Then she joined
the cat on the bed. The tomcat padded around in a
circle and settled down on the pillow to lick an oversize
paw. Hesitantly, Linna put out a hand to stroke the
soft fur and was rewarded by a loud purr.

"Where did you come from?" she whispered. "Do
you have a name?" The cat closed one eye. "Would
you like to spend the night?" The animal shut the
other eye and continued to purr. Linna laughed.
"Whatever your name is, I'll take you over a rat any
day."

Blowing out the candle, Linna stretched out on the
bunk, taking care not to disturb her new friend. *I could
have lain awake all night worrying about rats if I hadn't
gotten up to look,* she thought, listening to the steady
hum of the cat's purring. *The fear wasn't real—it was
all of my own making. Could it be possible that her
fears about Rory were also self-conjured? Would facing
those fears head-on dissolve them as readily?*

There was, Linna decided resolutely, only one way
to find out. She would have to confront Rory, and the
sooner the better. If theirs was truly to be a marriage
of convenience, it was better to know it now and go
into it with her eyes open.

Chapter 6

Captain Cabbot motioned to Jeremy, and the boy brought the serving platter to Linna's side of the table. "Have some more roast chicken, Mistress Desmond," the captain suggested. "It's the last you'll see until you reach the Colonies."

"No, thank you," Linna murmured. Usually, she looked forward to supper in the captain's quarters. It was a welcome break from the long hours alone with Mab in the tiny compartment. But, so far, this evening was a disappointment. Other than bidding her good evening, Rory had not spoken a single word to her.

What's wrong with him? she wondered. Linna knew she wasn't ugly, although some men were said to disdain red-haired women. She had taken pains with that red hair tonight, washing and curling it diligently, then tying it back with a wide silk ribbon that matched her blue camlet waistcoat.

There had been no room for bulky hoops or fine gowns in the single chest she'd brought from Mount Beatty. Instead, she had chosen two riding habits, a forest-green wool, and the one she was wearing tonight. The blue camlet habit was the finer of the two; the coat and waistcoat were trimmed and embroidered

with siver, and the matching petticoat boasted an in-
verted flounce. Her cravat was Irish lace, and the ele-
gant cocked hat which completed the outfit bore a
scarlet feather.

Linna had thought the powder-blue riding habit the
most beautiful thing she had ever seen when Sir Edmond had brought it home for Mary Aislinn on her
birthday last year. Now the riding habit was hers. Mary
Aislinn will have little use in a nunnery for the lovely
things in my sea chest, she thought. So why, then, do
I feel so guilty wearing them? She looked sideways at
Rory from beneath her lowered lashes. And why hasn't
he noticed me at all this evening?

With effort, Linna stifled a yawn as Captain Cabbot
continued on with his long, involved story of a whale
hunt in the North Sea that resulted in the loss of his
fingers and a friend's leg. Mr. Slaybough, who she
surmised had heard the tale more than once before,
was giving full attention to his baked beans. Rory
sipped at the good French wine and listened attentively
to his host, delivering appropriate comments during
the captain's theatrical pauses in his story.

Linna's left foot was asleep, and she wiggled it,
wincing at the sharp pains that shot up her ankle. The
chicken and the dusty bottle of wine had been the only
indication that it was Christmas.

"We'll have no pagan excesses on my ship," Captain Cabbot had declared early that morning as he'd
offered a lengthy prayer on deck before the assembled
crew. Sternly, he'd bidden them all to spend their spare
hours compiling and renouncing their sins on this day
of the Lord Jesus' birth.

When the captain had left the quarterdeck, Linna

had noticed that Mr. Slaybough had earned a rousing cheer from the crew by ordering a double ration of rum for all hands.

It was the worst Christmas Day that Linna could remember. Even when she had lived in the cottage with her mother and stepfather, there had been a celebration. She remembered music, dancing, and laughter. The family had gone secretly to hear Mass in a hollow beyond Cleary's Bog, and then everyone had shared bread and honey, dried fruit and fish, and apple cider. The priest had always managed a bit of golden taffy for the children, and sometimes even a holy relic or bit of ribbon. One year, Maggie O'Shaughnessy had given every boy a slingshot and every girl a rag doll. Poor or not, Linna had treasured memories of Christmas to ease the pain of this barren one.

"Mistress?"

Linna realized with a start that everyone was staring at her. "Pardon me," she offered.

"Plum pudding," the captain said. "Will you have plum pudding?"

What happened to the whale? she wondered. "No . . . ah . . . yes," she stammered.

"Before we conclude this meal," Rory said smoothly, "I'd like to present you all with a small token of the day." He removed three small cloth-wrapped objects from the pocket of his coat and placed them on the table. "This is for you, mistress," he said to Linna. "You, captain, and you, Mr. Slaybough. I noticed that both you gentlemen indulge in a pipe on occasion. This tobacco is from my plantation. I believe you'll find it ranks with the best grown in Virginia."

"Thank you, Master Desmond," the captain said.

Slaybough nodded agreement. "Thank you, sir."

Linna felt her cheeks flush. A Christmas gift. Rory had given her a gift and she had nothing for him. "Thank you," she managed. "I didn't expect . . ."

"Open it," Rory urged. "I've no chain for it, but I'll buy you one when we get home." Linna's fingers brushed his as she took the present, and he was shocked by the intense sensations that shot through his body. What was wrong with him to let this chit of a girl unnerve him so? She'd made it plain she'd have no bedding until they were wed by a priest. A priest! Rory forced his features to remain impassive. Wouldn't his mother be surprised to learn that the Protestant bride was actually a fire-breathing Catholic? Not that he gave a damn. Organized religion meant little to him anymore. He'd switched his religion to please his first wife and he supposed he could well switch back to suit this one.

Linna unrolled the bit of royal-blue velvet to reveal an oval ivory pendant engraved with a rosebud. "Oh," she cried, "it's beautiful." The ivory was smooth to the touch and the rose as real as any painting. "Where did you find it?"

Rory kept his voice light. "I'm glad you like it. One of the crewmen carves all manner of trinkets from the tusks of walrus and narwhals."

"You are too kind, sir." Linna swallowed hard and blinked away tears. "I will cherish it always."

Rory tried not to notice how the red-gold hair curled around her face and the flickering candlelight enhanced her classic features. It would be easy to let himself fall in love with this Irish colleen. The dancing flecks of gold in her cinnamon-brown eyes dared him to take

her in his arms and kiss her curving lips, taste that
tempting mouth and more . . . God but he wanted her!
It was why he stayed away, why he avoided speaking
to her as much as possible. If they were thrown together, he might not be able to stop himself from
quenching this fire growing in his loins. The captain's
words jolted Rory out of his reverie. Gaining control
of himself, he forced himself to give Cabbot his full
attention.

"Never approved of giving gifts on Christmas,"
Captain Cabbot said, "but I don't suppose it will hurt
to try your tobacco." He nodded to Slaybough, who
nodded to the cabin boy.

"The pudding, sir," Jeremy said, holding out the
bowl.

"Set it there," Mr. Slaybough instructed. "We'll
serve ourselves."

"Very good, sir."

"This is for you, boy," Rory said, tossing him a
shilling. "Merry Chirstmas."

Jeremy caught the coin in midair and looked apprehensively at Mr. Slaybough.

"Yes, it's all right," the first officer said. "You
may keep the shilling. You're excused until it's time
to clear away the dishes."

"I want to go over the charts with you, Slaybough,
after supper," the captain said. "If the Desmonds will
excuse me from our normal walk." He indicated a
pile of papers on his desk.

"Sir," Linna said hesitantly, "there is something I
wish to make known to you."

Captain Cabbot frowned. "Yes? What is it?"

Linna nibbled at her bottom lip. "The walks, captain,'' she managed. ''They will not do.''

''Will not do? What are you talking about, Mistress Desmond?''

Rory's eyes narrowed. ''What do you mean?''

She took a deep breath and stood up, flinging her napkin on her plate. ''I am not a rat, sir, or a mole. I cannot remain below decks like a keg of vinegar until we reach the American Colonies.''

Captain Cabbot's face reddened. ''But you walk— twice a day,'' he protested.

''No, sir,'' Linna corrected in her softly accented English. ''I do not walk—I am walked like some pet pony or spaniel. My . . . my husband paid a handsome price for our passage on your ship, and I am treated like a prisoner. I will not have it, sir. I will spend my day on deck in fair weather or . . . or . . .'' Linna thrust her wrists out before the captain. ''Or you may clap me in irons and lock me below in the hold with the rest of the cargo.''

Captain Cabbot cleared his throat loudly and glared at Rory. ''This is most unusual, sir. I had no idea your wife—''

''Neither did I,'' Rory said, coming to his feet. His mouth tightened and he stared at Linna coldly. ''You should have spoken to me about this first, mistress.''

''When, Master Desmond? When would I have time to speak to you about any matter of importance?'' Snatching her cloak and cocked hat from a hook, she threw the woolen garment around her shoulders and turned to the captain. ''I apologize if I have offended you,'' she said angrily, ''but I meant every word I said. No man on this ship has offered me any insult, by word or look. You are a gentleman and a fine captain, and I have no wish to question your authority, but I cannot continue this way. Have I your permission to walk freely about the ship or not?''

"I will discuss the matter with your husband, madam."

"Very well, do so," Linna retorted. "But if you wish to keep me below deck in good weather, you will have to lock me in my cabin. Good evening to you and to you, Mr. Slaybough, and a Merry Christmas to you both." Without waiting for a response, she hurried out of the cabin and up the narrow ladder to the deck.

Rory caught up with her on the bow of the ship. "Linna, stop." He grabbed her arm. "To what do we owe that little performance? If you were unhappy about something, you should have come to me."

"Aye, come to you," she agreed sarcastically. "When?" She tried to pull free and he trapped her in his arms. "Let me go!"

"Not if you're going to act like a spoiled child."

Linna stared at him in astonishment. "Me? By the bones of Saint Anne, 'tis you who are spoiled, Rory Desmond. I have been dragged about, nearly arrested by soldiers, half drowned, forced to live in a hatbox, and publicly insulted by the man who is to be my husband. And you have the nerve to call me spoiled? The devil take you, you are a foul-tempered, sullen man without an ounce of feeling. I should have thrown myself down the well before I agreed to go to the ends of the world with the likes of you."

Rory gave a low chuckle. "What have I let myself in for? I've picked a shrew and a scold for my life's mate."

"Picked? You picked nothing but my—" She corrected herself hastily. "My father's dowry. I could have been a dwarf or simpleminded for all you cared. You are marrying for money, Master Desmond, and don't you forget it.''

"And you, girl," he said lazily. "What are ye marrying for?"

"My mother—"

"Your mother, nothing," he said. "You came with me by choice, Linna. Why?"

A frisson of fear coursed through her. Rory must not learn the truth. What would he do if he found out she had deceived him? If he found out she was not the bride he had bartered for?

"I asked you a question," Rory said. "Why did ye come with me?"

"I don't know," she lied.

"And now you regret your decision?" He pulled her even closer and looked down into her face. "You made it clear that you didn't want to be treated like a wife. Have ye changed your mind, Linna? Do you want me to share your cabin?"

"No!" Why was he holding her so? His nearness made it almost impossible to think clearly. "Let me go—please," she insisted.

"Who are you, Linna?"

"What?" Her throat tightened and fear made her knees weak.

"Are ye the shy bride-to-be, obedient to her parents' will, or a tough, independent spitfire? You've a cool head, and you're smart. You faced danger without a word of protest, yet you'd have me believe you're a meek, frightened child. I agreed to marry you thinking you a Protestant, but we're not hours away from your father's house and you're demanding a priest. Is it any wonder I'm confused?"

Relief drained the tension from Linna's body and she felt herself go limp against him. "I'm as confused as you, Rory Desmond," she murmured. "Does it matter so much that I'm a Catholic?"

"Hell, no. Ye can be a Quaker for all I care. I've seen enough fighting over religion to last me a lifetime. Who says the words over us means nothing to me." One of Rory's hands slipped up Linna's shoulder to tangle in her hair. "I have been nothing but trouble to ye, haven't I, colleen?"

"Yes . . . no . . ."

Rory's mouth descended on hers. For an instant, she tried to hold herself aloof from the unfamiliar sensations that overwhelmed her, but the attempt was useless. Rory's warm, seeking lips wrought their own enchantment. Linna's arms went around his neck, and her lips pressed his eagerly, then parted as his kiss deepened. Her mind whirled as she savored the sweetness of his caress, reveling in the clean male scent of him.

A tiny glow of heat began in Linna's loins and spread up her belly, igniting her breasts with a tantalizing fire. She was acutely aware of her tingling nipples and the soft, velvet texture of his tongue against her own. Unbidden, a cry of delight rose in her throat as his left hand cupped the fullness of her breast.

"Come to my room, Linna," Rory murmured huskily. "I've thought of little else since we came aboard the *Betty Jane*. You are mine . . . you belong to me. There is no need for us to wait until—"

"No!" Frightened, she pushed him away. "A betrothal is not the same as a marriage," she cried. She turned to the ship's rail and clung to it, letting the icy wind blow the doubts from her clouded mind. "I cannot," she said. "You ask me to commit a mortal sin."

Rory's hand fell on her shoulder. "Linna, listen to me," he argued. "We are promised. If I got you with child, the babe would be legitimate under the law." He wrapped his arms around her waist, pushed the cloak back, and brought his lips close to her ear, placing a soft kiss on her neck. "Linna, I need you tonight. Slaybough will be occupied with the captain for hours. Come with me to my cabin."

Linna trembled beneath the heavy cloak as specks of salt spray struck her cheeks and throat. Sin or no sin, she wanted to go with him, wanted his beguiling caresses and the feel of his hard body pressed against hers.

"Ah, girl," he whispered.

"No, Rory." The taste of his name on her lips was strangely sweet. He kissed her again on the side of her neck and Linna's pulse quickened. "Please," she stammered.

"Please what?" he demanded, spinning her around and kissing her full on the mouth.

The intensity of Rory's searing kiss sent Linna's mind whirling. Unconsciously, her lips parted to receive his hot, questing tongue. Her fingers tightened in his hair, and she moaned deep in her throat as unfamiliar desire coursed through her.

"Linna, Linna," he murmured raggedly. His hands stroked her pliant body beneath the cloak, then spanned a hip and pulled her tightly against him. "I need you," he repeated over and over between kisses. "Sweet Linna."

Vaguely, she was aware of being led away from the rail. She knew she should resist, but Rory's hands were doing wonderful, shameful things to her body. Her breasts throbbed and the heat in her loins had grown to a fiery, all-consuming ache. His words were like honey, soft Gaelic caresses that filled her brain and drove out all thoughts of reason.

"I won't hurt you," he promised. "Ah, girl, I'll teach you such pleasure."

Linna felt the rough wall against her hand and knew they were descending the ladder. Rory's cabin was only a few feet down the passageway. Her breath was coming in ragged gulps as he caught her chin between his hands and traced the outline of her mouth with a hot, moist tongue. Her feet left the floor as Rory gathered her into his arms.

"Ah, Rachel," he said huskily.

Linna stiffened. *Rachel! Not Linna, but Rachel! It's not me he wants, but another.* With a cry of pain, she struck out at him. "Put me down!" she screamed.

Linna's backhanded blow struck Rory unaware, and he stumbled and fell back against the wall. "What the—" Linna wriggled free and backed away, her eyes narrowed in anger.

"My name is not Rachel," she declared. Waves of shame brought a deep rose flush to her throat and cheeks. She wiped at her mouth with the back of her hand. "Rachel is dead," she said.

Rory's face darkened. "I'm sorry," he said stiffly. "I didn't mean—"

"Ah, but you did, Rory Desmond. You kissed me, but it was another woman you felt in your arms," she accused. "I will be your wife when the time comes—if you still want me—but I will be Linna, not Rachel." Hot salt tears flooded her eyes as she fumbled for the door of her cabin. "I will come to your bed when the marriage lines have been signed and sworn to, but not before."

"Listen to me, Linna," he reasoned, taking a step toward her.

"No, I've listened enough. We have entered into a marriage of convenience, and that's what we both shall have."

"It's not that way," Rory protested, running a hand through his tousled hair. "You don't understand. She died a year ago today, Christmas Day."

"And your mourning ends today?" Linna said coldly. "You have my sympathy, sir, and the genuine regret that being at sea makes it impossible for you to find a whore to tumble. Do not suppose I will play the whore for you, Master Desmond. If you believe so, you are badly mistaken." Before he could reply, she flung open the door and dashed inside, slamming and locking it behind her.

"Linna!" Rory rapped sharply on the cabin door.

She sank onto the lower bunk and covered her mouth with her hands, ignoring the repeated knocks.

"What is it?" Mab asked. She let the petticoat she was sewing slide to the floor and came to Linna's side.

"Linna!" The door rattled.

"Go away," Linna insisted. "I have nothing more to say to you."

Another blow shook the door, and Rory cursed. Then all was quiet.

"What have ye done to anger him so?" Mab demanded.

"I'll not wed the fool!" Linna snapped. "I'd sooner marry a baboon."

"Fash, girl, are ye mad?" Mab muttered. "Ye are

promised to Rory Desmond for better or worse. A wise woman does not anger her husband before they are even wed.'' She made a disapproving clicking sound with her tongue as she returned to her sewing. "Such a fuss, and on the birthday of Our Lord.''

Linna slipped out of her coat and waistcoat, sliding the petticoat over her legs to the floor. She folded it carefully and tucked it away in the chest, taking a linsey-woolsey gown to sleep in. Mab must not see the tears. Dropping the gown over her head, Linna crawled into the bunk and pulled the covers up around her.

"Why did ye fight?'' Mab asked.

Linna buried her face in the pillow.

"Ye're makin' a mistake, girl, I warn ye. A new husband can be managed, but if ye get off on the wrong foot—''

"Enough, Mab,'' Linna said.

"Oh, so now ye think ye can put old Mab in her place, do ye, miss? Others may not know who ye really are, but I do. Do not take such a high road with me.''

Linna sat up and glared at the older woman. "You are part of the lie, Mab. If I am found out, so will you be—and what will become of you then?''

Mab drew in a deep breath and dropped her gaze. There was much in what the girl said. "Ye've changed,'' she answered. "Ye're not the Linna I knew at Mount Beatty.''

Maybe I'm not, Linna thought as she pulled the damp quilt tighter about her. But if I'm not Linna, who am I? The question haunted her into a dream-tossed sleep.

Chapter 7

The next morning, Linna rose in the early hours of dawn, struck a light, and dressed in the green wool riding habit. She was still tired after her restless night's sleep, but she could no longer tolerate the stuffy air in the windowless cabin. Despite her acute distress over the fight she'd had with Rory, she'd told the captain she would be on deck, and she meant to keep her word.

Mab stirred on the top bunk. "What is it? Be something wrong?"

"Nothing. Go back to sleep; it's early yet." Linna drew on her thick woolen stockings and heavy shoes, then wrapped herself in her cloak. She paused to blow out the candle, then slipped from the cabin and made her way down the passage to the ladder.

Something warm and furry brushed against her leg and Linna gasped, stifling a chuckle when her fingers encountered a long, silky tail. "Cat," she whispered in Gaelic. The cat greeted her with a husky *merowl* and rubbed his broad head against her hand. "Good morning to you," Linna said, switching easily to English. "I wondered where you'd gotten to." She crouched down and stroked the cat's back. "What's your name?'' she asked. ''I feel foolish calling you cat.'' The cat began to purr.

Linna looked up and down the shadowy passageway. The only light came from a lantern at the far end. Nervously, she glanced toward Rory's cabin door, listening for any indication that he was moving about. But the only sounds were the shifting and creaking of ship's timbers and the ever-present dull throb of the sea against the hull.

She took a deep breath and rose lithely to her feet. Would anyone try to stop her from coming on deck? What would she do if they did? With a final pat to the cat's head, she climbed the steps and pushed open the hatch.

The ship seemed wrapped in a silvery mist. A few quick steps brought Linna to the rail; she could barely see the water below. The air was cold, but so fresh and clean that Linna inhaled great gulps of it, hardly noticing the chill. Rays of shimmering golden light pierced the fog from the east, heralding fair weather. Standing perfectly still, she listened to the splash of waves and the rustle of rope and canvas.

''The sea and the ship make a strange music,'' Linna murmured half aloud. The vessel slipped through the water as silently as a dream ship. There was no shrill pipe of the bo'sun's whistle or slap of sailors' bare feet against the deck. The fog seemed to absorb and distort even the ordinary sound of the waves. Reason assured her that the water was beneath the ship, but to her ears the sound was all around her, above as well as below, like the breathing of some great sea monster.

Slowly, Linna moved to the bow of the ship and found a sheltered spot to curl up and watch the sunrise. As day slowly conquered the night, the mist dissolved and the blue-green expanse of water stretched before her unbroken by any mast or hint of land. Her cheeks and fingers burned from the cold, but Linna ignored the discomfort, spellbound by the haunting beauty of the sea.

"It's like a great church," she whispered into the glowing dawn.

"Aye, so it is."

Startled, Linna whirled to find Rory no more than a half dozen paces away. "Oh!" she cried. "It's you."

"And were ye expecting Prince George?"

"N-no," she stammered. "I thought I was alone here." She'd not wanted to face him so soon. Linna's heart began to pound as she tried to find the right words to say what she must. Damn him for that dark curling hair, those fierce eyebrows, and eyes as dark as peat—eyes that could charm the birds from the trees. Handsome as Lucifer himself must be, she thought— and as proud.

A sinking feeling in the pit of Linna's stomach made her suddenly light-headed. How dare she think she could deceive a man like this? She was the bastard get of a serving woman, not the highborn daughter of Mount Beatty's master. What right did she have to such a man, to such a life as he could offer?

"Ye realize ye are disobeying the good captain in coming up on deck alone?" Rory said. "Suppose ye had fallen overboard in the morning fog?"

Linna gazed at him suspiciously. Was he making fun of her or not? Was that the hint of a twinkle she saw in those brown eyes? "If I'd been fool enough to tumble overboard, then it would have been good rid-dance."

Rory laughed, a deep, warm sound. "Fair enough."

He offered her his hand and helped her to her feet. "It's a cold seat you've chosen. Your hand is like ice."

Linna pulled her hand back and tucked it inside her cloak. "I'm sorry for what I said last night," she blurted out. "Some of it, anyway. It was cruel of me to taunt you about your dead wife. 'Tis sorry I am for my foul temper."

Rory smiled grimly. "I fear I had it coming." He turned to the rail and stared out across the rolling water.

"It must be hard to lose someone you love," Linna said, coming to stand beside him. "And I was wrong to fault you for arranging a marriage with my father. If not you, he would have chosen another stranger to be my husband."

Rory glanced down at her without a hint of humor. "And he might have been a dwarf or feebleminded?"

"No, he thinks too much of Mar— of me. He would be concerned that my husband could father healthy children."

"Then perhaps Sir Edmond should have looked further. My only daughter, Anne, has been sickly since her birth."

"I'm so sorry!" Linna's rosy cheeks reddened even more. "By Mary's Son," she cried, "I did not mean to hurt you more. The devil take my tongue! Babes are born thriving or frail, dwarfed or straight, according to God's plan. It is not your fault or that of your dead wife. I only meant to say—"

He smiled with his eyes. "I know what you meant, Linna. And at least I am not a dwarf."

"No, you have the length and breadth of a man and a half. Not that being a dwarf is a bad thing. The cook at Mount Beatty is a little man, no higher than this." Linna held up a hand. "And he wed as pretty a colleen

as you'd ever want to see—or at least she was before
the babies started coming. She's put on a few pounds
now, but their three sons are as big as any boys their
age in the village.''

''Enough,'' Rory interrupted. ''I get up my courage
to apologize to ye, and you're babbling on about
dwarfs.''

Linna cast her gaze to the deck. ''I'm sorry.''

''I am not a man given to apologies, so you'd best
listen and remember this one. First, the issue of your
dowry,'' he said huskily. ''I would not have taken
another wife so soon if I wasn't badly in need of
money. In fact, I might never have married again. I
loved Rachel dearly.''

''I—''

''No.'' Rory threw up a hand. ''Be still until I'm
finished, because we won't speak of it again.'' He
cleared his throat. ''I made an agreement with Sir
Edmond for a bride, sight unseen . . . but if I hadn't
liked what I saw when I came to fetch ye, I would
have refused to go through with the ceremony. If ye
were a man, I think we could be friends—and I have
felt that about few men in this world.''

''What does my being a female have to do with it?''
Linna demanded. ''Couldn't we still be friends?''

''Must I put an iron on that tongue to silence it?''

Linna clapped a hand over her mouth.

''I did not lie to your father about my plantation in
Maryland. It is as fair a land as man ever laid plow
to. The soil is deep and fertile; there are no rocks to
speak of, and the rains come often. There are trees for
lumber and game in the forest for any man who will
hunt. I own enough land to make me a lord in Ireland—
but I am still in debt.''

''But—''

"Quiet! Did anyone ever tell you that a chattering woman is worse than a plague?" he demanded.

"No, but—"

"I have a motherless child to raise," Rory continued in a strained voice. "I also have a brother and my own widowed mother to support."

Linna's heart sunk. She would welcome an infant stepdaughter with open arms, but she hadn't expected a mother-in-law. Would she be able to pass herself off as Mary Aislinn before the older woman? Suppose Rory's mother hated her?

"My family lost everything in Ireland. My father lost his life," Rory said bitterly. "My mother deserves a home in her old age. I won't lose the plantation—I can't." He sighed. "We raise tobacco—good tobacco—and I'm a good planter. Two years ago, I lost my entire crop to pirates. And last year, heavy rains washed away most of the plants. I felt that marriage to a decent young woman would solve our problems. My child would have a mother, and the dowry would tide us over until next year's crop."

"And you, Rory Desmond? What do you need in a wife?"

Rory's brown eyes met hers. "I have a man's needs," he said frankly. "I want a willing woman in my bed."

Fear made her bold. "Just that?"

He took her shoulders in his powerful hands and pulled her so close she could feel his warm breath on her lips. "If I could choose, I would have a woman I could talk with at the end of a day. A woman who would laugh . . . and maybe sing a bit. I chose a Connemara girl because I thought we might have something in common. A man never loses the green of Ireland in his blood. Even in Maryland, I sometimes long for the soft speech and sweet ballads of Connemara.''

"If I were to sing, you'd think the crows had gotten into the house," Linna admitted. "But I can laugh, and you know I have a tongue to talk with."

"Aye, that I know."

Linna swallowed hard as flames of excitement ran down her arms. Rory's stare was enough to cause a girl to think of shameful things. "And children," she dared. "Do you want more children?"

"Rachel died in childbirth. The fever took her," he answered thickly. "For months I was dazed, half believing it was my fault. She was always delicate. But she wanted a babe as much as I did. Had I known what would come of it, I would have taken a serving girl to my bed and spared her."

"Risking her life in childbed is a thing a woman does," Linna answered, freeing herself and stepping back a few paces. "It was Rachel's right to have a baby."

"So my mother said. But a wailing child is poor substitute for my Rachel."

"You must want sons."

Rory shrugged. "I wanted Rachel's sons. Now . . ." His voice trailed off.

"I would want children . . . if we wed." What was wrong with her to say such things? What must he think? Not only did she fall into his arms whenever he opened them, but now she was asking him to give her babies! Saint Joseph in heaven! He'd think her a common slut. "I m-mean . . ." she stammered. "If God wills, I would welcome children."

"Catholic children, I suppose."

Dumbly, Linna nodded.

Rory laughed. "That should set my mother into a spin. She wraps herself in her newfound Protestant faith." He shook his head. "Don't trouble yourself about that now. When the time comes, if it comes, we will decide together—and I can assure you the decision will be ours, not my mother's. I love her dearly, but I will be master in my own house. Ye need not fear that I will place her over ye as mistress." .

"She lives in your house?"

"Yes, she and my brother, Donal. You'll like Donal; all the colleens do. He is but a little older than you, twenty-one on his last birthday."

"What is your mother's Christian name?" Linna asked. It was strange to be standing here, talking so easily to Rory of commonplace matters. Her fear began to fade, and her breathing slowed to normal. As long as he didn't touch her, she could keep her wits about her.

"Judith."

Linna moistened her lips and slid her hands under her cloak once more. The wind off the sea was cold, but a warm glow was spreading from her chest throughout her body. Rory wasn't angry anymore. They were talking like any betrothed couple. "Oh, it is a lovely name."

"My mother is a good woman, if somewhat strong-minded. You seem to share the same trait. Rachel was a gentle soul; she usually gave in to Mother whenever they disagreed."

"Oh?" Linna's lips pursed, and she clamped her teeth shut to keep from speaking. Was she to escape Lady Maeve's iron hand only to fall under another?

"Show Mother the respect she is due," Rory advised, "but use your own good sense. You are to be my wife, not a servant in the household." He turned back toward the sea. "You really prefer being up here in the cold to your cabin?"

"Aye, I do."

"Then Ty or I will try to accommodate you. I don't want you here alone. If ye will have a little patience, one of us will bring you up morning and afternoon."

"Thank you."

He held out his open palm. "Your hand, Mistress Beatty—" Blushing, Linna obeyed. With a wicked grin, Rory lifted it to his lips and kissed the tips of her fingers. "Since ye have made your wishes clear, I will try and restrain my"—he chuckled—"my urges until we reach home. Ye are ruining what might be a very pleasant voyage for us both."

"I think not, sir," she replied, looking up at him through thick lashes. "When I am truly yours in the eyes of man and God, I will try to be a good and obedient wife to you."

Rory threw back his head and laughed. "Ye will, will ye?" He gave her hand a comforting squeeze before releasing it. "Why do those sweet words give me so little comfort?"

The weeks that followed were dreamlike ones for Linna. Day after day, the ship danced across frothy, sunlit waves in weather so bright and clear that it brought murmurs of foreboding from Mr. Slaybough.

"Every day is the same," he'd said at supper. "Fair with steady wind. We'll break a record for crossing if this keeps up."

"And is that bad?" the captain had jokingly demanded. "I've known you to gripe about foul weather or a windless sea, but this? What ship's officer complains about a fast, safe voyage?"

"That's it, sir. It's too fair. When have you ever known a passage to go so smooth? No hands sick, no spoiled water, no fights among the crew. Makes me uneasy, it does."

"Pah, you're an old woman, Slaybough. A fast voyage makes happy owners," Captain Cabbot said. "It makes poor sense to borrow trouble; I'll take this over a rough trip anytime."

Linna agreed with the captain. Neither she nor Mab had suffered seasickness, and neither had any wish to succumb to it. Ignoring the cold, Linna spent most of each day walking on deck under the watchful eyes of her betrothed or of the taciturn Ty. And despite the broad-brimmed straw hat Linna wore, Mab's dire prediction that she would become as tanned and rosy-cheeked as a country milkmaid came true.

Linna's victory was not as sweet as she'd expected. Rory spent more time with her, and he refrained from pressing her to share his cabin with him. But the warm companionship and closeness they'd shared that morning on the bow of the *Betty Jane* had vanished. Once again, Linna saw glimpses of brooding mystery in the man she was to wed. Rory did not mention his first wife again, although he did speak enthusiastically of his baby daughter, Anne.

Grudgingly, Linna came to value Rory's friend, Ty. Rough though the frontiersman's appearance and manner might be, he exhibited his own sense of honor, treating her with the utmost respect. Ty rarely spoke to anyone but Rory, but when he did talk, he spoke fervently of the great wilderness that stretched from the western shores of the Chesapeake, across the mountains to a never-ending prairie, rolling across an unchartered continent.

Linna had little to do during the long days and nights

but think of the man she was to marry and, inevitably, of the deception she was playing on him. She was not Mary Aislinn Beatty; the lie taunted her. Memories of Rory's hard body pressed against hers and the feel of his caressing hands made her pulse quicken and her thoughts drift to those on which a chaste maid should not dare to dwell. Her lips ached for his kiss; her nipples were sensitive to the slightest brush of fabric. To Linna's shame, she could not sit or walk near Rory without trembling and experiencing the strange yearning for his touch. She could not keep from following him with her gaze or stop herself from tensing when she heard his husky voice.

This morning Linna had marked off the thirty-fifth day of the voyage as Rory had come to escort her on deck. The day was overcast, and a few flakes of snow had fallen in the night. The deck was slippery with patches of ice; frost sparkled on the rail and covered the masts with shimmering cloaks of white.

"Take care," Rory warned, supporting Linna's arm. "If you go overboard, you'll freeze solid before we can stop and pick you out of the water."

Linna looked at the dark gray water with respect. For days, chunks of ice had floated past the ship. She had no wish to test the temperature of the ocean, or to end her life so quickly. It was the coldest morning she could remember on deck, but the fresh air was as welcome as ever after the stifling confinement of the cabin. "I'll be careful," she promised. The bite of the wind tore through her thick wool cloak, and she knew she'd not be on deck long.

As they neared the bow of the ship, a sailor high in the rigging cried, "Sail ho!"

Another took up the shout, and Captain Cabbot

raised his telescope to peer out across the water.

"There, sir," the keen-eyed sailor shouted. He pointed to the east. "A square rigger."

"Can you make out her flag?"

The wind carried away the sailor's reply as Linna and Rory went to the rail to try and see the sails of the ship. They had not seen another vessel for weeks, and Linna could barely contain her excitement. "Does this mean we're getting close to America?" she asked Rory.

He shrugged. "Possibly."

They waited for what seemed to Linna like hours before the sailor, equipped now with the master's telescope, shouted again.

"She's flying the Union Jack, sir," he called. "And she seems to be in trouble."

"Say on," Captain Cabbot bellowed. "What's wrong?"

"Her staysails are beatin' back 'n' forth, sir. Her square sails are fillin', sir, but she ain't movin' right."

A dull boom echoed across the water.

"She fired cannon, and she's runnin' up a distress flag, captain."

The captain turned to shout at Rory. "You'd best see your wife below. She'll only be in the way if there's trouble."

"Please, Captain Cabbot, I won't," Linna cried. "I want to see the other ship. I won't move a step, I promise."

"It's on your own head, Desmond," the captain threatened. "She's your responsibility. Mr. Slaybough, I want all hands on deck, gunners at their stations."

Linna's eyes glowed with excitement. "Please,

Rory,'' she begged. "I want to see it."

Against his better judgment, Rory nodded. "But if I give the order," he warned, "you're to go below immediately."

Steadily, the *Betty Jane* gained on the square rigger. Soon, Linna could make out men on deck and the flapping Union Jack. "What's wrong, do you think?" she asked Rory.

"See how she's moving in the water? Something's wrong with her steering."

When the two ships were close enough for voices to carry across the water, Mr. Slaybough raised the captain's brass speaking trumpet. "Name your trouble," he shouted.

"Steering's broken," came the answer.

"Ask him why his ship's carpenter hasn't fixed it," Captain Cabbot insisted.

"Where's your carpenter?" Slaybough called.

"Dead! Can you send us yours?"

Captain Cabbot's brow furrowed. "What's the captain's name?"

"Who is the master?" Slaybough shouted.

"John Tanner out of Mystic."

The captain of the square rigger waved his hat. Captain Cabbot hesitated a moment, then nodded. "Tell him yes. We'll send a carpenter over by dory."

Slaybough relayed the message, but a longboat was already being lowered from the square rigger. The distance between the ships narrowed. Six men piled into the rowboat.

"Captain," Slaybough said hesitantly, "something doesn't look—"

Suddenly, a cannon roared from the square rigger. In seconds, the ordinary scene turned to one of utter chaos as gunshots echoed across the deck of the *Betty Jane*. Linna screamed as cannonballs smashed into the bow and splinters of wood flew up and struck her arm. Rory threw himself over her, forcing her to the deck. "Pirates!" he shouted.

The *Betty Jane*'s cannons spat fire and death as grapeshot and langrage tore across the enemy's deck. Her mouth dry, Linna raised her head to see a blast of bar shot whir into the pirate ship's rigging. "Below decks!" Rory ordered. "Keep your head down!"

Terror turned Linna's mind numb as she crawled along the icy deck toward the hatch. Men were running and screaming; a bloody sailor crumpled to the deck almost on top of her and rolled onto his back, staring blankly in bewildered death. The acrid smell of powder and blood filled Linna's nostrils, and her stomach pitched. She glanced back at the pirate ship one last time as her hand felt for the hatchway door. Fluttering over the square rigger, replacing the Union Jack, was a forbidding flag, a leering red skull against a field of black. Scrawled beneath the skull Linna read the chilling legend in French: *Ange de Mort—Angel of Death*.

Chapter 8

Rory flung open Linna's cabin door and shoved her inside. "I can't stay with you," he said. "I've got to give them a hand topside. Bar the door and don't come out—no matter what ye hear!"

Linna watched as Rory brought a musket from his cabin and ran down the narrow passageway toward the ladder. Loud rumbling of cannonfire and gunshots seeped through from the decks above. "Be careful," she called after him, then slowly closed the cabin door and leaned her cheek against the cold, rough surface.

"Lock the door," Mab ordered gruffly. She pointed toward the bottom bunk. "The cat's back. Trust a dumb beast to seek the safest place in danger."

Linna shot the bolt and stood with her back to the door. "Pirates," she said. "We've been attacked by pirates."

"I didn't think it was Quakers," Mab replied tartly. "How many ships did ye see?"

"Just the one." Trembling, Linna dropped onto the bunk and pulled the cat into her arms, hugging it against her breast wordlessly.

Mab pulled out her rosary and began to pray. "Holy Mary, Mother of God . . ."

A man's scream drifted down. Linna pulled a blanket over her shoulders, but she might have wrapped herself in a layer of ice for all the warmth it gave her. Her teeth began to chatter, and she couldn't stop shaking. "I'm scared, Mab," Linna admitted.

"Good, show's ye got a little sense left," the older woman snapped back.

Linna lost all track of time as the battle raged above, then she heard a tremendous shock and a crash. The cat leaped out of Linna's arms as the lantern tumbled to the floor. Mab screamed and threw something over the candle, plunging the small cabin into pitch blackness. The silence from the deck lasted only a few seconds, then Linna heard a roar of human voices, and the gunshots began again.

"We're being boarded," Linna whispered huskily.

"Shhh," Mab insisted.

Something thumped against the ladder, then sounds of men struggling came from the passageway. Steel clashed against steel. The women heard a shouted profanity, then a strangled moan. Wood splintered across the corridor. Mab gestured toward the cupboard and held a finger to her lips for silence. When crashing came from the cabin next to them, Linna rose from the bunk and pulled the wooden bucket from the cupboard and handed it to Mab. The older woman nodded and positioned herself behind the door.

Something heavy slammed against their door from the other side. "Open!" a man shouted in gutter French. "Open or Gaston will slit you from gullet to arse!" Another blow rocked the door. "Open!"

Mab nodded again and Linna slid the bolt and yanked open the door just as the man flung himself against it. The pirate charged into the tiny cabin, crashed into the top bunk, and fell heavily to the floor with twelve pounds of clawing, snarling tomcat on top of him. Linna stepped aside, and Mab brought the wooden bucket down across his head. The frightened cat fled through the open door; the man groaned once and went limp.

"Is he dead?" Linna cried.

Mab kicked at the pirate with the toe of her shoe. "No, I don't think so. He's still breathing." She bent to retrieve a bloodstained cutlass from his hand.

Linna pulled a pistol from his belt and wrinkled her nose. "By Mary's veil, he stinks like a midden! If he moves or starts to wake up, hit him again," she advised. Cautiously, she stepped around the man's crumpled form and out into the empty passageway.

Mr. Slaybough lay on his back, arms outstretched and eyes staring sightlessly in death. Linna shuddered and forced herself to keep walking.

"Where are ye going?" Mab demanded.

"Up on deck."

"Are ye mad, girl?"

Linna's voice cracked. "I'll not stay here like a rabbit in a trap! I can't! If this one found us, there'll be more of his kind."

"Linna!"

Linna whirled at Rory's shout.

"Linna," he called again as he staggered down the ladder, clutching his thigh. Blood seeped between his fingers and ran down his leg, soaking the cream-colored breeches. "Are you all right?"

Instinctively, Linna raised the flintlock pistol and aimed it in Rory's direction. Mab screamed as Linna pulled the trigger. The pistol spit fire and lead, filling the passageway with a cloud of smoke. Rory cursed once, then stared at the body of a pirate falling past him to the bottom of the ladder. A scarred boarding ax fell from the man's lifeless fingers and clattered harmlessly down the passage.

Linna dropped the pistol and ran toward Rory. "You're hurt."

"A damned sight less than I would have been if ye hadn't shot him." He indicated the dead pirate at his feet. "I thought ye said ye didn't know how to shoot a gun."

"I don't," Linna protested. "I saw him behind you . . . and I just . . . I think it fired itself."

"And aimed itself?" Rory leaned against her and exhaled loudly. "By God, woman, ye missed me by inches."

"Your leg, sir," Mab insisted. "We'd best stop the bleeding. Did ye take a musket ball?"

"Nay. A cannonball struck the rail beside me. The wood shattered, and I took a fragment in my leg. I pulled out the splinter, but it went in pretty deep."

Mab frowned. "Have the pirates taken the ship?"

Rory shook his head. "One of our cannonballs sent the pirate captain to hell in a thousand pieces. Our pious Captain Cabbot's New Englanders are a force to be reckoned with. There are a few pirates still fighting for their lives, but we've whipped them soundly. The *Ange de Mort* is afire. Those who don't surrender will be driven overboard."

"And your man Ty? Is he safe?" Linna asked. She kept her eyes away from the dead pirate—the one she had killed. She felt no guilt that she had committed a terrible sin. She was glad! And if she had the cannoneer that had caused Rory's wound in her sights, she would shoot him just as readily.

"Aye, when I saw him last. Oughh! Careful." Rory's already pale face whitened as the woman assisted him into their cabin. The first pirate still lay outstretched on the floor. "Thank God poor Slaybough got this one in time," Rory managed between clenched teeth.

"Mr. Slaybough was dead when this scum forced his way into our cabin," Linna said. "Mab hit him with the necessary bucket."

"One buccaneer dead and one captured—not bad for two women," Rory said wryly. Sweat broke out on his forehead as he eased himself onto Linna's bunk. The pain came in waves, threatening to make him faint.

Linna covered him with a blanket, leaving the injured leg exposed. Mab handed her a pair of scissors from the trunk, and carefully Linna began to cut away the material around the wound.

"Have ye had much experience doing that?" Rory asked. His mouth was dry, and his stomach was pitching to and fro like a flag in the wind. Linna's hands were gentle, but the wound burned. He was certain fragments of wood were lodged in his thigh. Rory took hold of Linna's arm. "I've my wits about me now," he said. "No matter what happens, no matter how bad the infection gets, you're not to let them take off my leg. Do ye understand?"

Linna winced as his fingers dug into her flesh. "What is this talk of cutting off your leg?" she soothed in her soft Connemara way. "I must wash the wound and look for dirt or pieces of wood still in it. This is no time to speak of such a thing as amputation. It's bad luck to borrow trouble, Rory Desmond. Now lay back and let me see to it before you bleed to death.''

"I'm serious, girl. These ships' surgeons know but one way to care for a bad leg or arm. I've a plantation to tend to and people that depend on me. I'll not be left a cripple.'' He released her, leaned forward, and braced himself on one arm. "I mean what I say. I'll have your word that ye won't let them take off my leg. Swear it!''

Linna moistened her lips. "If it comes to that, who would listen to what I say?"

"Ye are my wife—or at least they think ye are. Promise me, Linna.'' His features hardened. "And know that if ye betray me, I'll never forgive ye. I trust ye, girl. If ye give your word, ye'll stick by it.''

"I promise,'' she said hesitantly.

"Good. Have your way with me, Linna. Your hands, at least, are soft and clean.''

"Not so clean,'' she apologized. "Is there any water in the pitcher, Mab?''

Mab dug out a lump of soft soap and poured the water over Linna's hands, letting it fall into the bucket. "There's only a little water, and that's salt, but some say salt's the best for curing hurts.'' She offered Linna a towel.

"I'm just going to look at it now, and remove any foreign matter I find,'' Linna explained. "When it's safe to go on deck, we'll get water to wash it. Wine will have to do for now.''

"I think the wine would be better down my throat,'' Rory suggested. He was afraid he was going to be sick. "Ye'd best put that bucket near my head,'' he said.

"Lady Maeve—my mother," Linna corrected, "said that spirits of wine should always be used on open wounds. When my brother, Thomas, fell down the stairs and broke his arm, the flesh was broken and a piece of the bone sticking out. The physician wanted to take his arm off, but Mother insisted that he set it. She soaked it in wine for hours every day. The arm healed crooked, but it healed."

"I'd expect a highborn lady like your mother to be too delicate to concern herself with such matters," Rory said.

"Then you think wrong. She kept a corner of the garden just for medicinal plants. She grew wintergreen, chamomile, and columbine, to mention a few. She taught me how to dry the herbs and flowers and how to administer them to patients." Linna kept her eyes on the wound as she talked, gently swabbing at the welling blood and wiping away bits of torn cloth.

Lady Maeve had wanted Mary Aislinn to learn her healing arts, but Mary Aislinn had thought it disgusting to touch a sore or rash. She hadn't liked drying the herbs, either; she said they smelled bad. Eventually, Lady Maeve had given up trying to teach her daughter anything about herbs. Linna had never regretted the long hours she'd spent listening and watching as Lady Maeve mixed a salve or ground the fragile plants to powder. She'd done her best to remember everything Lady Maeve had told her. She'd even kept a journal of the plants and their uses. It was tucked into the bottom of her trunk.

"Ouch!" Rory cried out.

"I'm sorry." Linna moved her finger lightly over the wound until she felt something hard. "There's another splinter here. Just a minute." If she could only get a good hold on it . . . . "There!" With a quick motion, she snatched the fragment free, then poured the remainder of the wine over it.

"For the love of God," Rory moaned. "Ye could have warned me."

Linna was already pressing the wound together for Mab to wrap with clean linen. "You'll lose no leg from this, I promise you. For all the blood, it's not so deep. Rory? Rory?"

Rory's head fell back against the pillow and he went limp.

"Rory!" Linna cried.

"Hush, girl," Mab said. "The man's just fainted. I never saw a man yet that could bear the sight of his own blood. 'Tis a good thing God saw fit to have women carry the babes. There'd be few enough born if it was left up to the men."

Linna spent the rest of the day and night in the cabin caring for Rory. Nothing could have induced her to go on deck and witness the hangings. Every Frenchman who had survived the attack was taken before the captain and sentenced to death by the rope for piracy — including the unconscious man Mab had struck down. One by one, they were hanged and their bodies cast into the sea.

"God have mercy on their black souls," Mab said. "Frenchmen and pirates they may be, but some leave widows and fatherless children behind."

Ty had been less eloquent. "I'd not have wasted the rope or the time. My pappy used to drown rats."

Mr. Slaybough and the fallen crew members of the *Betty Jane* had been prayed over, wrapped in canvas, and consigned to the deep. Captain Cabbot had assured

Linna that their families would receive a share of the booty his men had been able to salvage from the French pirate vessel before she went down.

The healing herbs that Linna had brought in her sea chest were put to good use on Rory's wound. At Linna's request, Ty had helped him back to his own bunk the following morning. "He needs rest and quiet," she'd explained to Captain Cabbot when she'd refused the services of the ship's surgeon. "I will tend to my husband's injury myself. With proper care, he will be up and about in a few days."

"Pray God it shall be so, Mistress Desmond," the captain replied solemnly. "If the weather holds, we should sight land within the week." He nodded to Rory. "Now if you will excuse me, I have duties to attend to."

Rory lay back against the thin pillow and stretched his good leg as far as the cramped bunk would permit. "Ye continue to surprise me, little one," he said to Linna.

"Why?" She settled onto the stool she had carried from her own cabin, folded her arms across her breasts, and stared back at him as unself-consciously as a child.

Slowly, despite the dull aching pain that emanated from his injured thigh, Rory let his gaze travel over her, beginning at the tips of her sturdy black leather shoes that peeked out beneath her skirt. Linna's green woolen riding habit bore bloodstains along one sleeve and down the skirt, stains that gave evidence of an unsuccessful effort to scrub them away. The other sleeve had been torn at the cuff and neatly stitched with new thread. Linna had braided her hair, wrapped it tightly around her head, and covered it with a crisp linen cap. Despite her attempts at severity, red-gold tendrils of hair had escaped to curl impishly about her fresh-scrubbed face.

A sudden stab of desire brought a rush of heat to Rory's loins, and he stifled the urge to cup her cheek in his hand. The curves beneath that sensible woolen habit were soft and womanly. Her scent filled the cabin—a unique mixture of dried heather and healthy young female. The fact that Linna was innocent of her intense sensuality only made her attraction greater.

"Why do I surprise you?" she repeated.

"Ye would have made a rapparee, girl," he admitted. "My brother, Donal, warned me I'd be bringing home a spoiled, high-nosed heiress—one who would scorn my family and the Colonies. Wait until I tell him my bride is a slayer of French pirates."

Linna blushed. "I took a life. That is not a joking matter."

"Killing never is, but there are times . . ." Rory sighed and shut his eyes. "Go back to your own cabin and let me sleep," he said brusquely.

"But I—"

"Damn it, woman! Will ye for once do as I say without giving me an argument?"

Her Gaelic oath was cut off by the slamming of the cabin door. Rory opened his eyes and stared at the rough slats of the bunk above him. He'd hurt her unnecessarily; he knew it. Damn the fates that had brought them together!

The hurt came as it always did, but softened now by the passage of time. Rachel . . . His beloved Rachel was dust, part of the rich brown soil of the Tidewater country. Her blood and bone had mixed with the soul of the land, making it his in a way that went beyond understanding. And part of the love he'd felt for her had gone into his love for that bit of green earth beside the Chesapeake.

How much love did the Creator allot to each man? How long before his portion was used up? Rory had loved his father, and he'd lost him to an ugly death. Rory had loved Ireland with a young man's passion. He'd offered his heart and soul to Connemara, and Connemara, too, was lost, slipped through his fingers like dry sand. The crucible of those savage years in the American wilderness had completed the transformation. The idealistic rebel was burned away in the white-hot flames of reality. He'd killed too many men, red and white, ever to feel his hands would be clean of their blood. And when he'd come out of the woods and met Rachel, he'd been certain he was too weary, too cynical, to let himself be bound to another love so completely.

A dry chuckle rose in his throat to emerge as a low moan. He'd fallen for Rachel as though he'd been struck by lightning. Scottish, Church of England, shy, gentle Rachel had stolen his heart the first time he'd laid eyes on her. He'd changed his religion for her, hung up his rifle and become a farmer. He'd given her his name and his love . . . and that love had killed her. She'd died of childbed fever within a year.

Rachel's death had brought him near madness, but he had come back from that black pit. He'd taken up his life and responsibilities for the sake of Rachel's child and for his mother and brother. And now he had added the burden of a new wife to those responsibilities.

He desired Linna fiercely—in the way a man wants a woman. He valued her good sense and her humor. He was prepared to care for her and to honor her, to protect her with his life. What he was not capable of doing was loving her.

"Damn her to hell!" Why couldn't she have been a shrew with the face of a cow? He could have dealt with that easily enough. He wanted a wife—not a lover. "I'll not take that road again," Rory swore under his breath. "No more." If he let down his guard, if he let himself begin to love her, he would only lay himself open for the pain and heartache to begin again. "No more." He slammed his clenched fist against the bandaged thigh and welcomed the pain when it came.

He and Linna were making a marriage of convenience. It was that and nothing more; it would remain that way. It had to if he wanted to keep his sanity. *She's falling in love with me,* a voice within him warned. *I can't let that happen.* It wouldn't be fair to Linna. They could be friends—no more. "There's no love left to give her," he murmured.

What he felt was lust, Rory assured himself. It had been too long since he'd lain with a woman. The physical part of their marriage would be easy enough to satisfy. When children came, Linna's life would be full enough. If he was kind to her, wouldn't—

The door banged open. "Are you asleep?" Linna demanded. "It doesn't look like it to me." She thrust a mug of foul-smelling liquid toward him.

"What is it?" he asked suspiciously.

"Just drink it. It will keep your fever down and help you to sleep." Linna's gaze dropped to his thigh and she gasped. "It's bleeding again!"

"It's nothing," Rory said, taking a sip of the potion. "Ugh! What's in this stuff? Rats' droppings?"

"It would serve you right if it was," she retorted. "What have you done to my clean bandage? I'll have to wrap it again. Mab said I should sew the wound shut, but I thought—''

"No sewing!" Rory yelled. "For the love of God, it's a scratch, nothing more. Can you leave me in peace?" He shuddered as he remembered his last ordeal of being sewn together. It had taken three warriors to hold him down while an Iroquois squaw had stitched up the results of his accidental encounter with an angry bear. He'd slept on his stomach for months after that while his back healed, and he still had nightmares about the procedure.

" 'Tis more than a scratch and well you know it," Linna scolded. "I'll not be saddled with an invalid husband if I can prevent it." Ignoring his grumbling, she began to unwind the bandage. "You'll be in no shape to tend that precious plantation of yours when we get to Maryland if this doesn't heal right."

Rory swallowed the remainder of the herb tea, sat the empty mug on the floor, and turned his face to the wall. "Have your own way, then, woman. You'll give me no peace until you've completed your witchery."

"Stop your senseless braying," Linna flung back. " 'Tis luck for you I'm not a witch, for if I was, I'd turn you into the jackass you sound like! Oh," Linna choked as she felt the heat rise in her face. "I'm sorry . . . I didn't mean . . ."

Rory's warm chuckle eased the tension between them. "Nay, Linna. No apologies. You've the right of it. I do sound like an ass. Do what ye like, Linna. But I give ye fair warning—once I've wedded and bedded ye, you'll dance to a tune of my choosing."

Chapter 9

January 1754

It was snowing when a seaman aboard the *Betty Jane* lowered the Dutch flag and raised a British one off the mouth of the Delaware Bay. "We want to be certain of our welcome," Captain Cabbot explained to Rory.

"And is it possible you have other flags in your cabin?" Rory asked innocently. He was well aware of British law that forbade Colonists from purchasing the cheaper Dutch trade goods. The switching of flags only confirmed his opinion that the *Betty Jane* was a smuggling vessel.

"Naturally not!" the captain roared back. "Do you take me for a dishonest master?"

Linna didn't miss the wink that Captain Cabbot gave Rory as he turned to go below.

A few hours later the ship dropped anchor at the small town of Lewes to allow Rory Desmond and his party to disembark. "You'll have no trouble finding passage to the Chesapeake," Captain Cabbot assured them. "Good weather or foul, ships touch at Lewes on the way to Annapolis and Chestertown. The Widow

Brinker sets a good table. She'll give you lodging and meals until you get a ship. Just follow the main street until you come to a house with a blue door. There's no sign, but she can always make room for a few more guests.''

A longboat was lowered to carry Linna, Rory, Ty, and Mab to the dock. At the last minute, Linna had carried the one-eared cat on deck and begged Captain Cabbot to let her have him. ''Please, sir,'' she said. ''I'll give him a good home. I promise.''

''And what will we do for the rats?'' the captain asked.

Rory laughed and tossed him a silver penny. ''You'll send your cabin boy to pick up another cat on the streets of Philadelphia.'' Quickly, he handed Linna and the cat down the ladder to Ty in the boat.

The cat crawled inside Linna's cloak and settled as peacefully in her lap as though being rowed ashore were an everyday occurrence.

Snow was still falling as they trudged up the street to the Widow Brinker's house. A blanket of white covered the neat houses and yards and muffled the sounds of an occasional barking dog or passing horse. Linna's first impressions of America were of the cold and the blowing snow.

The Widow Brinker provided ample, well-cooked meals and clean bed linen. the women were housed over the kitchen on thick cornhusk pallets, sharing the single room with the four Brinker girls. The men bedded down on the kitchen floor before the fire. The cat was exiled to a storeroom.

''I'll charge nothing for the cat,'' the widow had said. ''He can pay for his keep by ridding the place of mice.''

The snow fell for four days, and on the first clear

morning, Rory found passage for them on a sloop bound for Oxford on the Eastern Shore. The small ship was laden with cargo and even carried a pig and a crate of chickens. The single cabin was so crowded that Rory and Ty were forced to spend the days and nights on deck, coming below only to grab a bowl of hot corn mush and portions of bacon.

Linna spent as much time as she could on deck, trying to view the coast of America off the starboard side of the sloop. For a long time, there was only sand which then gave way to a thin line of trees.

"We're entering the mouth of the Chesapeake," Rory said. "We'll soon be home."

"Not soon enough for me," Mab grumbled. "Another few weeks of ship's biscuit and I'll lose every tooth in my head."

"Ty tells me that the plantations all have names," Linna said to Rory. "What is yours called?"

Rory leaned back against a large wooden crate and rubbed at his bandaged thigh. As Linna had promised, the wound had healed without becoming infected. He wasn't sure if Linna's herbs had done the trick, or if it was the salt water she had poured over the injury every few hours. In any case, he was on his feet and walking with only a little stiffness to remind him of the accident.

"I asked you what you call your plantation," Linna repeated, stroking the cat. "I've decided to name him Brigand. Don't you think that's a good name for a sea cat?"

"I didn't know cats had names." Rory pulled his cloak tighter around his shoulders and strained his eyes for familiar landmarks. "The plantation I call Connemara."

"Atcch, Rory, I love it," she cried. "With such a

name it'll feel like home—I know it will.''

" 'Twas to please my mother,'' Rory said. There
was no need to let Linna know how homesick he'd
been for Ireland during his first years in America.
"The house is nothing like Mount Beatty, but 'tis no
hovel I bring you to,'' he assured her. "Connemara
is small, but I think she has her own beauty.''

"I didn't expect a house like Mount Beatty,'' Linna
replied. In truth, she'd not known what to expect.
Mary Aislinn had insisted Linna would be going to
live in an Indian hut, and Mab had said they'd be lucky
if the inhabitants of Maryland didn't live in caves.

"The house sits on a rise,'' Rory explained. "It's
bounded on two sides by water—the Choptank River
and a small creek. We have our own dock on the creek.
The nearest town by land is Talbot Courthouse and by
water a place called Oxford.'' He laughed. "Our roads
are worse than those in Galway, if that's possible.
You'll find we travel by boat most of the time.''

"And will we leave the ship at this Oxford?'' she
asked.

"Nay. Our creek is deep enough for oceangoing
vessels. I've made arrangements for the captain of this
sloop to take us directly to our own dock.''

When will we ever reach Maryland? she wondered.
The journey had stretched on for so many weeks that it
had been easy for Linna to believe it would go on
forever. Now that they had almost reached their destination, her fears came rushing back. Rory and Ty had
accepted her as Mary Aislinn Beatty. Would Rory's
mother be as easily fooled? What would they do to
her if they found out the truth?

Ireland seemed another world. Was it possible she
could put that world behind her? The slurs and hurts
that had been directed toward the bastard child of a

serving woman could never touch Rory Desmond's new bride.

She'd miss the smells and sounds of Connemara, the azure-blue sky and the whitewashed cottages against a field of green heather and gray stone. She'd long for the earthy fragrance of peat and the heady scent of roses in early summer. The vivid colors of columbine, buttercups, and wild violets would remain forever imprinted on her mind. Linna would mourn the loss of all those bright memories, but she'd gladly close the door on the pain and deprivations of her childhood.

Nothing in the Colonies would make her long to return to Ireland. She would commit herself—body and soul—to this man beside her and to this place. Unconsciously, Linna's fingers reached out to catch hold of Rory's hand. She looked up at him shyly. "Will your family like me, do you think?"

Rory turned her hand palm up and gazed at it. Rachel's hands had been soft; he'd watched her rub scented oil and honey into them at night. The bones beneath Rachel's skin had been fragile, like the bones of a bird. There'd been no cracks or calluses, no chapping or broken nails like the hand he held now. Linna's fingers were as strong and tough as those of a farmwoman; her palm showed the mark of leather reins and scars of briars and old scrapes and blisters.

"A man would think you had no servants at Mount Beatty," he mused, ignoring her question. "Did you work in the fields beside your father's cottagers?"

Blushing, Linna snatched her hand back and tucked it into her cape. "I like to work in the herb garden," she said, "and with the flowers. Does it displease you?"

"You ride?"

"Of course." An angry retort rose to her tongue and she bit it back. "Don't Maryland ladies ride?" she managed.

"Aye, they ride, fast and furious. You'll be in good company. Mother doesn't, at least not for sport. But I'll see you have a suitable mount."

"Thank you, sir," she said stiffly. She glanced sideways at him under her lashes and cursed herself for forcing her attentions on him. Her hands were not those of a lady; Mary Aislinn had told her so enough times. Her bitten fingernails and rough skin were not suited to fine embroidery. She had spent too many hours at the loom and in the kitchen, and the chilblains she had suffered as a child had left their traces. Fear clouded her mind. Did Rory suspect anything?

Giving a hasty excuse, Linna went below deck to huddle beneath a blanket in the single cabin. She tried to pray, but her lips would not form the words. How could you pray that God would help you to live a lie? Linna realized that she was exhausted, so tired that she could barely keep her eyes open. She leaned back against her sea trunk, pulled her legs up under her, and surrendered to the mental and physical fatigue that had suddenly overwhelmed her.

Voices surrounded her. Linna wanted to open her eyes, but it took too much effort. Her limbs refused to obey her sleep-fogged mind. Vaguely, she was aware of Mab's soothing voice and one she didn't recognize. Strong arms lifted her. "What's . . . Who are . . ."

"Shhh," the comforting male voice assured her.

Rain spattered against Linna's face. Cold. It felt so cold. Someone was carrying her. Was it Rory? She knew she should protest, but her head ached and she was so weary. It was easier to float in this half-awake, half-dreaming state.

"Welcome home, Linna." A man's lips pressed against hers tenderly.

The rain on her face stopped. Where was Rory taking her? They seemed to be climbing. A knot of nausea formed in the pit of Linna's stomach, draining her last reserve of strength.

"Put her down here," Mab said.

Slowly, the air around her became warmer. Mab tugged insistently at Linna's clothing. Was she in a bed? Linna snuggled down into a soft, clean feather tick and gave up the struggle to retain consciousness.

"Wake up, girl. Ye've slept long enough."

Linna opened one eye, then clamped it shut as bright light came flooding in. Cautiously, she opened both eyes. She was in a great four-poster bed with embroidered satin hangings.

"Ye've slept a day and night and most of this day. What ails ye?" Mab fussed, fluffing at the pillows.

Linna's eyelids felt as though they were lined with sand. The headache was gone, but her mouth was dry and her tongue seemed swollen. "I'm thirsty," she murmured. "Is there something to drink?"

Mab turned to a young black girl holding a tray. "Let me have that tea," she ordered. "Sip some of this, mistress." Mab put an arm under Linna's shoulder. "Sit up. Ye'll choke to death if ye try to drink like that. It's good China tea, and I've sweetened it for ye."

Linna tried not to stare at the black serving girl as she sipped the delicious tea. Lady Maeve had said there were many blacks in the Colonies. Linna had seen only two in Ireland, and they were at a distance. The girl was wearing a neat gray homespun gown and a crisp white apron. She must be a servant, Linna thought. That is why Mab is being so polite to me, because a stranger is in the room.

"I slept a whole day?" Linna asked.

Mab nodded. "Leave the tray, girl," she said, dismissing the maid.

The black girl bobbed a curtsy and hurried out of the bedchamber.

"Gather your wits about ye," Mab urged. "Ye've frightened me half to death. I thought ye were taken by ship's fever."

"I'm sorry . . . I didn't . . ."

Mab waved impatiently. "No need for that. Ye were worn to the bone, that's all. But ye must rise and dress and meet the family. There's no time to coddle yerself; we've come to a house in mourning."

Linna sat bolt upright. "What's happened?"

Mab's lined face wrinkled with concern. "Yer stepdaughter, Anne—the baby. She died in her bed not two weeks after Master Desmond set sail for England."

"Rory," Linna said thickly. "He didn't know until . . ."

"How could he? His family had nowhere to send word."

"How is he?"

"Taking it hard. He went to the grave this morning. Poor babe. The girl that was just here, Daisy, said the child was sickly from birth. But she wasn't ill. They just found her dead in her cradle."

Linna threw back the covers and slid from the bed. "I must go to him," she said. "Quickly, my clothes."

"Ye'll go not a step until ye've bathed and washed yer hair," Mab replied sternly. "I'll not have ye meet yer new mother-in-law like a gypsy. There'll be time enough to give comfort to the master. For now, ye must establish yer place in this fine house."

There was a timid knock at the door; then two women came in carrying a tin bathtub, followed by the black girl Daisy with a bucket of steaming water.

"This is yer new mistress," Mab informed the women. There were shy murmurs of greeting, and all three curtsied again. "Mistress," Mab said gravely, "this is Daisy"—she pointed to the black girl—"Edna, and Bessie."

Linna returned their greeting and smiled. She judged Daisy to be a few years younger than she was, and Edna to be about the same age as herself. Bessie had traces of gray in the black hair at her temples.

"We'll need more water," Mab urged. "Hurry. And Edna, bring more wood for the fire. I won't have Mistress Linna taking a chill."

In the next hour, Linna was bathed and powdered and dressed in borrowed petticoats, old-fashioned hoops, and a fine gown of dove-gray. Mab washed Linna's hair and brushed it out before the fire until it was dry. Then she gathered the unruly tresses into a delicate lace snood and pinned it firmly at the back of her head.

"No curls today." Mab lowered her voice as the serving women carried away the bathwater. "The lady of the house must have no cause to find fault with ye."

"Rory's mother? What is she like?" A dozen questions rose to Linna's lips. "Is she—" Linna stopped in mid-sentence, drawing a sharp intake of breath as a strange man appeared in the open doorway.

"So, you've decided to join us," he said, stepping into the room. A wide grin split the darkly handsome face. "We've already met, although you may not remember." Quickly, he strode across the room and bent to kiss her soundly on the lips. "Greetings, sister," he said. "Welcome to Connemara."

Linna blushed, unable to stifle a small sound of confusion. "You must be Donal," she stammered. "Rory's brother."

Donal chuckled. There was no mistaking the Desmond men's laugh. "Aye, so you do remember. I carried you up from the sloop."

"You?" she asked stupidly. *He kissed me then! I do remember. But I thought it was Rory.* "I remember nothing," she lied. Recalling her manners, she extended her hand. "But I am very pleased to meet you, Donal."

"So formal," he teased, dropping easily into a high-backed chair. "And I love your accent. Don't ever lose it as the rest of us have. It sounds like home."

He looks like Rory, she thought. Slender, almost as tall. His hair and eyes were the same—no, not the same. Donal's brown eyes were flecked with gold; they were laughing eyes. It was impossible to feel ill at ease with the owner of such dancing, mischievous eyes—even when he was lounging, uninvited, in a lady's bedchamber.

"Is Rory—"

"Gone. Off to Talbot Courthouse on business. He'll not be home until morning. I'm to act as your escort, fair lady. I'll stand beside you when you confront the lioness in her den." Donal grinned insolently. "Mother," he explained. "You must pass muster. She'll never forgive you that she didn't get to check your teeth and gait herself before the bargain was sealed.'' He settled back and folded his arms over his chest. ''You're far too pretty for a bartered bride, you know. Mother was expecting a long, thin aristocratic nose and tiny feet. Do you have tiny feet?''

Linna giggled. ''I'm afraid not.''

''Ah,'' Donal sighed loudly. ''What's to do?'' He scratched his head and pursed his lips, then raised one eyebrow roguishly. ''Now, if you don't suit mother as bride to the heir, perhaps she'd consent to let me have you. A second son can wed where he pleases— within reason, of course.''

Mab cleared her throat in disapproval.

Donal chuckled again. ''Peace, old marsh hen. I'll not compromise your chick in my brother's house, although I'm not saying it wouldn't be fun to try.'' He leaned forward and gave Linna a penetrating look. ''Don't let my mother intimidate you,'' he cautioned. ''She'll try. She's got a good heart beneath that prickly crust, but she fancies herself a dragon.''

''I thought the marriage was her idea,'' Linna said.

''Aye, and so it was. Your dowry is to save Connemara from the brink of the sheriff's gavel. We've had a bad turn of luck lately. Annie's death was the worst of it.''

''I'm so sorry to hear about the child,'' Linna replied.

''Her loss cut my mother deep. We'll all miss her, wee sprite of a baby that she was.'' Donal's eyes clouded with emotion. ''The best thing you can do is to give Rory another child—boy or girl. Girls are valued highly here in the Colonies, you know. There's such a shortage of unmarried females that a maid too ignorant to read her own name can have her pick of landed suitors.''

Linna blushed again. ''Your brother and I are not

wed yet; it is too soon to speak of children.''

''It is never too soon to speak of children.'' An unfamiliar Gaelic voice filled the room.

Linna rose to her feet as a tall, gray-haired woman swept into the room. ''Madam,'' she murmured and dropped to a graceful curtsy.

''Daughter.'' Cool lips brushed Linna's cheek. Strong fingers closed around Linna's hand and lifted her up. ''You don't look to be sickly,'' Judith said, switching back to English.

''No, madam, I'm not. I'm afraid the journey—''

''I remember the ocean journey all too well; I would not wish to make the trip from Ireland again.'' Faded blue eyes bored into Linna's brown ones. ''The wedding must be postponed for a few weeks. Rory needs time to adjust to the shock of Anne's death. I'm certain you understand that, Mary Aislinn.''

''Yes, of course, madam. I—''

''Linna, Mother,'' Donal interrupted. ''Rory said she prefers to be called Linna.''

''This is a much simpler household than you were accustomed to in Ireland,'' Judith stated flatly. ''I detest 'madam.' You may call me Judith, or Mother Desmond, as you please.'' She frowned. ''Rory tells me that you wish the marriage to be performed by a Catholic priest.''

''Yes, ma— Yes, I do. I am a practicing Catholic.''

''Your father led me to believe otherwise,'' Judith said sternly. ''Well, there's little to be done about it now, I suppose. Rory changed his religion once for his first wife; he'll have to endure the switch back for you. When will your father send the dowry?''

''I don't know.'' Linna fought to hold back her rising anger. ''I was not consulted about the arrangements, and Rory and I had to leave quite suddenly.''

''Humph.'' Judith sniffed. ''I've seen the betrothal agreement. It seems legal. Is Sir Edmond in the habit of breaking his word?''

Linna stiffened. ''No, madam, he is not.''

''Good, then I see no reason why we can't go on with the wedding as planned, after a proper mourning period—a few weeks at most. You will have much to learn if you expect to take your proper place as Rory's wife. I trust you are not lazy.''

''No, madam, I am not.''

''Then we will get on well enough. The mistress of a Tidewater plantation works harder than any indentured kitchen wench. I will be happy to have your assistance. If you are modest and truthful and willing to learn, I will be pleased with Rory's choice. Donal will show you about the house and grounds. Rory had to leave the plantation on important business. You must accustom yourself to his absences.'' She paused for breath and then plunged on. ''I noticed how few belongings you brought with you, and I have instructed Daisy to provide you with some of my things until yours arrive. This is to be your room. Is it satisfactory?''

Linna glanced about the spacious bedchamber. It was sparsely furnished, but what was evident was quality. Two broad windows gave light and a view of fields running down to the river. ''It is quite satisfactory,'' she said.

''Then I bid you good afternoon. It is past teatime, but one of the girls can bring you something to eat if you are hungry. Supper is promptly at eight.'' With a frosty nod, she left the room.

Donal caught Linna's eye and winked. ''What did

I tell you? The only thing lacking is fire and smoke, and you'll see that if she gets mad enough.''

Mab made a sympathetic click with her tongue.

Linna wished that they would all go away and leave her to gather her wits about her. Why had Rory left her alone to face his mother? He must have known how Judith would behave. She gave Donal a shy smile. At least she had one friend in this strange house. The question was, would her bridegroom be as supportive?

''Come, little sister,'' Donal said, rising and holding out his hand. ''I know for a fact that there is fresh apple pie in the kitchen, and a wheel of aged cheese. If I hadn't eaten for two days, I know I'd be starving.''

''Yes,'' Linna agreed, ''I am.'' Suddenly, she wanted to see the rest of the house, she wanted to see it all. The sooner she began to settle in, the sooner they would all come to accept her—wouldn't they? With a silent prayer to Saint Patrick to give her courage, she allowed Donal to take her hand and lead her out of the chamber.

Chapter 10

March 1754

Linna stood before the open window and stretched as the early morning sun spilled into the room. Brigand, the one-eared cat, licked lazily at an outstretched paw and narrowed his eyes as he gazed at the trilling mockingbird on a tree branch outside the window. "Just don't get any ideas," Linna warned in Gaelic. "The tree's too far away." She scratched the top of the tomcat's head and leaned both hands on the windowsill, letting her eyes drink their fill of the beauty that stretched before her.

In the weeks that had passed since Linna had come to Connemara—New Connemara, she called it in her mind—she had watched the plantation turn from winter gray and white to spring green. "Could I have appreciated the wonder of it all if I had come in summer?" she asked the cat. Ignoring her, Brigand began to groom his other front paw. "Scoundrel!" Linna teased. "You'll not have my mockingbird."

She leaned from the window and inhaled deeply, reveling in the soft, salt-tingled air. " 'Tis a fairyland," she murmured as the pale greens of new grass and sprouting leaves warmed her heart. A shiver of excitement passed through her and she laughed out loud. What was there about this magical place? She'd always loved spring, but she couldn't remember ever feeling so alive. The tiny leaves on the majestic oak just beyond her window seemed to grow as she watched. "A new land," she whispered. "A new, fresh land . . . and a new beginning."

Across the sweeping lawn, down near the water, Linna could see two figures on horseback. It was too far to make out the men's faces, but by the color of the horses they rode, she knew it was Rory and his brother, Donal. Suddenly subdued, Linna shut the window and turned back to finish dressing.

If there was a shadow across her new life, it was her relationship with the man who would become her husband in two days. Linna dropped onto the bed and lay back against the tumbled covers. Since they had arrived in Maryland, Rory had distanced himself from her. Their meals had been in the company of his family and the servants; Rory's leisure time had consisted of a few isolated periods in early evening in the great hall, again as part of the group. They had enjoyed no private time together, no lovers' whispered sweet talk, no snatched embraces or shared laughter.

It had been Donal who had taken her riding, who had shown her about the plantation, who had introduced her to the servants. Donal joked with her and tried to make her feel a part of the family.

"What's wrong?" Linna had asked Rory one morning when they'd passed each other in the yard. "Have I done something?"

He'd given her a strange look. "Nothing's wrong," he'd answered. "I've been working."

"I know there was much to do when—"

"Aye, much to do." A fleeting expression of concern crossed Rory's face. "If the fields are not prepared properly, we'll have no crop this year." He'd laid a hand on her shoulder. "Has Mother been giving you a hard time?"

Linna had smiled and shrugged. "It's you I—"

"I've set a date for the wedding. What more do you want?" Rory pulled off his cocked hat and ran a hand through his hair. "For God's sake, girl, I've been working eighteen hours a day. We had a mare foaling half the night, and I've not had a bite to eat since yesterday. What is it ye want of me? Love sonnets?"

"Nothing, sir!" she'd snapped. "I want nothing of you." She had turned and run to the barn and hidden in a corner, trying to compose herself before Donal came to take her riding. She'd not cried, not outwardly; the tears had remained within and turned hard and cold.

Linna rolled over onto her stomach and buried her face in a pillow. She and Rory were to have an arranged marriage; it was the custom. Few women chose their own husbands for any reason other than securing a roof over their heads and food in their bellies. The gentlefolk might pretend otherwise, but a girl's dowry was far more important than her wit or even her face. Linna was lucky to have any husband at all—let alone a landed gentleman. She had chosen this man. She loved him, she had loved him since she was a child.

Memories surged over her, memories of the ragged child she had been and the handsome young rapparee she had risked her life to help. So long ago and yet so vivid in her mind. Would she ever be able to tell Rory that she was the child who had saved him?

Linna had sacrificed her only shift, ripping it to the

knee and using the wadded-up cloth to press against the stranger's bleeding shoulder. Too poor to own a petticoat, she'd known when she'd done it that her stepfather Gill would beat her for ruining the shift.

Linna rolled on her back again and stared at the embroidered bed hangings overhead. When she'd refused to tell Gill how she'd ripped the shift, he'd broken a stick the size of his thumb over her back and forced her to wear the shift for weeks. The other children, urged on by her stepbrother Sean, had taunted her about the indecent garment, laughing and calling her crude names. Worse, Sean had trapped her one night in the corner by the hearth, running his dirty hands up her thigh. She'd struck out at him with her fists and feet, earning a black eye and a bloody lip from his hard fists. But a well-aimed kick had struck Sean in an undefended area of male vulnerability and he had limped for two days, a potent reminder not to try his filthy tricks with her.

Swallowing her pride, Linna had gone to Father Joseph in tears. "I need a shift," she'd said, "but Gill's forbidden my mother to make me a new one." She'd been too ashamed to mention Sean's harassment.

"Leave this to me," the priest had said. The following day, he'd returned, producing a patched blue woolen shift and petticoat.

"What if Gill won't let me keep it?" she had asked.

"I'll tend to Gill," Father Joseph had assured her.

Linna never learned what he had said to her stepfather, but although Gill had glared at her malevolently, he never said a word about the new clothing.

Linna fingered the fine linen shift she wore now, letting her fingers slide over the delicate embroidery. "All that fuss over a ragged shift," she whispered.

The cat jumped up on the bed beside her and curled into a ball, purring.

"I've come so far," Linna murmured. "Is it wrong to ask for more?"

She remembered how she'd sat beside Rory Desmond throughout that long night, praying for his life with all the fervency of a child. She'd held the makeshift bandage over the wound until her fingers went numb, and wept silent tears over his still face when a British patrol passed within yards of their hiding place. And in the muffled gray mist of dawn, she had made her way back to the old woman's cottage and told her of the young rapparee.

Maggie O'Shaughnessy had listened to every word, then fetched her donkey from the pound, and the two of them had gone to bring the man to Maggie's house. Linna had watched as Maggie washed the bullet wound and wrapped his shoulder in clean linen. "The ball's gone clean through, praise God," Maggie had said. "If he lives, he has you to thank for stopping the bleeding."

Linna had stayed in Maggie's cottage all day. No one cared enough to come and look for her. When night fell again, they carried him, still unconscious, up to the hills on the donkey. Maggie had refused to say where they were going. After doubling back and forth, they reached the mouth of a cave at last.

"There is food and water inside," Maggie had said. "You must swear on your immortal soul never to reveal this place to any man or woman that draws breath."

"I do," Linna had promised. She hadn't needed Maggie to explain that this was one of the many hiding places of the rapparees.

"He will need care. I can't come every day,"

Maggie had continued. "Will you help?"

Maggie's words were as clear in her mind here in America as they had been that night so long ago in Ireland. Will you help? Could she have done anything else? The young rapparee was hers! She had saved him. She would fight for his life with every ounce of her strength and will.

"He'll not die," she'd promised Maggie. "I won't let him."

Linna sighed. She'd kept that promise. Gill's beatings and her mother's tears had not kept her in the house. She'd crept from it in the night, stealing bits of food from the pot and ointment from her stepfather's stores of horse medications. If it's good for a horse, it must be good for a man, she'd reasoned. She'd kept faith with Maggie and with the man she would come to know as Rory Desmond. She'd cared for Rory through nights of fever and days of delirium, spooning broth into his mouth and nursing him as she would one of her little sisters or brothers. And long before he was well enough to take his first wobbling steps from the cave to relieve himself, she knew she loved him.

"And I still do," Linna said into the empty room. "Stiff-necked, brooding bastard that he is, I still love him."

Linna stood in the middle of her bedchamber on her wedding day, clad only in a dainty cambric shift and quilted satin petticoat. She took a deep breath and put both hands over her ears. "Out!" she cried. "Everyone out!"

For a moment, no one seemed to hear her in the confusion. Daisy and Edna continued to empty the contents of the huge wooden chest. Bessie clapped her hands to chase Brigand off the mantel, and Mab and a serving girl Linna had never seen before kept moving armloads of gowns from one place to another.

A ship had docked at Connemara the night before to deliver Mary Aislinn's bridal goods and personal belongings to her new home. Not only did the shipment contain the long-awaited dowry in good English silver, but there was furniture and china and more clothing than Linna could wear in a lifetime.

Sir Edmond's personal letter to Mary Aislinn lay crumpled on the bed. In it, her father had assured her of his love, told her how much he had regretted not being there when she and Rory had to flee Ireland, and wished her much happiness in the future. Those painfully scrawled and ink-spotted pages had brought tears to Linna's eyes when nothing else could.

. . . You think me a harsh and unfeeling father. Nothing could be further from the truth. I want only what is best for you—a good husband, children, and God's blessing. I do not doubt that this will reach you long after your wedding to Master Desmond, and that you no longer hold any desire for a religious life.

As further proof of the love your mother and I bear you, I have taken steps to assure that you and your new husband will never be troubled by a repeat of that horrible flight from Mount Beatty. I am not without influence. Without going into details, or taking unnecessary risks, I can truthfully say that the wanted rapparee is dead. His name has been removed from certain records, and his case closed.

The villain who reported the presence of such a

nonexistent person, one Sean Flynn, son of my gamekeeper, Gill Flynn, has been duly punished. I had the rascal publicly whipped and driven from Mount Beatty. His name has been listed with the authorities as a liar and troublemaker. You need have no fear that he will endanger you or your family anymore . . .

It is lonely here at Mount Beatty without you, especially now that your brother, Thomas, has gone to school in Dublin. Your mother worries about him, but I am certain that the discipline and routine of boarding school will make a proper man of him.

I am told that riding is of the utmost importance in Maryland. Your mother insists that you must have a mount as fine as any. Therefore, when my dapple-gray mare, Shamrock Lady, foals, I will breed her to Ballinasloe's Might and send her and the weanling foal to you as a gift for your coming birthday. I am certain that Master Desmond will appreciate the breeding and stamina Shamrock Lady carries in her. In time she should improve your stable and provide an extra means of income for you.

I trust that you will remember us in your prayers, that you will be a credit to your upbringing, and that you will inform us of the birth of our first grandson.

> Written this day, of Our Lord
> January 2, 1754

> Your loving father,
> Edmond Beatty

Linna had read the letter over twice. He didn't mention me, she thought. All this for Mary Aislinn and nothing for me! Sir Edmond was her father, too, and he hadn't acknowledged her existence with a single word. Her vision clouded as tears welled up in her eyes.

"Please, all of you, just go," she insisted.

Startled faces looked up. Mab's face reddened. "You heard your mistress," Mab said. "Out. I'll call you when we need you."

Linna turned away as they filed from the room. Mab shut the door and came to stand beside her. "I've never seen a bride on her wedding day who didn't snap like a stray dog. 'Tis why they say it's bad luck for her to see the groom. If they saw each other, there'd likely be no marriage."

Linna indicated the crumpled letter on the bed. "He didn't mention me, Mab. I might never have been born." A single tear dampened her cheek. "Is it foolish of me to wish he would?"

"Now, now," Mab soothed, putting an arm around Linna's shoulder. "Ye must not blame him. He knows ye're alive, girl. I've seen him looking at ye many a time. He's watched ye grow from a mite."

Linna wiped at her eyes with the back of her hand. "I can't do it, Mab. I can't go through with it. I'm not Mary Aislinn. I've got to tell Rory the truth."

"Are ye mad?" Mab exclaimed. "Ye cannot falter now. There are others to think of beside yerself. Why, the master could have ye clapped into jail! If they have not found ye out by this time, they never will. Sir Edmond has sent the dowry, Mary Aislinn is safe in France in her convent."

"How do you know that?" Linna covered her face with her hands and sank into a chair.

"Use your wits. If she wasn't in the convent, would

Sir Edmond have sent the dowry?''

"You're right, I suppose. But—" Linna's eyes met Mab's faded ones. "It was my stepbrother who betrayed Rory at Mount Beatty. Sir Edmond had him whipped from the estate."

"Sean Flynn is the devil's spawn. No better than the sot that fathered him." Mab threw up two fingers in the ancient folk sign to ward off evil. "Good riddance, I say. Mount Beatty is the better without him."

"I should have known it was Sean. He'd sell his own soul for a pint. But if Sean knew about Rory, did he know Mary Aislinn and I switched places?"

"Linna, Linna, think!" Mab scolded. "If he knew, he would have told Sir Edmond. Your secret is safe, child. Ye have only to act yer part today, and ye will become Mary Aislinn Desmond, a great lady."

Linna swallowed hard. "If I tell the truth—"

"If ye tell the truth, ye ruin us all and destroy Mary Aislinn's chance at a religious life. How long do ye think it would take Sir Edmond to yank her from that nunnery?"

"But I love Rory," Linna whispered. "How can I betray him?"

"The milk is spilled, girl," Mab chastised. "It's too late for tears. Be the wife he deserves. It is the only way to atone for yer sins. Do ye honestly believe Mary Aislinn would have been a better wife for him?"

"Mary? No, but—"

"No buts. Wipe yer eyes and wash yer face. I'll call back the women and prepare ye for yer wedding day. Ye must hold fast, Linna. Ye planned this, now ye must have the courage to carry it through."

"Then I must begin our life together with a lie," Linna said huskily.

"Ye'll not be the first woman, or the last," Mab said tartly. "Women must ever look out for themselves in this world."

"And in the next world, Mab? What of that?"

"Worry about heaven or hell when the time comes. For the present, ye must worry about your life here and now."

Slowly, Linna shook her head. If she told Rory, she would lose him, but if she didn't . . . "I'm sorry, Mab," she whispered, "but I can't go through with the wedding." Ignoring the older woman's protests, Linna seized a lavender damask dressing gown from a pile of clothing on the bed and threw it around her.

"Where are ye going? Ye're not dressed! Ye can't go out like that!" Mab shouted. "Wait!"

Linna threw open the door and dashed out bare-legged into the hall, nearly colliding with Daisy. "Where is Master Rory?" Linna demanded of the startled maid. "Is he in the house?"

"Yes," the girl squeaked. "In his room—dressing for the wedding."

Linna crossed the hall and flung open Rory's bed-chamber door. Rory, shirtless in the center of the room, whirled to face her. "I must talk to you," she cried. "Now!"

Rory dropped his boots and padded to the door in stocking feet. "Come in, then." He glared at Daisy. "Is there something you want?"

"No, sir," Daisy managed, and fled down the hall.

Trembling, Linna stepped into the room and waited as Rory closed the door behind her. "I'm sorry to break in on you this way, but—"

"It's all right, girl, I'm glad you've come. I wanted to see you before the wedding." He put a protective arm around her shoulder and led her toward a chair. "Sit down. Ye are as pale as December milk."

"No." She shook her head and pulled free. "I . . ." The words caught in her throat. "You must listen to me. Please . . ."

Rory's eyes darkened to shards of jet and a muscle jumped along the line of his jaw. Then, without warning, he caught her in his arms and pulled her urgently against him.

"I can't marry you, Rory," Linna blurted out. "I'm not—"

Rory's searing kiss stifled her words. His arms crushed her against him, molding her body to his. "Linna, Linna," he murmured, trailing hot kisses along the soft curve of her throat.

"Oh, Rory," she whimpered. "Don't . . ."

His lips met hers again, and Linna moaned as his kiss deepened, sweeping away all conscious thought from her mind. His searching hands slipped beneath the damask gown to caress her unclad flesh, and sweet sensations of intense pleasure sapped the strength from her muscles.

"God, woman," he said huskily. "If ye only knew how I've wanted ye here in my arms like this."

Rory's hot tongue plundered her mouth, and she clung to him as intense throbbing desire coursed through her. The force of his hard, bulging manhood against her bare leg sparked a smoldering flame in her own loins, and she drew a long shuddering breath.

"Rory, please," she begged. "I . . ."

"No," he insisted. "Not now." His mouth claimed possession of hers once more as he pushed the dressing gown off her shoulders and lifted her in his arms. "I want ye, Linna. I need ye."

"You don't understand," she murmured. "I must tell you—"

"Nay! I'll listen to no more." He carried her to the bed and laid her back against the pillows, tangling his fingers in the glory of her unbound hair. " 'Tis I who must tell you, sweet Linna," Rory said raggedly as he lowered his weight onto her body. "And this is not a time for words between us."

Chapter 11

Linna clamped her eyes tight as Rory fumbled with her petticoat strings and slid the quilted garment off over her ankles. Her lips were bruised and tingling from his kisses, and her mind was whirling. What they were doing was wrong—it had to be. But why did it feel so good?

Sharp sensations of delight skittered beneath her skin wherever Rory touched her; she'd never felt so warm inside, so cherished. All her life Linna had heard of what a man does to a woman, but no one had told her that a woman felt such bubbling joy. She wanted to laugh and cry at the same time, she wanted Rory to keep on holding her, caressing her with his hands and lips.

"Linna."

Her pulse quickened at the sound of her name on his lips. She opened her eyes and looked up at him; his face was barely inches from hers. Linna's heart was beating so hard she was certain he must hear it. Her breath came in slow, ragged gasps.

"Let me take off your shift, sweet," he whispered. "You're so beautiful. I want to see all of you." He cupped her breast in one hand and bent to kiss the hard, erect nipple through the thin linen. "You want me, darling," he coaxed, "as much as I want you."

Linna caught her breath at the spurt of sweet pleasure. Her breasts felt tight and swollen, and her nipples ached for his caress. Shamelessly, she moved beneath him, unable to quell the low moan in her throat. She hadn't meant this to happen. She'd come here to tell him she couldn't wed him—to confess her deception. She knew she should put a stop to his lovemaking before it was too late . . . but she was powerless to control her own emotions. When he'd enfolded her in his arms, her willpower had been washed away in a flood of unfamiliar desire.

"I've dreamed of having you here like this," Rory murmured, sliding a hand slowly up her leg to stroke the inside of a silken thigh.

Linna trembled at his touch, and he brought his mouth down on hers in a slow, sensuous kiss. Her lips parted; their tongues touched provocatively, and Linna's arms tightened around his neck, pulling him closer. Somehow, her shift was up around her waist, and she felt the throbbing heat of Rory's engorged flesh against her bare skin. She moaned, arching beneath him as a curious excitement grew in her loins.

With a single motion, he pulled the shift over her head, leaving her body exposed in the full light of day. Shyly, Linna buried her face in his chest, letting her fingers explore the bulging muscles of his upper arm and shoulder. He gave a contented sigh and lowered his head to kiss one rosy nipple. Linna's fingers continued to trace the lines of rippling sinews across his broad chest, lingering at the swollen nub of a male nipple when Rory's sigh turned to a sharp intake of breath.

"Woman, woman," he moaned, forcing himself to slow the tide of passion that threatened to sweep him away. Rory knew that this time it wouldn't be enough to satisfy his own physical longing. Linna was no lightskirt, no willing wench taken easily and as easily forgotten. He knew he must make this act of love—her initiation into full womanhood—an experience of wonder for her.

She flicked her tongue teasingly across his bottom lip and Rory groaned again. For all her obvious innocence, he'd never known a woman who was so completely sensual. She was a seductress, as guileless as Eve . . . and as bewitching.

He'd meant to go to her before the wedding—to try and make her understand why he'd held her at arm's length all these weeks since they'd come to Maryland. He'd paced the floor all night, trying to deny the truth to himself. He'd tried with all his heart and soul not to love her. Hadn't he sworn by heaven and hell that he'd never give his heart to another? Loving meant pain . . . and God knew he'd had pain enough to last a lifetime. But somewhere in the stillness between the witching hour and dawn he'd realized he was fighting a losing battle. In spite of everything, he had fallen hopelessly, irrevocably in love with her. And one look at Linna, clad only in a revealing thin dressing gown, standing in the doorway of his room, had sent all thoughts from his mind but the overwhelming desire to possess her sweet body.

Linna ran her fingers through Rory's curling dark hair and sighed softly. His big hands were doing wonderful things to her body as his lips whispered Gaelic words of love; their limbs entwined in the tangled covers. There was nothing for Linna but the sound of Rory's voice and his clean, male scent that filled her brain. She wanted him . . . wanted something more . . .

The aching in her loins grew to a pulsing, incandescent heat, and he arched her hips to meet his powerful thrust, crying out as he plunged inside her. The brief flash of pain was lost in the rapture of oneness. The sheer intensity of their unbridled passion propelled them into a firestorm of shared rapture that suddenly exploded in a shower of falling stars. The world fell away and Linna drifted on a cloud of warm, safe joy, coming gently to rest with her head on Rory's shoulder.

His arms tightened around her. "Darling," he whispered huskily. "Sweet Linna." He brushed his lips against hers in a feather-soft kiss, then kissed away the single tear that rolled down her cheek. "Did I hurt ye? I'm sorry, but there's always pain for a woman her first time. It won't be that way again, I promise."

"No," she protested. "It was nothing." She sighed and snuggled against him. "I didn't expect . . ." Linna felt the flush of blood in her cheeks. "No one told me . . ."

"You're a woman made for love," he said. *Different than Rachel.* He pushed the disloyal thought away quickly. "I've wronged ye, little Linna," he said softly. "I'd not have blamed ye if you'd refused to wed me today. But now"—he grinned and rolled her over on top of him—"now I've got ye." He caressed her back with a slow, circular motion. "You're a ruined woman," he teased. "Ye have to marry me to save your reputation."

Linna's head snapped up. "That's why you made love to me?"

"No, little goose. I made love to ye because I am madly in love with ye and because I desired your soft body." He chuckled. "I've been a fool, Linna. A thickheaded fool."

Linna pushed herself up and leaned on her elbows against his broad chest. "I did come to tell you I couldn't marry you," she began hesitantly.

"Hush," he said, pulling her down to kiss her soundly. "Ye weren't the first." He turned over on his side, adjusting Linna's position so that her softly rounded derriere pressed against his naked loins and he could fondle her silken breasts. "My mother told me two days ago that I shouldn't go through with the wedding until I persuaded ye to be married by a Protestant minister. And Donal came to me this morning."

"Donal doesn't want you to marry me?"

"No."

Linna's heart sank. "But I thought he was my friend."

"Silence, woman. If ye keep chattering, you'll never hear my abject apology and confession of idiocy."

"But Donal—"

Rory chuckled warmly. "Donal's smitten—he thinks he's in love with ye. He wants me to release ye so he can press his suit. He wants to marry ye himself. He offered to give me your dowry if he can have the blushing bride."

"Oh!" Linna emitted a squeak of protest. "Am I to be handed back and forth like a milk cow? Doesn't anyone care what I think?"

"No, Linna, nobody cares." Without warning Linna bumped him sharply in the groin with her bottom. "Ouch! Would ye destroy the Desmond line and doom us to an existence without heirs?"

Linna wiggled and raised a hand threateningly. "I warn you."

"Peace, sweet," he gasped. "Ye have me at a disadvantage." He pulled her against him and kissed her tenderly. "I want ye, girl," he whispered, suddenly serious. "I tried not to. I loved Rachel and I lost her. I loved baby Anne and she died, and I wasn't even here with her when it happened. So I had this crazy idea that if ours was just a marriage of convenience, if I buried myself in the work of the plantation and didn't let myself love ye, I couldn't be hurt like that again."

"Rory," Linna sobbed. "You don't understand. I—"

"No, Linna, I was wrong. When I first saw ye, I knew ye were a threat. I do love you and I'm asking your forgiveness." He pushed her away and stared hard into her bright eyes. "Will ye do me the honor of becoming my wife today?"

Linna's throat tightened. Now was the time to tell him. If he loved her, maybe it wouldn't matter if she wasn't Mary Aislinn. If Rory loved her for herself, maybe . . .

"Well, woman," he demanded. "Will ye or won't ye have me? Or would ye rather consider Donal's request?"

Linna hesitated. *Tell him,* her inner voice cried. *Tell him now that you are not Mary Aislinn!* Linna's fingers balled into fists so tightly that her nails cut into the palms of her hands.

"Yes," she whispered. "I'll marry you. Today."

Rory and Linna were married by a Catholic priest, Father Francis, in a tiny forest chapel on a neighboring plantation. Only the family members, a bevy of servants, and their hosts, John and Mary Kennedy, witnessed the brief ceremony. Even Rory's best friend, Ty, was absent, gone north into the wilderness to trade with the Indians for furs. Afterward, the wedding party and guests returned to the plantation house at Connemara to celebrate the occasion.

If Judith had had reservations about the wedding, she had none concerning the reception. Neighbors and friends had been invited from miles away for an evening of dancing, good food, and shared merriment. Linna, splendid in her Parisian gown of sapphire figured silk, was whirled from dance partner to dance partner, unable to keep names and faces straight. Musicians played country reels and formal minuets with skill and enthusiasm. Whole families joined in the festivities, from stately grandfathers down to unweaned babes.

Linna was astonished at the groaning tables of food that Judith's servants had prepared for the guests. Roast beef, venison, spring lamb, and suckling pig shared the honors with turkey and wild duck. There were platters of raw oysters and clams, crab cakes and baked fish. The long table of delicious-smelling vegetables included many that Linna was unfamiliar with, such as sweet potatoes and succotash, a combination of dried lima beans and corn.

"It is an Indian delicacy," Donal explained, handing Linna a plate. "That and the spiced crab. Try it."

Numbly, Linna shook her head. If it meant her life, she couldn't have eaten a bite of anything—not even the myriad cakes and pies and tempting sweets. Her gaze fixed on Rory caught between two ancient dames across the room; he saw her and smiled, and her insides flip-flopped crazily.

I am his wife. I am Mary Aislinn Desmond.

The reality of those words in her mind swept away any lingering regrets. Mab had know what she and Rory had done in his room just before the wedding; the servants must surely guess, and if they knew, it would be only a little time before word spread to her mother-in-law. But it was unimportant. All that mattered to Linna was Rory, and that she belonged to him . . . forever.

Donal handed the plate to a servant and caught Linna's hand to lead her out onto the dance floor. As he inclined his head toward her, Linna caught a whiff of strong spirits. It was obvious to Linna that he had been partaking of something other than the claret punch she'd been sipping.

"Stop eating Rory with your eyes," Donal whispered. "It's not considered good taste to be so taken with your husband." His fingers lingered at her waist for a fraction of a minute too long before he released her to catch another partner's hand.

Linna concentrated on the intricate steps of the dance, smiling stiffly at each partner and laughing when the others laughed. Rory had said that Donal wanted to court her. She'd been grateful for Donal's friendship since she'd come to Maryland; he was the brother she'd never had, and she couldn't bear to hurt him. In truth, the thought that Donal had desired her for himself was flattering. If she hadn't loved Rory, there might have been a real chance for them.

Donal caught her hand and led her beneath the arched hands of the other dancers. Suddenly feeling very grown up and matronly, Linna smiled warmly at him.

"Do you know how beautiful you are?"

Linna blushed, missing a step in the final notes of the song. "You mustn't," she protested. Donal's reply was drowned in the enthusiastic clapping at the end of the dance.

"Sir Roger de Coverley," a red-cheeked elderly gentleman called. Immediately, the musicians struck up the first notes of the lively new reel.

"I'll dance with my bride, if ye don't mind, brother." Rory draped an arm possessively around Linna's shoulders. "There are enough young ladies present for you to find your own."

Startled, Linna glanced apprehensively at Rory. Was that a note of jealousy she'd heard in his deep voice? Surely, she'd done nothing amiss in accepting a dance or two from her new brother-in-law when her bridegroom was occupied with his guests.

"Come, sweet," he said, guiding her toward the hall and out on the front step. "I'd like a moment alone with ye."

As the door closed behind him, Rory crushed her against him and kissed her ardently. "Let's send them all away," he murmured, "so I can have you to myself."

The bite of rum was sharp on Rory's lips and Linna suppressed a shiver. Rory was drunk, or nigh onto it. His words slurred faintly as he whispered immodest suggestions in her ear. Unconsciously, Linna's muscles tensed and she turned her face away.

"What's wrong, colleen?" he demanded, catching her chin and tipping her face up to his. "I am your husband. Ye need not be shy with me."

"We . . . we should get back to our guests." She

tried to pull free, but he held her. "Let go." Her voice strained. "You're hurting me, Rory."

Instantly, he released her. "Something is wrong, Linna. Tell me. Has someone insulted ye—spoken amiss?"

She shook her head. How could she tell him the truth? "It's nothing," she lied.

"Aye, nothing," Rory repeated huskily. "Married three hours and my bride turns to frost. You were hot enough for my kisses this afternoon."

Linna's hand flew to her mouth and she shrank back. "That's unfair and you know it!" she cried. Trembling, she yanked open the door and stepped back into the wide hallway.

"Linna. Wait." Rory caught her arm and spun her around. His dark eyes caught the glow of candlelight, and for an instant she could read the pain in their depths. "I'm sorry. I didn't mean to—"

"Ah, there you are," Donal called from the doorway. "I wondered where the two of you had gotten to. No sneaking off early." He bowed formally. "May I have the honor of the next dance, Mistress Desmond?"

"No," Rory said.

"I didn't ask you," Donal replied. "I asked the lady. Sister?"

Linna nodded. "Yes."

"The hell you will!" Rory said. "You and I are having a private discussion. We'll finish it before there's any more dancing with him or anyone else."

Donal flushed with rising anger, his body becoming rigid as he turned his gaze from his brother to Linna. Bright spots of color tinted her cheekbones, and her hands nervously smoothed her skirts. "What did you do to her?'' Donal demanded. ''Give her a taste of the famous Desmond temper?''

''Stay out of this, little brother,'' Rory warned. ''This is between my wife and me. It's none of your business.''

''Maybe I'll make it my business,'' Donal threatened.

''No,'' Linna stammered. ''Please, Donal, don't. It's all right.'' She swallowed her tears and extended a trembling hand to Rory. ''I don't want to fight with you,'' she said. ''Can we join the others?''

''As you wish,'' Rory said coldly. ''But I'll have an explanation before the evening is out, mistress. Is that clear?'' He fixed hard eyes on Donal. ''Linna is my wife. She doesn't need you to fight her battles for her.''

''You're damned protective of a woman you've barely spoken to for weeks,'' Donal flung back.

''If you have a problem, take it up with me tomorrow—in private,'' Rory said. Holding Linna's arm, he ushered her back into the party. Instantly, they were surrounded by enthusiastic well-wishers.

''We thought you two had made your escape,'' said a middle-aged woman. She stood on tiptoe to kiss Linna's cheek. ''Welcome to Maryland, my dear. We were so happy when we heard Rory was marrying again. Some of the ladies in . . .''

The woman's words blended into a babble in Linna's ear. Rory was furious with her, and she had nearly caused a fight between the brothers. She hadn't meant to compound the problem by agreeing to dance with Donal. She'd only wanted to get away from Rory, to keep from answering his questions.

Rory's arms were around her as he laughed and

talked with his friends and neighbors, but his embrace was no longer warm and comforting. Linna's fear increased with each passing moment. Men were offering repeated toasts to the bride and groom, and Rory was matching them drink for drink. No matter how long the celebration lasted, when it was over and the guests all left, she would have to go up to Rory's bedchamber with him. What if he was still furious with her? What would she do if Rory became violent?

Dark memories of her childhood swept over Linna as she stood in the midst of laughter and bright swirling gowns. As she retreated mentally into her past, the joyful music of her wedding reception gave way to memories of drunken curses and the sound of her mother weeping. Her stepfather Gill had been a sour, mean-spirited man when he was sober, but under the influence of strong drink he became a sadistic bully.

Doll-like, Linna nodded to Rory's friends, smiled, and made the correct responses, but her mind was far away in the tiny whitewashed cottage, remembering . . .

"Woman!" Gill's angry voice filled the cottage, waking Linna's mother and the children sleeping in the loft above. "Woman, I want you! Now!"

"Please, Gill, the wee ones."

"The little bastards will stay in their beds if they know what's good for them!"

"No, Gill. No more of that. Come and sleep. It's late."

"I'll do what I want in my own house! Ye think I'm drunk, don't ye? Ye half-witted slut!"

First came the shouting and then the beating. Linna would stare through the cracks of the boards until she could watch no longer, until she covered her ears with her hands to shut out the sound of her mother's crying. Even as a young child, Linna had known what Gill was doing to her mother. When Finola was cowed and sobbing for mercy, her stepfather would take his rutting pleasure on her broken body.

Linna had dreamed of doing something to stop it, running for Father Joseph or even hitting Gill over the head with the cream pitcher and knocking him cold. But, in the end, she had been too frightened. She had never actually done anything to help her mother; she had only wept and cultivated a hatred for Gill in her heart. And then, when Mary Aislinn had offered her a way out of the pain and poverty, she had ridden away to Beatty Hall and never looked back.

In coming to America, she had pushed her mother and half brothers and half sisters farther into the past. She had believed that in becoming Mary Aislinn, she could forget. But she had carried the bitter memories with her, as surely as if she had locked them in her sea trunk, and now they were rising up to come between her and her new husband.

"Last dance," someone called. "Dance with your bride, Rory."

Woodenly, Linna let Rory lead her out onto the floor, fingers as cold as ice. Hesitantly, she raised her eyes to stare into his accusing gaze.

He bowed. "My lady." His voice was deep and precise.

Linna curtsied prettily. "My lord." Step by step she followed the dance, oblivious of everything but Rory's unspoken disapproval. The musicians ended with a flourish, and Rory pulled her to him and brushed his lips against hers, to the delight of the onlookers.

"We'll leave now," he whispered in her ear.

"There's a carriage at the back door."

Linna's eyes widened in alarm.

"Didn't Mother tell you? We're not spending the night here. We're going to Sherwood." Lacing his fingers firmly through hers, Rory pulled her through the crowd and into the hallway. "This way," he insisted.

Ignoring the ribald cries of the guests, Linna followed Rory through the kitchen and out the back entranceway. An open carriage waited by the garden gate. In one easy motion, he caught her by the waist and swung her up into the vehicle.

"Go!" Rory shouted to the driver. The old man slapped the reins over the backs of the team and the carriage rolled out of the yard. Rory slid onto the seat beside her. "We're going to the other house. I told ye we had two. The house at Sherwood is smaller; I thought it would be a better place to spend our wedding night than down the hall from Mother."

"Oh," was all Linna could manage. Rory's arm was around her shoulder; every jolt and bump of the carriage on the rough dirt road threw them against each other. Soon they would be alone and Rory would expect her to receive his attentions. She was his wife; she belonged to him. It was his right. But it was not his right to beat her. It was not his right to take her in a drunken rage. If he tried . . . God help her—what would she do if he tried?

Chapter 12

Rory stared up into the dark Tidewater sky arching overhead. Stars, as brilliant and sparkling as diamonds, pierced the velvet canopy, adding to the golden glow of the huge crescent moon. The March air was soft and damp against his cheek, and the chirping chorus of thousands of spring peepers rose above the thud of the horses' hooves and the creak of the carriage. He could hear Linna's steady breathing in the darkness; it did not alter when he removed his arm from her shoulders and slid away on the carriage seat.

What's in God's name had come over Linna? Rory wondered. When she'd come to his room and they'd made love, he'd been certain she'd accepted his apology. She'd seemed happy and as physically satisfied as he had been.

Mentally, he went back over the wedding and the celebration that followed. Everything had gone smoothly; his neighbors had all made Linna feel welcome. She had been fine until he'd taken her outside and kissed her. What had he done or said that set her off?

Damn Donal and his silver tongue! A stab of jealousy

knifed through him. He'd been a fool to allow his brother so much time with Linna since they'd arrived. Surely, she didn't prefer Donal over him! His little brother had a way with the ladies for certain; God knew he had enough time to dally with them—he did little else. Part of the reason Rory had been so busy since he'd gotten back to the plantation was because Donal had let things slide in his absence.

His brother had sweet-talked Rachel, too, but she had never taken him seriously. She insisted that Rory and Judith spoiled the boy, and she'd been right. After his father had died, his mother had clung to Donal. Rory had been away, first in the mountains with the rapparees and then in the American wilderness. Donal had grown up surrounded by women and sheltered from the realities of the world by his mother's protective hand. Now Donal was almost too old for Rory to chastise, except for serious matters like Donal's compromising an indentured dairymaid last summer.

Since there had been no question of Donal wedding the Welsh baggage, Rory had been forced to give the girl her freedom and arrange a marriage for her with a blacksmith in Annapolis. The dowry Rory provided was enough to set the couple up in their own shop. He would have forced Donal to support the child, but the girl miscarried the babe in her fifth month. The expense of Donal's misadventure had been a severe blow to the plantation's slim financial resources. But despite Judith's protests that the wench was as guilty of fornication as Donal, Rory had felt honor bound to do no less for the girl.

If Donal had caused Linna's upset, his brother had best find another object for his affections. Perhaps it was time that Donal took a wife of his own. A wife and children might settle him down, and now that Linna's dowry had eased the burden of Connemara's debts, they could support another family household.

The carriage rolled to a stop at the front entrance of Sherwood. The driver turned around. "Help ye down, sir?"

"No, Harper, we'll be fine," Rory answered, getting down out of the carriage. "Ye take the horses back to the stable and go on to bed. I'll send a lad for ye when we want the carriage." Rory offered Linna his hand. "Mistress."

A woman in a starched white apron flung open the front door and cried a welcome. "Come in, Master Rory, Mistress Desmond. The big chamber's ready. I even lit a fire for you t' take the chill off the room. Will you be needin' anythin' else, sir?"

"Nothing more tonight, Ethel, thank ye," Rory replied as he led Linna into the front hall of the house.

Sherwood was frame Dutch gambrel with a two-story addition on the south side. It had belonged to Rachel's father before he died. The house was much smaller than the one at Connemara, but crafted of the finest material and well laid out. A narrow staircase led to the bedrooms on the second floor.

"This way, mistress," Rory said to his bride. Linna's fingers were like ice. Surely, she wasn't afraid of being alone with him—not after they'd already bedded. He led the way upstairs and opened the door to the master bedchamber.

As Ethel had promised, a cheery fire glowed in the small brick fireplace that dominated one paneled wall. Linna hesitated in the doorway, glancing around the spacious room. A huge poster bed, two straight-backed chairs, and a round mahogany table were the only furnishings. A worn Turkey-red carpet lay on the polished floor in front of the hearth.

Rory blew out the candle on the landing and followed Linna into the chamber, closing the door behind him. She stood just inside the room, her hands twisting together, her face flushed and eyes sparkling with unnatural brightness.

"Now, my lady," Rory said, "perhaps ye can give me an explanation of this behavior. Just what the hell is going on?"

Linna's face visibly paled and she stepped back.

"Have I insulted ye? Have I hurt ye in any way?" Rory demanded. Linna dropped her gaze to the floor and shook her head. "Has anyone else?"

"No," she whispered.

Rory let out a sigh of exasperation and glanced around the room. A tray on the table held a bottle of wine and two pewter goblets. "Are ye thirsty? Would ye care for a bit of wine or—"

"No, nothing."

Rory poured himself a goblet of wine, tasted it, then placed it back on the tray. Turning his back to Linna, he removed his coat and began to tug at the knotted stock at his throat. "I regret there is no maid to help ye undress. It was an oversight. I had supposed that I might have that pleasure tonight."

Linna let out a muffled sob, and he whirled on her fiercely. "Please," she murmured. "I can't—"

"Can't! Can't what? Isn't it a little late to play the frightened virgin?" With two strides, Rory crossed the room to loom over her, the torn stock dangling forgotten from his hand. "For the love of God, Linna, what have I done to ye?"

Linna's eyes fastened on his clenched fist with numb incredulity, the taste of fear strong in her mouth. Primitive instinct bade her run, but her legs refused to obey her brain and she stood her ground.

Rory sensed her terror, and the seams of his gray satin vest strained at the shoulders. His face flushed as he fought to control his rising fury. "Damn ye, woman."

Linna threw up an arm to protect herself and frantic words burst from her mouth. "Don't—don't you dare!" she warned. "If you hit me, I'll—"

"Hit ye? Why in the name o' all that's holy would I strike ye?" he roared. "Are ye mad?" Turning away, he seized the wine bottle and threw it against the back wall of the hearth.

The shatter of glass and the loud sizzle of the flames as the wood was drowned in wine broke through Linna's haze; she swore softly in Gaelic. "Ye drunken sot, will ye throw the bed in the fire next?"

"Mayhap I should. It's the first sensible word I've had out of your mouth in hours."

Linna stared into Rory's face with open surprise. The anger was gone; in its place was black humor.

"Not the bed? Perhaps the goblets then." Rory's fingers closed on the goblets and he tossed them, one after the other into the fire. "Now," he mused. "What . . ." His gaze dropped to his satin coat, draped over a chair.

"No!" Linna grabbed the coat and whisked it to safety. "You call me crazy? You're as mad as a hatter, Rory Desmond! And wicked, too. The price of this coat would feed my family for the whole winter."

Rory laughed wryly. "Not any family I ever knew—and certainly not yours, mistress. Your mother wore a ring on her pinky finger that would have equaled my year's profit in tobacco."

"Not my . . . I didn't mean my family," she stammered, putting the coat behind her back and edging toward the door. "I meant a cottier's family . . . in Connemara."

"There ye go, shaking like a lamb at butchering time again." He eyed the bed. "Maybe those hangings."

"No!" Linna shouted. "You'll burn nothing more. If you . . ." Suddenly, she realized he was grinning at her. Feeling foolish, she let the coat drop from her fingers. "You aren't drunk, are you?"

"Not as far as I know."

"And you didn't really mean to burn the coat, or the satin bed hangings."

"Nay, not when I knew I'd have to replace them by my own sweat."

Hesitantly, she took a step in his direction.

"Perhaps we should talk now, Linna," he said quietly.

"Yes."

Somehow, she was in Rory's arms and he was guiding her to the bed. Obediently, she sat beside him and leaned her head against his chest.

"What is all this about, darlin'?" Rory asked in their native tongue. "From the beginning."

Tears came before the words; they spilled out of her eyes and stained Rory's embroidered gray vest. Her body shook with uncontrolled sobs and then silent weeping as the memory of a terrible afternoon filled her mind.

"It was . . . my birthday," she managed finally. "My fifteenth birthday . . ."

She had gone riding with Mary Aislinn and two of Mary's friends. They had taken a groom and a basket of food to share. No one had remembered that it was her birthday, but it didn't matter. The holiday from lessons and chores, and the chance to ride out on a bright, sunny day, had been present enough.

"I . . . I was riding with friends," she said. "Our groom's horse had thrown a shoe, and we rode on without him. It seemed a silly lark. We thought we were recklessly daring, riding out alone."

Mary's friends had begun to tease her. One girl, Anna Gilbert, demanded to know why Mary's maid was riding with them at all.

"There was an argument, and I rode back toward the house alone." That much was true. Mary Aislinn, Anna, and Kathryn McCarthy had taken the basket of food and rode on toward the spring that was their original destination.

"Your friends left you?" Rory asked. He began to unlace Linna's gown at the back; she made no protest. Suddenly, it didn't matter anymore.

"I was no more than a mile from Mount Beatty, riding through a small patch of trees when a man came out of nowhere." A man. Her own stepbrother Sean, drunk as a lord and mean as the hounds of hell.

"Who was it? Did you know him?" Rory slipped the gown over her head.

"No," she lied. "Just a man. Big, coarse-looking." Linna shivered. "He grabbed me and pulled me from my horse. I screamed." Screamed and cursed him with every profanity she'd ever heard.

Rory undid the petticoat and pulled it down, then

began to unroll her stockings. "Did he hurt you?"

"He . . . he tried to . . ." The tears came again as Linna remember Sean's whiskey breath in her face, and the pain of his rough hands on her breasts. She'd fought him with every ounce of her strength, kicking and biting, but it had been useless. He'd thrown her back against the rocky ground and her head had struck a rock. She'd been only half conscious when he'd yanked her skirts up and tried to rape her. Sean had thrust his thick tongue deep in her mouth until she gagged, struggling for breath. She remembered the feel of his hands on her throat and the sour taste of the whiskey on his breath.

Rory pulled back the covers. "Under," he ordered. Linna was naked except for a thin cambric shift. Quickly, Rory stripped off his own clothes, blew out the candle, and slid into bed beside her.

"I fought," Linna whimpered. "I tried to stop him . . ."

"Shhh, darlin'," Rory crooned, enfolding her in his arms. "It's all right. That was long ago, and you're safe here with me now."

"But I fought him," she protested.

"I know ye did, sweet." Rory's lips brushed her hair and he cradled her against his bare chest.

"He tasted of whiskey," she murmured. "And all the time he kept taunting me, saying terrible things." Things too awful to repeat.

"Ye came to me a maiden this day," Rory reminded her. "He did not succeed."

Linna moaned, deep in her throat. "Because he . . . he couldn't," she rasped. "He tried . . . but he couldn't." He'd been so infuriated by the failure that he'd struck her with his fists. She'd known he meant to kill her, and sheer terror had given her the strength to break free and run. "The groom heard me scream," she whispered. "He shouted, and I ran toward him."

"The man?" Rory asked with hard, clean precision. "Did they catch him?"

"No. I was hurt . . . bleeding. The groom carried me back to Mount Beatty. Lady Ma— My lady mother put it about that I had fallen from my horse. She forbade me ever to speak of the incident again."

"But your father? You did tell him? They searched for the rogue, didn't they?" Rory's muscles tensed.

"No. She said I would be damaged goods if I told." She had lied to everyone, even to Mary Aislinn. "She said I would never get a husband if it was known that I . . ."

"That you'd been assaulted, almost murdered?" Rory swore a foul oath. "The fault was not yours, girl. If he'd taken your virginity, it would have been nothing to me. A man—a real man—would not judge a woman by such a thing." He pulled her tightly against him and laced his fingers through her hair. "Ye should have told me, sweet. 'Twas the taste of drink on my lips, was it not?"

Linna murmured assent, and he caught her chin with his free hand and lifted it, brushing her lips with his. Rory's kiss was gentle. The tension eased from her body as she cuddled against him. "It's all right," she whispered finally. "You can—" She broke off, unable to say the words.

"Make love to you?" Rory chuckled. "No, little one, not tonight." He began to massage her shoulder and the back of her neck. "You'd find little pleasure in my embrace this even'. Go to sleep now." He pressed a soft kiss on her forehead. "You're tired. We have a lifetime of nights and days before us.''

Timidly, Linna slipped an arm around his neck. ''You don't mind?''

Rory groaned. ''Damnable wench, of course I mind. Would ye spoil my noble speech? Go to sleep, I say, and quit wiggling against me. I am not made of stone, and you are soft and sweet-smelling enough to tempt a saint.''

She tucked her head under his chin and let her fingertips slide slowly across his chest. ''What we did before . . .'' she whispered shyly. ''I liked it. You didn't frighten me then. It was just that later . . . at the party . . . when you'd been drinking, I thought . . .'' A tiny moan escaped her lips. ''My fears have robbed you of every man's right. I'm sorry, Rory, truly I am.''

''Nay, Linna. Never apologize for fear. I am not a monster to take your body without thought of your mind. I care for your thoughts and fears. But ye must tell me. I can abide anything but lies between us.''

A chill ran down Linna's spine. ''I . . . I didn't lie,'' she protested.

''I asked ye what was wrong,'' he reminded her, ''and ye said nothing. I was nigh on to leaving you to sleep in a cold bridal bed. Would that have solved things between us?'' He leaned up on one elbow and stared down at her pale face in the flickering firelight. ''What a woman does not say can be as much a lie as what she does. I am a man who expects the truth from his friends, and I will forgive much if ye do not break that trust.''

''I was afraid because you were drinking,'' she hedged. ''I have seen naught but violence come from a bottle.''

'' 'Tis true that I like a drop as much as any man,''

Rory conceded, "but I am no drunkard. I will not come to our bed *ar meisce*," Rory promised, "but I cannot swear ye will never taste liquor on my lips."

"You seemed so angry with Donal."

"My brother and I are at odds over some things. Ye must keep him in his place, Linna. I love him, but he is not all he should be. Donal gives his heart too freely and too often where colleens are concerned. I trust you; it is Donal I do not trust."

"He is my friend," she said. "Nothing more. And if he were, I would never betray you . . . not ever."

"Nor I you," he said simply. "I took no other wench while Rachel lived, and I shall do the same for you. If I have fallen from the grace of the Church, some things I still hold dear."

Linna sighed and snuggled closer. She would not think of the terrible deception she was living. "Rory," she whispered.

"Aye."

"What we did before . . . when you touched me and asked me to touch you."

His voice deepened. "Aye."

"Would you mind if . . ." The tip of her tongue flicked against his bare chest. "I'm not certain I . . ."

Rory groaned again and let his hand slip down to caress her rounded bottom. "Linna," he warned. Her amused chuckle warmed his heart and he bent to kiss her lips. "Linna."

"If I could practice a bit," she whispered, "I'm certain I could get it right." Her teeth closed gently on his lower lip and she nibbled teasingly as shivers of desire began to radiate through her body. "I am not afraid now," she murmured. "Is it too late to—"

With a mock growl, he rolled her over and nuzzled

her throat. Laughing, she moved against him, welcoming his gentle touch and thrilling to the growing pressure against her thigh.

"Linna?"

"Yes. Oh, yes."

Tenderly, he cupped a full breast in his palm and lowered his head to taste the sweetness of her nipple. Linna groaned and arched her back as pure joy spilled through her veins. "Ye have the most beautiful breasts," he whispered hoarsely. "Made for a man to love."

Their lips met again, and Linna's fear melted away as Rory's soft words of love washed away the hurt and terror of that frightened fifteen-year-old. Their limbs entwined, and Linna's breath came in ragged gasps as desire flared within her.

Unashamed, she let her hands explore his body, finding pleasure in Rory's cries of passion. When his hand closed over hers to guide her in a more intimate investigation, she was awed by the throbbing potency of his engorged silken shaft. The curious hot excitement grew as Rory returned favor for favor until their heated flesh glistened with a faint sheen of moisture.

"Linna," he moaned. "Precious Linna. Let me love you."

Swept up by the rising tide of love, she opened to him, arching to meet the thrusting proof of his male virility, reveling in the sheer power of their shared passion. Waves of rapture caught her, swirling her round and round until, breathless, they reached the peak as one soul, then gently drifted back to rest on a velvet shore of contentment.

"I love ye, woman," Rory murmured, breaking the silence. "Now and always, I will love ye."

"And I love you," she swore. "I do."

But the joy of the precious moment was tempered by the bitter knowledge of her secret—a secret that she must carry within her heart fovever. I can't tell him who I really am, she cried inwardly. I want to, but I can't.

"I do love you," she repeated as she thought silently, I've loved you since I saved your life on that stony piece of ground in Connemara.

Chapter 13

May 1754

Linna sank down into the lush green grass and lay back against the warm earth. Above her stretched a blue sky laced with gossamer clouds of the purest white. She raised a hand to her cheek, wincing at the tenderness. She'd not believed she could burn from the sun, not after so many days at sea, but the climate here was so different from that of Connemara; it seemed almost tropical.

She rolled onto her stomach and untied the ribbons of her straw hat. Keeping her face covered had not prevented her sunburn; she might as well enjoy the freedom of the breeze blowing through her hair. Linna tossed the hat beside the bouquet of wildflowers she had picked.

From the position of the sun, she could tell it was past noon; she knew she would be late for dinner if she didn't hurry back to the house. Lazily, she reached for a blade of grass, snapped it off, and put the end in her mouth. The sun-kissed morning had cast its spell over her, and she had no desire to face Judith's censure.

The Tidewater country was a garden of Eden. Instead

of harsh stones and windswept moors, there were fertile fields and primeval forests. When the land was cut by plows, Linna could thrust her hand into the rich earth up to her elbow without reaching the bottom of the precious topsoil. The waters of the bay produced fish and clams and oysters and crabs without number, and the woods yielded all manner of game. Rory had told her of the migrations of great flocks of geese and ducks, and even of pigeons, so numerous that they could be knocked from the trees with sticks. Here in the Maryland Colony was food for master and servant alike; she had seen no children with hungry eyes and swollen bellies. Instead, the little ones, even the children of slaves, were tall and sturdy-limbed, with bright, inquisitive eyes.

Linna chewed thoughtfully on the stem of grass. Rory was a husband any woman would be proud to call her own. A shiver of happiness ran down her back as she remembered the unabashed passion they had shared the night before. Rory had shed the moodiness that had troubled her so on the ship; he was a tender lover and a laughing companion. Although he often worked from sunup until sundown, he still found time to take her with him occasionally, and to share the day's activities with her in the warm darkness of their poster bed.

Donal was Donal. He had not changed since she had wed his brother. He still teased and joked with her. It was Donal who had taken her fishing the first time in the plantation sloop, and who had defended Brigand when Judith wanted to exile the cat from the house.

Her mother-in-law was the thorn in her side who would not permit Linna to be completely happy at New

Connemara. Judith made it clear in dozens of petty ways that Linna was her son's pampered plaything, not fit to be mistress of the plantation.

Linna leaned her chin on her hands, kicking off her soft leather shoes. Everyone worked at Connemara. From the eight-year-old boy who carried wood for the kitchen hearth to old Margery in the weaving house, each person had assigned chores to do—all but Linna. Even Donal had daily responsibilities, some of which he managed to carry out to Rory's satisfaction.

"I know how to weave," she had told Judith eagerly. "I can instruct the women in the weaving house, if you will tell me what is required and what your priorities are."

Judith had stared at Linna as though she had suggested strapping on wings of wax and flying from the roof of the tobacco barn. "I hardly believe Margery, or Cora, or any of the others would take orders from a girl."

Linna had had no better luck in offering to help with the herb garden or the kitchens.

"I have my own way of doing things, Linna," Judith had insisted. "In time, perhaps . . . when I have properly trained you . . ."

But weeks had passed and then months without Judith giving over any of her authority. Linna had not wanted to complain to Rory about his mother; it seemed a sneaky, underhanded thing to do, but the idleness was driving her crazy.

"I am a wife with none of the wifely duties," she had confided reluctantly to Donal at breakfast. "Mab cares for my clothes and my hair. I've nothing to do but feed my cat, and he's gotten so fat lately, I know they're giving him tidbits in the kitchen."

''Poor little princess,'' he'd replied. ''I warned you about the lioness. You frighten her. You're a threat to her position. She means to be the only queen in this house.''

Mab had been even worse. ''Are ye never satisfied then, puss? Ye are wife to the master. Save yer energy for yer marriage bed. when ye give him a son and heir, he may take from his mother to give to ye. Until then, bid yer time and step softly.''

''But I must have something to do!''

''Be a lady.''

''You know better than that. When did Lady Maeve sit idle?'' But Mab had only shrugged and went on with her sewing.

Linna tugged at another blade of grass. A line of ants marched along the ground only inches from her face. Most of them were carrying bits of something in their mouths. ''Even you have something to do.'' Linna sighed deeply.

Suddenly, a savage war whoop split the air. Linna screamed as strong arms clamped around her.

''If I'd been an Iroquois, you'd be my captive,'' Rory cried, rolling her over onto her back and pinning her wrists against the grass with his big hands. ''And a tasty little pigeon of a captive, too.'' Laughing, he nuzzled her neck.

''Rory! Don't you ever—'' Her protests were cut off as his mouth descended on hers. He released her wrists and slipped a hand beneath her skirts. ''Rory, stop!''

''A man comes home for his dinner and finds no wife,'' he murmured between kisses. ''Sarah said she saw you come this way.''

Linna's arms tightened around his neck and she giggled. "For shame to accost me in broad daylight," she protested halfheartedly. "How did you sneak up on me? I didn't even hear your horse."

"I told you I lived with the Indians." Rory's smoldering gaze held her prisoner as his fingers inched provocatively up her thigh. "Long enough to learn their ways. They called me Mishkwe-Tusca."

Linna drew in a ragged breath as her heartbeat slowed to almost normal. Tenderly, she tangled her fingers in his dark hair, and her voice dropped to a husky caress. "You're as wild as a red man, Rory Desmond."

"And how many have ye known, colleen, that ye can share your vast knowledge with me?" he teased, taking her lower lip between his teeth and nibbling gently.

Linna gasped as Rory's exploring hand brushed the triangle of curls at her most intimate spot. "We cannot," she cried in earnest. "Not here!"

"Why not here?"

Bright spots of color flamed across Linna's cheekbones. "In broad daylight? In the open? Rory, what if someone—"

Rory's lingering kiss muffled her protest, and Linna felt the familiar thrill of sweet desire spill through her. The taste of his mouth, the maddening sensations of his hard, masculine body pressing against hers, drove all thoughts but Rory from her mind.

Linna awoke with a gasp to find Rory leaning over her, grinning. A feather dangled from his fingers just above her nose. "Fiend," she whispered and snuggled her head against his chest. "If anyone saw us . . ." Her voice trailed off. She didn't care. Nothing mattered but Rory. Hastily, she pushed her skirts down modestly over her bare legs and moistened her lips with the tip of her tongue. "Am I a wanton to take so much pleasure in our loving?"

For a long moment, Rory scrutinized her, his face impassive. Then his expression softened and he cupped her chin in his hand. "If so, then 'tis a good wantonness. I cannot see ye walk or catch sight of that red-gold mane without wanting ye, Linna." Rory's voice held the lilting caress of Connemara, and Linna's heart thrilled to the tone. "Ye are a fire in my blood, girl, and the more I give my love to ye, the hotter it burns."

Linna swallowed and blinked back the moisture that welled in her eyes. This afternoon, this minute was the best in all her life . . . and she wanted it to last forever. "I love you, Rory," she whispered. "With all my heart and soul." God forgive me for my sins against you, she prayed silently. I cannot tell you . . . not now, not ever. "I will love you always," she promised.

Rory sighed. "I do not know what spell ye have cast over me. I never thought to know such joy. There is a serenity about ye that makes a man content."

Linna traced his jaw with her finger. Rory had shaved at first light, but a faint shadow of beard showed across his face. "It is this place," Linna said. "I was lying here, listening to the wind. It reminds me of home, but there is a difference. At home in Connemara when I was a child, I used to think the wind made music. It was a sad song; sometimes it made me cry. But the song of your Chesapeake wind is light and laughing. I think I like this song better.''

Rory laughed. "Trust a woman to think of such fancies. I suppose ye believe in leprechauns and fairies, too.''

"No, I do not," she replied, coloring. "Nor ghosts, nor banshees. I believe in nothing I cannot see or touch—other than the teachings of the Church," she added quickly. Her greenish-brown eyes lit with mischief. "But I do hear music in the wind."

"If it gives ye pleasure, ye can hear music in the well." He ran a hand possessively over her hip. "We should get back," he admitted. "I sent Donal to oversee the lumbering near the creek, and I should be certain he is there. Cutting timber is a dangerous operation I won't have my laborers hurt for lack of proper overseeing."

"You are hard on him."

"Aye, I am. 'Tis a hard land. Donal is not a boy. If he does not take his work seriously, he will make mistakes that cannot be rectified."

"Sometimes you must show a person what to do and stand back and let him do it," Linna said thoughtfully. "A person learns by making mistakes."

"Donal doesn't need you taking up for him," Rory answered lightly. "My mother is very adept at it." He kissed the tip of her nose, then rose to his feet and pulled her up. "Ye must be starving; I know ye have not eaten since early this morning."

Linna followed him toward his horse grazing a short distance away. Rory swung up into the saddle and offered her his hand. "Come, I'll give ye a ride back to the house." He lifted her up behind him, and she wrapped her arms around his waist.

Linna's leg brushed the saddle holster containing Rory's musket and she sobered. "Why do you carry a gun with you all the time? We're not in danger from the savages, are we?"

Rory covered her hand with his. "Aye, girl, we are, but not the ones you're thinking of. The Eastern Shore is relatively safe from Indian attack, but there are still pirates, ships' deserters, human scavengers. 'Tis what I was thinking of when I told you I'd teach you to shoot a gun." The muscles tightened in his shoulders. " 'Twas why I let Donal guide you about the plantation. My little brother may be a stranger to work, but he's no coward. He has a temper like the rest of the Desmonds, and he's hellfire in a fight. I knew ye'd be safe enough with him at your side."

Linna frowned and rested her head against the smooth leather of Rory's vest. Judith had warned her not to go too far from the house, and Donal trailed her steps like a puppy. They had all known of the danger, but no one had thought to explain it to her. They were treating her like a child.

"I'll not have ye worrying yourself sick about pirates, Linna. Ye are my wife; 'tis my job to protect you."

"And my job, Rory, what is that? Am I to have any duties other than warming your bed?" Linna flared.

He laughed. "Aye, ye are to provide me with a son as soon as possible."

"A son, is it? Before, when I mentioned children, it was you that—"

"Hush, woman," he interrupted. "Forget that nonsense. I had a living child when I spoke those words. Now I have none." Rory reined in the bay and swung her forward onto his lap. "I would have your sons, Linna—a handful. The Desmonds trace their bloodline unbroken back through time to the Geraldines of Kildare, and before that, the royal line of the Ui Neill," he said proudly. "My mother's family claims descent from Conn of the Hundred Battles. Our son will be the first to be born outside of Ireland. It is a new land and a new beginning. Give me strong sons and daughters and I'll ask no more of ye."

Linna's features hardened. "No matter what you think, I am more than a brood mare. I must have something to do." She balled a fist and tapped his chest soundly. "Hear me, Master Desmond. I am no fancy piece. Connemara women have had to be strong, or there would be no Irish left on that stony ground. I will give you children, if God wills it, but the hours I do not spend with you will mean something."

Rory sighed. "My mother. She is a hard one to live with, I know. Would ye have me take the reins from her hands by force? Could ye honestly say ye could take her place if I did?" He caught her wrist gently and placed a kiss on her forehead. "I will order it done, if ye ask, Linna. I respect my mother, and I will care for her, but you come before her in all things."

"No," Linna replied quickly. "That would solve nothing. It would make us enemies and bring discord to your household."

"You see my dilemma."

"I do. But I will not be satisfied to . . ." Her words trailed off as excitement began to sparkle in her dark eyes. "There is something, Rory," she said eagerly. "I mentioned it to Donal, but he said you would never consider it."

"Did he, now?" Rory grinned lazily. "What is this

thing that I would not allow?"

"A school for the children. I could teach the little ones—the ones too young to work in the fields or the kitchen. If they knew their sums and a little reading . . ." Linna's lips parted and she stared at him beseechingly. "Rory, please. I'd need little. At home, we . . . the children used slate or wax to write on. I wouldn't even ask for any books. I'd keep the children out of the way, I promise."

"And what would persuade mothers to send their children to be forced to learn?"

"You."

"Who would ye teach, just the children of free parents, or slave and indentured children?"

"Does it matter?" Linna's heart began to beat faster. "You could tell the slave and indentured parents that the children had to come for an hour a day. If the children liked it and they learned something, the other mothers would demand that their children be allowed to come, too."

Rory pursed his lips. "This means a lot to you, does it, colleen?"

She nodded.

"Have your school then, one hour a day, every day but Sunday. Tell Donal I said to have the old cooper's cabin cleared out for ye. There are benches stored in the old barn." He frowned. "I suppose ye meant to teach boys and girls under the same roof?"

"Girls at nine, boys at ten o'clock."

"Good. It will make less trouble with the mothers. You may have those five to eight years of age for three months. At the end of that time I will come to your school and judge their progress. Agreed?"

"Agreed!" Linna threw her arms around Rory's

neck and hugged him tightly.

"Hmmm," he murmured. They rode in silence for a few minutes until he reined in the horse at the end of a field.

Rows of men and women stooped and crawled in the fresh-turned dirt, planting green shoots. Boys followed with buckets and gourd dippers carefully watering each new plant. A few workers waved or called a greeting, but most continued their slow progress down the field.

"This is the last of the tobacco," Rory explained. "This is a new field, cleared just last summer. It should produce a good crop."

"Are these the same plants that you grew in the woods?"

"Aye. We start them there, then transplant to the open fields. Tobacco is a hard crop. It takes careful tending. Sarah!" he called to a plump, copper-skinned woman near the end of a row. "Bring a plant for Mistress Linna to see."

Gracefully, the young woman rose from her knees and came toward them. She was dressed in a short woolen dress with fringe at the bottom and wore her hair in two midnight braids. A thin strand of leather was twisted about her forehead.

"Sarah is a Christian Indian," Rory murmured. "I bought her indenture last year. She's one of my best tobacco planters, and she's skilled in weaving as well."

"Good afternoon, Sarah," Linna said. "I don't believe I've seen you before."

The woman smiled, revealing even white teeth. "I have been working at Sherwood. We are finished with the tobacco there." She offered a tobacco plant for Linna's inspection.

Linna took the plant, trying not to show her surprise at the Indian woman's excellent English. There was only a trace of a soft accent in her clear, precise tone. "Do you like planting tobacco?"

Sarah smiled. "I like to see things grow. Corn is better than tobacco, but I like tobacco, too." She held out her hands for the plant and cradled it between her palms. "This is rich earth. It will give good harvest."

"My husband tells me that you are an Indian. I have never met one of your people before. Perhaps you would be willing to tell me about your home in the wilderness someday."

Sarah nodded. "I would like that." She glanced at Rory, then turned back to her task.

"What an unusual person," Linna said, when Sarah was too far away to hear. "Her eyes are slanted, almost like a person from the Orient, but I thought an Indian's skin would be darker."

"Some are." Rory nudged the horse with his heels. "Sarah's from the north. She's a Shawnee from the Ohio River country. Very few of them have become Christians. Most are fierce fighters, the men and women alike."

"But how did she get here?"

"Ty says she was captured by Iroquois and sold into slavery. I bought her indenture from a Dutchman. Ty likes her, but she'll have none of him." Rory chuckled. "She says he's a savage."

"Indians are not all alike then?"

"Nay, girl, no more than Irishmen. 'Tis God's truth the tribes fight among themselves like our countrymen."

For a while, Linna was content to lean against Rory's

chest and watch the bobbing of the horse's head. She was intrigued by the Indian woman; there was a grace about her that belied her position as a servant. Linna wondered if it might be possible to make her a friend.

The horse broke into a trot as he spied the barn. "Rory," Linna asked, clinging to him for support, "what was that you said the Indians called you? Miskee-something?"

"Mishkwe-Tusca. Indian words don't always translate well into English," he explained, "but it means of the blood of a warrior, or one who is born a warrior."

Despite the hot sun, a shiver passed down Linna's spine, and she felt goosebumps rise on her arms. "I hope not," she whispered. "I pray your days of fighting and danger are gone forever."

"Amen to that," he said, swinging down from the animal and raising his arms to catch her. "I'm satisfied here on the Tidewater with nothing more exciting to deal with than one of Mother's screaming tantrums. I've seen as much bloodshed as I care to in this life. From now on, I'm just a peaceful, law-abiding tobacco planter."

Chapter 14

August 1754

Linna watched from the shade of a three-hundred-year-old oak tree as men and women chopped off the mature tobacco plants close to the earth and impaled the butts on sharpened stakes. When the stakes held five plants, they were loaded onto a wagon drawn by oxen. There was no school today; all nonessential activity on the plantation had stopped for the tobacco harvest. Boys and girls ran back and forth across the rutted field carrying gourds of water from the well for the sweating workers.

Rory and Donal were among the cutters, stripped to the waist in the hot August sun, slicing the plants free with razor-sharp cutlasslike knives. Even Judith had come to the fields in a broad straw hat and hoopless dress. The erect blue-clad figure was clearly visible on the far side of the field, directing women in setting out a huge noon meal beneath the trees.

Snatches of song and laughter drifted on the breeze. The hard work was tempered by the workers' knowledge that half the crop was already hanging in the tobacco barns. The rich new soil of the freshly cleared land had cradled the tobacco, and the gentle kiss of summer rain and sun had given Rory the crop of his dreams. The tobacco was of the highest quality, and the days of harvest had gone well.

Bend and slash, bend and slash. Linna's heart thrilled as she watched Rory move down the field, his muscles rippling across his back and shoulders like those of some heroic Greek athlete. Twice she had crossed the field to bring him cider, and twice he had threatened her life if she stirred from her seat in the carriage again.

The cat, Brigand, padded up into her lap, made two circles, and settled down to lick a fat paw. "Enjoy your cushion," Linna said. "There won't be room for you there long."

Rory straightened up, rubbed his back, and turned to wave at her. She waved back and he grinned. Ripples of laughter and teasing banter spread down the field; it was clear to every member of the plantation that Rory was as full of joy as his young wife.

Linna was certain that she had become pregnant early in June; her illness had begun almost at once. For weeks, she hadn't been able to keep down solid food. Her breasts had swelled and become so tender she could hardly bear for Mab to lace up her gowns. Linna had been light-headed, and twice she had fainted dead away. She would have disregarded those things as minor if it were not for the bleeding.

Rory had summoned a physician from Annapolis four times. Dr. Hodges had been gentle and reassuring, but he had been unable to tell her why her body was reacting so to the pregnancy, or, indeed, if she had miscarried the child. The doctor had advised bed rest, a potion that was so foul-tasting Linna had dumped it spoon by spoon into the chamber pot, and a rich diet that included blood pudding and daily doses of claret.

Rory had held her head over a china basin when she was sick, washed her face with warm water, and rocked her against him when she was wracked with bouts of weeping. It was Rory who had sent away the untasted platters of food and tempted her with fresh strawberries and tiny portions of chicken breast cooked with wild mushrooms and chives. He had gotten up willingly in the middle of the night to scramble an egg with a bit of cheese, or to fetch her a cup of tea and dry biscuit.

Mab had overheard a terrible fight between Rory and Judith in the library. Mab couldn't make out what the master was saying to his mother, but, as she told Linna, she was certain Master Rory had warned Judith against upsetting Linna in any way. Not once after that did Linna's mother-in-law say or do anything that would indicate that she felt Linna was at fault in being ill.

By the first of August, Linna had reached the end of her patience. Doctor's orders or not, she had dressed and come downstairs. Within two days, she had decided to reopen the school. "Two hours," she had told Rory, "will not overtax my health." She had hidden her weakness from them all, ignored her headache and churning stomach, and plunged into the task of teaching the children to read. At the end of two weeks, most of her symptoms had faded.

"The mistress wants to know will you join her in a cool drink before the noon meal?"

Linna turned to see a smiling Sarah standing beside the carriage. Sarah was wearing a man's flat straw hat, and the hem of her patched linen skirt was tucked into a sash at her waist, revealing neat copper-brown ankles and bare feet.

"Shall I fetch a man to drive the carriage around?" Sarah asked. "The dinner's about set."

Linna's eyes widened as she hastened to share her good news with her friend. "Oh, Sarah, I feel so much better today." Linna motioned to the seat beside her. "Come, sit here and rest with me a minute. You've been busy since dawn."

Sarah shook her head. "No, I cannot. What would the other women think? They would be angry with me." Sarah's almond eyes narrowed as she smiled warmly. "I am certain you will carry your baby to the end of your term." Her soft voice dropped to a whisper. "Among the Shawnee we have a belief that each child has a spirit protector. Some children decide to stay with the mother and be born; others do not. If you wish, I will bring you a potion that Shawnee women take to make good babies. It will not hurt you; it is made of living things of the forest and field." She looked at Linna questioningly. "Would you want me to bring it?"

"Is there any blood in it?"

Sarah laughed. The story of the white doctor's blood pudding had made its rounds in the servants' quarters. "Not a drop," she promised.

"Then I will try it," Linna agreed.

"And you must eat wisely," Sarah cautioned. "A little honey is good if you have a desire for something sweet, but cornbread and greens—do not your people call them *salad*?—are best for a mother. Venison and wild duck are recommended, but eat rabbit only sparingly if you do not wish your child to be timid."

It was Linna's turn to laugh. "Now I know you're joking. The animal flesh a pregnant woman eats can't affect the personality of her baby. That's just superstition."

"Maybe so for English babies. I know only Indian babies."

"What if the mother eats mutton?" Donal called, walking jauntily toward the carriage. He grinned disarmingly at Sarah and dropped his tobacco knife to the ground. "Come to think of it," he said, "I have seen some sheep-faced children in that hedge school of yours, Linna."

Sarah averted her eyes, but she could not hide the flush that rose to her cheeks. She picked up a gourd dipper and ladled out a cup of cider from the crock. "You are thirsty?" she asked shyly.

"Thanks." Donal took the cup and drank the cider in three long gulps. "Whew." He leaned back against the open carriage and wiped his forehead with the back of his arm. "Hot work, cutting tobacco. Rory's the devil to keep up with."

"Aye, but you've done well this day, little brother." Rory joined them, waving away the offered cider and picking up a water bucket. Stepping back, he dumped it over his head to wash away the sweat and grime of the tobacco field. "I'm hungry enough to eat a horse and chase the rider," he admitted. "I hope Mother has enough for dinner."

"She'd have had more if you'd let me do my share," Linna insisted, climbing down to lock her arms around Rory's damp waist. She wrinkled her nose; he smelled of dirt and man and green tobacco, good earthly smells.

"And risk my son? Not likely." Rory bent over and kissed her. "Are ye well, Linna? Not tired by the sun and dust?'' He caught her chin in his big hand and tilted her face up to meet his gaze.

"I'm fine, I know it. I'm even hungry."

Rory let his hands slide to her waist. Before she could protest, he lifted her up onto the carriage seat as carefully as if she were spun glass. "In that case, me darlin','' he crooned, untying the lines and climbing up to the driver's seat, "I shall drive ye in state to dinner.'' He glanced back at Donal. "Brother? Will ye ride or walk?"

Donal laughed. "I'll walk. I'm not about to catch hell from Mother for muddying up her go-to-church carriage."

Rory clicked to the team and guided them slowly away from the field and out onto the dirt track that ran through the trees. "It's a good crop, Linna," he said proudly. "But what you're carrying means more to me."

A bubble of happiness warmed Linna as she settled back on the cushioned seat. She untied the ribbon of her stylish straw hat and laid it on the seat. The orange cat promptly curled on top of the hat and began to chew the green silk ribbon.

Linna sighed. Her baby was alive and well; she knew she would carry it beneath her heart and deliver it safely next spring. Rory loved her. She was happy in her new home here in the American Colonies, happier than she could ever have imagined. She drew her legs up under her and hugged herself. Who would have thought it?

Saving Rory Desmond from the British soldiers had changed her life. It had given her the courage to follow Mary Aislinn to Mount Beatty and to survive the transformation from illegitimate child to lady's companion.

Remembering the young rapparee's raw determination as he fought to survive the gunshot wound had helped her through lonely nights and long days of learning the customs of another world. She had never expected to set eyes on Rory again, yet she'd remembered and loved him just the same. Now he was the center of her world once more, and she had miraculously changed from lady's maid to lady of the manor.

Without warning, Rory reined up the horses. Linna sat bolt upright to see an apparition step into the road. Rory cursed and jumped down from the seat to throw his arms around the man in buckskins.

"Ty! Ye old woods bison! I thought your scalp was dangling from a Huron longhouse! Where the hell have ye been?"

Linna's heartbeat slowed as she recognized Ty. His hair hung loose below his shoulders, and a scruffy black beard added to his savage appearance. He was dressed all in beaded buckskins with quillwork moccasins that came to his knees. His open vest was worked in heathen designs, and he wore a necklace of bearclaws around his bronzed neck. A musket was slung over one shoulder, and a hatchet dangling from a rawhide thong on one hip balanced the oversize skinning knife on the other. A fresh scar traversed his face from his left eye to his lower lip, giving a satanic twist to his face.

Ty nodded in Linna's direction. "See you survived Judith so far."

"Linna's expecting a baby," Rory declared, slapping Ty on the shoulder with a blow that could have broken a bone in a lesser man. "Damn ye, ye Welsh bastard, I thought ye were buzzard meat."

"Shawnee come close to makin' an end to me, and that's a fact," Ty answered, slapping Rory back with equal vigor. "A pilgrim can't walk two days without smelling smoke or hearing drums. It ain't natural, I tell ye. The wild tribes is riled as bee-stung bears."

"How's Sweet Water and the boy?"

Ty's dark face sobered and he stared at the ground. "Gone. Took by measles last fall. Fifteen people died in a week. Too many to give decent burial to—had to pile 'em in wigwams and burn the bodies."

Rory's hand tightened on his friend's shoulder. He glanced up at Linna. "Sweet Water was Ty's Menominee wife."

Linna felt a rush of compassion for Ty. "Your wife and son died while you were on your way to England?" The sun-dappled lane suddenly became too cool and she shivered. "I'm so sorry."

Ty stared into her eyes. "The boy was hers by a French trapper, but we liked each other right enough," he admitted gruffly. "Sweet Water wasn't much to look at, but she was a good woman just the same."

The cat jumped out of the carriage, strolled over to Ty, and began to sniff at the toe of one moccasin. The big man bent and scratched the animal's stumpy ear. "Still got this good-for-nothin' cat, I see," Ty said.

"You went north for furs," Rory said. "Bring back anything worthwhile?"

Ty shrugged and folded his arms across his chest. "See any furs?" He grinned and fingered the foxtail at the end of the hatchet. "This is as close to prime pelts as I got."

"What about the sorrel gelding I lent you?"

Ty grimaced and scratched his head. "Ate him."

"You mean to tell me I outfitted you with enough trade goods to buy off the whole Shawnee Nation, gave you a horse, bought you a new knife and a good British musket, and you come back after seven months with one worthless foxtail and tell me you ate my horse?"

Ty yawned and scratched his neck. "No sense yellin'. I got the musket, don't I?" He scratched harder. "Spent the night with a dadblamed Quaker north of here. Think I must've picked up lice in his stinkin' lean-to."

Involuntarily, Linna took a step backward. Ty winked at her and pinched something between his fingers. Grabbing Brigand, Linna hurried back to the carriage and climbed in. Behind her, the two men switched from English to Indian. Linna strained her ears, but the mumbled words were incomprehensible. What could Ty possibly have to tell Rory that he didn't want her to know?

They stood for several minutes talking. Ty's back was to Linna, but she knew by the strained expression on Rory's face that something was wrong. Finally, Rory slapped Ty on the shoulder again, and the woodsman turned and entered the forest the way he had come. Rory returned to the coach.

"What is it?" Linna demanded. "What did Ty tell you?"

Rory frowned and picked up the reins. "There's going to be a war," he said reluctantly. "Between the French and the English."

Linna smoothed the folds of her chintz skirt nervously. "There's always a war somewhere with the French," she said, keeping her tone light. "It shouldn't mean anything to us, not here in the Colonies.''

Rory shook his head. "This is different, Linna. The French are stirring up the Algonquin-speaking Indians north of here. Ty says there's going to be bloodshed between the British settlers and the Indian tribes. The French are giving the Indians whiskey and guns.''

Linna's face paled. "Are we in danger here?''

"No, the Eastern Shore is protected on three sides by water. None of the wild tribes would bother to cross the Chesapeake, and we're too far south to worry about a war party coming down the Susquehanna and crossing over to the peninsula.'' He drew a deep breath. "We can't depend on the government to look out for our interests. There's talk of forming a militia to protect the smaller plantations north of here.''

Linna moistened her lips with the tip of her tongue. "It isn't just what Ty said, is it? You knew about this before?''

"He just confirms the rumors we've been hearing.'' Rory frowned. "Now, don't go pouty on me, Linna. I didn't tell ye about it because I was concerned about the babe. You've been ill; there was no need to trouble ye with an Indian scare.''

"Will you have to fight?''

"Not unless a war party sets foot on the Eastern Shore.'' He shook his head. "Stop worrying, girl. I told ye, it's my job to look after ye and the family.'' He grinned. "If I don't get ye to dinner, Mother will be sending out a search party.''

Linna nodded, but her appetite had vanished. Her world, which had been so bright, had suddenly taken on the tangled shadow of the thick intertwining canopy of branches overhead.

October 1754

Linna yawned, tucked her legs under her, and laid the book of poetry down on the small mahogany table beside her. The coziness of the fire and the soft rhythm of rain against the windowpanes made her too sleepy to read. Contentedly, she patted her rounded stomach and laughed. Not even the looser gowns Mab had sewn could hide the curves of Linna's pregnancy.

Lazily, Linna rose, stretched, and went to the window. Mist and gently falling rain muted the bright colors of autumn; even the gold and red leaves of her oak tree were less vibrant. "The rain should remind me of home," she mused, "but October in Connemara brings chilling blasts of wind, not this teasing melody."

Brigand followed her to the window and jumped up on the sill, eyeing the tree branches anxiously.

"No birds today," Linna murmured, running her hand down his silky back and up the arched tail. "You're becoming positively domesticated for a sea cat." She smiled. Sarah had shown her a white cat's new litter in the barn, and one of the kittens was an orange male with an unmistakable black patch covering one eye.

Linna's breathing had fogged the window. She rubbed a spot clean and stared out. The fields were empty, the greens of summer fast turning to browns and grays. The creek was a silver ribbon of mist winding toward the bay, its surface marred only by the caprice of the wind.

Despite the rain, Rory had assured her that he would have no trouble taking the sloop to Oxford for supplies and returning safely before dark. Donal and Judith had

gone with him, Judith to attend church services and
Donal, no doubt, to attend to some mischief of his
own. Linna had intended to go with them, but Rory
had forbidden it when the weather turned wet.

"I'll not have ye coming down with an ague," he'd
pronounced firmly.

Linna turned from the window and picked up Rory's
gray coat from the chair where he'd left it. She sniffed
the fabric and laughed; it smelled of tobacco and
licorice. Rory, she'd discovered in recent months, had
a childish passion for licorice and went to great pains
to secret supplies of the sweet in various hiding places
around the house. "That's why you had to go to Oxford," she murmured. "You were probably out of
licorice."

When Rory had said she couldn't go with them,
she'd been disappointed. They'd come close to arguing
over it when Judith had entered the room.

"In my day a decent young woman wouldn't think
of leaving her home in your condition," Judith said
coolly.

"Stay out of this, Mother," Rory had warned. "This
is between my wife and me."

Linna had stayed at Connemara, and after an hour
or so was glad she had. The day had been so peaceful
and relaxing. Because it was Sunday, most of the servants had the day off. Mab had brought her a pot of
hot chocolate and a tray of delicacies for her noon
meal just before she had gone to spend the afternoon
with a friend.

Linna had definitely recovered her appetite. Before
she'd realized it, she'd eaten three of the flaky biscuits
with slices of ham, a cherry tart, and a huge, crisp,
yellow apple. The illness of her pregnancy had passed

in the fourth month; she felt wonderful, and the baby was kicking lustily every day.

She yawned again. She wanted to plan a lesson for Monday morning's classes, but the bed looked so inviting with the quilt turned back. Perhaps it wouldn't hurt to just— A knock on her bedroom door startled Linna from her reverie. "Yes. What is it?"

The door opened and Daisy bobbed a curtsy. "There's a strange man to see you, Miss Linna." Daisy's disapproving tone made it evident that she felt the request was highly improper.

"For me? Are you sure?"

"Yes, Miss Linna, I'm sure. He said 'the young Mistress Desmond.' That's you."

Linna pursed her lips. "That's me, all right. But who could it be? I don't know anyone in Maryland other than—"

"This ain't the kinda person you would know, Miss Linna." Daisy grimaced. "He's not quality. I said he'd best go and come back when the master was here. He said, 'Step and fetch your lady, girl,' like I was common." Daisy put her hands on her hips. "Will you come or should I call Samuel to throw him out of the kitchen?"

"No, that's all right," Linna assured her. "I'll come." Drawing on a rust-colored polonaise over her plain woolen sacque, she followed Daisy downstairs and through the hallway to the kitchen.

A big man in a rain-soaked surtout and broad-brimmed felt hat crouched before the hearth warming his hands. His sagging striped stockings showed gaping holes, and his tattered Indian moccasins were split down the back. His surtout was patched at the elbows and obviously too short for his long arms. Hairy wrists thrust out of the cuffs as he snatched off his hat and whirled to face them.

"Mistress Aislinn," he began, his tone thick with the speech of Connemara. "I've come to beg a—" He broke off and stared at Linna. "Not ye," he growled. "I want nothin' from ye. 'Tis the Mistress Desmond I ha' business with."

Linna's hand flew to her mouth, and the earth tilted. It was months since she had seen him, and his countenance was bruised and scarred, but that leering face and arrogant voice could belong to only one man on earth. Sean!

"Mind your tongue!" Daisy snapped. "This *is* Master Desmond's wife! Speak your business or begone, before I set the dogs on you!"

Shock and disbelief spread across Sean's face. He blinked twice, obviously trying to comprehend Linna's change of status. "I can see I've made a mistake, Mistress Desmond," he said at last. He clapped the shapeless hat back on his head as he backed toward the door. "A mistake," he repeated ominously. "Mine . . . or yours." He threw open the door and dashed out into the rain.

"Lock the door, Daisy," Linna ordered softly. "And then go and lock the front entrance."

The black girl slammed the iron bar in place. "The front is always kept locked when the master's not here, Miss Linna. Shall I call some of the men? I've only got to ring the bell and they'll come runnin'."

"No. No need," Linna insisted. "He's only a poor madman. He's gone and he won't be back."

"But he looked at you like he knew you, Miss

Linna. I ain't never seen him around here before. He don't belong to no plantation I know. Talks like an Irishman, though.''

"I've never seen him before," Linna lied. "He must have heard that Master Rory was away and thought to beg from us." Linna's heart was beating so fast, she could hardly breathe. Her stepbrother Sean . . . How had he gotten to Maryland? How had he found her? Linna's hand tightened on a chair as she fought back the terror.

"You're white as tallow, Miss Linna. Best you sit down a spell." Daisy put her arm around Linna's waist. "I knew I never shoulda let that crazy man in this kitchen. Just it was rainin', and he talked like he—"

"It's all right, Daisy. You did right," Linna said. "I'm fine. He's gone, and we'll both be fine." She stepped back. "I think I'll go upstairs and lie down for a bit. You can bring me some tea."

"Yes, Miss Linna. I'll bring the tea."

Linna could hear Daisy grumbling in the kitchen as she made her way slowly up the stairs. She had to think. The walnut banister was cool on the palm of her hand and she clung to it lest the dizziness return. "Sean. Here in Maryland," she whispered. "Damn his black soul to hell." What would she tell Rory? If Sean hadn't known about the substitution of brides before, he knew it now. Linna's trembling lips moved in silent prayer. "Holy Mary, Mother of God, what will I do now?"

Chapter 15

Despite the search parties sent out by Rory and the inquiries to neighboring plantations, the men found no trace of the intruder who had confronted Linna and Daisy in the kitchen at Connemara.

"If ye both hadn't seen him, I'd have thought he was a product of Daisy's overactive imagination," Rory said as he removed his soaking cloak and hat and handed them to a servant. "A stranger that size . . . It's beyond me why someone hasn't seen him." Rory's voice was muffled as he pulled his wet shirt off over his head and added that to the other clothes.

"Whoever the poor soul was, he's long gone," Linna soothed, draping a towel around her husband's shoulders and beginning to dry his neck and back. "There's no excuse for you to catch pneumonia riding up and down the shoreline hunting for him."

"It's my fault," Rory insisted. "I should never have left ye here unprotected." He dropped into a chair and motioned to the cook's boy to help remove his sodden leather boots. "When I think of that madman here in my house . . ." He swore softly. "If he'd laid a finger on ye, Linna . . ."

Linna handed Rory clean woolen socks to replace

the wet ones. "Well, he didn't. You're making a great fuss about nothing." She forced herself to smile. "I'm not a child."

Daisy poured a pewter mug of mulled cider and handed it to Rory. "Drink this, sir," she suggested. "It will warm your insides."

"You're not to let anyone you don't know into the house," Rory warned. "Do ye understand?" His scalding gaze encompassed the entire kitchen staff.

"Aye, sir."

"Yes, sir."

The cook's boy nodded vigorously as he stuffed old rags into the master's boots. "Sir," he mumbled.

"Three days you've driven yourself and the men searching," Linna said. "It's enough, Rory."

He drained the last of the cider, stood up, and pulled on a loosely woven linen shirt and dry leather vest.

"There are clean breeches and boots here," Linna murmured. "If you'd like to change before the fire . . ."

He shook his head. "No, I'll go up to our room. That cider took off the worst of the chill."

Linna watched as Rory ducked to avoid the low doorway and strode off down the hall. Daisy hastened to wipe up the puddle of water he had tracked into the kitchen. "He's not angry with you, Daisy," Linna said.

The outside door opened, and Mab entered the room, wet but smiling. She hung her cloak on the peg, spoke a hasty greeting to the other servants, and followed Linna from the kitchen.

At the foot of the stairs, Linna paused, her eyes reluctantly meeting her friend's. Despite her terror,

Linna had told no one the truth about Sean's coming, but she was certain that the shrewd old woman had her suspicions.

"I need to speak to ye," Mab said quietly. "About an important matter."

Linna put her finger to her lips. "Judith is in the great hall," she whispered. "We can't talk here."

Mab shrugged. "She'll know sooner or later. I wanted to talk to ye alone first, but if she overhears, it will make no difference." She laid a work-worn hand on Linna's arm. "I am leaving ye, Linna. Jonas McCarthy of Oxford has asked me to become his wife."

For an instant, Linna stared at her. "M-married," she stammered. Mab hadn't guessed, then. This had nothing to do with Sean's coming to Connemara—or her deception. "But how . . . when?"

Mab laughed. "It is quick, I know, but how often does a woman of my years and position fall into such good fortune? Master McCarthy is a wheelwright with his own shop and a good solid house in Oxford."

"You are to be married?"

"Didn't I just say so?" Mab could not contain a chuckle. "A fine figure of a man, if I must say so. He is a God-fearing Catholic widower with five children to look after." Mab's tone softened. "The eldest boy is but twelve, and the youngest babe has never known a mother's hand. She is a precious little mite with hair as black as a crow's wing and soft as angel down."

Linna sat down on the stairs in astonishment. "You're marrying a man with five children? How old is he?"

Mab sniffed. "That, my fine young miss, is none of your business. Master McCarthy has asked for my hand and I have accepted. The sooner we are wed, the sooner we will both be pleased, but I told him I have a duty to stay with ye until ye can find another to take my place." Mab folded her arms across her chest. "Fash, girl, must I speak to ye like a simpleton? At home in Connemara I was lucky to have a place in the big house. I came with ye because I knew ye had a good heart, and I thought that ye might provide for me when I was too old to work. In Connemara there are too many widows and too many old spinsters. Here, in the Colonies, women are as scarce as hen's teeth."

Mab sat down beside Linna and put her arm around the younger woman's shoulder. "I have watched ye since ye were a young thing, and ye know I love ye like my own flesh and blood. But ye do not need me now. Ye are a great lady with house and servants and a tall, handsome lord to wait upon. This is my chance, Linna. Master McCarthy is tired of being both mother and father to his little ones. He is as broad as one of his own wagon wheels and most of the hair God gave him has slipped away. We have spoken to each other only four times, and two of those were at Mass with the priest standing by." She sighed heavily. "This is no great love match, child. Ye know it, and I know it. But Jonas and I need each other, and in the long run, that may make the best marriage of all. Give us yer blessing, Linna. I would not wish to leave ye with hard feelings."

Linna blinked back tears as she slipped her arms around Mab's neck and hugged her tightly. "Of course you have my blessing. I can train Daisy to take your place. You must marry your wheelwright as soon as the banns can be cried.'' She pulled away and wiped her eyes, then said mischievously, ''Five children?''

''Five,'' Mab repeated, chuckling. ''It's senile I've become in my old age, and that's for certain.''

''Mother Mary protect you.''

''I'll need her protection,'' Mab agreed. She exhaled sharply. ''I dreaded telling ye, Linna. But the chance will not come again. I must accept Master McCarthy before he realizes the folly of his offer.''

''Folly!'' Linna's chin firmed. ''Not by half! He's a lucky man, Mab. You'll set his household right and give his children the mother they need.'' Her eyes grew serious. ''He's not just looking for a drudge, is he?''

''No. There is a house servant and a man of all work for the yard and barn. Jonas is lonely. He told me he wants a wife, one of his own faith. He doesn't care that my hair is gray or my body sags. We hit it off from the first moment I caught him starin' at me. He's a jolly sort, Linna. Ye'll like him and the children.''

''Linna! I can't find my black boots.'' Rory's voice came from the top of the stairs, and Linna rose to her feet. ''Are ye coming up?''

''Yes, Rory. I'm coming,'' she answered. She gave Mab's hand a squeeze. ''Don't worry about me,'' she said. ''I'll be fine. You must promise to visit me often and bring your new family.''

''Linna!''

''Coming.''

*　　*　　*

For days, Linna did not venture from the house unescorted, not even to go to the school. Rory had relieved the Indian girl, Sarah, from most of her outdoor duties and bid her accompany her mistress and sit with her through the daily lessons. At first, Linna was uncomfortable with Sarah's shadowy presence, but gradually, she came to feel at ease and finally almost to forget that Sarah was sitting in the back of the room watching.

The weather cleared and turned colder, and the children's laughter echoed across frozen fields. Rivers of geese and ducks poured overhead, lending their piercing cries to the ever-present Chesapeake winds.

"Where are they all going?" Linna asked Sarah one crisp morning as they hurried across the yard toward the school.

Sarah shaded her eyes with a bronzed hand and gazed up toward the great flock of geese passing over the house. "They come from the north," she said in her soft, accented English. "They will winter here in the Chesapeake lands and there"—she motioned eastward—"on the shores of the great salt sea. It is said that they mate and raise their young beyond the mighty lakes and forests of the north, but I do not know this for certain. It is only what the old hunters say."

"Your home is in the north, isn't it?" Linna asked.

Sarah's expression grew pensive. "The Ohio country. It is a time of snow and ice." Her sloe-black eyes clouded with memories. "A time of song and stories."

"Rory says there will be war on the frontier. Will your people fight against the English?"

Sarah shrugged. "Among the Shawnee there is always war. Against the French, against the English, against the Iroquois. *Ne-gau nis-sau*—'I will kill.' Do men know any other song?''

"But Rory says the war won't touch us here."

Sarah allowed the barest trace of a smile to grace her lips. "War seeps like blood into every crack and hollow. If the great war comes, you will feel it. Has not your husband's friend, Ty, gone to scout for the English?" Sarah's eyes glistened with moisture. "But if the English bear fights the French wolf for Indian land, who will suffer most?"

A chill ran down Linna's spine and she shivered, in spite of the fur-lined, hooded cloak she wore. What Sarah said was true. She had heard Donal and Rory arguing about a coming war with the French, and she knew he was worried for Ty's well-being. "At least you'll be safe here with us," she said quickly.

"Perhaps." Sarah sighed. "Perhaps not. Life is always better than death . . . but it may be that there are many kinds of death."

Linna touched Sarah's arm. "You want to go back to your people, don't you?"

Sarah's almond eyes turned fierce. "I will go back. When my indenture is finished, no one will keep me from going. My place is there with my people."

"Even in war?"

"Better to die with one you love than to lay your bones in a stranger's land."

"We were all strangers here once," Linna reminded her gently. "If you gave the Tidewater a chance, it might become home."

"Yes," Sarah agreed solemnly. "And the French and English might sail back across the ocean and leave Indian land to the Indian . . . but I do not think so."

Sarah's words troubled Linna throughout the day and into the night. War with France and with the Indians was not a subject she wished to dwell on. She had a more pressing fear, one that remained a constant companion.

Now that her stepbrother Sean was aware of her deception, Linna knew he would never go away and leave her in peace. As a child in the village, Sean had been her greatest enemy. He never forgot and never tired of a game until the object of his torture was dead or defeated.

On the first of December, Mab left Connemara to be married in the small Catholic church near Oxford. Since the bridegroom's house was already well furnished with household items, Linna dowered her friend with good English silver, a trunk of Flanders' wool, and a milk cow. Tucked into the layers of wool were needles and thread, scissors, and silver goblets that had been part of the gifts to Mary Aislinn from her father in Ireland.

"Ye've no need to give me so much," Mab had crooned privately to Linna in Gaelic. " 'Tis a sin to rob yer own unborn children for the likes of me."

Linna tugged at the waist of the neat plum-colored woolen gown she had helped Mab to stitch for the wedding and bit off a loose strand of thread with her teeth. "Fash on you," she teased. "You have stood by me, Mab. Since I was a ragged urchin you have offered a shoulder to lean on. My debt to you can never be paid." She brushed a kiss against the older woman's wrinkled cheek; Mab smelled of nutmeg and cinnamon. "I wish you happiness with your wheelwright, but if he ever mistreats you, or if you are in need . . ."

"I have looked out for myself these two score and ten years," Mab scoffed. "Is it likely I'll need ye now?" Her faded eyes glistened with moisture as she bustled about the room, straightening what had been already in place and rechecking her packed belongings.

"You are a radiant bride," Linna assured her. "And the sun is shining. Happy is the bride the sun shines on, so they say."

Mab pursed her mouth. "A few drops of rain for luck is what I heard."

"Promise you will come to see me."

"Oxford is not Araby," Mab scolded. "If ye've a mind, ye can bring yer babe to visit me when ye come to town to do yer dealin'."

The cook's boy rapped at Mab's chamber door. "Master says come on, or ye'll be late fer the weddin'." He held out his arms for the bundle Mab dropped into it. "Master said don't worry 'bout the heavy stuff. He'll have a man fetch it to Oxford fer ye."

Linna caught Mab's hand and pressed an ivory rosary into it. "It was Mary Aislinn's," she whispered. "She'd want you to have it."

"Not likely," Mab replied, "but I'll treasure it all the same. Thank ye, Miss Linna." Together, they descended the steps and hurried across the lawn toward the dock.

To Linna's relief, she and Rory returned from Oxford without Judith. Donal had taken his mother on to Chestertown to visit friends for two weeks. It would mean that Linna and Rory would have precious time alone, time in which Linna could be mistress of her own home.

She had taken great pains in planning meals; she

wanted to be certain that nothing but Rory's favorite foods were served. In the evening, they shared a simple supper of cold chicken and gooseberry tarts, and played cribbage until Rory dropped his cards on the table and threw up his hands in surrender.

"You win," he admitted. "How can I concentrate on the cards with the firelight dancing on your hair?" He covered her hand with his own. "Come to bed with me, woman," he murmured huskily. "There's a bit of gooseberry tart on your lower lip I'd like to taste."

Linna laughed and patted her rounded middle. "Surely you jest, sir. What man would desire a wife so fat and ugly?"

"Ugly? Ugly? I'll show you ugly!" With a feigned growl, Rory leaped to his feet and swept her up into his arms. Her arms went around his neck, and they fell onto the bed in a flurry of tossed skirts and laughter. Leaning over her, Rory lowered his lips to hers and kissed her tenderly. "I love ye, woman," he said. "And we'll have no more talk of ugly." His hand dropped to caress her swollen belly. "You carry our child, and that makes you beautiful to me." He bent close to Linna's ear, tonguing it, and whispering lecherous suggestions until she dissolved in laughter.

"Get off me," she protested weakly, pushing him away with both hands. "You'll make a pancake of your son."

"Does he complain?" Rory laid his cheek against her belly. "I don't hear—ouch! The little beggar kicked me!"

"Rory, stop it," Linna insisted, wiping the tears of laughter from her eyes. "If you're going to act like a fool every time I carry a child . . .''

He grinned lazily. "Can I help it if ye drive me mad with passion, woman?" He cupped a breast in his hand. "If I—"

The loud ringing of the kitchen bell brought them both upright as the cry of "Fire" rang out through the house. Rory was off the bed and halfway to the door before Linna could realize what was happening. "Stay where you are!" Rory ordered. He flung open the door and stepped out into the hall.

"Master Rory!" a servant cried. "It's the prize house! The prize house is on fire!"

"Rory!" Linna called. "Be careful!" Quickly, she rose from the bed and threw a cloak over her gown.

"Stay with your mistress," Rory commanded the manservant.

Daisy was still pulling the bell rope when Linna reached the kitchen. "There's a fire!" she shouted.

"Go and find out what's happening," Linna ordered. "Come back and tell me as soon as you know something."

With a nod, Daisy dashed out the door. The manservant, Peter, stood red-faced in the middle of the kitchen.

"I'll be all right, Peter," Linna assured him. "They'll need you to help put out the fire. You go ahead."

Peter shook his bald head. "Don't know, mistress. Master Rory said—"

"There's no fire here," Linna insisted. "I'll be fine. You go and do what you can. Look after your master. Don't let him do anything dangerous."

"Master said—"

"Master Rory isn't here and I am," Linna said sharply. "I'll take the responsibility. Now go where you can do some good!"

Peter yanked at his forelock, grunted a response, and followed Daisy across the yard. Linna stepped out on the kitchen stoop and stared in the direction of the prize house. She could see nothing from the step but a glow in the darkness.

Pandemonium reigned in the farmyard. Dogs barked and horses whinnied. Men and women shouted and called to one another. "Fire! Fire at the prize house!" There were sounds of people running and pounding on doors as others were roused from their beds.

Linna stepped off the stoop and hurried around behind the woodshed. From there she could plainly see red-gold flames shooting into the air. Frantically, she looked around; the prize house sat alone near the dock. There was no other building close enough to catch fire from the blaze.

Something furry brushed against Linna's ankle and she jumped, nearly tripping over a pile of split firewood. Linna glimpsed a movement in the shadows as she regained her balance. A cat hissed and she let out a sigh of relief. "Brigand! You scamp! Is that you? You frightened me—"

A stick snapped behind her and Linna whirled to face a man's form looming over her. Before she could jump back, iron fingers closed around her wrist.

"Going somewhere, sister?" Sean taunted in Gaelic. He pulled her close to his chest, twisting the arm behind her back. "Just like your mother, I see, swollen like a bitch in pup."

Linna gagged at the wave of foul odor that engulfed

her. "Let go of me," she cried. "You smell like a pig!"

Sean's hand found the opening of her cloak and closed roughly on her throat. "Still a spitfire for all your haughty ways?" He laughed and brought his wet mouth down on hers.

Linna twisted her face away and slammed her free fist into his ear with all her might. Sean swore and shoved her backward. An inhuman snarl split the air as twelve pounds of clawing, biting tomcat leaped off the top of the woodpile onto Sean's head. Linna hit the ground and rolled, coming to a stop at the base of the stacked firewood. She scrabbled frantically for a weapon and her fingers closed around a discarded ax handle.

With a foul oath, Sean managed to get a grip on the cat's fur and flung it away. "Damn you to hell!" He wiped at his bleeding face and advanced on Linna. "Witch!"

Linna flinched at the thud of Brigand's body hitting the ground. The cat yelped in pain and tore off into the darkness. Linna backed up until she felt the solid wall of the woodshed behind her. Her breath was coming in long shuddering gulps, and she was trembling so hard she could barely hold on to the ax handle. "Don't come any closer," she warned.

"Such bravery," Sean exclaimed. "Not like last time, Linna." He stepped into the circle of lantern light that shone from the back step, his hooded eyes glittering malignantly like those of some demon from her nightmares. "Do you remember the last time I touched you?"

White-hot fury rose within her. "I was a child then,

Sean.'' The words fell from her lips in cold, precise syllables. ''I'm not a child anymore, and I'm not afraid of you.'' She raised the ax handle menacingly. ''If you come near me, I'll kill you.''

Sean rubbed his bleeding lip and stared at her, shifting his feet uneasily. A frown creased his wide brow, and he spat noisily on the ground. ''High and mighty witch.'' He uttered a blasphemous malediction. ''Witch or no witch, I'll wager Master Desmond don't know he'd got a crazy woman's bastard for a wife. You've lied and cheated your way into his bed,'' Sean surmised shrewdly. ''He came for Lady Mary Aislinn and he got you. What have you done with the Lady Mary? She's not at Mount Beatty, I know that much.''

''My husband will kill you if he finds you here,'' Linna threatened.

''Rory Desmond is a fool. It's easy to get around him. I almost got him hanged in Connemara, and I can do the same here, if I tell what I know.'' He spat at her feet again. ''I set his barn on fire,'' Sean bragged. ''If I don't get what I want, next time I might burn the house.''

''What do you want?''

''Silver. Enough to make me a rich man. Enough so no man would dare to lay hands on me again.'' He made a crude sound. ''They took me for a sailor. Did you know that? A press gang caught me in Galway. They beat me like a dog and chained me in a ship's hold until we were out to sea.'' He took a step toward her. ''But they couldn't keep me. As soon as the ship anchored in Philadelphia, I ran away.''

''I'll not give you a penny,'' Linna cried. ''But I will see you in your grave if you don't get away from here.''

"You'll pay all right," Sean said. "You'll bring me a horse and two hundred pounds tomorrow night. Bring it to the woods by the crook in the river. And come alone or I'll tell your precious husband and everybody else that he's married a whore's daughter." He took another step closer. "Be nice to me, Linna, and I may give you something to—"

Suddenly, Linna swung the ax handle with all her might, slicing it down to slam into Sean's knee. He howled with pain and doubled over. Before he could gain his senses, she dodged past him and ran back to the house. She threw open the door and ducked inside, slamming the bolt securely behind her.

Panting, she leaned against the door. Realizing she was still clutching the broken ax handle, Linna opened her numb fingers and let it clatter harmlessly to the floor. She reached for the bell rope, then stopped. If she rang the bell Sean would know they were searching for him. It was better if he believed she would bring the money.

Slowly, Linna carried a chair over to the door, stood on it, and took down the musket cradled on the rack. Sean would not try to enter the house. If he did, she would shoot him; it was that simple.

She pulled the chair away from the door and sat down with the loaded musket in her arms. A single tear rolled down one cheek, and she brushed it away ruthlessly. The time for tears had passed . . . but Linna knew in her heart that the time for pain was just beginning.

Chapter 16

"It was arson," Rory repeated as the two serving men carried the tin tub from the bedchamber. "There was no way that fire could have started accidentally." He wrapped a towel around his middle and stood close to the hearth. "The building was a total loss. We'll have to have a new press."

Linna offered him a dressing gown.

"No." Rory rubbed at a raw spot on the palm of his left hand where a blister had formed and broken. "By the king's royal cod!" he exploded. "Why would anyone want to burn my prize house?"

Linna turned away and stared out the window into the moonless night. No sign of the fire remained. Rory had formed the plantation workers into bucket brigades, hauling water from the creek and throwing it on the burning building until the last of the flames were extinguished. He had returned to the manor house barely an hour ago, exhausted, his clothes scorched, his hair singed by the fire. Tired as he was, he'd been too filthy to fall into bed; he'd insisted the servants bring him a bath.

"I've set a guard on the other buildings," Rory explained, sinking heavily into a straight-backed chair.

"In the morning I'll send messengers to warn the neighbors. It was not one of our people who set the fire, I'd wager my soul on it."

Linna bit her lower lip until she tasted the salt of her own blood. She didn't know how long it had taken Rory to put out the fire, minutes or hours; she was past all reason.

She clearly remembered unlocking the kitchen door at the sound of Daisy's voice, and if the maid had wondered about Linna's disheveled hair and dirt-smeared cloak, the black girl had asked no questions. When Rory appeared safely in the kitchen doorway, Linna knew she had flung herself into his arms and clung to him until he'd put her gently aside, insisting that he was unharmed. Silently, she had followed him up to their bedchamber and watched as he bathed by the fire. Now, they were alone, and she knew she must tell him the truth about Sean.

"I'll find out who did it," Rory promised vehemently. "Ye need have no fear of that."

Linna turned back toward him, slowly, as though in a dream. "I know who it was."

"What?" His head snapped up. "What did ye say?"

Linna willed her body to obey. She crossed the room until she was close enough to smell the acrid scent of his singed eyebrows and see the dark circles of worry beneath his eyes. Her mouth was dry and tasted of ashes; her tongue felt swollen to twice its normal size. Clutching the folds of her gown, she swallowed hard and forced herself to meet Rory's fierce gaze. "It . . . it was the same man who informed on you in Connemara."

"Bull."

Linna's spine stiffened and she knotted her fingers

together. "I'm telling you the truth," she insisted. "His name is Sean Flynn." Hot tears gathered behind her eyelids and she blinked them back. "I saw him. I talked to him."

One second Rory was sitting in the chair staring at her in disbelief, and the next he was towering over her, naked, his powerful fingers gripping her shoulders. His voice shook with anger. "What nonsense is this?" he demanded.

"It's true," she answered hoarsely. She could no longer hold back the tears and they spilled down her cheeks. "It's true. The man who came to the kitchen . . . before. It was Sean." She dropped her eyes in shame. "I hoped he would go away . . . but he didn't. He set the fire, Rory."

"Have ye taken leave of your senses?"

"No." She swayed as waves of faintness threatened her equilibrium. "It was Sean Flynn."

"Who in the name of Beelzebub is Sean Flynn?" Rory demanded. "And why would he burn my prize house?"

Linna tried futilely to pull free, but he held her in an iron vise. "Please, Rory," she stammered. "You're hurting me."

Slowly, with deliberate effort, Rory relaxed his grip on her and stepped back. He exhaled sharply and ran a hand through his unbound hair. "Have ye gone mad, woman?"

She shook her head. "No. It's true, it was Sean."

"And who is this . . . this Sean?"

"My stepbrother."

Rory's hands balled into fists at his sides. "There is more to this than a burned building."

She nodded. Wordlessly, he turned away. Opening

a cabinet door in the fireplace wall, Rory took out a flask of rum. He unstoppered the cork and took a long drink of the fiery liquid. When he spoke again he had gained control of his voice.

"Don't keep me in suspense, Linna," he said sarcastically. "Tell me more of this *brother* who carries a different name from that of your father. The night is old, but this tale is too fine to wait for daybreak." His eyes narrowed dangerously as he drank again from the bottle.

"Have the decency to put on some clothes," she snapped. "I'll not be cross-examined by some drunken satyr."

Rory's features hardened. "Damn you, Linna. I'll have the truth. I've not hurt you—ever. I think you owe me an explanation, drunk or sober."

The child moved within her, and Linna stifled an urge to cover her belly with her hands. She swallowed again, fighting the pitch of her insides as a sharp pain knifed through her lower back. She caught the bedpost for support and took a deep breath. "I am not Mary Aislinn Beatty," she uttered tonelessly. Her voice seemed to come from far away; bright spots of light flashed in her brain and the floor seemed to sway.

Glass shattered against the brick hearth as the blackness threatened to consume her. Strong hands caught her in midair and laid her back against the soft feather tick. "Linna, for the love of God," Rory swore. "Have you lost your mind?"

Lost your mind . . . lost you mind . . . lost your mind. The words blurred one into the other as the bed hangings swam before her eyes.

"Hush . . . hush. You don't know what you're saying."

Her eyelids were made of lead. She was hot . . . so hot. Why was she so hot? Was the room on fire? Linna forced back the darkness and opened her eyes. Rory's face was inches above, so close she could feel his breath on her hot face.

"Not the one . . ." she murmured. "Not Sir Edmond's legal daughter. Not Lady Maeve's Mary Aislinn." Linna blinked. The pain was back, grinding, drawing her knees up. "Finola's bastard," she cried. "Sir Edmond's daughter . . . but not the right one. Lied to you . . . cheated you."

Rory stiffened as numb disbelief clouded his expression. With a smothered oath, he rose from the bed and backed away. Linna covered her ears at the sound of splintering wood. There was another crash and the tinkle of glass. Frightened, she uncovered her eyes and looked up as a blast of cold air brought her to her senses.

Rory stood before the window gripping one hand in the other. A broken pane lay scattered on the braided rug at his feet, a rug that became blotched with the dark stains of Rory's blood.

"Holy Mother of God," Linna cried. Oblivious to her own pain, she scrambled from the bed, snatched up her nightgown from a chair, and wrapped it around his bleeding hand. "What have you done?"

"What have ye done?" he echoed. Veins stood out on his wide forehead; his face was the color of old ivory. "Once before I asked ye who ye were," he agonized. "Maybe now ye will answer that question . . . if the truth is in ye."

Linna lifted his poor hand and cradled it against her cheek. "I had a sister," she began. One by one, the words tumbled out like rushing water over a dam. Lady Maeve . . . Mount Beatty . . . Linna's real position in her father's house . . . Mary's desire to join a religious order. Through it all, Rory listened, saying nothing as she poured out her confession of lies and deceit.

"I could not know I would come to love you," she said in anguish, "or that Sean would follow me here and threaten what we have."

"Ah yes, the brother." Rory's voice was as hard as gravel. "I had nearly forgotten Sean's part in this tale. It is a nice twist."

"Would you rather I paid his blackmail?" Linna cried, dropping his hand and backing away. "You do not know me if you think me such a fool! He is a cruel man and as mad as any hatter. Give him one shilling, and we will never be rid of him."

Rory returned to the cabinet and removed a second flask of rum, taking care not to step on the broken glass on the hearth. He held out his cut hand and poured the amber liquid over it, then took a deep swig. He gave her a long, penetrating gaze. "What would ye have me do with him?" Rory asked.

"Seize him. Turn him over to the authorities." She sank into the bed and hugged her belly. "I don't know. But I do know he will kill someone if he isn't stopped."

"Ye spin such a story it is hard to know what is true and what is fancy, Linna. I've never known such an accomplished liar. Doubtless, Sir Edmond has enjoyed many a laugh at my expense."

"Sir Edmond . . . my father . . . knows nothing of this. He signed the betrothal in good faith. He believes that it was Mary who wed you."

"And the dowry?"

"Paid for Mary."

Rory turned and stared into the dying fire. "Would ye have told me—ever?"

"Probably not."

"Then I am wed to the daughter of a serving wench . . . and my son, if it is to be a son, can add that to his noble lineage."

Linna's chin went up. "Yes."

"Ye know what ye have told me is grounds for annulment or divorce?"

"I know."

Rory took another drink, threw open a chest, and pulled out stockings and a pair of breeches. Linna watched as he began to dress.

"Who else knows that Sean is your stepbrother?"

"Mab."

"And she knows about his coming here?"

"No. I didn't tell her."

Rory yanked on a vest over his shirt. "I will send someone to mend the window and clean up the mess. Ye will not leave this room. Not tonight, not tomorrow. Do ye understand me, woman?"

Linna nodded.

"I will go to the woods and wait for this Sean Flynn. If he can be made to see reason, I will spare his life. If not . . ."

"Don't go alone," she begged. "You don't know him like I do. He can't be trusted."

"I can see that that is a family trait." Rory took a small pistol from the chest and tucked it into a shoulder holster beneath the vest. He paused by the bed. "Ye need have no fear for your safety, Linna. Whatever ye have done to me and to our marriage, ye carry my

child." His voice dropped to a whisper. "I trust it is
my child," he added in Gaelic.

"Bastard," she flung back.

"That is the point, is it not, sweet wife? A woman
who would lie to her husband, who would make her
whole life a lie—would such a woman shrink from
adultery?" He took a deep breath. "If it is not my
child, never tell me. I don't know if I could keep from
killing you if I found out you'd betrayed me in that
way, too."

Fresh tears of anger stained her cheeks. "This is
your child," she cried. "On his unborn soul, I swear
it." She covered her face with her hands and sobbed.
"I love you, Rory . . . I've always loved you."

"Aye, madam, perhaps you do," he replied coldly.
"But you pick a damned strange way to show it."

Linna shivered as she made her way on foot across
the moonlit field and into the shelter of the trees beside
the creek. The ground was crunchy-hard beneath her
feet; the numbing cold seeped up through her stout
leather boots. Nevertheless, she strode on staunchly,
ignoring the sting of the biting air on her face and
fingers and trying not to be intimidated by the eerie
howling in the distance.

"It's nothing but a dog," she murmured to herself.
The shadowy word *wolf* formed in a dark corner of
her mind, and she pushed it firmly away, wishing
she'd been able to take a horse from the stable instead
of having to walk.

Damn Rory for his stupid male pride! Going alone
to meet Sean was foolhardy. Rory had not spoken a
word to her all day, but she had seen him leave the
manor house just before dusk. He'd ridden out of the

farmyard, jumped the pasture fence, and turned his horse northeast toward the sharp bend in the creek. If only Donal was at Connemara! She would have told him everything and sent him to help his brother. But Donal was in Chestertown, a day's journey away, and no matter how angry Rory became at her for disobeying his orders, Linna had to follow him.

Linna pulled the woolen cloak tighter around her and gingerly fingered the flintlock dueling pistol she had taken from Donal's room. She hoped the weapon was loaded; Rory had promised to teach her to shoot a gun, but he'd never found the time. Still, loaded or not, the pistol made her feel braver. If she needed it to bluff Sean, he wouldn't know if the gun was empty, either.

Far above, a vee of geese arced across the cloud-strewn sky. Their plaintive cries cut the cold winter air, increasing Linna's sense of loneliness. She stumbled over a tree root, caught herself against the tree trunk, and bit back a cry of alarm. The backache that had nagged her all day was still there, but she had experienced none of the pain that she'd felt the night before when she had confessed her deception to Rory.

"I'm sorry," she whispered to the child in her womb. She patted her belly and leaned against the tree until she stopped shaking.

Doubts spilled into her mind like icy needles of rain. Suppose she was too late? Suppose Sean had lost his nerve and hadn't come at all? What if Sean had lain in wait for Rory and ambushed him? Would she be walking into a trap, too? What if she lost her way in the night and froze to death? Rory had called her mad; maybe she was losing her mind. If anything happened to her unborn child because of her impulsive decision to follow Rory . . .

Linna shrugged away her apprehensions. It didn't matter if Rory hated her and wanted to put her away. She loved him. She could never live with herself if she let harm come to Rory because of her. Sean was her personal Lucifer; he had come to New Connemara because of her. She would have to deal with him.

Unfamiliar rustling in the woods caused goosebumps to rise on her arms. Rabbits, she assured herself. *Wolves!* argued the demons in her mind. Her heart was beating so fast that it made her breathless. "Just think of Rory," she murmured. "Rory." Resolutely, she put one foot ahead of the other and kept walking.

Suddenly, she caught a fragment of a human voice on the wind. Linna began to run, heedless of the branches that snagged her hair and clothing and scratched her face. The whinny of a horse rang out, just ahead and to the left. Linna turned toward the sound, stumbling over a fallen log and gouging her hand on a snag. Now there were two male voices, clearly raised in anger.

"Sassenach lickspittle!" a man cried in Gaelic— Sean's voice.

"No!" Linna protested.

The roar of a musket split the air, then a man's scream, and then a second shot exploded in the night. A horse whinnied and bolted into the woods, almost running her down.

Linna dashed into the clearing in the woods. The moonlight made the circle of fallen logs and knee-high grass almost as bright as day. She fumbled for the pistol as Sean's giant form lurched toward her. Beyond her stepbrother, a man's form lay sprawled in the grass.

"Linna!" Sean shouted in Gaelic. His hand came up and metal gleamed in the moonlight. "I'll kill you, you Sassenach bitch!"

Linna whipped the flintlock from the folds of her cloak as a pistol cracked again. Sean stopped in his tracks, his eyes wide and bewildered. The pistol tumbled from his massive hand. Sean moaned once and fell facedown in front of her.

Still clutching her unfired weapon, Linna ran past him and dropped to her knees beside Rory.

He swore and caught her in his arms. "What in the name of the Twelve Apostles are ye doing here, woman?"

"You're hurt!"

"Aye, but I'll live, and that's more than ye can say for that bastard." Rory put her from him and tried to stand, but his leg buckled.

Linna tore a piece of cloth from her shift to staunch the blood running from his upper thigh. He jerked the material from her and balled it up, pressing it tightly against the wound.

"Is he dead?" she asked, motioning toward her stepbrother.

"He should be. I shot him once in the chest and once in the back when he came at ye." Rory drew a long, shuddering breath. "This hurts like hell," he admitted. "I think ye'd best catch that horse and ride for help."

"I can't leave you here."

"Linna," he rasped. "I've got a ball in my leg. I think it's nicked an artery. Will ye sit here sniveling while I bleed to death, or will ye go and fetch the men to carry me home?"

Trembling, Linna got to her feet. "I'll go."

"What were ye thinking of, to come out here?"

"I brought a pistol." She retrieved the weapon from the grass and gave it to him.

"I told ye to stay in your chamber." Rory's voice cracked as he switched from English to Gaelic. "Ye risked the child for nothing."

"Not for nothing," she answered softly. "For you."

Rory shook his head. "Your coming doesn't change the way I feel about you."

"I didn't expect it to."

"We needed your dowry money for the plantation." He winced as he pressed the cloth harder against his thigh. "I'll send it back to Sir Edmond—what's left. The balance I'll owe him. The dowry was for your half sister; I'll not keep what's not rightfully mine."

Linna nodded. "I never thought of that."

"It's a matter of honor, something you'd know little about."

"Don't speak to me of honor!" she lashed out. "A man's honor! A man's world!" She swore a Gaelic oath. "Sir Edmond took my mother's honor when he got a child on her, and he ground it into the dust when he refused to give me his name or his protection. I could have starved for all he cared!" Linna marched back to the spot where her stepbrother lay and nudged him with the toe of her boot. For a long moment she stood, looking down at Sean's still form. "Sean was the man who tried to rape me on my fifteenth birthday," she cried. "Where was my father's honor when no one punished him? When they let Sean come back to work on the manor as though nothing had happened?" She sniffed. "Honor? You're right, Rory Desmond. Honor is something I know little about." She spun on her heel and started into the forest in search of the horse.

"Linna—wait," Rory called. "I want you to know Sean shot me first. We were arguing, but I didn't want to kill him. We'll have him buried in holy ground if you wish."

"You can bury him in a pigsty for all I care," she retorted soundly. "He's bound straight for hell anyway."

"Say nothing to the servants of who he was."

"Do you want me to go for help or not?"

"Aye. You'd best. Be careful with the horse in the dark," Rory admonished.

"Why should I?" she demanded. "If I fall off and break my neck, you'll be well rid of me."

Rory's cursing scorched her ears as she plunged into the woods. "Damn him," she muttered. "Damn him to hell!"

The horse was no more than a few hundred feet away, his bridle reins tangled in a tree branch. Linna spoke soothingly to the frightened animal and patted it as she approached. She realized with a jolt that there was no sidesaddle; she'd be forced to ride astride.

Getting on a horse without the assistance of a servant and without a mounting block was harder than it looked. Nervously, she led the animal to a fallen tree, climbed up on it, and scrambled awkwardly into the saddle. "I like this no better than you do," she informed the horse. Holding tightly to the saddle, Linna leaned low over the horse's neck and touched his sides with her heels. Without hesitation the horse began to walk in the general direction of the manor house. Linna slid sideways until one toe caught in an iron stirrup, and she took a firm grip on the reins.

The finality of Sean's death settled over her, and she whispered a hasty prayer for his black soul. The saints forgive her, but she could spare no sympathy for his passing. He had been an evil boy who had grown into an evil man, and the world would be a better place without him. Rory's wound worried her more. Surely, the injury was not mortal. What dying man could rage at her as Rory had?

When they left the forest, Linna urged the animal into a slow canter. And for the hundredth time she wished Donal was home at Connemara.

A fortnight passed before Donal and Judith arrived, and by that time Sean was buried and Rory on his feet and walking again with the aid of a cane. In all those days, Rory had spoken to Linna only when necessary, and not at all about what concerned her most—their future as man and wife. What he had done was to move his belongings into another room.

He sent Daisy to Linna's bedchamber when Donal's boat docked at the landing.

"Master Rory says will you come down to meet the family?" Daisy asked.

Linna laid down her book, put Brigand off her lap, and followed the maid downstairs. Rory stood waiting just inside the front door.

"Will you tell them, or shall I?" he asked her coldly when Daisy returned to the kitchen.

Linna forced herself to meet Rory's gaze squarely. "I'll tell them myself."

"They have a right to know."

"I said I'd tell them," she snapped.

"Linna." He reached for her hand and she stepped away from him. "I have no wish to be cruel."

"Nor do I."

"I'm hurting," Rory said. "I loved ye and I trusted ye. God, woman! I would have trusted ye with my life."

"Am I any less the woman you married because I'm not Mary Aislinn?"

"You deceived me."

"Yes." Linna stiffened. "I did. And if I had it to do over again, I'd do the same thing."

The front door banged open and Donal stepped into the entrance hall, arms laden with bundles. "What the hell happened to our prize house?"

Chapter 17

"You little guttersnipe!" Judith sputtered. Her face swelled with blood and turned a mottled puce as she advanced on Linna, hand lifted to slap the younger woman across the face.

"None of that, Mother," Rory said, placing his muscular form solidly between the two women. "It's done, and we must find a—"

"A civilized way to deal with it?" Donal finished sarcastically. He shrugged and arched a dark eyebrow wryly. "The question is, of course," he mocked, "what would Father do?"

Judith's voice was shrill. "The marriage must be annulled!"

Rory took his mother by the arm and led her firmly to a chair. "Madam, if you will be so kind." Judith's brow creased in a frown and she stiffened. "Mother, sit!" Rory ordered. "No one will stir from this room until we have reached a workable situation."

"Aye," Donal agreed. "And I've the perfect answer. You dissolve the marriage and I'll wed her." He winked at Linna. "Agreed?"

"I'll have no kitchen wench's offspring in my family," Judith railed, trying to sidestep Rory. "She must be sent back to Ireland at once!''

Linna glared back at her. ''And your grandchild! Am I to take the baby with me?''

Judith gasped at the outrageous suggestion. ''Indeed, not. Common blood aside, the child will be a Desmond.''

''Only half,'' Donal reminded his mother as he dropped into a chair, stretched his long legs out before him, and crossed them at the ankles.

Linna tried to keep from shivering. The family had gone into the great hall as soon as Judith had come up the hill from the dock, closing the doors to keep the servants from overhearing their conversation. Since the elegantly furnished room was kept for special occasions, no fire had been lit there for several days, and the chamber was chilly and damp. Linna crossed her arms defiantly. ''No one will separate me from my child,'' she declared. ''If I go, I take the baby.''

''I've lost one child; I'll not lose another,'' Rory stated with a calm relentlessness.

Linna shifted her gaze from Judith's sour face to Rory's. There was no mistaking the torment in her husband's eyes; she wondered if he could read the bittersweet anguish in her own. I still love you, she cried silently. Please . . . Rory . . . don't send me away.

Rory turned to his mother. ''The baby remains in Maryland on Connemara. If Linna is content with our marriage, there will be no annulment.''

''I don't recall hearing what Linna wants,'' Donal said coolly.

Rory spun around. ''Well, woman? What shall it be?''

Linna fought her own rising anger. Did he think to

make her beg in front of his mother, in front of Donal? The babe kicked as she found her voice. "We were wed in the Church."

"Nay, Linna," he insisted. "I asked what ye wanted."

Judith scowled. "She wants to stay—what else would she want? She thinks to continue her farce of being a lady. In Ireland she would—"

"Silence, Mother," Rory warned, turning hard eyes on Judith. "This is not your affair. If we are seeking blame in this matter, ye are not lily-white. 'Twas your doing from the first. I had no wish to marry again. Ye made the match." Rory glanced back at Linna. "If ye desire your freedom from the marriage, say it now."

Linna's lower lip quivered. "No. I do not." For an instant she was certain she saw relief in Rory's gaze, then his dark eyes narrowed and his expression became impassive again. He squared his shoulders and held out his hand to her. Trembling, she extended her fingers until they rested lightly on the back of his wrist.

"The matter is settled, Mother. If ye cause Linna grief over what cannot be undone, we will move out of the house and take up residence at Sherwood. Do I make myself clear?"

"Plainly," Judith replied crisply.

"Donal?"

"Don't look at me," Donal answered. "She's the first breath of life on Connemara in years. I've been her champion from the first."

"Good. Then it is settled," Rory pronounced. "I have written to Sir Edmond and made arrangements for the return of Linna's dowry. I tell ye this so that ye will understand our financial situation and the need for personal sacrifice from all of us.''

''Return the dowry!'' Judith cried. ''You can't! We've spent—''

''It will be repaid—every penny. And I will hear no more of the matter.'' Giving his mother a sharp nod of dismissal, Rory led Linna out of the room to the foot of the stairs. ''If Mother is unkind to ye, I want to know it,'' he said softly. ''This family has weathered a lot of storms; I don't intend to let it break over this one.''

Linna removed her hand from his. ''If you don't want me here . . .''

''As ye said, Linna, we were married in the Church. We will soon have a child to—''

''Damn you!'' Choking back tears, she slammed a balled fist against his chest. ''Not the Church! Not the baby! You!'' He caught her wrists and held her effortlessly as she began to weep. ''I . . . want . . . you, Rory. Forgive me. Please.''

With a groan, Rory enveloped her in his arms, muffling her sobs against his shirt. His lips brushed her hair, and he breathed deeply of her intoxicating, heady scent. ''Linna,'' he murmured. ''Linna.'' It would be so easy to give her what she asked, to return to her bed and the comfort of her arms. What difference would it make if he no longer trusted her? How many men did trust their wives?

''Don't hate me, Rory,'' Linna whispered. ''I can't bear it if you hate me.''

A shudder passed through him as he released her and stepped back. ''I could never hate ye, Linna.'' Pain knifed through his gut. He had only to stare into those green-flecked brown eyes and he would begin to weaken. "But I cannot lie to ye," he said. "Ye ask too much of a man. Not only did ye betray our marriage vows, but ye have brought us close to financial ruin." He shrugged. "They say time heals all things. Perhaps it will be so for us. For now . . ." His deep voice trailed off.

"You will not forgive me," she whispered.

"Nay, Linna," he answered in Gaelic. "Not will not . . . cannot."

"Then ours will be a marriage in name only?"

Rory rubbed unconsciously at the healing bullet wound on his thigh. "It's all I have to give ye. If it's not enough . . ."

"You're a fool, Rory Desmond," Linna flung back. "And if your heart is so small that it cannot forgive a wrong, God help you!" Whitely resolute, she turned and began to ascend the wide staircase. At the landing, she hesitated and glanced back. Rory was still standing motionless at the base of the steps. "You may stop loving me, but as long as I draw breath, I will love you," she vowed. "And I will never, never give up on our marriage."

The ache in his gut subsided to a dull throb as Rory turned and walked swiftly toward the door, Linna's parting words echoing in his brain.

Winter wrapped the Tidewater in a cocoon of ice and snow. Fierce storms swept down from the north, churning the Chesapeake into an impassable body of water. Ships were trapped at anchor by the thick ice, and travel by land became impossible as heavy snow drifted across the roads. For weeks, the Eastern Shore was cut off from the outside world.

Daily, Linna listened to the servants' gossip of lost men, of frozen and starving livestock, and—even more frightening—tales of packs of wolves that had crossed the bay to prey on the outlying farms.

For the most part, Linna remained in her room, waiting for word of Rory and Donal's safety. From dawn until long after dark, the two men directed emergency measures to keep their people and animals warm and fed through the unnatural cold.

Linna could see nothing through the icebound windows of her bedchamber. Although the roaring fire and warm clothing kept her reasonably comfortable, she paced the floor in constant apprehension. Not even Brigand's companionship could ease her foreboding.

"You will bring harm to your child," Sarah warned. Linna had asked that the Indian girl be permitted to act as her maid, and Rory had agreed. With Mab gone to her own home and Judith more distant than ever, there was no one for Linna to talk to. "Your husband is not a child to be lost on his own plantation."

"But the storm . . ."

"He is not one of these soft, powdered Englishmen," Sarah observed from her place near the fire. "He has lived among the Shawnee and knows their ways. A Shawnee grandmother could not become lost in her own backyard." Smiling, Sarah bent her dark head over her sewing.

"You know he is very angry with me," Linna admitted. "We do not even share a bed anymore."

Sarah kept her eyes on the mitten she was patching.

"His mother hates me."

The Indian girl looked up. "She does not hate you— she is afraid of you."

"Of me?"

Sarah bit off a piece of scarlet thread and slipped the wooden egg out of the mitten. "She thinks you have taken her sons away."

"Her sons?"

"I have seen Donal watching you."

"He is my friend—nothing more," Linna flung back.

"Perhaps."

"He is the only friend I have here now, except you, Sarah. You don't understand Donal."

"I think I know more of men than you do. Red or white, a man is a man. His eyes tell what his tongue will not." Sarah rolled the pair of mittens together and tucked them into a basket.

Linna raised her hand aimlessly to smooth a stray lock of hair away from her face and dropped to her knees beside Sarah. "And what do you see in Rory's eyes? Will he ever forgive me for what I have done?"

Sarah's face remained impassive as she considered the question. "Your man is not as easy to read as his brother. Knowing his heart is as difficult as tracking a cougar over rock, but this I believe." She inclined her chin toward the hand-carved walnut cradle that stood empty at the foot of Linna's bed. "When your man-child lies there, things will be different in this house. There will be great change."

"For the better?" Linna demanded.

Sarah sighed and spread her delicate hands, palms up. "To know that, we must wait the will of God."

April 1755

Early on a Sunday morning, on the second day of April in the year 1755, Linna gave birth to the first

Desmond heir to be born in the American Colonies. The labor was short and without complication; a healthy baby boy was born before his father could be summoned from Sherwood Plantation.

When Rory reached the bedchamber, Linna had already been bathed and dressed in clean clothing. She lay propped up on pillows in the great bed, tired but content, her small son cradled in the crook of her arm.

"May I come in?" Rory asked. Linna nodded, and he strode across the room to stand beside her. "Are you—"

"She's fine," Judith said, beaming. "Who would've thought it?" She folded her arms over her chest. "Two hours. A fine boy with less fuss than some women make over their moon days. We'd have called you sooner, but I didn't think she'd birth it before evening." She bent and picked up the crying infant. "Are your hands clean?"

Rory nodded dumbly.

"Good. Here, get the feel of him." Judith thrust the baby into his father's arms, then turned toward Daisy and Sarah. "Out, both of you. We've got to leave them alone."

Hastily, Judith followed the women toward the door. She stopped suddenly, spun around, and nodded briskly. "There's good blood in you somewhere, Linna," she said curtly. "Blood will out, and you have your children like I had mine—no nonsense." With a final nod, she stepped out the door and closed it firmly behind her.

Linna covered her mouth with her hand and giggled. "Give him to me," she insisted. "You're holding him like a chicken."

"Nay, not yet," Rory answered in Gaelic. "I must

get a good look at my son. You're certain it's a boy—he's got all his parts?''

"Look for yourself," Linna replied in the same tongue.

"He's not overly small?"

Tiny fists beat the air as the infant wailed angrily, eyes wide open and minute legs kicking in the folds of the blanket.

"No."

"Is he supposed to be red like this?" Rory raised his voice to be heard above the screaming, and the baby cried harder.

"Give him to me, you great ninny! You'll frighten him."

Rory brushed his lips across the downy dark fuzz on the infant's head and handed him over. Linna cuddled him against her breast and whispered soothing mother sounds. Gradually, the wails turned to hiccups.

"Ye do that like ye know what you're doing," Rory said, sitting on the edge of the bed. "You're all right? You're certain?"

"I'm fine." Linna hugged the baby against her and tried not to cry. She'd had this crazy notion that when Rory saw the baby everything would be fine between them. She swallowed. "What will you call him?"

"Ye carried him for nine months; ye brought him safely into the world. As long as it's not Donal, ye can name him whatever ye choose."

"Colin Patrick."

"Colin Patrick Desmond it is, then," Rory said huskily. He stood up. "I would have been here with ye, had I known."

Linna nodded.

"I sold the bay stallion and two breeding mares at

Sherwood . . . but it won't be enough. There's been no word of our tobacco shipment.''

Linna closed her eyes.

''I'd not upset ye, but Ty's returned from Virginia. He says that Major General Edward Braddock is leading an army of regulars and provincials north to capture Fort Duquesne from the French. They're desperate for guides who speak the Indian languages, and they're paying good English silver. I mean to go along with Ty to Williamsburg and see for myself.''

Linna's eyes widened. ''No!'' she cried. ''Don't go! Please. Don't leave us here.''

''I've not said I'd go yet. I'm only going to talk. I know a few Virginians who went along with young Washington last summer. I can find out from them what we're up against.''

''Rory . . . please.''

His expression hardened. ''I'd not leave Connemara and . . . the boy . . . if I didn't have to. But without the tobacco money, we stand to lose the land.''

''We wouldn't if you hadn't insisted on sending my father back the dowry,'' Linna said. ''It's your damned pride that got us in this. I'll not have you going off to war because—''

''It's not your decision. If ye ever had any say in what I do, you've lost it.''

''It's easier to run away than it is to stay here and try and mend what's between us, isn't it?'' The baby began to fuss, and Linna rocked him against her. ''We need you, Rory. I need you.''

''Damn you, woman, don't ye understand? I'm doing this for all of us.''

''No, you're not! You're doing it to punish me.''

''And ye think it doesn't punish me, too?'' Rory

turned away and stood squarely, shoulders trembling with emotion. "You've got to give me time, Linna. I want to be a husband to ye . . . but I can't."

"Pride, again?"

He turned back and glared at her with icy calm. "Nay, Linna, the fault is trust. I cannot be husband to a woman I cannot trust."

"Then go and be damned," she cried. "But don't be so certain we'll be here waiting when you get back!"

"Stay if ye choose, go if ye must," he retorted, "but my son remains on Connemara. If ye take him so much as a step off this plantation, I'll track ye to the ends of the earth to get him back."

Two weeks later, Colin Patrick was baptized in the same chapel where Linna and Rory had been wed the year before. Friends and neighbors were invited back to the manor house to celebrate the arrival of a male heir for Connemara. Linna's joy in the day was dimmed by the knowledge that Rory had signed on as a civilian guide for General Braddock's campaign against the French.

The guests could talk of little else.

"I hear Braddock's a stubborn, coleric bastard," said one old gentleman. "By the book, do or be damned!"

"Aye, I'd say he was, from what little I saw of him," Rory agreed. "But he's got forty-three years in the Coldstream Guards behind him. He's tough, and he's experienced."

"And not afraid of the devil himself," Ty put in.

At the sound of Ty's raspy voice, Linna glanced down the table at her husband's friend. The frontiersman's usual hunting shirt and fringed leggings had been exchanged for Rory's second best satin coat and breeches. The spotless linen stock was knotted so tightly about his neck that Linna expected him to choke at any minute. Ty's black mane had been trimmed and was tied back neatly with a scarlet ribbon.

Judith leaned close to Linna's ear. "There's the devil's right-hand imp. He's as near to savage as a white man can get, but he's loyal to Rory. He'll not let harm come to him."

"Pray God," Linna murmured silently. She looked sideways under her lashes at her mother-in-law. Judith was attempting to eat with Colin balanced on her lap. The baby was sleeping contentedly, seemingly unaware of the dinner for twenty-five going on around him.

The change in Judith since Colin's birth had been almost miraculous. Her behavior toward Linna bordered on pleasant, and it was hard for Linna to remember past slights when the older woman so obviously doted on Colin's every breath.

Linna couldn't get over the fact that Judith didn't blame her for Rory's decision to join the attack on Fort Duquesne.

"My son's a fool," Judith had said when she'd heard of Rory's plan. "He's not going off to save Connemara—it's merely to run around in the woods and play Indian. It's too dull here on the Tidewater for the young scamp. He's always been a roamer. He ran off to America, and we didn't hear a word out of him for years. Don't let him try and put the guilt on you. He's going because his head's full of guns and glory."

"What do you propose we use for money, Mother?"

Rory had demanded sarcastically. "The ship carrying our tobacco was lost from the fleet and hasn't been heard of since. Without that revenue, Connemara's finished."

"Poppycock!" Judith had flung back. "I never would have returned Sir Edmond's money. We'd have had plenty then!"

Colin's hungry wail brought Linna from her reverie. "I'll take him," she offered, holding out her arms for the baby.

Judith gently placed a knuckle against the rosebud mouth, and the infant began to suck frantically. "He's hungry," she said, indicating the long table spread with all manner of meat and vegetables. "All this food and none for him." Ignoring Linna, Judith motioned for a servant. "Take him to the wet nurse," she instructed. "Then see that he's bathed and dressed in the blue muslin—no, make it the silk with the embroidery. Bring him back here for the guests to admire." She kissed a tiny fist and handed the baby to the maid. "Nothing you can do for him, Linna," she said. "Not so with me. My late husband, the boys' father, used to say I was as well endowed as a Saxon peasant."

Linna flushed and looked down at her plate. Being unable to breastfeed Colin was a great disappointment. She had had milk at first, but then it had dried up without reason. An indentured woman with a baby girl had been brought from the quarters to stay in the house as long as Colin needed her. The woman was clean and gentle with him, but Linna still felt left out and looked forward to the time when Colin could be switched to goat milk.

"A toast to our Indian fighters," someone cried.

"Yes, a toast!"

"To Ty and Rory! May they send the Frenchies to hell!"

Glasses clinked all around as men and women alike lifted their goblets in salute.

"Drive the French into the sea and be back in time to cut tobacco, Desmond!" a red-haired planter cried.

Linna's gaze met Rory's across the table, and for an instant, she stared into his naked soul, reading uncertainty in his dark eyes. Then he turned abruptly away, leaving her desolate as if their thoughts had never touched. Oh, Rory, she cried silently. God help us both.

Chapter 18

Linna lay awake all through the night listening for a squeak of a board, the turn of the doorknob, or the deep lilt of Rory's voice calling her name. She hoped and prayed that he would come to her—this last night before he left for the campaign against the French. Her recent childbirth would prevent sexual intimacy between them, but it didn't matter. All Linna wanted was for him to hold her in his arms and tell her he still loved her.

Shortly after the hall clock had struck the hour of three, Colin woke and began to cry hungrily. Gingerly, Linna rose from her bed and picked him up. "Hush, sweeting," she whispered. "Don't cry." Joy coursed through her at the feel of his strong little body squirming against her. She kissed the back of his neck, where the hair grew in downy whorls, and smelled the sweet scent of him.

The baby jammed one fist into his mouth and began to suck noisily. Linna opened her gown and offered him a breast. The tiny mouth seized her nipple and began to tug, first eagerly and then in frustration. He spat out the nipple and began to wail.

"I've let you down, too, haven't I, Colin," Linna crooned. "All right, little one." Barefoot, she padded down the hall to the small room occupied by the wet nurse. "Mabel," she called softly.

"Yes, ma'am," came the sleepy answer. "Is he awake?"

Linna heard the rustle of sheets and heavy breathing as Mabel pulled a shift over her nude body. Colin continued to fuss and suck on his fingers.

"I'll take him, Miss Linna," Mabel said. "He wouldn't wake ye if ye'd jest let me keep his cradle in here wi' baby Jane 'n' me."

Linna kissed her son's head again and passed him to the wet nurse. Within seconds Linna was rewarded by the sound of Colin's lusty nursing. "Bring him back to my room when he's finished," Linna instructed firmly. "And be certain you change his linen." She knew that Mabel let her infant daughter sleep in her bed. It was a dangerous custom that often resulted in a baby's death by suffocation when the mother rolled on the baby in the night. Linna was unwilling to risk Colin's life in such a manner. Besides, she liked having him near her at night; it was comforting to hear his strong, regular breathing.

Linna returned to her room and waited. Three quarters of an hour passed before a yawning Mabel placed Colin in his cradle. The baby was asleep, but Linna stared wide-eyed at the dark recesses of the bed hangings. When the first streaks of dawn spilled across the purple sky, Linna was still awake. And when she summoned her courage to go to Rory's room in the half light of the still morning, she found the chamber empty.

A note with Linna's name on it was lying on the

mahogany desk by the door. With trembling hands, she opened it and read the bold script.

Linna,

I thought it better for us both if there were no good-byes. God keep you and our son safe until my return.

Your husband,
Rory Colin Desmond

Silently, Linna crumpled the parchment. Any reconciliation—if there was to be one—would have to wait until Rory came home . . . and that could be months . . . or years . . . or never.

The days at Connemara fell into a pattern, one after another like so many leaves drifting on the salt bay wind. With Colin to care for and the children at the school to teach, Linna felt she had purpose—and if she fell into bed at night exhausted, it was a good exhaustion.

The Indian girl Sarah had become her friend, and Linna had enlisted her help at the school. Even though Sarah could not read or write, she could help in keeping order and in amusing the children with games and stories. Because Linna refused to be parted from Colin, Sarah had fashioned a Shawnee cradleboard for her to carry the baby in.

Despite Judith's vocal misgivings, the sturdy infant spent most mornings in the company of his mother. Strapped safely into the cradleboard, his hands free to play with the dangling toys, he was amiably content to ride Linna's or Sarah's back, or to be propped against a wall to laugh and coo at the admiring children.

Linna and Judith had found a common ground on which to build their wary friendship. Both women loved Colin, and both wanted what was best for him. Judith's tongue had lost none of its sting, but Linna learned to ignore the remarks that were directed to her, and to countermand any order regarding Colin's welfare with which she did not agree. Surprisingly, when Linna was firm, Judith usually gave in with only a token protest.

Three weeks after Rory's departure, a sloop from Oxford brought a message from the Desmond's factor in London. The ship carrying Connemara's tobacco had been greatly damaged in a storm. The captain had limped back to the sea lanes and had been found by a whaler out of New England. With the aid of that ship, the merchant vessel had reached the coast of North America and a shipyard. Repairs took weeks, but eventually the ship sailed again for England. The cargo was intact, and the tobacco had been sold for six times what Rory had expected. The money had been deposited in the Desmonds' account, and was immediately available for their use in the Maryland Colony.

Linna's relief at the improvement in their financial condition was tempered by the fact that Rory had gone to war without good cause. It did not make the waiting any easier for her, but it did improve Judith's disposition.

With Rory gone, Donal was responsible for the planting, the lumbering, the direction of workers, and the thousand and one jobs a plantation master must oversee. Linna saw little of him. Between Connemara and Sherwood, he was so busy that he often missed dinner.

"Donal's done better than I would have expected," Judith stated one afternoon as she and Linna finished eating. "The responsibility is just what he needed to make a man of him." She waved away a pot of chocolate a servant offered and reread the letter she had received by postrider that morning. The missive was from a lady friend, Mistress Ann Sinclair in Williamsburg. "Ann says that we are worrying about Rory needlessly," Judith repeated for the second time. "Captain James Sinclair of the Maryland Blues is her nephew. She says Rory will report directly to Captain Sinclair." Judith tapped a long fingernail sharply on the table. "Linna, are you attending?"

"Yes, of course," Linna answered hastily. Her attention had been focused on Colin, sleeping soundly in a wicker basket near her feet. One starfish hand was flung carelessly over his head, and the tiny pink lips were sucking soundlessly. "You were speaking of Captain Sinclair."

"Captain Sinclair is Ann's godchild. They are quite close. Captain Sinclair says that Major General Braddock commands fourteen hundred Redcoats and four hundred fifty militia from the Carolinas and Virginia as well as Maryland. The general has ordered a road cut from Fort Cumberland at Wills Creek to Fort Duquesne. Captain Sinclair is present at staff meetings with General Braddock, and the general assures him that they have every reason to believe the French will desert the fort before the army gets anywhere near it."

Linna exhaled slowly. "Sarah says that if the French have roused the tribes, there will be Ottawas,

Caughnawagas, Hurons, Abenakis, Delaware, and Potawatomies, not to mention the Shawnee and the Iroquois.''

''I distinctly heard Rory say that the Iroquois will stand firm for the British.''

''Sarah says Indians do not think the way we do. Their leaders cannot command them; each man does as he thinks fit. She believes that some of the Iroquois will fight with the French. It is the English who bring settlers to cut down the forests and build farms on Indian land.''

''Sarah is an ignorant savage. You spend far too much time with her. I don't believe she is a good influence on the baby. Who knows what diseases he might contract from her?''

''Smallpox, measles, cholera and the French pox are all European diseases. Sarah says the Indians have no resistance to them.''

''Hush!'' Judith's eyes flew to her sleeping grandson. ''What are you thinking of, to mention such evils in this house?'' Unconsciously, Judith began to cross herself, then stopped and tucked her offending hand under the table. ''We've had no outbreak of those things here, and we're not likely to, as long as we stay away from the ports and common people. Fortunately, I had smallpox as an infant. You cannot catch it a second time, you know.''

Linna nodded. ''I had it when I was seven. I've a pox scar on the back of my knee and another at my waist. Two of my half brothers died of it.''

Judith sniffed. ''Puny children, likely. Cottier stock. I'm surprised that you did not contract cowpox. Many country folk do. Dairymaids are quite immune to the smallpox.''

"We were too poor to have a cow then," Linna admitted. "We had one, but my stepfather traded it for *fuisce*."

"Ah, *poitín*. Rory's father was always fond of his drop. Not that he was an abuser. He just liked good whiskey." Judith motioned for Daisy to pour her a small measure of brandy.

Linna put her hand over her glass. "My stepfather Gill would drink anything and did. Once, he lay in a stupor for three days straight."

Colin stirred in his basket, and Judith pursed her lips. "Daisy, take the babe to Mabel. It's time for his feeding." Judith turned her gaze on Linna again. "Put on an apron and come with me to the bakehouse. You can supervise the breadmaking today. At my age, I really should not be doing everything around here, you know. It's time you shared some of the responsibility as mistress of Connemara."

Linna lowered her eyes to keep her mother-in-law from reading the amusement she knew they must reveal. For some reason, known only to Judith, the less favor Linna found with her husband, the more Judith seemed to approve of her.

Fort Duquesne
July 1755

Early in July, General Braddock wearied of the slow progress of his three hundred axmen, the cumbersome wagons, the sick and motley assortment of women and noncombatants. At Little Meadows, the general divided his forces and continued on with twelve hundred soldiers and nearly two hundred axmen. Hacking their way along Indian and game trails, the army reached

Turtle Creek, eight miles south of Fort Duquesne, on July 7, 1755. The army crossed the Monongahela River and traveled down the far bank.

The heavily guarded expedition was accompanied by Sir John St. Clair's artillery as well as Lieutenant Horatio Gates and Lieutenant Colonel Thomas Gage. Colonial militiamen and scouts flanked the noisy procession of regulars, packhorses, tumbrils, wagons, and herds of cattle. The general's aide, Lieutenant Colonel George Washington of Virginia, was suffering from a fever and had to be carried prone in a wagon along the makeshift road.

On the morning of July 8, two hundred and fifty French and French-Canadians left the protection of Fort Duquesne under the command of Captain Hyacinth de Beaujeu. With them went six hundred and fifty Indians, an assortment of fierce warriors from ten different tribes including Shawnee, Ottawa, Menominee, and Ojibwa. The Ottawa were led by the fearless Chief Pontiac.

On July 9, at one p.m., General Braddock's army crossed the Monongahela again. Lieutenant Colonel George Washington had recovered enough to sit a saddle and took his place in line near General Braddock. Although the army had expected an ambush at the river, they had forded without incident. The soldiers fell into line and advanced smartly to the fifers' air of ''The Grenadier's March.''

Lieutenant Colonel Thomas Gage and his scouts rode at the head of the column, leading the perilous way through a narrow ravine. On the far side, they heard the shout of Harry Gordon, an engineer; he had spotted a white man wearing Indian clothing. His warning cry was drowned in a savage war whoop and heavy volleys of musket fire from the woods surrounding the road.

Raw courage could not stand against the hail of death from the forest. Despite General Braddock's attempts to rally his ravaged troops, the Redcoats fell like ripe wheat before the farmer's sickle. The Virginia and Maryland militiamen took to the woods, dropping behind the trees and stumps to fight "Indian fashion." English cannon roared, deafening ally and enemy alike, but the cannonballs were useless in the heavy forest.

When British regulars attempted to join the Virginians, their officers, including the major general, beat them back into the road, insisting they fight in the traditional European manner. The Virginians were fired upon by their own troops and were forced to leave their strategic position and return to the bloody track.

General Braddock's bravery was without question; four horses were killed under him. Lieutenant Colonel George Washington was unscathed but suffered the loss of two mounts. Artillerymen fired again and again through the hot afternoon, sometimes shooting their own comrades in the confusion.

Seeing all was lost, Braddock signaled retreat. Before he could reach a place of safety, the general was mortally wounded. The retreat turned into a rout; screaming horses and soldiers fled through a sea of tangled gore, leaving the wounded, the artillery, ammunition, wagons, cattle and even their weapons. It was left to the shattered Colonial militia to try and save the wounded and put up a token defense against the blood-crazed Indians. Captain Steward carried the fallen general away with the aide of a militiaman.

The panicked remains of Braddock's army swam

and waded the Monongahela and did not stop until
they reached Great Meadows, fifty miles away. The
Maryland and Virginia provincials suffered terrible
losses as they tried to bring some order to the retreat.
When an account was made, it was found that over
eight hundred and fifty men had been killed and
wounded. Major General Braddock died four days
later; he was interred in the road, and the army marched
and drove over it to keep the Indians from finding and
mutilating his body.

Connemara Plantation
August 1755

Linna knelt in the herb garden, ruthlessly ripping at
weeds that sprouted in the dry soil around her lavender
plants. Her hands were dirty, her nails broken; her
eyes were red and puffy from weeping.

Word of the massacre on the Monongahela had been
trickling in for more than three weeks. Judith had received a letter from her friend in Williamsburg telling
of the death and gruesome scalping of her nephew,
Captain James Sinclair of Chestertown. The first re-
ports to reach the Eastern Shore said that General Braddock's forces had been totally annihilated. There were
rumors of French and Indian attacks all along the frontier.

Donal had taken the sloop and gone first to Annapolis
and then to Williamsburg to try and find information
about Rory and Ty. He'd returned with only sketchy
facts about the ill-fated expedition and no word of
either of the two men.

"The Virginia and Maryland militiamen suffered

the worst,'' Donal had explained in desolation. ''When
the Redcoats broke and ran, it was the Colonials who
tried to save the wounded and protect the rear of the
retreating army. I talked to dozens of people. No one
could tell me anything about Rory or Ty. I met one
man who'd crossed the Monongahela with Rory that
morning. He'd had trouble with his pack mule, and
Rory and another Blue had given him assistance. The
other man was dark, with long hair and a deerskin
shirt. It could have been Ty.''

Judith's face had shown the strain of her fears for
her missing son. ''None of Rory's officers—?''

''All dead according to the posted list in Annapolis.
I could go to Captain Sinclair's home in Chestertown
if you want.''

''No need to do that,'' Judith had replied. ''Captain
Sinclair's widow has her own grief.''

Linna had listened in silence. And when she could
bear it no more, she had taken Colin from the nurse
and run upstairs to her room. She had rocked Rory's
son and murmured love words in the baby's ear. Donal
and Judith had talked as though they thought Rory was
dead, but she didn't accept that.

Linna hadn't believed it then, when Donal had returned from Williamsburg, and she didn't believe it
now. ''He's not dead,'' she whispered. ''He's not. I'd
know it if he were dead.'' She continued to tear at the
weeds with a vengeance, pulling up lavender and
rosemary without seeing them. ''Rory is not dead,''
she repeated stubbornly.

''No,'' a soft voice said behind her. ''Mishkwe-
Tusca lives. I have seen him.''

Linna whirled to find Sarah standing a few paces

away. "Where?" Linna cried, scrambling to her feet. "Where is he?"

Sarah shook her head. "I do not know. But I saw his face . . . in a vision. He lives. I know he does."

Goosebumps rose on Linna's arms, and she drew in a deep breath. "You have the sight?" In Ireland, she had heard of many people who could see into the future or bear witness to things that happened at a great distance. "Are you a witch?"

Sarah crossed herself hastily. "I am not!" she declared. "I have received Christian baptism." She lowered her voice. "But sometimes I see things . . . not in dreams, but waking. I have seen your man. He lies wounded, but he does not smell of death."

At the moment, the back door of the manor house flew open and Daisy shouted Linna's name. "Come quick, mistress!" the black girl cried. "There's a sloop at the dock! Come quick!"

Linna dashed in the door, down the formal center hall and out the front entranceway of Connemara with Sarah right behind her. An unfamiliar sloop was moored at the dock at the bottom of the hill. Donal and several others were there, helping to remove a man on a stretcher from the boat.

"Rory!" Linna's heart thudded wildly and she ran down the slope toward the small party of men. "Rory!" The joy turned to despair as she got close enough to recognize the injured man—it was Ty.

Donal caught her as she ran past him.

"Let me go!" Linna insisted. "Let me go! I've got to find—"

Donal shook his head. "Rory's not here," he said. "Ty's lost a leg."

Pulling free, Linna pushed through the men and caught Ty's hand as they carried him down the dock. "Ty," she whispered, blinking back tears. "You're alive."

"Hell, yes, I'm alive," Ty grated. His face was pale beneath the nut-brown tan, and his obsidian eyes gleamed fiercely out of a shrunken face. He squeezed her hand. "Part of me is." He waved toward the bandaged stump.

Linna tried not to shudder as her gaze traveled down his ravaged leg. Below his left knee was nothing. "Indians did that to you?" she murmured.

"Injuns, hell! Braddock's artillery! Damned Redcoats were too stupid to tell the militia from the enemy." Ty cleared his throat and wiped his eyes with a dirty sleeve. "Damned wind," he muttered. "Dust in my eye."

The men bearing the stretcher stopped, and Linna noticed for the first time that one of them was an Indian. The man was small and muscular and wore nothing but a cut-off pair of leather breeches and a scarlet vest. A stone amulet dangled from a thong around his neck, and his hair was worn in two long braids.

"This is Tumme Uoote—Wolf Belly," Ty explained. "He's a nephew to the great Chief Scarroyaddy. We would have had some help from Scarroyaddy if the general hadn't insulted him and his people at Wills Creek."

The Indian nodded, grunted, and repeated the name, "Scarroyaddy."

Ty answered Tumme Uoote in his own language, then looked directly at Donal. "He don't speak no

English, or claims he don't, but he's a damned good friend. He carried me ten miles on his back, then yanked a running Redcoat off a mule and tied me to it. I'd never have seen Fort Cumberland alive if it wasn't for Tumme Uoote. You'd be doing me a favor if ye'd give him some presents and see he gets a safe escort a day or so west of Annapolis. White folks is spooked. Had two men wanted to scalp him today jest because his skin is red.''

"I'll see to it," Donal promised.

Linna's hand tightened around Ty's until her knuckles turned white. "Rory?" she mouthed silently.

"Alive when I last set eyes on him, girl," Ty said hoarsely. "It were bad out there . . . bad." His dark brown eyes took on a faraway cast. "Worst I ever seen." He rubbed his head, as if to wipe away the memories. "Heat and smoke, men and horses screaming, Injuns howling, and lead flying like a hailstorm in hell. We was near the front of the column when we come through the ravine. Tumme Uoote and me followed some savvy Virginia Blues up the hill and found us some cover behind a windfall of logs. God, it was hot! Some of them Redcoats saw what we was doing and tried to get behind trees, but the general would have none of it. He was bound on going to glory and takin' us with him.''

"Rory. Where was Rory?" Linna demanded.

"He'd been on patrol, across the road. I caught sight of him maybe halfway through the skirmish. By that time the artillery had blasted us out of our hideyhole and I was hurting too bad to have all my senses about me. I saw the lieutenant colonel go down—that young Washington from Virginia. Bold as brass, that

one. If he was leading us, we'd not have come to such
sorrow. Anyway, the lieutenant colonel's horse took
a musket ball and went down. I seen Rory standin'
over Washington until he got his bearings. A black-
painted Huron charged out of the bushes screaming
like nothing you ever heard. He was too close to shoot,
but Rory made some Huron squaw a widow with the
butt of his musket.'' Ty sighed and lay back against
the litter. "I never seen him after that, but Tumme
Uoote swears he saw Rory during the rout. After the
general was killed, the regulars turned and ran. What
was left of the militia boys tried to hold them together.
They left their wounded, their guns and their supply
wagons. They dropped everything and ran like . . .''
Ty swore under his breath. "You never seen nothing
like it." He gripped Linna's hand with both of his.
"The militia was tryin' to get the wounded out. You
couldn't leave 'em—not to that pack of . . .'' His
words trailed off.

"Rory?'' Linna begged.

"Soon as this leg is strong enough to fit a peg, I'm
goin' after him,'' Ty promised. "If he's dead, I'll
bring his bones back to lie on Connemara . . . and if
he's alive, I'll find him.''

"But if your . . . your friend saw him alive, why
doesn't anyone know what happened to him?'' Linna
protested. "If he was alive after the battle . . .''

"Fifty mile,'' Ty said. "Fifty mile they run, through
river and woods and thicket. Fifty mile of wilderness.
Maybe . . .'' Ty's eyes dropped and the faintest tinge
of color stained his cheeks.

"What else, Ty?'' Linna demanded. "What else do
you know? Tell me.''

"Tumme Uoote talked to another Delaware scout that was with us. He said . . . he said he saw Rory fall, and two Injuns, one of Pontiac's Ottawa braves and a Shawnee war chief called Uingaokuee, was standin' over him."

Tumme Uoote spoke again in Algonquin. Ty nodded. "He claims they was fightin' over which one would have the right to lift Rory's scalp."

Chapter 19

Linna waited in the moonlit shadows of the formal garden for the first sounds of Sarah's approach. Linna had bid her friend to meet her here when all the house was asleep. She felt only a calm numbness; the overwhelming rush of emotion she had experienced at Ty's arrival was past. Around her, fireflies danced like fairies in a child's tale, and the air was thick with the sounds of frogs and insects and night birds. An owl hooted twice from the cedar tree, but Linna wasn't afraid. She merely sat on the thick grass with Brigand in her arms . . . and waited.

"Linna." Sarah's voice, so low that it might have been the whisper of the wind. "Linna . . . are you here?" A shadow detached itself from a clump of boxwood.

"Here," Linna called quietly. Brigand strolled across the brick walk, still warm from the August sun, and rubbed against Sarah's ankles.

The Indian girl lowered herself crossed-legged onto the grass, close enough for their hands to touch. "Why do you want me?"

"You heard?"

"I have spoken with Tumme Uoote."

"Rory is alive." Linna caught Sarah's small hand

and squeezed it. It was a hard hand, callused from work in the field and weaving house, but warm and caring.

"Did I not see it?"

Clouds scudded across the ivory moon, veiling the bottom half of Sarah's face in ebony shadow; only the slanting eyes gleamed above high, golden cheekbones. Linna hesitated, her breath caught in her throat, seeking the right words.

"You will go for him," Sarah said. It was not a question but an acceptance of fact. "You want me to take you."

"Don't tell me it's crazy, Sarah." The words tumbled out, half in English, half in Gaelic. "Don't tell me Rory is lost in a wilderness—that there is a war. Don't tell me he may already be dead. Only say that you'll take me there. Please!" Linna's voice broke. "I can wait no longer. If I wait . . . he'll die. I know he will."

"If I go with you, I break my bond," Sarah answered guardedly. "I could be hunted . . . branded like an ox."

"No, you won't. I'll leave a message saying that I forced you to go. I'll have Rory free you when we find him. I give you my word, Sarah."

"Ty has said that he will search for your husband when he is well enough to sit a horse. Would it not be wise to wait?"

Linna rose to her feet and hugged herself in silent, rocking anguish. "I need you," she murmured hoarsely. "But I will go—with or without you."

Sarah tilted her head as the shadows covered her face completely. "And your man-child? Will you take him on your back like an Indian papoose?"

The reply was wrenched from Linna's core. "No.

I will leave him here on Connemara. Judith loves Colin; she will care for him until I return.''

''And if you do not return?'' The words fell like leaves.

''Then she will raise Rory's son to be master here.''

For a long time there was silence between them. Crickets chirped and a waking mockingbird sounded a sleepy call; Brigand wrapped himself around Linna's ankle and purred. Linna waited, knowing instinctively that arguing would not influence Sarah's decision.

''We may well end up as slaves of the Mohawk—or meat in their cooking pots,'' Sarah warned at last. ''They are not called 'eaters of men' for nothing.''

''I must go,'' Linna repeated and seized a half truth. ''The wind sings to me, Sarah . . . the wind off the Chesapeake. It tells me I must find him.''

''Shaakhan, the wind. The old ones believe that each of the four winds has a powerful spirit. But not all the wind spirits are kind. Which one calls you? Is it a call to rescue the man you love . . . or your own death song?'' She made a clicking sound with her tongue and stood up. ''It does not matter, does it? A call of the spirits must be answered. We cannot escape the great plan.'' She reached for Linna's hand and clasped it between her own. ''Tumme Uoote knows of Uingaokuee, The Raven. He is a powerful Shawnee war chief.''

''Do you know him? Do you know where to find his tribe?'' Linna could not still her trembling. Would it be so easy?

Sarah laughed, a light tinkling murmur that Linna had never heard. ''I do not know him. I have been away from my people''—she paused—''more than seven years. But the Shawnee are not like the English—

you are like the sands of the ocean. There are only a few of us, fewer now than yesterday, and fewer tomorrow. When I lived among the people, Uingaokuee would have been a young warrior. I do not know him,'' she repeated, ''but I know his clan and his tribe. Tumme Uoote says that The Raven makes his home in the Valley of the Green Willow beside the Ohio.''

''What if it was Pontiac's Ottawa that captured Rory and not this . . . this Raven?''

Sarah shrugged. ''The Ottawa take no prisoners.''

''Rory is alive! I know it.''

''Then we will search out Uingaokuee. Have you thought how you will persuade a war chief to give up his prisoner if you find him? A warrior such as Mishkwe-Tusca would be a great prize.''

Linna took a deep breath. ''I will buy him back. I know what Ty took to trade with the Indians; I have collected needles and scissors and thread as well as beads and dye.''

''Hmmm.'' Sarah nodded. ''It could work. Forget the beads—take powder and shot.''

''To use against my own people? No.''

''Steel fish hooks, then, and pocket knives, leather awls and good wool blankets.'' The Indian girl sighed. ''We will need food and weapons, tough shoes and horses to carry us away from the English settlements. Once we are in the great forests, we must walk. Do you know how many days' walk it is from here to the Ohio country?''

Linna shook her head. ''I have seen maps, but they are so vague . . .''

''Maps.'' Sarah sniffed. ''English maps will be of no use to us. Tumme Uoote will lead us part of the way, and then we will follow the sun. When we reach the Ohio, I will know it. Then we will follow it until we come to one of the tribes.''

"Tumme Uoote? You already asked him to take us?'' Linna said in astonishment.

"Why not? He is my cousin.''

"Really? Your cousin?''

Sarah laughed again. "Not the son of my aunt. He is Delaware—Lenni-Lenape. I am Shawnee. The Shawnee are kin to the Delaware. Tumme Uoote is of the Turkey Clan; that makes us closer. He could not refuse me.''

"How did you know I would go?''

"I did not say anything about you, Linna. I asked Tumme Uoote to put my feet on the trail. I was going home before you ever asked me to take you.''

Another day and night passed as Linna secretly prepared for her journey. She knew it was vital that neither Judith nor Donal suspect what she was about to do. They would never agree to let her go, and might even physically prevent her from leaving.

Fortunately, Ty had been placed in one of the upstairs bedrooms in the manor house, and the household was in a flurry over his care. Daisy and the other servants ran up and down the stairs with buckets of water and hot soup under Judith's steely gaze. In the confusion, it was easy for Linna to collect the trade objects she wanted to take with her.

Donal had summoned a physician from Annapolis to examine Ty's leg. The primitive amputation, done under the rudest of conditions, had left the woodsman with fever and infection that threatened the rest of his leg and even his life. The doctor's dire warning had produced only amusement from Ty and his Indian companion.

"Ain't killed me yet, ain't goin' to,'' Ty said. "I'll

be walkin' on it in a couple of weeks, and sittin' a horse before that.''

Tumme Uoote said nothing. He remained seated on a blanket on the floor by Ty's bed and occasionally smoked his pipe. He did not even glance at Sarah or Linna when they came into the room.

Linna had spent hours sitting with Ty, but he refused to say anything more about the battle. ''Only worry ye,'' he said. ''I'll fetch Rory home before snowfall.''

There were many questions Linna wanted to ask, but she did not dare. To show undue curiosity about the wilderness or about the Indians might tip off the shrewd woodsman to her plan. She would have to put her trust in Sarah . . . and in God.

Leaving Colin behind was the hardest thing she had ever had to do. Even knowing how Judith doted on him, Linna still felt as though she was abandoning the baby. ''I love you,'' she'd whispered to him as she held him against her for the last time. ''I love you, but your Papa needs me more, right now. You be a good boy for your grandma.''

On the night she and Sarah planned to leave, Linna insisted that the baby's cradle be taken into the wet nurse's chamber. ''There's no sense in both of us waking for Colin's night feeding,'' she said to Judith. ''But I've warned the woman, I'll have the hide off her back if she dares to take him into her bed to sleep.''

Judith only gave Linna a look of disdain, and went about her duties.

Linna chose her departure well. Donal had gone back to Annapolis with the doctor to obtain medical supplies for Ty and to inquire further about Rory's whereabouts. He wasn't expected home for two days.

It was past the hour of ten when Linna carried her

bundles down the back stairs and out of the kitchen. Quietly, she tiptoed past a sleeping maidservant on a pallet by the cold hearth. Brigand tried to follow her out the door, but Linna closed it firmly. His loud meows of protest followed her down the walk and into the moonless night.

Sarah waited in the orchard with four horses and the Indian brave Tumme Uoote. He made no sound as the women strapped the bundles to the animals. Just before she mounted, Linna handed a new English musket and powderhorn to Tumme Uoote.

"He will not take it if it is a reward for bringing his friend home," Sarah warned. "You will insult his manhood."

"Tell him it is not payment. I give this as a token of my friendship," Linna whispered. "Tell him it is a custom in my own land of Ireland, across the sea."

"I accept, Matshipoii," the man replied in soft lisping English. "I am sorry that you were born white instead of human. You are *olamaalsu hokkuaa*, a brave woman, and I will take your gift—even if you are crazy."

"What did you call me?" Linna asked, too astonished at the Indian's command of English to be afraid of him.

He laughed quietly. "Matshipoii—Red Bird. Your hair is like his bold coat."

"Come," Sarah whispered. "There is no time for talking. We must put many miles behind us before the dawn."

Linna swung cautiously up into the man's saddle. Beneath her skirts, she had donned a pair of Donal's breeches that she hoped would keep her legs from rubbing raw against the leather. To ride so far into the wilderness on a sidesaddle would be impossible; she would have to learn to ride astride as they went. She had chosen her stoutest boots and a plain gray cloak of wool. Her hair was braided like Sarah's and she wore no jewelry but her wedding ring and, for luck, the ivory pendant that Rory had given her aboard ship.

The footfalls of the horses sounded loud in Linna's ears and they rode through the orchard in the darkness. The animal's hooves crunched fallen apples and the air was full of the smell of green fruit and honeysuckle. Linna looked back over her shoulder at the shadowy outline of the house. Her lips formed the silent words, "Take care, little one. I love you."

Then she straightened in the saddle, fixing her gaze on the horse's head. Rory was waiting somewhere ahead of her. She must put her son out of her mind and think only of her husband. If she thought only of Rory, she could almost banish the feel of Colin's warm, sweet-smelling body against hers. Almost . . .

Linna, Sarah, and Tumme Uoote followed the rough dirt road until violet hues of dawn began to pierce the canopy of branches overhead; then they entered the forest and continued on foot, leading the horses at a slow, steady pace. Linna was all too glad to dismount. She considered herself a fine horsewoman, but riding astride had chafed raw the insides of her legs in three places, and her neck and shoulder muscles ached from being in the saddle so long.

Tumme Uoote had not spoken since he had thanked her for the gift of the musket. He signaled to Sarah with hand and body motions, and she passed the commands on to Linna.

"I didn't know he was familiar with the Eastern

Shore,'' Linna whispered when they took an abrupt turn in the thick woods.

"He isn't. This tells him.'' Sarah indicated her stomach. "It is . . . I do not know your English word.''

"Instinct?''

Tumme Uoote turned and glared at them, and Linna fell silent. Their guide had made it quite clear that he didn't approve of talking on the march.

At noon, the three skirted a cornfield and crossed a river. There was no ford; Tumme Uoote and Sarah let their horses swim, and they held on to the animals' tails. They didn't stop to give Linna instructions or question whether she would follow. Tumme Uoote's horse was already finding solid ground on the far side of the river when Linna gathered her courage and drove her bay into the water.

The tide was running hard, and the bay was skittish. After what seemed an eternity, scared and dripping wet, Linna mounted and urged her horse into a canter to catch up with her Indian companions.

"You could have waited for me!" Linna said hotly as she reined in behind Sarah's animal. "What if I'd drowned?''

Sarah shrugged, then turned her head and flashed a brilliant smile. "Tumme Uoote thinks you will go back.''

"And you? What do you think?''

"I have bet Tumme Uoote my silver earrings against his copper bracelet that you won't.'' She laughed. "It was only a *tongeetu siipu*, a little creek. You cannot cross the Susquehanna if you are unable to swim such a baby river.''

Tumme Uoote gave no hint that he had heard them speaking or that he was in the company of two women.

He rode in an easy slouch, more part of the animal than a rider.

Linna glanced apprehensively at the Delaware brave. "How far will he travel with us?" Linna asked. A blister was forming on her left heel, the insides of her legs felt as if they had been skinned, and she was so tired she was seeing spots before her eyes—none of which she had the slightest intention of admitting.

Sarah shrugged again. "Until he decides to go."

They rode on in silence until the hottest part of the afternoon. Linna had drunk from the river before crossing, but she'd become thirsty again almost immediately. Strapped to her saddle was a goatskin water bag. It sloshed against her knee with every step the horse took, but no one else had taken a drink from his water bag. If they did not drink, Linna wouldn't, either. It was a matter of pride.

Then, without warning, Tumme Uoote raised a bronzed hand, reined in, and slipped from his horse's back. Without speaking to Sarah or Linna, he proceeded to hobble his sorrel, took a long drink from his water bag, and climbed a tree.

Linna stared as the Indian made his way hand over hand up the big oak tree until he was hidden by the branches. When she saw Sarah dismount, Linna did, too.

"We will rest now," Sarah said softly. "Tumme Uoote will sleep up there." She pointed to the treetop. "That way, he will hear someone coming from a long way off."

"He'll sleep in a tree?" Linna echoed dumbly. "Won't he fall out?"

Sarah laughed. "He is a Delaware of the Wild Turkey Clan. Where does the turkey sleep? Or a Squirrel?"

She shook her head at Linna's ignorance. "Does a turkey fall out of a tree?" Sarah hobbled her horse and the other animals. "We will leave them saddled. The rawhide can be pulled from their front legs quickly."

"Do you think Judith will try to stop us?"

Sarah nodded. "She will not wait for your brother's return. She will send riders, but I do not think they will find us."

Linna sighed as she spread a blanket on the ground and eased her aching body into a sitting position. The water in her bag was warm and the cornbread dry and crumbly. She ate and drank in a stupor, then lay down and fell into a deep sleep.

Sarah shook her.

"Uumph . . ."

Sarah placed two fingers on Linna's lips. "It's time," she said.

Wearily, Linna opened her eyes. It felt as though each eyelid contained a pound of grit. Stretching, she sat up and looked around.

Dusk had fallen over the forest. Linna blinked at the shadowy forms of the horses against the tree trunks. Had she slept for hours? It seemed only minutes, yet the oppressive heat of the afternoon had given way to a pleasant coolness. If she had slept, why didn't she feel refreshed? Her bones felt as if they were made of broken glass; they seemed to cut into her flesh as she tried to move. Dusk had also brought mosquitoes; Linna discovered that her arms and face bore itching welts.

Tumme Uoote said something to Sarah in Algonquin. Sarah nodded her agreement and replied in the same tongue.

"He says I should have given you a remedy for insects. They did not bother us the first night because of the direction of the wind." Sarah dug in her saddlebag and came up with a birchbark container and offered it to Linna. "Rub a little of this ointment on your face and arms. I have nothing for the bites, but watch for honeysuckle vines or . . ." She exhaled in impatience as her fingers drew the outlines of the weed in the air. "It grows in fields—plantain! Either will do. You chew the plant, then rub it against the bites. It will stop the itching."

Tumme Uoote was already removing the hobbles from his horse.

"If you must be alone . . ." Sarah suggested.

Taking the hint, Linna hurried into the trees, relieved herself, and returned to gulp down a long swallow of water before swinging up into the saddle. Her legs were so sore that just sitting on the saddle brought tears to her eyes, but she didn't complain. The long journey was only beginning, and though her muscles were stiff, they would toughen.

As Tumme Uoote led the small procession through the forest into the gathering darkness, Linna allowed herself to picture the face of her tiny son. Was Colin well? Did he miss her? If she didn't return, would he believe she had abandoned him?

"Judith will take care of him as though he were her own," Sarah called back, seeming to read Linna's mind.

"How did you know what I was—"

"Once I had a son," Sarah offered. Her face was lost in the shadows, but her voice revealed an irrevocable loss.

"A baby? You had a baby? I didn't know," Linna said. "Did he die?"

"No."

"Where is he?"

"With the Iroquois."

"But why—"

"Silence!" Tumme Uoote ordered. "You chatter like *hahees* in a cornfield!"

Sarah emitted a bubble of laughter and was still.

"Hahees?" Linna asked.

"Hahees—crows," Sarah said.

Tumme Uoote grunted.

Sarah giggled again and they rode on in silence.

On the third day it rained. The downpour began with an ear-shattering clap of thunder in the west and continued with occasional flashes of lightning and intermittent rumbling that spooked the horses and made even Tumme Uoote uneasy. The great trees swayed and groaned in the wind, and the rain muffled all sounds but the storm around them.

Linna shivered in her woolen cloak, even though the rain was warm. She was wet through and through; her braids hung against her shoulders like sodden ropes. Even her boots were soaked through to her stockings. She looked back with sympathy at the packhorse plodding behind her, head down. "I know just how you feel," she murmured.

The rain was depressing. Linna was cold and damp, and she couldn't remember when she had last slept. They had eaten no hot food since they had left Connemara. She had no idea where she was, and she hurt all over. Worse, she was afraid—afraid for herself, afraid of the wilderness they were riding into, and afraid that Rory was already dead and she was on a fool's errand.

Linna had put all her trust in Sarah and Tumme

Uoote. If they betrayed her to the Indians, or just abandoned her in the forest, she would be as helpless as a child. Nothing in her life had prepared her for the emptiness of this magnificent wilderness.

All her life, Linna had been surrounded by people. In Ireland, there had been stone walls and roads, towns and villages. The Tidewater seemed much larger, but on the plantation there were boundaries of plowed fields, farm lanes, and fences. The lapping waters of the bay had framed Rory's plantation of Connemara as the sea had defined the shoreline of western Ireland.

Here there were no civilized people—they had not laid eyes on a living soul since they'd begun their journey—and there were no boundaries. The unbroken forest seemed to stretch forever, full of wild animals and savage Indian tribes—some of whom were reported to be eaters of human flesh.

Thoughts of what lay ahead, of empty forest and raging rivers, terrified Linna and memories of what she had left behind tore at her heart. Still, she did not consider turning back. If there was the slightest chance that Rory lived, she must take it. She must subdue her cowardly fears and her ignorance, and push on.

Linna clamped her eyes shut against a surge of heavy rain, letting the horse follow the others. In the darkness, the image of Rory as she had first seen him so long ago in Ireland formed behind her closed eyelids. Rory's face had been as smooth and unlined as an angel, and his crow-black hair had felt like silk to her chapped, raw fingers. She had lost her heart to him in that moment, and nothing, not even death, would break that bond.

"Rory, my rapparee . . ." she whispered into the beating rain. I loved you then . . . and I love you now. No matter what's happened between us. "I'd follow you anywhere, Rory Desmond," Linna murmured, "even to the gates of hell."

Chapter 20

Linna, Tumme Uoote, and Sarah crossed the Sus-quehanna River late on a Sunday afternoon. As they neared the far bank of the rocky, fast-rushing body of water, the carcass of a wild turkey tumbled past them in the shallows. Linna was so intent on getting her footing on the slippery bottom that she nearly missed seeing the misshapen bundle of feathers. Sarah pointed to the dead bird as it floated by and placed her fingers over her lips in an unmistakable warning to be silent.

Tumme Uoote led the women and horses a few hundred feet from the river and signaled a halt in a grove of trees. Unsmiling, he hobbled the horses and began the familiar chores of setting up the rude camp.

Linna glanced at Sarah for some explanation. Tumme Uoote's face was pale beneath the bronzed skin, and his eyes revealed an apprehension Linna had not seen there before. Sarah frowned and shook her head.

Tumme Uoote gathered twigs and started a tiny fire. "Stay here," he said. Taking his musket, he entered the thickest part of the forest.

"What's wrong?" Linna asked when the Delaware

was gone. "Are we in danger?"

Sarah shrugged.

"Does it have something to do with that dead . . . whatever . . . in the river?" Linna persisted. She pulled off her wet dress and donned a dry one from her pack. Spreading the damp garment on a rock to dry, she began to rub her bare arms with the insect repellent Sarah had given her. Linna moved out of the shade of the trees and into the warm sunshine. August or not, the Susquehanna had been icy cold, and she was glad for the chance to change her garments and get warm.

Sarah unsaddled the packhorse without answering.

"I have the right to know." Linna folded her arms over her chest and planted herself in front of Sarah.

The Shawnee woman looked uncertain.

"Sarah, please . . ."

"Tumme Uoote is afraid."

"Afraid of what?"

"The dead turkey in the water." Sarah piled the pack saddle with the others. Her face was as smooth as a blank page with no hint of what she might be thinking.

"By all the saints! Must I drag it from ye like a rotten tooth? Tumme Uoote is a hero—a brave warrior. Why would he be afraid of a dead bird?"

"The turkey is his totem. It is a bad sign for him."

"You can't believe that? Turkeys all die sooner or later." Linna shook her head in amazement. "You can't tell me he's never eaten one."

"Tumme Uoote would rather starve than eat his totem." Sarah chewed at her bottom lip. "Besides, the turkey was in the water. Wild turkeys live in the forest . . . on land. The turkey was a messenger."

Linna rolled her eyes. "Yes, and I'm a leprechaun."

Sarah squatted beside the fire and began to feed twigs into the flames. "Say nothing to Tumme Uoote. To talk of the turkey will only make it worse."

A single shot reverberated through the trees, and Linna flinched. Sarah continued to add sticks to the fire. Within minutes, the Delaware brave returned carrying a fat young doe. He dropped it by the fire and grinned at the women.

"The gun is true," Tumme Uoote said. He pointed to the hole in the deer's head. "One shot," he bragged.

The animal had already been gutted and washed. Linna watched as Tumme Uoote began to skin the deer.

"It is this year's fawn," Sarah explained. "Too young to mate. A doe is better eating than a buck, but a grown doe may be carrying a little one."

"Such a beautiful thing to die," Linna said sorrowfully.

"When I creep through the woods," Tumme Uoote said, motioning in the air with his hands, "I see deer." He held up four fingers. "All female—no bucks." He rolled the carcass over to remove the hide from the other side. "Old doe sees me. Ears go up; tail go up." Tumme Uoote's ebony eyes sparkled as he related the story of the hunt. "The young deer see the old one signal—they run. This one"—he nudged the dead animal with the toe of his moccasin—"does not run. She stops to look." He shrugged. "She is foolish, and we will eat her flesh."

"Everything that lives must die," Sarah said. "Trees, grass, people. Some die sooner."

Tumme Uoote grunted and began to cut the tenderloin from the doe. Sarah took the liver back to the river and washed it again, then sliced it into thin strips. She skewered the strips on green branches and handed them to Linna to broil over the fire.

Linna's sympathy for the doe faded as the meat began to cook. The smell of the venison was tantalizing, and she'd had no meat since they'd left the plantation.

"We will cook and eat as much as we can," Sarah explained patiently as Tumme Uoote wrapped the bones, head, and feet in the skin. "In this heat, the meat will spoil quickly unless it is dried. But this camp is not safe. We cannot remain here long enough to smoke all of the venison."

Tumme Uoote took the bundle back to the river and threw it in, taking care to wash thoroughly before he returned to the camp. The choice pieces of venison were all rinsed free of blood and cut into small pieces for cooking.

"To waste any meat is a sin," Sarah murmured. "But because we must travel quickly, it is not so great a sin. Tumme Uoote has sacrificed to the spirit of the deer and has given the hide to the river." Sarah's high cheekbones tinted rose against her flawless copper-colored skin. "The spirits of the forest and river are practical. They know that even a good man is sometimes forced to break the laws."

"And a good woman?" Linna asked softly. "What happens when a woman is forced to sin?"

"If her heart is true, she is forgiven," Sarah assured her.

"Matshipoii!" Tumme Uoote admonished. "Turn the meat before it burns. I did not hunt this deer to feed it to the ants."

Linna snatched the liver from the flames. Sarah laughed and said something to Tumme Uoote in Algonquin. In a few minutes they were all laughing and chewing the good, hot venison.

The sun sank in the west, and darkness fell over the campsite. The three sat around the fire for a long time, telling stories and staring into the flames. Tumme Uoote sang a hunting song, and Sarah countered with a Dutch hymn. After much coaxing, Linna shared an old rhyming song in Gaelic from her childhood. Then Tumme Uoote told a Delaware story about a turtle that carried his people from the east across the great ocean.

It was late when Tumme Uoote kicked dirt over the fire and rolled up in his blanket. Sarah had prepared a bed of leaves, carefully spreading blankets over it. She motioned Linna to a place beside her. Sarah fell asleep almost before her head touched the blanket, but Linna lay awake long into the night, staring into the night sky.

In the morning when the women awoke, Tumme Uoote, his horse, his gun, and his blanket were gone.

"He will not be back," Sarah warned Linna. "If we go on—we go alone."

Linna was stunned. Regardless of what Sarah had said before they left Connemara, Linna had come to rely on the Delaware brave. Without Tumme Uoote's quiet strength, the journey ahead seemed much more ominous.

"It doesn't matter," Linna lied. "We've come this far without any trouble." She gazed directly into Sarah's troubled face. "If you leave me, I'll keep going by myself. I can't go back to the Tidewater without knowing if Rory's dead or alive."

"He's dead, Linna. You might as well face it."

Linna whirled toward the sound of the familiar voice. "Donal!"

Her brother-in-law stepped out of the trees and strode toward them, a musket cradled in his arms.

"How did you find us?" Linna demanded. She took a step backward, bumping into the packhorse. The animal snorted and nipped at her. "Stop that!" she said sharply to the horse. Attempting to regain her composure, Linna stared directly at Donal. "You weren't due back from Annapolis until—"

"What in God's name did you think you were doing?" Donal roared. "Two women going into the wilderness alone?" He glared at Sarah. "I thought you had more sense. You know what it's like out there." He motioned north. "You could have been killed . . . or gotten lost and starved to death."

"Don't blame Sarah! It was my decision."

"I don't know how you got this far without coming to harm." Donal scrutinized the campsite and the forest around the clearing, then leaned his musket against a sapling. "Ty says there are white men in the woods as bad as the Indians."

"We had three days start on you. How did you catch us?" Linna asked.

"Ty said you'd cross the Susquehanna near here. I took a sloop up the bay, then rode north. I near killed my horse to do it." He swore softly. "Have you lost your mind, Linna? You've a baby at home. What did you think to do out here besides get yourself killed too?"

"You came alone?" Sarah asked in disbelief.

"Mother organized a search party the day you left. I have two men with me now; one's riding the far side of the Susquehanna, the other's a few miles south on this side." Donal scowled. "I guess I got lucky."

Linna turned her back on him and picked up a saddle blanket. Throwing it over the nearest horse, she arranged the blanket carefully. "Now that you're here, you'll have to come with us," she said.

Donal grabbed her arm and turned her to face him. "We're going home to Connemara," he insisted. "All of us. You've got to accept Rory's death and start thinking rationally."

Linna stiffened. "Rory's not dead. I'd know it if he were dead." She tried to pull free from Donal's grasp, but he held her fast. "Donal . . ."

Grief flooded the dark Desmond eyes, so like her husband's and yet so different. "Linna . . ." The words were dragged from deep within, rough and gravelly. "He's dead. Accept it."

"No. Unless I—"

Donal lowered his head and kissed her full on the mouth, a kiss of desperate yearning. His hands fell away from her and he stepped back and swallowed hard. "I'm sorry. I shouldn't have done that."

Linna trembled, raising her fingertips to brush against her bruised lips. She caught his arm when he would have turned away, forcing his shamed gaze to meet hers. "I love you, Donal," Linna said softly. Joy flared in his eyes to flicker and dim as she finished. "But as a brother. You are as dear to me as my own son." She squeezed his arm. "And I will cherish your love for me always."

"A sister's love," he rasped.

"Your sister and your friend."

He turned his back to them, unwilling to expose his anguish. Sarah moved into the trees, leaving Linna and Donal alone in the bright morning sunlight.

"Don't," Linna pleaded. "I could not bear it if you

turned against me. I need you, Donal.''

He straightened and looked back. ''But not as a woman needs a man.''

''Nil neart air,'' she replied, lapsing into Gaelic.

''And if you find his body, what then?'' The cruel words hung between them.

''Then I will keep on loving him, and he will be my husband all the same.'' A single tear trickled down her cheek. ''Donal . . . come with us. Help us find him.''

''You're mad! There's a hell out there you know nothing of. And if he were alive, how could you find him? These damned woods stretch halfway across the world. There are a dozen Indian tribes who would burn you alive—when they were finished with you.''

''Sarah says rape is a European custom. The Indians don't assault women; they think it's bad medicine.''

He scoffed. ''And they don't scalp and murder either, I suppose. They didn't butcher nine hundred men under Braddock? Or torch the frontier and massacre men, women, and children, from New York to Virginia?'' He picked up his musket again. ''Get your things together. We're going home.''

''If Ty could walk, would he be out searching for Rory?'' Linna took a saddle from the pile and threw it over the horse, slowly drawing the cinch strap through the iron ring and knotting the leather. She twisted to glance back at Donal. ''Sarah is Shawnee; she speaks the language of most of the tribes. Not all of the Indians are at war with us. We didn't just run off without a sensible plan.'' She tested the tightness of the cinch. ''Rory lived with the Shawnee. If this Raven that Ty spoke of captured Rory, he may well be alive.'' She wiped her hands on her skirts. ''We brought trade goods to exchange for Rory. Sarah says it's common practice.''

"Ty said Rory was down, maybe dead. There were two Indians over him. What if you're guessing wrong? What if they took his scalp and left his body for the wolves?''

Sarah moved across the clearing behind Donal as silently as a shadow. She raised her fingers to her lips, warning Linna to make no sign that she saw her.

Linna averted her eyes. "And if I'm right, if Rory's alive, would you let him die if you could save him?''

"Damn it, Linna," Donal said hoarsely, "you know I'd move heaven and earth to have him back, but—"

"No buts." Sarah poked Donal in the spine with the barrel of her musket. "Drop your musket," she ordered softly.

"Do as she says, Donal."

Donal let the gun slide to the ground.

"Good," Sarah said. "Now back away from it. Over there." She motioned with the musket.

Slowly, Donal obeyed. "You'll get her killed, Sarah.''

"Maybe so, maybe not." Sarah held the musket level, her finger on the trigger. "But you will not stop us.''

"Linna, for God's sake!''

Sarah's fierce expression softened. "I am a free woman," she said. "According to Shawnee law, Linna is a free woman. We go where we please. You will not stop us.''

Linna began to saddle another horse. "You can come with us, Donal, but you can't keep us from going.''

"I'll come after you.''

Linna whirled on him in anger. "Damn you to hell,

Donal Desmond! 'Tis you who are mad! I'm going after my husband, and nothing, no one, will stop me. You can come or stay, but if you follow me, Sarah may take you for the enemy and put a musket ball between your eyes. Make up your mind. You've got about as long as it takes for me to tie these packs on the horse.''

"I'll go with you.''

"It's a trick,'' Sarah warned.

"No.'' Donal sighed. "I still think you're crazy, but I can't let you go alone. I'll come.''

Linna glanced at Sarah questioningly.

"Strap his musket to my horse,'' Sarah said. "Then get some thongs and tie his hands behind his back.''

With an oath Donal lunged forward, then stopped in his tracks as Sarah cocked the hammer of the musket. "Whoa,'' he protested, holding up a hand. "If you think I'm going to let you—''

"She's right,'' Linna agreed. "I don't trust you either. If you're coming with us, you can consider yourself a prisoner . . . at least until we're far enough away for you to be as lost as I am.''

Reluctantly, Donal extended his hands. "At least tie them in the front. I can't very well ride through the forest with my hands behind me. My horse is back by the river.''

"He's telling the truth, I saw the animal,'' Sarah said.

"You won't be sorry,'' Linna promised. "We'll find Rory alive—I know we will.''

Donal nodded. "I hope to hell you're right, Linna. I hope to hell you're right.''

For two days they rode as fast as the horses could

carry them through the trackless forest. Sarah took her bearings from the sun and from the moss that grew on the north side of the ancient trees. When the sun was shadowed by clouds or darkened by night and they found no moss, she led them by instinct alone.

The thick woods that had awed Linna on the Tidewater were dwarfed by these primeval forests. Oak and hickory towered above the narrow game trails; sweeping hemlock and blossoming laurel brushed the pungent earth and touched Linna's Irish soul with their beauty. The horses' hooves sunk into the soft topsoil of the forest, dislodging the fallen leaves and mold, filling the air with the rich, heavy scent.

They kept to the trees, avoiding the occasional open valley or cleared patch around a settler's cabin. Once, they heard the sound of an ax ringing in the cool morning air, but it was far away and soon faded. One night, Sarah left Linna and Donal with the horses for an hour and came back with an armful of sweet corn. They ate it raw, savoring the sweet juice, and washed the remainder of the dried venison down with spring water.

When they crossed the Juniata, Sarah untied Donal's hands. He remained sullen for another day, but gradually his spirits lifted and he began to laugh and talk with the two women.

"For a land filled with savages, we have seen precious few," Donal quipped as they made camp one evening. The mosquitoes had been particularly bad, worrying the horses into a sweat with their constant whining and biting. He swatted a blood-filled mosquito on his arm. "If I'm murdered out here, it will probably be by the insects."

Sarah motioned for silence and moved close to

whisper to Linna and Donal. Sarah's dark slanted eyes were dilated with fear. "We have been followed for the last two hours. I hear birds that are not birds. Please." She grasped Linna's arm. "You must trust me."

Linna nodded. "What do we do?"

Donal pulled his musket from the saddle holster. "Indians or white men?"

"No!" Sarah laid her hand on the musket barrel. "No guns. Huron are there." She pointed. "And there." Sarah gazed beseechingly at Linna. "If we try and fight them, we will die."

Donal looked unconvinced. "What's your plan?"

"I think we are safe. It is your scalp, Donal, they will take."

"He can hide," Linna suggested. "Climb a tree . . ."

"No. They have tracked us. They know how many we are." Sarah slid her hand down the stock of the gun to touch Donal's hand. "If they believe you to be crazy—touched by God—they may not harm you. The Huron may pass us by without bothering us. Can you pretend to be mad?"

"You're right," Linna cried. "I heard Rory say the same thing once. He told me about an old French priest who walked through an Indian camp with a pot on his head. Rory said the tribe was angry with the French because a trader had brought measles. They murdered the French trader, but they didn't harm the old priest."

"You want me to pretend to be crazy?" Donal swung down from the horse and roughly shouldered Sarah away. "How can you expect—"

"We don't have time to argue with you!" Linna said. Digging in her saddlebag, she came up with a

crumpled linen shift. She ripped it long ways and
handed it to Donal. "Here, wrap this around your
head." The shift was bloodstained. Linna blushed as
she realized what Donal might be thinking. "It's not
from my courses," she mumbled, lapsing into Gaelic.
"The saddle leather rubbed my legs raw the first few
days. If the Indians see the bloodstains, they'll think
you have a head wound. It will give you a reason to
be crazy."

Sarah nodded, not understanding the language, but
comprehending Linna's meaning. Quickly, she
scooped up a handful of dirt and leaves and rubbed it
across Donal's face. Before he could protest, she tore
the front of his shirt and smeared dirt on his chest.
"A madman is not so handsome," she said.

"I must be a madman to agree to this."

Sarah looked pointedly at the musket.

"No," Donal said.

Linna pulled the musket from his hands. "Who
would give a madman a gun?" She pointed to a tree.
Her hand was shaking. "Sit over there and try to look
stupid. Sing. Eat dirt . . . I don't know. You put on
a good enough act when you want a new woman."

Donal looked pained. Mustering what dignity remained to him under the stained turban, he plopped
down under the aspen. "Banshee," he muttered.

Linna glanced at Sarah for instruction, and the Indian
girl motioned toward the horses.

"Set up camp as we always do. They must not know
we have seen them."

Waves of fear washed over Linna as she unsaddled
the horses and hobbled them. The hair rose on the
back of her neck and her skin prickled as she imagined

a painted warrior leaping out from behind every bush and tree. "What do I do with Donal's musket?" she asked in a hushed voice.

Sarah answered her in a normal tone. "The bay seems to be favoring his left hind leg." Then she whispered, "Wrap the gun and powderhorn in a blanket." When Linna had done as she asked, she moved to the edge of the camp and pushed aside the lacy boughs of a hemlock. Swiftly, she buried the gun in the leaves and returned to her task of starting a fire.

Water trickled down the hill from a spring just above them. When there was no creek, it was Linna's chore to carry water in a folding leather bag for the animals. She looked at Donal; his eyes were shut and he was mumbling to himself. I'm a coward, Linna thought. I can't do this. But she forced herself to untie the water bag from the packsaddle and walk toward the spring.

Leaves rustled and Linna froze, a cry of alarm caught in her throat. A squirrel scampered across the ground just ahead of her, his beady black eyes snapping with indignation at her invasion of his forest glen. She smiled at her own foolishness. She hadn't seen any Indians. Maybe Sarah was wrong. Maybe the Indians had gone away.

Linna reached the spring and knelt beside it, scooping the leaves and sticks out of the natural basin of rock. She bent and drank from the steady stream of water; it was cold and sweet, better than any wine she had ever tasted. She splashed a little over her face, and then drank again. A twig snapped behind her and she whirled about, still on her knees. Something struck her from the back, and she fell facedown in the leaves.

Inches from her face Linna saw a man's bare legs.

Before she could raise her head to look up, she was shoved back down. Her nose brushed the toe of a quill-worked moccasin.

A man's harsh voice spoke, but Linna didn't understand the words. She lay still, hardly daring to breathe. She heard other men's voices down the hill in the camp, and then Sarah's angry reply.

The man standing over Linna barked an order in heavily accented French. "Get up." He grabbed her arm and yanked her to her feet. "No speak! Make scream—you die!"

Linna swallowed hard and raised her head to stare into the black and yellow striped face of a Huron warrior. One sinewy hand was raised high. Clutched in that hand was an English trade hatchet . . . and the steel blade was stained with fresh blood.

Chapter 21

Cold numbness seeped up through Linna's knees, and she clenched her fists at her sides to keep from screaming. The sickening smell of dried blood filled her nostrils; her stomach churned. Still the painted savage stared into her face with relentless, cold black eyes.

Linna had seen eyes like those before—not in any human, but in the sharks that had circled the ship on her voyage to America. The realization that this man could dash out her brains with as little feeling as a shark brought Linna to the brink of sanity.

Anger gave her courage. If she was to die, she would not die cringing and begging for mercy.

Unconsciously, Linna's spine stiffened and her dark eyes narrowed. *"Mishkwe-tusca,"* she accused him. "Mighty warrior. *Tout est perdu hors l'honneur!"*

Doubt clouded the Huron's malignant glare, then he threw back his head and whooped with glee. A second warrior standing behind Linna joined in the laughter. Still chuckling, the yellow and black painted brave tucked the hatchet into his belt, gave Linna a shake, and pushed her downhill toward the camp. The second man, really little more than a boy, said something to his companion in the Indian tongue and both men roared with amusement again.

Linna stumbled down the incline with as much dignity as possible. She counted seven Huron below—tearing apart the contents of the saddlebags and digging through her trade goods. Two warriors held Donal suspended between them; he was clapping his hands and singing a child's nursery rhyme in Gaelic. Sarah stood in the middle of the camp, arguing loudly with a thin, dark-skinned Indian in a red military jacket.

Ignoring the hostile stares, Linna hurried to Sarah's side. Sarah put an arm protectively around her shoulder.

"Say nothing," Sarah warned Linna. "They speak French and perhaps a little English. The Huron tongue is much like the Shawnee. I have told them that Donal is my husband."

The warrior in the jacket reached out to touch one of Linna's braids. She tried not to tremble. He thrust his face close to hers. "Do you have a husband?" he demanded in crude French.

"Oui."

The Indian tugged at her braid playfully. *"Rouge. Jolie laide."*

Linna slapped his hand away and he laughed.

"What did he say?" Sarah asked.

"He called me good-looking ugly woman." Linna eyed the brave warily. "He wanted to know if I was married."

"I told him that we were searching for your husband—that he was captured during Braddock's rout," Sarah explained in English. "Try not to make them angry. This is a war party. Their belts are heavy with English scalps."

Red Jacket barked an order to the two men holding

Donal. They released him, and Donal sat down on the ground cross-legged and began to draw circles in the dirt. He continued to hum loudly.

"Silence!" Red Jacket ordered in French.

Donal looked up at the Indian, blinked twice, and grinned broadly. "If I had my musket, I'd blow you away—you great lump of donkey dung," he said in the Irish tongue.

Linna averted her eyes. They all seemed players in some monstrous nightmare.

Sarah dropped to her knees beside Donal and cradled his head against her. "Be good," she hissed in English.

He hugged her tightly. "Shall I kiss you, wife?"

"Donal—please." Sarah patted his shoulder and stood up, placing herself between the white man and the leader of the war party. "Leave us in peace," she begged the Huron war chief. "There is no bad blood between the Shawnee and the Huron. This man, my husband, is not English—he comes from another land. He has been touched by the spirits. He can do you no harm."

"And the flame-haired woman?" Red Jacket let his glance stray to Linna.

Sarah shrugged. "You travel too fast for a prisoner. Take our guns and horses. I give them to you freely as a gift. Take all that we have, but leave us in peace."

He nodded. *"Kihiila."* He motioned to a brave holding the packhorse and gave an order. The man untied a turkey from his belt and threw it on the ground. Red Jacket looked back at Sarah. "Do not say that the Huron accept gifts without giving in return."

Quickly, the warriors gathered up the packs and saddled the horses. They filed from the camp as silently as they had come. Red Jacket mounted the bay and balanced Sarah's musket across his lap. "I think I will regret not taking this ugly woman," he said.

Sarah shook her head. "She would only fill your lodge with the buzzing of a thousand angry wasps. Her temper is as hot as her hair."

"It may be as you say," the war chief agreed. He raised a hand in salute. "Tell your husband to clean the musket beneath the leaves well—otherwise it may blow up in his face and cause him further injury." Chuckling, he rode away into the trees.

Linna stared after the Huron, straining to hear until all sounds of their passing had faded and the birds began to sing again. Then, slowly, she slid to the ground and buried her face in her hands. "Thieves," she murmured raggedly. "Murdering thieves."

Donal stood up and dusted off his breeches, exhaling loudly. "Whew! You're some woman, Sarah."

"And you," the Indian girl accused, "play your crazy part too well." She went to the hemlock and knelt to retrieve the buried musket.

"Well enough to fool those bloodthirsty savages," Donal replied as he went to Linna and put his arm around her shoulder. "It's all right, they're gone now. Don't cry."

Linna pushed his hand away. "I'm not crying." She got to her feet, walked over, and picked up the turkey. "Damn them—why did they have to take my trade goods? How can I get Rory back from the Shawnee if I have nothing to give them in exchange?"

"The Huron didn't steal from us," Sarah explained. "I gave them everything."

Donal glared at her. "You what?"

Sarah shrugged. "They wanted to take Linna." She handed the musket and powderhorn to him. "The

Huron leader said to clean the gun well.''

Donal ran his hand along the barrel. ''They saw you hide it under the leaves and they didn't take it? Why?''

Linna began to pluck the feathers from the wild turkey. ''The Huron didn't believe Donal was crazy, either, did they?'' Her voice was strained. She would not allow herself to think what might have happened. The loss of the trade goods stunned her; she regretted losing the needles and scissors and the other things even more than the horses and their supplies.

Ignoring Linna's question, Sarah began to gather twigs for a fire. With the Huron war party so close, no one else would move in the forest tonight. ''We will eat and sleep,'' she said softly. ''Morning will be time enough to continue our journey.''

''With only one musket between us?'' Donal demanded. ''Without horses or blankets—without even salt?''

''We've come too far to go back,'' Linna said stubbornly. ''Sarah said we'd have to walk part of the way.''

From a doeskin bag at her waist, Sarah took flint and steel and began to strike a spark. ''The horses would be a danger to us. They make too much noise.'' A tiny column of smoke rose from the tinder; Sarah leaned over and blew gently on it, feeding the resulting flame with a bit of dry bark. She glanced sideways under her lashes at Donal. ''We will need green branches to cook the turkey.''

''Is that an order, captain?''

Sarah flashed him a smile. ''Among the Shawnee, it is not considered a shame for a warrior to aid a woman. I will find the branches if you do not wish to." She offered him her hand and he helped her to her feet. "If you will tend the fire, I will find something to eat with the turkey. I saw blueberries growing a short ways back along the trail."

The pile of feathers grew around Linna as she continued to pull them from the wild turkey. "It's a fat bird," she murmured. Linna wondered if she were losing her mind. Less than an hour ago, a Huron warrior had threatened to tomahawk her. The three of them were alone in the wilderness, lost and helpless. She had abandoned her baby to hunt for a man everyone said was dead . . . and all she could think about was how good roast turkey would taste. Methodically, she plucked the feathers one by one, and a child's game rose tantalizingly in the back of her mind. Rory loves me . . . he loves me not. He loves me . . . he loves me not. He's alive . . . he's dead. He's alive . . . he's dead.

"Linna." Sarah repeated her name.

With a shudder, Linna broke from her trance and stared into her friend's concerned face.

"Linna, are you all right?"

Wordlessly, Linna held out the turkey. It was plucked bare and the skin was torn off in patches. "I . . . I . . ." She blinked back tears. "I didn't . . ."

"Shhh," Sarah soothed. "Let me take the bird and put it over the fire. Come and sit down." She took Linna's arm gently. "See, Donal and I have picked his hat full of blueberries for our supper."

Linna blinked. She had not seen them leave the camp, had not been aware of the passage of time. Suddenly weary, she went to the fire and sat down, leaning back against a tree. "I wish Tumme Uoote were here," she said.

"If he were with us, the Huron would have killed

him,'' Sarah replied softly. "There is bad blood between the Huron and the Delaware.''

"Then . . .'' Linna's eyes looked baffled. "The turkey we saw in the river really was . . .''

Sarah shrugged. "Who can say? But we are Christians, not superstitious pagans. We will enjoy every bite of this fat turkey.''

"And the blueberries,'' Donal reminded her. "I risked my life to get these berries. We saw a bear back there. I'd have taken a shot at it, but Pocahontas here wouldn't let me. She shouted and waved her arms to chase it off.''

"If you had killed the bear,'' Sarah chided, "who would have had to skin it? Besides, we have food. We do not need a bear.''

"I'll bet I could have killed it with a single shot. I had it dead in my sights.''

"Sit, mighty hunter of bears,'' Sarah teased, "and rest your legs while we prepare the feast. You will have need of your strength tomorrow.''

"And the day after that?'' he quipped.

"Every day,'' Linna whispered. "Every day until we find Rory and take him home.''

Ohio River Country
September 1755

Linna lay on her stomach and stared at the mist rising off the river. It was the time between dawn and day, and the forest around her was hushed. Above the rushing water, she heard the familiar cry of an osprey, but his form was lost in the thick haze. Here and there, a fish jumped, the splash adding to the magical song of the tumbling water.

She had crept down the bank to wash her face and

hands, and to drink. Now she was content to stretch out on the still warm earth and wait for the others to rise.

The arduous days and nights of the journey had forged a bond between Linna and Sarah, deepening the friendship to something Linna could only describe as a sisterly love. It was Sarah who had fed them from the forest and kept them from danger as they traveled through country where no man—white or red—was safe. She had found them thickets and rock overhangs to sleep in, and she had raised their spirits when Linna and Donal despaired of ever finding Rory alive.

The time in the wilderness had changed Donal, too. Linna closed her eyes and tried to think back to the first moment she'd realized that her brother-in-law had shifted his romantic interest from her to Sarah. The two had been discreet, finding logical reasons to slip off for an hour or two until, finally, Linna could find no fault when they began to sleep nestled against each other.

Linna sighed. Living so close to death had brought her a strange inner peace. If Sarah and Donal could find solace in each other's arms, she was happy for them. It didn't matter that the two came from different worlds; it didn't matter that if they survived this ordeal, Donal would most likely abandon the Indian girl as he had his other women. What did matter was that the love that shone from their eyes as they looked at each other was genuine.

They had reached the Ohio River early in the morning of the preceding day. Sarah had insisted that the sensible thing to do was to set up camp and wait for one of the local Indian tribes to find them. Linna, exhausted from the weeks of walking, had readily agreed.

The three had spent the rest of the day swimming

in the river, washing their hair and ragged clothing, and resting their blistered feet. Donal had caught fish in the river, using one of Linna's hairpins for a hook and a line that Sarah fashioned from inner tree bark. Linna thought the fish was delicious—even without salt. They had washed it down with water and something Sarah called tea berries. It had been a day of laughter and celebration, a day that ended with Linna settling down by the warmth of the fire, and Sarah and Donal going into the forest darkness hand in hand.

The two had not returned until nearly dawn. Linna had been careful not to wake them when she rose to come down to the river.

A rhythmic splashing caught Linna's attention, and she opened her eyes. Coming out of the mist, not more than ten yards from the riverbank, was a canoe with two Indian men and a woman in it.

Linna got slowly to her feet and walked toward the water. *"Jai-nai-nah,"* she called, using the Shawnee word for brother that Sarah had taught her. *"Jai-nai-nah."*

The brave in the bow of the canoe dropped his paddle in the boat and reached for a musket.

Linna stopped in her tracks and forced a smile, trying desperately to remember the proper Shawnee greeting between friends.

"Matchele s'squaw-o-wah!" the man at the stern cried as he notched an arrow in his bow and pointed it directly at her.

Linna held out her hands, palms up to show that she held no weapons. Her mind was blank with fear, then a single word formed on her tongue and she blurted it out. "Uingaokuee!" Uingaokuee—The Raven. Why had she said that?

Before Linna could cover her stupid blunder, the

Indian woman cried something to the man with the gun. He lowered the musket, picked up his paddle, and guided the boat toward the shore with one powerful thrust.

"Uingaokuee," the woman repeated.

The rest of what she said was meaningless to Linna, but Linna continued to smile and nod. To her relief, Sarah's voice came from behind her, speaking to the Indians in the same tongue.

Warily, the first man climbed from the canoe and scrambled up the bank, musket in hand. He exchanged a few words with Sarah, then lowered the gun and called to the others.

Sarah turned to Linna. "It's all right. They are Shawnee. I don't know any of them, but the woman is half sister to Uingaokuee, The Raven." She twisted to wave at Donal. "Put down your weapon," she advised. "These are friends." Sarah spoke softly to Linna. "They want to know if we are free of sickness. There is smallpox in some of the Indian villages, and many have died. I told them we are not sick."

Donal came forward from the trees to stand beside Sarah. "Ask them if they know of any white captives," he said.

Sarah laid a hand on Donal's arm. "I have told them that you are my husband. Because I am Shawnee, that will give you safe passage among them as long as you do not break the peace. They are not from Uingaokuee's camp, but they say it is a day's journey south of here. If we will return with them to their fishing camp, Aatu—the man with the bow—will guide us to Uingaokuee."

"What of English captives?" Linna demanded. "Do they know if this Raven has any white men in his camp?"

Sarah asked the woman.

Uingaokuee's sister shrugged and answered in Shawnee.

"She says," Sarah translated, "that she heard of two prisoners. One died and another was traded to the French for guns. She does not know if your husband was ever in her brother's camp or if he is still alive."

Shrieking taunts, the boys circled the man and flung stones with varying degrees of accuracy. One stone struck the captive's forehead, and the thrower let out a yelp of delight.

Blood trickled down Rory's face as he raised his head and glared into his tormentor's face. "Begone," he threatened softly in Shawnee. "Or I will raise a faceless ghost to creep down your throats in the night."

Laughter ceased and the taunts died away. One by one the boys slipped away until only the youth who had drawn blood was left. "Traitorous dog," the boy hissed. "You will howl a different tune when you go to the stake."

Rory bared his teeth and laughed—a harsh, rasping sound. "If I die, Namiis, I will become a ghost and yours will be the first soul I seek to drag down into the swamp." He laughed again. "You need have no fear of me by day, but by night . . . By night I will ride the wings of an owl, and I will find you, Namiis."

The boy's eyes widened in fear. He threw the last stone halfheartedly at Rory. It flew wide, and the boy turned and ran toward the river.

Rory sagged against the leather thongs, wincing at the pain that shot down his arms and into his shoulders. How many days had he spent like this—suspended by his wrists between two trees? He couldn't remember. He had lost any sense of time after the massacre. Days, weeks . . . He couldn't be sure. The head wound had left him foggy, and the ill treatment he'd received at Uingaokuee's hands hadn't helped.

He'd been only half conscious when they'd carried him to the French fort and then through the forest to Uingaokuee's village. He'd been too ill to speak to the other captives—too ill to care deeply when the British officer was put to death. He didn't know what had happened to the Virginian. Rory had awakened one morning to find he was alone in the prisoners' wigwam. He'd asked the old woman who brought his food, but she had only laughed and gone away mumbling to herself.

Gradually, Rory's wound had healed, and his mind had cleared. At dusk, every day, the Shawnee took him down from the trees and gave him food and drink. He was permitted a few minutes to see to his bodily functions, and then taken to the wigwam and bound hand and foot. Again, in the purple haze before dawn, he was allowed to walk to the river—to drink and wash. Always, Rory was guarded by armed Shawnee warriors. They never spoke to him at night, but they were never cruel.

At dawn, he was taken to the trees; as the first sunlight fell across his face, he became an enemy of the Shawnee. He became *cut-ta-ho-tha*—he who is condemned to death by burning at the stake!

Rory knotted his fists and flexed his spine. He never slept at night. Instead, he lay awake, flexing his arms and legs, straining against the rawhide, and mentally running, jumping and practicing with knife and bow. Rory knew the days tied to these trees would cripple him if he didn't stay mentally and physically alert.

Uingaokuee, The Raven, was trying to work on his

mind. He wanted to destroy Rory's will and take him
to the stake broken in spirit and crying out for mercy.
So far, Uingaokuee's plan hadn't worked.

Rory opened his eyes and stared into the mist rising
off the river. He and Uingaokuee had been enemies
long before Rory had marched down Braddock's road.
When Rory had lived among the Indians, they had
vied for the same woman—Gimewane of the waist-
length hair. Pretty Gimewane had chosen Rory over
Uingaokuee, and the Shawnee brave had challenged
him to a fight to the death. Rory had refused. By Indian
law, Shawnee did not fight Shawnee. Rory had gone
to the council for settlement of the issue, and the council had ordered Uingaokuee banished from the tribe
when he would not accept their judgment.

It had been a stupid argument from the first, and
Rory regretted that he'd made an enemy over a woman
for whom he had no deep feelings. Gimewane had
been as fickle as she had been beautiful; she'd stayed
with Rory for only a single turning of the moon before
she left him for a passing French trapper.

That Gimewane had scorned both Uingaokuee and
Rory meant nothing. The issue was Uingaokuee's
pride. He had sworn a blood oath to kill Rory, and it
looked like The Raven might finally get that chance.

Because Rory had been adopted into the tribe and
was considered a Shawnee by tribal law, his sin in
following Braddock had been worse than that of an
Englishman. Uingaokuee and some of the tribe considered Rory a traitor. It was that traitor who was
tortured and taunted by day. By night, Rory, the Shawnee warrior known as Mishkwe-Tusca was given the
respect due one of the People. No matter what he had
done, no one could take his warrior status away. He

would live—and die—a *lenni-lenape*, a human being.

The cut from the stone the boy had hurled hurt. Rory thought the cut had stopped bleeding, but he couldn't be sure. He couldn't touch it until his hands were untied at dusk. Damn the brat! The blood would draw insects and they'd pester him all day.

Rory closed his eyes again, allowing himself to think of Linna and his infant son. He'd been a fool to leave them to follow Braddock; he'd known it before the expedition left Wills Creek. A man with any sense would have quit and gone home.

Linna's face hovered behind his eyelids. God, but he loved her! No matter what she'd done—how she'd lied to him and deceived him—he still wanted her. Pride and stubbornness had kept him from forgiving her, had driven him hundreds of miles into the wilderness to share in a bloodbath caused by English stupidity and monumental incompetence.

Rory had had time to think in the long days and nights since he'd been taken captive. He didn't blame the Indians or the French for Braddock's massacre; the seeds of that defeat were sown in English drawing rooms and cultivated by the pride and stiff-necked obstinacy of Major General Edward Braddock. The French and their Indian allies had merely taken advantage of a golden opportunity. English had murdered English, and the Colonists who had followed British orders against their own better judgment had signed their own death warrants.

Rory sighed. He'd been a fool, all right. He'd forgotten that the English were his true enemies. If he lived to get back to his wife and son on Connemara, he'd stay there and let the cursed Sassenach fight their own battles.

Rory pushed the thoughts of Braddock's bloody road from his mind and tried to concentrate on Linna. He had cried her name aloud when he was standing knee-deep among the bodies of his comrades, when he'd fired and reloaded, fired and reloaded until his musket had become so hot it had raised blisters on his face and hands. He'd murmured her name when he'd hung suspended between reality and madness, and it was the magic of her name that shielded his spirit from Uingaokuee's daily attacks.

Rory's head snapped up as the wind carried shouts from the riverbank. The rising sun shone directly into his face, and he squinted to see what all the commotion was about.

Men and women were running toward the beach. A canoe touched the bank and the crowd surged around the newcomers. A musket shot rang out, and a boy on a horse galloped toward Uingaokuee's wigwam at the far side of the camp. "English-manake!" he shouted.

Rory strained against the leather thongs and blinked to see. The cries of the people had turned ugly. Two men had seized one of the strangers. Suddenly, a white woman broke from the knot of Shawnee and ran toward the camp. Rory groaned deep in his throat as the morning sun sparkled on the bright crown of her red-gold hair.

Uingoakuee burst from his wigwam directly into the woman's path. He threw out his arms to catch her and she dodged him, turning sharply and dashing toward where Rory was tied. The Shawnee warrior sprinted after her. Laughing, he seized the end of one thick braid and jerked her around to face him.

The woman struck out with both fists at Uingaokuee, wiping the smirk from his face with a hard blow to the Indian's nose. Uingaokuee's massive arms closed around her, and she cried out once in Gaelic.

Linna! A red haze of fury possessed Rory. Muscles bulging, he threw himself against the ties. One braided thong snapped. With a cry of rage, Rory pulled the other free and launched himself across the space that separated them.

A Shawnee woman called a warning, and Uingaokuee slammed a fist against Linna's jaw and flung her aside like a broken doll. Whipping a knife from the sheath at his waist, The Raven crouched to meet Rory's wild attack.

Seconds before it was too late, Rory's brain flooded with cold reason. He slowed his suicidal charge and circled Uingaokuee with deadly calm.

"The coward has a voice!" Uingaokuee taunted, flashing the blue-steel blade in the sun. "Come closer and we will see if it is a bark or a bite."

Chapter 22

"You have something of mine," Rory answered softly in the Shawnee tongue. "You have my wife. Give her to me, or your women will cry your death song this day."

"A dog owns nothing but the dust of his grave!" Uingaokuee replied harshly. "I claim this flame-haired English *s'squaw-o-wah* for my own."

Dazed, Linna sat up in the tall grass and tried to gather her wits. The blow had stunned her, but the pain in her jaw meant nothing. "Rory . . ."

"Stay where you are," he warned.

Uingaokuee slashed at Rory with the knife, and the Irishmen sidestepped and drove a balled fist into the Indian's belly. Uingaokuee gasped and fell to one knee. Rory followed with a blow to Uingaokuee's head, and they went down in a blur of arms and legs.

Uingaokuee's knife cut a gash across Rory's forearm and Linna screamed. Then, suddenly, the three of them were surrounded by Indians. Angry warriors pulled Rory and Uingaokuee apart, holding them fast.

Uingaokuee's eyes were hate-filled as he glared at Rory. Blood ran from the Indian's nose, and one eye was rapidly swelling. "You are too dangerous to live," he threatened Rory in Shawnee. "Tonight, we light the fires of your death."

Sarah pushed through the crowd and knelt beside Linna. "Are you all right?" Linna nodded and Sarah pulled her to her feet.

"It's Rory—he was nearly—"

"I know."

"What are they saying?" Linna begged.

Uingaokuee shook off his captors and approached Rory. He thrust his incensed face close to the white man's and closed his fingers around Rory's throat, squeezing tightly.

Rory stared through the war chief as though he were invisible. Uingaokuee tightened his grip.

"Coward!" Linna cried. Before anyone could stop her, she dove past the two braves in front of her and pushed between Uingaokuee and Rory, striking the Indian's hands away from Rory's throat. "Choke me!" she dared.

Her brown eyes flashed sparks of fire. One auburn braid had come undone and her hair fanned wildly about her face. A smear of dirt covered one cheek and the other side of her face was swelling from Uingaokuee's blow.

"You dare to call yourself a man!" Linna cried.

Uingaokuee raised his hand to knock her away, and an imperious female voice called his name from the crowd. Uingaokuee flushed and stepped back.

"You bring shame on us!" a gray-haired woman admonished.

Linna whirled and threw her arms around Rory, burying her face in his neck. "Rory, Rory," she murmured in Gaelic. "My love, my darling man . . . I thought you were dead."

Rory cleared his throat and blinked, trying desperately to maintain his composure. "Nay, Linna," he growled. "Don't . . ."

Uingaokuee barked an order, and the men holding Rory dragged him to a post in the center of the village and bound him to it. Linna followed, dry-eyed and numb. No one seemed to notice her. "Rory, please . . ."

His features hardened and he turned his head away from her, staring toward the river.

Uingaokuee and the older woman exchanged heated words, then The Raven angrily stalked away, followed by most of the Shawnee. Linna looked around for Sarah, but could no longer see her or Donal.

The gray-haired woman came toward Linna and spoke to her in English. "You are wife to Mishkwe-Tusca?" Linna nodded. "And you come to Shawnee land in time of blood to find your man?"

"Yes."

The Indian woman looked about at the remaining Shawnee. She clapped her hands twice and said something Linna couldn't understand. Without protesting, the remaining braves and the staring women and children hurried away.

The woman turned her attention to Linna once more. "I am Melassa, mother to The Raven. I am also clan sister to the mother of the Shawnee woman you call Sarah."

"You're Sarah's aunt?" The Indian woman was slight and unimposing. She wore a white deerskin skirt and a fringed cape that covered only one breast, leaving the other bare. Around her wrinkled neck was a string of purple wampum. In her ears were gold Spanish coins that had been drilled and hung with silver wire.

The gold of the earrings glittered brightly against the thick gray braids.

Melassa shook her head patiently. "Not as the English know." She held up her left hand and clasped the fingers with her other hand. "A clan sister is not blood, but the same."

"When we touched the beach, my husband's brother Donal was taken prisoner. He—"

Melassa's eyes narrowed shrewdly. "This English-manake, this Do-nal, he is a soldier?"

"No. He came with me to find his brother. We meant to trade with you, but my trade goods were stolen by the Huron." Linna paused for breath, then added, "And we are not English. We are Irish. The English are our enemies, too. They have stolen our land across the sea."

The older woman chuckled dryly. "It seems the Irish cannot keep their things from being stolen." Her eyes twinkled, and then the warmth of her gaze turned to frost. "If the English are your enemy, Mishkwe-Tusca has betrayed more than the Shawnee when he marched beside Braddock. He has betrayed those you call Irish."

Linna gazed at Rory. His face was as immobile as an Indian's. Blood still dripped from the knife wound on his arm. "I need water and cloth to tend his wound," Linna said matter-of-factly. "It may have to be stitched."

"You are a brave woman," Melassa observed.

Linna shook her head. "No, I'm not. I'm afraid." She stared into the Indian woman's ebony eyes. "Will they kill him?"

Melassa spread her hands palm up. "Sarah and her husband will not be harmed. Of Mishkwe-Tusca, I cannot say. The decision must be made by the council. My son wants to burn him.''

"No," Linna protested. "They can't. It's not human."

"White men burn," Melassa answered softly. "They bring diseases to kill our children in their mothers' arms. They rape our women and slaughter our old people like cattle. They fence the water where Shawnee have come to drink for time out of time and say we can drink no more. They cut *ake*, the earth, with their plows and build their towns on our burial places." She shook her gray head sadly. "We think the white men are not human." With a regal nod of dismissal, Melassa turned and walked away.

Linna surveyed the Indian village about her. She and Rory were alone in the center of a hard-packed dirt clearing. The nearest hut, or wigwam as Rory had told her they were called, was at least a hundred feet away. She tried to gauge the number of wigwams in the village, and therefore guess how many people were wandering about. Some of the wigwams were round at the top, almost like beehives, and covered with bark. Others, high peaked, were covered with animal hides. Here and there was an occasional larger hut, rounded at the top and two to three times as deep as the others, with heavy posts set into the ground for support.

Although there seemed to be no order to the arrangement of the wigwams, the area around each house was neat. No garbage lay about, and as far as Linna's sense of smell could tell, there were no open pits for human waste. It was a far cry from Dublin or Galway, where the stench of butchers' offal and emptying chamber pots was an accepted fact of life.

Linna counted more than three dozen wigwams from

where she stood. South of the village were cornfields and gardens with women working in them. Birchbark canoes and clumsy wooden dugouts were drawn up on the riverbank. Two boys and their dogs were playing a game in the shallow water, throwing a big leather ball and knocking it back and forth.

Linna gathered her courage, moving close to Rory, and placing her hand on his dirt-smeared cheek. "Rory, please," she begged. "Say something to me."

He raised his head and glared at her with icy rage. "What the hell are you doing here?"

Linna stepped back and blinked away the tears that rose in her eyes. "I came to find you."

"Our son?"

"Colin's well. I left him in your mother's care."

"Mother knows you've come here?"

"By now she does." She touched the wound on his arm; it was an ugly gash, encrusted with dirt and grass. "I've got to clean this. I told Me—"

"Melassa."

"—Melassa that I needed cloth and—"

"For God's sake, woman! Can't you get it through your head? You're a prisoner. Melassa is a council member—very high rank. She's married to the chief and full sister to the shaman, the medicine man of the tribe. Melassa is royalty! You don't tell her what you want and expect to get it."

Linna exhaled sharply. "If I'm a prisoner, why aren't I tied to a post like you are?"

"Where the hell are you going to go? Upriver? The Shawnee camp there is riddled with smallpox. West? There's no civilization until you come to China. They haven't tied you because you can't run away."

"Oh . . ."

"You've ruined any chances I have of escaping by

coming here. Raven hates me, and he'll use you to get revenge. He'll never let you go, Linna. You'll live out your days as his slave . . . or maybe as his third wife."

Linna made a small sound. "I thought Melassa was his mother. How can she be his wife and his mother at the same time?"

"By holy Saint Joseph! Who said she was Raven's wife?"

"You did." Linna kicked aimlessly at the dirt. "You said she was wife to the chief."

Rory swore softly. "Iron Shirt is high chief here. The Raven is a war chief. He has a lot of influence with the young bucks, but not as much power with the council. If Raven was high chief, he'd have boiled me down for soap the first week I was in the camp."

A young squaw with a baby on her back approached Linna cautiously and held out a birchbark container of liquid. "Melassa say you clean arm," she said in halting English.

"Thank you," Linna answered gravely. She flashed an I-told-you-so smile at Rory as she accepted the bowl and the packet of soft skins. "I am called Linna," she said to the girl.

Solemnly, the woman spoke her own name. "Siike."

"See-kee? And is this your child?"

Siike nodded vigorously. "Make well Mishkwe-Tusca. I come for you."

"Mishkwe-Tusca is my husband. Do you understand?"

"Yes, *uikiimuk*—husband." Siike motioned toward Rory. "Make quick. Uingaokuee no wish you talk."

The Indian girl turned away, and Linna caught a glimpse of a round little face and two currant-black eyes peering over the rim of the cradleboard. Linna's heart was heavy with longing for her own baby son as she watched Siike stride gracefully toward the nearest wigwam.

Linna picked up the bowl and without speaking began to wash the wound on Rory's arm.

"Ouch! Be careful!"

The water in the bowl was pale brown and gave off a faintly astringent odor. Linna wasn't certain what the solution was, but she reasoned if Melassa had ordered Rory tended to, she wouldn't order poison to do it. In place of a washcloth were handfuls of soft, fluffy cattail down and seeds. "I didn't come to make things harder for you," Linna explained painfully. "Everyone said you were dead. Ty told me—"

"Ty's alive?"

"Very much alive. A Delaware Indian brought him home to Connemara."

"Tumme Uoote?"

"Yes." Linna poured the rest of the liquid over the clean wound, covered it with a pad of clean rabbitskin, and began to bind the bandage with thin strips of leather. "Ty wanted to come looking for you himself, but . . ." She raised her eyes to meet Rory's angry ones and lapsed into Gaelic. "He lost a leg. There was infection. I know he'll heal in time, but I couldn't wait that long. I can see now that it was an idiotic thing to do. I've come across a wilderness to hunt for a man who didn't want me."

Rory started to speak and she raised a hand for silence. "No! You'll hear me out! I came because I loved you . . . because I didn't want to think of living in a world that you weren't a part of. It's been like that for a long time, Rory Desmond." Linna paused and drew in a long, ragged breath. "I thought . . . in time . . . you'd forgive me. But if you can't, then that's your loss—and if I end up as some Indian's squaw, maybe he'll value me more than you have."

"Damn ye, woman, can ye ever cease your blabbering long enough for me to say my piece!"

Linna gazed up at him through tear-filmed eyes. God knew he looked as rough as any savage. His hair hung loose below his shoulders, and his face looked as if he'd been shaved with a hot iron. He was shirtless, and the remains of the breeches he wore would shame a beggar. In place of his fine leather boots, his feet were covered with worn leather moccasins. "You're not the man I first saw, and that's for certain," she admitted.

"Linna!" a familiar voice called. Sarah hurried toward them. "I have only a minute," she said breathlessly. "They're letting Donal and me go free." Sarah hesitated, then went on in a rush of words. "They think we're married. I'm taking him to my village. I'd take you, too, Linna, but The Raven won't let me. He's claiming you as his prisoner. I'm sorry . . . I never should have brought you here." She threw her arms around Linna and hugged her tightly. "If I could help your man I would."

"Sarah," Linna murmured, "you can't blame yourself. I'd have come without you."

"And drowned in the first creek," Sarah teased.

"Probably."

"Get my brother to safety," Rory said.

"I will try." Sarah gave Linna a final squeeze. "Only one thing more I can give you—a law of my people."

"What is it?"

"Anything but honor may be bought," Sarah answered. "Anything—even a blood price, a death sentence—can be exchanged for something of equal worth."

Rory strained against the leather bonds that held him to the post. "Don't fill her head with nonsense," he growled. "Linna has nothing left to trade."

"A woman is never without resources," Sarah said softly. "And it is up to her to decide if that which she desires most is worth the price she must pay."

Linna sat in the semidarkness of the wigwam and waited. The young squaw, Siike, had returned without the baby and taken Linna to a secluded spot along the river to wash. Siike had given her a crushed dogwood stem for brushing her teeth and a handful of unfamiliar herbs to use as shampoo for her hair. While Linna was waist-deep in the water, Siike exchanged Linna's tattered shoes and dress for a fringed dress of soft doeskin and white quillwork moccasins.

When Linna came from the river, dripping wet, Siike had stared curiously at Linna's pale skin. They had sat together on a broad rock while Linna's hair dried in the sun. From a leather bag, Siike had produced a large wooden comb and an exquisite beaded headband. She had indicated that all these things were gifts from Melassa.

Linna was intelligent enough to know that ordinary prisoners would never receive such gentle treatment. She had asked Siike questions at the river and again when the Indian woman had led the way to the wigwam. Siike's only answer had been an enigmatic smile.

Sarah and Donal were gone. Linna had seen them walking down toward the canoes. If Sarah's tribe was not at war with the English, perhaps someone would help Donal return to the nearest white settlement. There had been no opportunity to talk to Donal, but Linna was confident that Sarah would look after him if it were humanly possible.

Just before dusk, Siike returned again with a bowl of hot stew and a bundle of firewood. She knelt beside the cold hearth and lit a fire, letting Linna's questions slide off her back as easily as a duck sheds water. When the tiny sparks burst into flame, Siike glanced up from under her dark lashes. "Do you wish to piss?"

Linna felt her cheeks grow hot. She nodded dumbly. She had been uncomfortable for the last hour, but had been afraid to venture from the wigwam.

Siike nodded and led the way out of the wigwam and into the forest beyond the cornfield. All over the camp, families were gathering for the evening meal. Smells of stew and broiling fish were heavy in the air. Mothers called to their children, and they filed wearily home.

Linna was struck with the similarity of this Indian village to the village she had grown up in at home in Ireland. Although she couldn't understand the language, the immature voices of the children showed the strain of the long day's hard play in the bright autumn air. The mothers' voices revealed the impatience of mothers everywhere. It was time to seek out the children, feed them, and settle them for the night.

As she followed Siike into the woods, they passed a hunter returning from the chase with a young deer slung across his shoulders. The man was no taller than Linna, dark of skin and thin-lipped. He averted his eyes and strode on with the pride of a prince, making not the slightest sound as his moccasined feet touched the ground.

Linna tried to catch sight of Rory when they returned

to the wigwam, but it was impossible. Half a camp separated the cleared space from this hut. Siike raised the deerskin curtain that served as a door and stood back for Linna to enter.

"Do you have a child?" Siike asked.

Linna paused and met the ebony stare. "Yes."

"Mishkwe-Tusca is father?"

Linna nodded. "We have a son."

Siike sighed, a sad, soft sound like the sighing of the wind. "I have sorry for you," she answered. She motioned toward the interior of the wigwam and Linna obeyed.

The stew had cooled, but Linna ate it eagerly, licking the wooden spoon like a child when every drop of the good juice was gone. It had tasted like venison, but it didn't matter. If it had been dog, she would have eaten it. Linna knew she needed every ounce of strength she possessed for what might come in the next hours. The water in the skin bag was warm and tasted faintly of iron, but she drank deeply of that too.

The wigwam was small, not more than eight feet across. The fire pit was in the exact center of the hut; above it, a hole in the roof allowed smoke to rise straight up and out of the wigwam. The floor of the front half of the wigwam was hard-packed dirt, swept as clean as any housewife's pine floor. Baskets and bags hung from the interior framework of saplings. Linna was curious as to their content, but was unwilling to pry into another's possessions, especially as she was certain that none contained a weapon of any kind. A copper kettle sat just inside the doorway and beside that a woven basket of corn. Beyond the fire, the entire space of the wigwam was taken up by a raised sleeping platform heaped high with silver-tipped wolf pelts. The furs gave off a faintly musty odor, not unpleasant, that blended with the bite of the burning cherry kindling and the smell of drying herbs and corn.

Linna placed the empty stew bowl beside the copper kettle and crouched before the fire. One by one, she fed finger-size sticks into the growing flames. With the coming of darkness the air had taken on a sharp bite, and she was glad for the heat of the fire.

Sometime after dark—just when Linna was not certain—a drum began to beat. Voices, far off, took up a low, wordless chant. Gooseflesh rose on her arms and her throat grew dry. She tried to fix Rory's face in her mind's eye, but Uingaokuee's malignant features overshadowed Rory's. The Raven's bitter threats sounded over and over in Linna's ears, all the more frightening for being part of her imagination.

When her legs stiffened from kneeling, Linna rubbed away the pins and needles and moved to lie across the sleeping platform, her face buried in her arms. She could not bear it if the Indians killed Rory, not now, not after she had come so far and suffered so greatly to find him. Sarah's parting words lurked in the corners of Linna's mind, and she knew that she would do anything to save her husband . . . anything.

"If I have to sleep with the devil himself . . ." Linna murmured into the silky pelts. Nothing mattered, not her life, not her immortal soul, only the man she could not wrench from her heart. If Rory no longer loved her or no longer wanted her to be his wife, she would learn to live with his rejection, but she would not live without knowing he was alive.

The ghostly cry of an owl sounded from a tree just outside the wigwam, and Linna shivered. The drumming stopped, and she could no longer hear the chanting of the Shawnee. Tree branches creaked in the rising wind; the soft patter of rain against the bark roof did nothing to soothe Linna's growing panic.

She rose to a sitting position, straining to hear any human noise in the night. And after what seemed hours, she was rewarded with the murmur of voices and the soft thud of footsteps.

A man spoke in the Indian tongue, just beyond the entrance flap, and Linna's heart skipped a beat as she recognized Uingaokuee's deep voice. A scream gathered in Linna's throat, but she choked it back. She would not cry out—would not give The Raven the satisfaction of hearing her fear. She rose to her feet, cold hands clenched at her sides, and fixed her frightened gaze on the deerskin.

The curtain was brushed aside and the sinewy bulk of man's naked, oiled shoulders filled the low entrance-way.

"Linna."

Linna swayed, fighting to keep the whirling blackness from drowning her mind. She blinked, balling her fists until her nails cut into the palms of her hands.

"Linna?" The naked hunger in the husky voice was as clear as Connemara spring water. "Colleen—"

"Rory!"

Her husband caught her as she fell, lifting her in his arms and crushing her against him. "Linna," he agonized. "Come back to me, my darling. Come back to me . . ."

Chapter 23

"Linna."

Rory's voice caressed her . . . luring her from the safety of the black void into which she had fallen. She could feel his warm breath on her face . . . smell the sharp man-scent that was his and his alone.

"Linna . . ."

She had dreamed of him holding her like this, had wanted it so badly that she feared this was nothing more than a dream. Linna's heart quickened with bittersweet joy. If she opened her eyes, she would see Rory's eyes staring into hers . . . or would she? If this was a dream, she would lose him. He would slip through her fingers like the ethereal, translucent mist of Galway Bay.

"Linna!" Rory's voice demanded. "You were never a fainting woman. Must you choose tonight to—"

Her eyes snapped open. The face above her was no painted savage. "Rory?" she dared. "Rory!" Her arms went around his neck, pulling him fiercely to her. Her mouth met his, and suddenly Linna was laughing and crying and kissing him all at the same time.

"Ah, Linna," he moaned and laid her gently on the bed of wolf pelts. "My darling."

Her mouth opened to his and passion flared between them as hot and bright as the flames of the crackling fire. Linna twined her fingers in Rory's unbound hair and drank in the sweet headiness of his all-consuming kiss.

"Don't cry," he murmured hoarsely as he lay down beside her and urgently pressed her back against the soft furs. "No tears tonight, my darling."

"But how? Why did—"

"Shhh. Not now, Linna."

Rory's hard hand spanned her hip possessively as he claimed her with another searing kiss.

Linna sighed as a knot of tingling desire formed in the pit of her stomach and radiated outward, making her pulse quicken and her breath come in slow, ragged shudders. She let her fingers trace the rugged features of Rory's face, sliding down the length of his jaw to brush the hollow of his throat. "Darling Rory," she whispered. "Are you real?"

"I'm real enough," he answered, and his kisses trailed down her neck to linger on the rising mound of her breast. "I want you, Linna," he moaned. "I want all of you. I want to touch you . . . to taste you . . ."

Willingly, she lifted her hips as he slid the deerskin dress up and over her head. Linna raised shining eyes to his as Rory caressed her naked body with his tantalizing gaze. He moved above her, and the firelight reflected off his oiled, muscular body. Linna's hand moved down Rory's sinewy thigh and tugged at the thong that held his loincloth.

With a low cry he yanked it away, revealing the

proof of his potent male desire.

Linna caught his shoulders and pulled him against her, rubbing her swollen breasts provocatively against his broad chest, arching against his straining loins. She moaned deep in her throat as he lowered his head to flick her nipple with his hot tongue and then to gently suck and nip at first one aching breast and then the other.

She buried her face in his thick, dark hair. "I love you," she murmured. "I love you."

The warmth of the fire . . . the silken sensation of the wolf pelts beneath her naked body . . . Rory's slow, tantalizing seduction of her willing body . . . all flowed together into a river of sweet, throbbing enchantment. Time slowed for Linna and then seemed to stop. She was filled with the poignant beauty of this joyous, incomparable moment, filled with the heady scent of love and the taste and smell of this man who was everything to her.

"Linna," Rory breathed huskily, licking her ear. "I need you." He captured her small hand in his and guided it to caress his engorged and throbbing shaft.

A thrill of excitement shattered her heavy-limbed languor. "Love me," she cried. "I want you, Rory. I want you . . ."

She opened to meet him as a flower opens for the morning sun, and they blended like dry earth and spring rain. Their cries of passion merged as his powerful thrusts filled Linna with the love and oneness she desired above all else. They rose together in an all-encompassing spiral, higher and higher until they reached the summit of passion . . . and fell and rose again, lost in their own world of beauty and rapture.

*   *   *

The crescent moon was no longer visible through the smoke hole of the wigwam when Linna opened her eyes and stared up at her lover. "I thought you were a dream," she whispered sleepily. She raised her hand to cup his rough cheek. Rory's long hair hung over his rugged face like that of some ancient Irish hero. "You look like Conn of the Hundred Battles," she teased. "Have they made you a savage, too?" Her fingertips brushed his firm bottom lip and she sighed contentedly. "If this is a dream, don't wake me."

Laughter rumbled in his throat, and he kissed her full on the lips. "You make a proper savage yourself," he teased. Rory touched the rose pendant that was Linna's only garment. "Is this a magic talisman that protects you from all evil, little witch?"

She smiled up at him. "If it is, you are the warlock who gave it to me."

Rory fingered the carved ivory bauble. "My charms are as child's play to yours, woman. You've held me in your spell since I first laid eyes on you in your father's hall."

"That's not what you said before." Linna rose on one elbow. "Outside . . . before, when I tried to tell you why I'd come, you wouldn't—"

"Damnation, woman, you're at it again." Without warning he threw her back against the furs and pinned both wrists above her head. "You will not stay silent long enough for a man to apologize!" he grumbled. "Bite that sharp tongue of yours and listen for a change."

"But I—"

"I said, listen!"

Linna squirmed until her knee grazed Rory's inner

thigh. It was pleasant to have him so close, even if he was holding her hands and scolding her.

"Stop that and listen to me," he warned.

Linna shook her hair from her face and laughed. "Pray go on, husband. I would hear this apology from you. It is such an occasion, I wonder that we shouldn't have thunder and lightning from heaven to announce it."

"Will you—"

Linna shifted so that her bare breast rested against Rory's left arm. "Silent as the grave," she promised.

"A damned poor choice of words considering our predicament," he grumbled.

"How am I to know? You won't answer any of my questions," she badgered. "I'm not even certain you mean to apologize. I—"

He stopped her words with a kiss.

"Are we to make love or talk?" she demanded when he stopped kissing her and took a deep breath.

"Both, I think," he conceded, lapsing into Gaelic.

"By rights, it is no favor you do me to apologize," Linna said loftily. "You owe me that and more, no matter how I deceived you by pretending to be my sister."

"What twisted feminine logic is this?" he growled.

"I saved your life."

"Which time?"

"In Ireland."

"The coach doesn't count. You were afraid the soldiers would arrest you if they found me." He released one of Linna's wrists and cupped a round breast gently in his big hand.

She tried not to giggle. "What are you doing?"

"Looking for a witchmark. If you're a witch, you're bound to have one somewhere. Ah-hah!" He nuzzled her breast. "What's this?"

"That's my nipple. Stop that." The delicious feeling was beginning to trickle through her veins again. She laughed and twisted away, coming to rest sitting upright on top of Rory while he lay flat on his back. "Now who won't listen?" she demanded. "I'm telling you something important. Do you remember when you were wounded by the soldiers—before you came to America the first time?"

"Of course." He slid her down his torso until she was astride his loins. "What of it?"

"Do you remember the little girl who saved you?" Linna leaned forward, resting her elbows on his chest and her chin on her entwined fingers. "Her name was Linna, too."

"Girl? I don't remember any girl. There was a boy, a dirty, ill-tempered little urchin. He smelled of pig—ouch!"

Linna gave Rory's chest hair another sharp tug for good measure. "You knew!" she accused. "All this time I was planning how to tell you and you—"

Laughing, he pulled her down and kissed her. "I only recognized you after you confessed who you really were," he confided. "There are many red-haired, freckle-faced Linnas in Connemara. You've grown up since you were that child in the cave." He hugged her tightly against him and stroked her back in slow, circular patterns. "Ah, Linna girl," he whispered huskily, "I thought of that child many times in the years that followed. I thought of her and I wondered if she'd ever find a man who was worthy of her . . . who would love and care for her as she deserved." Rory kissed Linna again tenderly. "Did you think I could forget her?"

"But you didn't say anything."

"And ruin my image as a complete ass? I was ashamed of the way I treated you. And I was angry."

"You were still angry with me when you saw me here at the camp."

"Of course. I still am." He caught her shoulders and forced her to face him. "I'm angry because you're in danger, Linna. I wanted you safe in Maryland, on Connemara with our son. I wanted to know that no matter what happened to me, you would go on living."

"Oh." She sniffed as her eyes filled with tears. "I thought . . ."

"You thought I still cared about wedding the wrong woman. I didn't, Linna. I married the right woman. I knew that before we marched away from the first fort on that damnable expedition. My pride kept us apart. I couldn't go home and face you after what I'd put you through."

"I am sorry, Rory," she said. "I never thought you'd have to return the dowry. I didn't want to hurt you. I would never have forgiven myself if you lost the plantation. Besides, your tobacco got safely to England. They gave you a fantastic price for it."

"Atcch, woman. You are as mad as a hatter. Do ye think I care a thimble for the plantation without you? If we lost it, we could go west of the Chesapeake and claim new land. We could start over again, if . . ." Rory trailed off, and Linna sensed something terribly wrong.

"Rory? What is it? What aren't you telling me?"

He grinned wryly, taking a lock of her hair and winding it around his finger. "We aren't out of the woods yet, my little optimist witch. There's an entire Shawnee Nation out there."

"But they let you come to me. I thought—"

"Don't think anymore tonight, Linna. Just love me and let me love you."

Fear rose in Linna's throat, pinching her voice. "Uingaokuee is going to kill you in the morning," she said. A silent scream of agony ripped through her. "Rory, no. He can't . . . not now . . . I won't let him."

"If you know any real witchcraft, this might not be a bad time to cast some of your spells."

The tears spilled over, running down her cheeks to dampen his shoulder. "Rory, Rory," she murmured. The weeping became a torrent.

"Shhh, shhh," he soothed. "I'm not dead yet. Don't cry."

"It's not fair," she wailed. "I need you."

"Stop crying. Uingaokuee is outside. He'll hear you."

Linna gave a shuddering sigh. "He . . . he's outside? Why?"

"Because, my little innocent, he's taking no chances on my making an escape." He kissed her tear-filled eyes and the tip of her nose. "Nothing's been decided yet. The high council will probably be in session all night. The Shawnee would rather argue issues of tribal law than eat."

"But if Uingaokuee wants you dead and Melassa thinks you're a traitor . . ."

"Melassa is undecided. Iron Shirt will probably vote the same way she does. If they do decide I deserve to die, they may not put me to the stake. They might decide to let The Raven and me settle our old score in the circle."

"Fight? You mean with weapons?"

"Knives probably, or hatchets. If it comes to a fair battle between us, I think I can take him."

"You think you can? That's not much consolation for me."

"I'd a hell of a sight sooner face The Raven than the flames of the stake. There's no use thinking about it, Linna. You can't understand the way an Indian mind works. They don't think like we do. We've got tonight. Let's make the most of these hours together."

"But, Rory, I—"

He silenced her with a kiss. "Just love me," he said.

There was no sleep for either of them that night. After they had made love a second and then a third time, they lay close together and talked until the first shafts of purple morning light spilled through the smoke hole of the wigwam.

"I'm so afraid," Linna whispered softly. "Why are the Shawnee doing this to us? Why did they allow you to bathe and come to me last night? Why—"

"For a witch, you are oddly full of questions," Rory teased. He lifted her right hand and positioned it palm to palm, finger to finger against his own larger hand. "How can you be so like me and yet so different?" Rory mused. "I have never met a woman like you." He lowered his head to kiss the tip of her nose, then enfolded her hand in his and brought it down to press against his chest. "I want years with you, Linna . . . enough years to see our son grown with children of his own. But . . . if we don't have them, if this is all there is for us—"

"Don't say that!"

"No, listen." He laid two fingers over her lips. "I am a condemned man. The drums last night promised a trial of courage. If I don't survive, I want you to promise me that you will. I want you to escape and find your way back to our son. He needs you."

"I don't want to live without you."

Rory rained gentle kisses on her eyebrows and forehead. "All my adult life I have sought a violent death for some noble cause," he murmured. "I welcomed it . . . until now. If you fight as I did—first the English soldiers, then the Iroquois and the Ottawa—not being afraid of death but seeking it boldly makes you invincible. Men who don't care if they live or die have an advantage in battle over those who do."

He inhaled deeply, drinking in the scent of her hair and skin. "I was wrong, Linna. Life is better than death. I want to grow old with you, to see these copper tresses turn to silver. But if I die today, I want you to promise you'll live your life to the fullest. I want you to find a man who'll care for you and marry again. Hell, you can marry Donal if you want to—but don't give up on life. I can't think of anyone who deserves happiness more than you."

"You're still jealous of Donal!" Linna wrapped a few strands of Rory's chest hair around her finger and gave it a yank. "I can't believe you're jealous of your little brother."

Rory laughed. "Here I am giving my deathbed confession and you haven't heard a word of it."

"Yes, I have. It's nonsense, and I won't pay any attention to it. You want me to marry Donal and have a dozen kids."

"I didn't say anything about having Donal's babies," he said gruffly.

Linna punched him teasingly. "I love you, you woodenheaded Irishman. Donal is a brother, nothing more. Not now, not ever." She smiled up at him. "Besides, I think Donal's lost his heart to Sarah."

"Sarah?"

"She's a special person, Rory. Sarah's smart and sensible—she saved our lives more than once on the trip here."

"God knows he needs someone with common sense, but Donal's romances last about as long as August showers." Rory rose from the sleeping platform and stretched. "Sun's coming up," he observed. Linna's eyes followed him as he crossed to the entranceway and drank from the water bag, then poured water over the wound on his forearm. The bandage had been lost sometime in the night, but neither of them had noticed.

"Oh, your arm." Linna pulled the discarded dress over her head and hurried to his side. "Let me see," she said.

Rory shrugged off her concern. "It will heal if I live long enough." He found his headband tangled with Linna's on the floor near the fire pit, separated the two, and handed one to Linna. The other he tied around his head.

Linna began to comb out her hair. "You look like an Indian," she said. She blinked back tears. She would not ruin these precious moments with weeping.

"Here, let me do that," Rory offered. Leading her back to the bed, he seated her in front of him and tenderly began to comb the tangles from her auburn hair.

Linna sat like a statue, her eyes fixed on the blackened ashes of the cold fire pit. The steady, rhythmic tug of the wooden comb on her hair and the pressure of Rory's thigh against her leg comforted her.

"Tell me about our son," Rory urged. "Are his eyes still blue?"

"Blue?" She smiled in spite of herself. "Colin's eyes are as brown as Connemara peat. And his lashes—"

"Mishkwe-Tusca!" The Raven's command shattered the quiet morning. "Come out, Mishkwe-Tusca!" he shouted in English. "Come and meet your death!"

"No!" Linna cried. Twisting around, she threw herself against Rory's chest. "No! I won't let you go!"

Rory's mouth descended on hers in a brief, desperate kiss, and then all too swiftly, he pushed her aside. "Be strong," he said huskily. "Uingaokuee can make you a slave if I die, but he can't force you to his bed."

Before she could answer, Rory was across the wigwam and stooping to push aside the deerskin flap. Linna dashed after him.

Outside, the tribe waited in rows, the warriors in front, the women behind. Even children stood and stared, their copper-brown faces peeking wide-eyed from behind their mothers' fringed skirts. The braves were heavily armed and painted. As one, the Shawnee people began to chant, and the solemn dirge gave Linna gooseflesh.

A bear-man danced forward, shuffling back and forth, his body encased in a thick hide, his face covered with a wooden mask and the head of a massive black bear. The teeth of the bear gleamed like old ivory; the eyes were startlingly white shells from some distant sea.

The Shawnee gave a great sigh as the bear-man

shuffled in and out among them, dangling front paws sweeping the ground, his magnificent head swaying to and fro.

Linna could not take her eyes from the bear-man. The chanting seemed to seep under her skin and touch the marrow of her bones. She blinked as her eyes played tricks on her. She knew that the bear-man was not real, but with each turn, with each dip of the body and shake of the head, the figure became less human and more animal.

Two women stepped from the crowd to take her arms, but there was no need. Linna was rooted to the earth, unable to move, caught up in the spell of the twisting, swaying bear.

The chanting grew louder and louder, and the bear-man increased the speed of his movements until he was spinning, pirouetting.

Only Rory seemed unaffected by the bear-man's dance. He stood motionless, his arms folded across his chest, and stared straight ahead. He paid no attention when the bear circled and dipped around him, grazing his chest and legs with the yellow-white claws.

Then, when Linna thought she could stand it no longer, the Shawnee men and women gave a great shout and were silent. The bear-man froze in his tracks, emitted an unearthly growl, and rose to his hind legs directly in front of Rory. An object appeared in his teeth as if by sorcery. One second, there was only the gaping ivory-toothed maw, and then the bear held something in his mouth. He dropped the gray-brown object onto the grass at Rory's feet, shook his front paws defiantly, and moved away, losing himself quickly in the trees at the edge of the camp.

"Ho!" roared the Shawnee tribe in one condemning voice.

Proudly, Rory lowered himself to one knee and picked up the bear-man's offering. He held the object high so that all could see, then fastened the leather thong around his neck.

The Shawnee people gave a great shout of triumph, and Rory turned, giving Linna a clear view of the gruesome token. It was a wolf's paw strung on a necklace of beaten copper disks.

The warriors surged forward in a howling wave and caught Rory, hoisting him on their shoulders and bearing him away toward the cornfields. The women and children ran after the men with hooting cries and the measured clapping of wooden rattles. Drums and barking dogs added to the savage cacophony.

Linna broke from her trance and threw herself against the woman on her right. To her surprise, both squaws loosed their hold on her arms. Linna whirled and tensed her muscles to run after the crowd.

"Wait!"

Linna stared up into the orange and black streaked face of The Raven. With a cry, she tried to duck past him and he stepped in front of her. Running into that bronzed muscular chest was like hitting an oak wall. Linna recoiled and would have fallen if he hadn't caught her. His hand tightened cruelly around her arm.

"It is better if you do not see," Uingaokuee said in precise English. His eyes above the band of orange paint were faintly mocking.

Linna regarded him warily. Pain shot up her arm and she set her teeth together to keep from crying out.

"Mishkwe-Tusca is a dead man," The Raven said.

The words tore from her throat. "What are they doing to him?"

Raven laughed. "Guiinska Tumme, the Dance of the Wolf."

"I don't understand."

"It is the judgment of the high council. Mishkwe-Tusca must prove that he is worthy to be a Shawnee. If he is *olamaalsu*—brave—and Wishemenetoo, the Great Spirit, favors him, he will live. If not"—Uin-gaokuee shrugged—"he will die and his flesh will be meat for the crows." He brought his face so close to Linna's she could smell his foul breath. "But no man has come out alive from Guiinska Tumme."

"Take me to him," Linna insisted. "I will see this Dance of the Wolf."

"As you wish, flame-haired woman. Watch your man die if it pleases you, but soon you will come to my wigwam and heed my commands." The Raven's gaze traversed her body with unconcealed lust. "You belong to me. The council upholds my claim of capture."

"I belong to no one," she flung back defiantly. Her eyes met his stubbornly. "In my own country, I was known as a witch, and men there have sense enough to fear what they cannot control."

Raven sneered, but he let go of Linna's arm. "Go and see if you have the taste for blood, witch!" He stepped aside, and Linna dashed past him to the spot where the screaming crowd milled and stamped.

Heedlessly, she pushed her way through the chanting, jeering Shawnee. She caught sight of Rory, head and shoulders above the old men around him. "Rory!" she called and threw herself forward.

A warrior's hand shot out and jerked her rudely back. *"Mat-tah!"* he shouted in her ear, and pointed to the pit that yawned at her feet.

Trembling, Linna dropped to her knees and clamped her lower lip between her teeth. A deep hole had been dug in the soft, sandy soil of the cornfield. Rory stood on the far side of the pit between two grizzled old warriors, head bowed. A woman—Melassa—was painting Rory's face black. He turned toward her and opened his eyes. For an instant, their eyes met, and then a heart-stopping snarl drew Linna's horrified gaze to the bottom of the pit.

The great gray wolf drew back his lips and snarled again. The animal's bloodred eyes gleamed with hatred for the howling men that surrounded his prison as he paced in ever smaller circles.

"Guiinska Tumme! Guiinska Tumme!" screamed the warriors.

Rory smiled faintly, took a deep breath, and leaped empty-handed down into the pit.

Chapter 24

The Shawnee tribe fell silent as Rory landed at the bottom of the hole, rolled, and came up on his feet. Flattening his gray ears against his head, the wolf crouched low to the ground and growled ominously. Rory backed away a few steps and began to circle the animal.

Still kneeling on the rim of the pit, Linna held her breath as man and beast stalked each other in a primeval battle for survival. Hackles raised, the old wolf bared his teeth; his scarred belly brushed the sand as he challenged the man with slitted eyes and a blood-chilling snarl.

Linna screamed as the wolf sprang at Rory. The animal struck the man full in the chest, and they both went down in a gray blur of fangs and slashing claws. The wolf gave out a high-pitched yelp, and suddenly Rory and the animal were apart. Blood ran down Rory's arms and chest. Again, man and beast circled each other, eyes locked, muscles tensed for the inevitable confrontation. The only sound was the soft crunch of sand beneath Rory's feet and the heavy breathing of man and animal.

Linna watched the carnivore's unblinking eyes take on an unholy gleam as his brain filled with the scent of human blood. In the instant before the wolf launched himself for the kill, Linna seized a spear from the warrior beside her and hurled it into the pit. "Rory!" she shouted.

Rory heard her cry and looked up. The spear flew through the air and landed just beyond his reach. Rory grabbed for the weapon as the wolf began his attack.

The Indian brave gave an angry cry and swung his open palm at Linna. She ducked the blow and threw her shoulder against the man's knee. The force of the Indian's swing carried him over the rim of the pit, and he tumbled into the hole with Rory and the wolf.

The warrior struck the wolf with his hip as he fell, and the animal twisted in midair, sinking his teeth into this new and terrifying enemy. Rory's hands closed around the spear; he lifted it high over his head and plunged it deep into the wolf's broad chest.

The wolf gave an agonizing cry and the fierce light in his slitted eyes dimmed and went out. The beast slumped over the Indian, gave a final surge, and then lay still. Bleeding and shaken, the brave staggered to his feet and backed away. Rory stood facing him, still holding the now bloodied spear.

For what seemed like an eternity, there was silence, and then Rory threw back his head and rent the air with an ancient Gaelic war cry.

It was late afternoon of the same day when Siike came to lead Linna to the council meeting. Linna had been dragged away from the wolf pit before she could exchange a single word with Rory or even see how badly he was hurt. A stern-faced warrior had shoved her into the wigwam and left her there alone with her worst fears.

Siike's expression was not reassuring. Her slender

hands trembled as she offered Linna a plate of corn cakes. "Eat," the Indian woman commanded. "I take you council."

Linna forced herself to chew and swallow two of the flat circles of bread, washing them down with water Siike had brought her. There was no way of knowing when or if she would be allowed to eat again. "Can you tell me what they've done to my husband?" Linna asked.

The girl shook her head. "Iron Shirt and Uingaokuee say Mishkwe-Tusca burn at the stake. Melassa speak for his life. She say your man face wolf with open hands. Mishkwe-Tusca come from pit alive. Wishemenetoo spare him. It make bad luck put him to death." Siike raised her eyes to meet Linna's gaze. "You throw spear. Some want you die alongside Mishkwe-Tusca. Uingaokuee call you witch." Siike's eyes narrowed. "He not want you die."

"The Raven is a blackhearted bastard," Linna murmured.

"Uingaokuee great warrior. It honor he want you in his bed," Siike said with a gentle relentlessness.

"I love my husband," Linna answered. "I do not want The Raven's honor."

Linna shivered as Sarah's last words echoed in her mind. *Anything but honor may be bought. Anything— even a blood price, a death sentence—can be exchanged for something of equal worth . . . A woman is never without resources . . . If that which she desires most is worth the price she must pay.*

"Good."

Linna blinked and stared at the Indian woman.

"Uingaokuee my husband—father my child."

"I'm sorry," Linna stammered. "I didn't know."

Siike shrugged. "As long as you not want Uingaokuee you not need sorry. Come now. Council wait.'' She turned and led the way from the wigwam.

A few old women and children stared as Linna and Siike walked through the village. As they passed one wigwam, Linna could hear the sound of a woman weeping. ''What's wrong?'' Linna asked.

Siike stopped. ''The black demon you call smallpox. Brave who bring you downriver sick.''

''Aatu?'' Linna could not remember seeing the man since they had arrived at the village. ''He's here?''

''He want marry woman this village. He stop, talk. Now sick—maybe die. Maybe all catch black demon . . . woman, man . . .'' Siike's voice cracked. ''. . . baby.'' Anger distorted her features. ''White man's demon. Kill Shawnee. All white man demon same. Powerful demons.''

''Are you sure it's the pox? He seemed healthy enough before,'' Linna insisted.

Siike nodded, and Linna could see the fear in her eyes. ''Fire in head, fire in—'' She broke off as the English words evaded her. ''Demon leave his mark.'' Siike touched Linna's neck and face. ''Aatu bad sick. Shaman make medicine.'' Siike sighed. ''I think Aatu die.''

A child came running toward them and shouted something to Siike.

''We go,'' Siike said to Linna. ''Council speak.''

A noisy crowd of people pressed tightly around the entrance to the largest of the wigwams. Reluctantly they parted to allow Siike and Linna to pass.

The interior of the dwelling was many times larger than that of the wigwam in which Linna had been held prisoner. Center posts held up a high, bark-covered roof, and a small fire burned in the center of the single room. Men and women were packed tightly along the walls. The wigwam was dimly lit and smoky, and thick with the odor of so many humans all gathered together.

Linna blinked to adjust her eyes to the light, then caught sight of Rory sitting cross-legged at the far end of the lodge. His hands were bound behind him, but he seemed alert and unharmed.

Siike nudged Linna in the side. Melassa had risen from a group near the fire and was speaking to Linna.

"Inu-msi-ila-fe-wanu protect you," Siike murmured. With a nod of respect to the circle of elders, she found a seat on the floor near the entrance.

Melassa held out her hand to Linna and spoke first in the Shawnee tongue and then in English so that Linna could understand. "Wife of Mishkwe-Tusca," she intoned clearly, "you have broken a law of the Shawnee. What do you have to say for yourself?"

Linna drew in a deep breath. "Mishkwe-Tusca faced the wolf," she said. "His hands were empty."

A gray-haired man jumped to his feet and shouted angrily at Linna.

"Iron Shirt, my husband, says that you brought the wrath of the Great Spirit down upon us by throwing the spear to Mishkwe-Tusca. He says that you caused the smallpox to seize the body of the warrior Aatu. What say you to this, white woman?"

A wave of irate muttering rose from the onlookers. *"Cut-ta-ho-tha! Cut-ta-ho-tha!"* several chanted, demanding death by fire for Mishkwe-Tusca and his witch woman.

Melassa silenced them with an icy stare. "Speak," she ordered Linna.

Uingaokuee rose from the council circle, his

bronzed, muscular chest gleaming with sweat from the heat of crowded room. "She cannot speak," he said in the Indian language. "She is a witch. With her own mouth she has condemned herself."

"My son says that you are a witch," Melassa translated. "Is this true?"

Linna's gaze locked with Rory's for one brief second. He shook his head.

"Hahhah!" Linna declared, using the Shawnee word for yes. "It is true. I am a witch."

"No!" Rory cried. He leaped up and tried to throw himself between Linna and the council circle, but two warriors stepped from the crowd to seize him firmly between them. "She is not a witch!" Rory shouted. "She lies to protect me."

Iron Shirt raised his fist and roared for order in the council lodge. Melassa's face turned ashen.

"I have the right to speak," Linna said. "Melassa, Iron Shirt, is this true?"

Reluctantly, the old chief nodded. "Speak, witch."

Linna's knees felt as though they were made of water, as it was hard for her to breathe. Her mouth was as dry as sand, but she folded her arms over her chest in imitation of Tumme Uoote and raised her head proudly. "Mishkwe-Tusca is a mighty warrior," she said. "He faced Guiinska Tumme, the Dance of the Wolf, without fear. He entered the pit without a weapon and he killed the wolf. If the Great Spirit had been angry with him, Mishkwe-Tusca's blood—not that of the gray wolf—would turn the sand red. By Shawnee law, Mishkwe-Tusca is proved innocent."

Linna took another breath while Melassa repeated all she had said in the Indian tongue.

Uingaokuee growled a reply. He raised his arms over his head, fists clenched, and shouted to the onlookers. *"Mishkwe-Tusca, cut-ta-ho-tha!"*

"My son says that Mishkwe-Tusca killed the wolf by witchcraft," Melassa said.

"The Raven is an old woman with an old woman's superstition!" Rory yelled. "Shawnee steel killed the wolf, not magic but a lance of wood and steel!"

A figure rose from the shadows, a slim, dignified man of indeterminate age. Around his shoulders was a mantle of lynx skins, and encircling his throat was a bearclaw necklace. He wore no paint, and his hair hung straight to his shoulders. Rawhide leggings and breechcloth covered his body from the waist down; his scarred chest was bare.

The man moved to stand beside Melassa, and Linna detected a strong resemblance between them. Could this be the shaman, the man she had seen before concealed in a bear costume?

The room grew quiet and the man nodded. "Mishkwe-Tusca killed the wolf with a spear," he said softly. The lilting voice carried easily to those in the back of the room. "I am the one to say there was magic. I, Atchmoloh Calumet, shaman, say to you I saw only a warrior's skill."

An old woman cackled. "I saw the spear thrust," she agreed. "I said so from the first. Magic? Bah! These young men see magic if a dog pees into the wind."

The shaman stared at Linna. "Do you still say you are a witch?" Melassa translated his words.

"Yes," Linna repeated. "I was a powerful witch in my country. I have come here because Shaakhan, the wind, sang to me. You hold my husband, and I hold the magic that will protect you from the black demon, smallpox! In Ireland, the country of my birth, we know the secret of fighting off this demon. If you will release Mishkwe-Tusca unharmed, I will give you the magic.''

"Linna, no!" Rory cried. "For God's sake, you don't know what you're saying."

The Shawnee men and women began to talk all at once, some calling for Linna's death and others speaking in her favor. The Raven stared stonily at Linna's face.

Melassa grabbed Linna's arms and pulled her close. The Indian woman's dark eyes were fierce. "Do you speak the truth?" she demanded. "Lie to me and I cannot save you from the flames."

"You know I did not bring the black demon," Linna continued, "but I can send it away. I will trade the secret for the life of Mishkwe-Tusca."

"Hoo!" Iron Shirt clapped his hands for silence. Hesitantly, he glanced at the shaman. "Atchmoloh Calumet? You must pass judgment on the witch."

The shaman dropped to his knees before the fire, flicking his fingers over the coals. A bit of dark powder fell and there was a great flash of light and blue smoke. A woman screamed, and there were frightened murmurs from the crowd. The shaman rose and faced the council circle. "If Shaakhan spoke to this woman, then we must listen. The black demon runs among us. We will see this magic. If it is good magic, then she is a good witch and deserves to live. If a single Shawnee dies of the pox in this village, then we will know her magic is evil and she shall die."

"And Mishkwe-Tusca?" The Raven called. "What of him?"

Atchmoloh Calumet laughed wryly. "The husband of a powerful witch has enough trouble without us adding more. If the woman's magic is true, Mishkwe-Tusca goes free."

Melassa repeated the shaman's words to Linna. "Do you understand that both you and your husband will die if you fail?" she asked sadly.

Linna nodded. "I do. But if I am to save your people, you must do as I say, and I must have the help of Mishkwe-Tusca. I cannot work the magic without him."

Melassa looked at Iron Shirt.

"It shall be as you ask," the old chief said. "But work your magic well, or you shall feel the flames of the stake."

In the privacy of their wigwam an hour later, Rory shook Linna until her teeth rattled. "Are you mad?" he demanded. "The Shawnee never put women to death unless it's in the heat of battle." He shook her again, then yanked her against his chest and held her so close she could feel his heart beating. "My God, Linna," he whispered. "You've condemned yourself to burn at the stake." Rory kissed the top of her head and stroked her hair. When he spoke again, his voice was husky with raw pain. "If I was man enough, I'd kill you with my own hands . . . but I'm not. I love you understand that both you and your husband will die if you fail?" she asked sadly.

Linna wiggled free and backed away from him, hands of her hips in exasperation. "Mary, Joseph, and Holy Jesus," she cried. "Will you never learn to trust me?"

"You said you could cure smallpox!" he flung back. "That's a bald-faced lie, and if you believe you can do it, you're crazier than I thought!"

"You bog-headed Irishman, I never said I could cure the pox! I said I could work magic to keep the Shawnee from getting it."

"And that's not the same thing?"

"No! It's not! Did you think I made the whole thing up? I'm going to inoculate them, using the pox from the sick man."

"Inoculation? I heard they were trying it in Boston, but most physicians consider it little better than murder. Patients die from—"

"No, they don't. Lady Maeve brought a young physician from London when I was thirteen. He inoculated all the family and servants. I had already had smallpox as a child, but Lady Maeve insisted I be inoculated just the same. Mary Aislinn and one of the maids were sick, but no one died. And when there was an outbreak of pox in the village, no one at Mount Beatty caught it. I watched the physician do the inoculations with a goose quill. I can do it, Rory, I know I can."

"It's no good if a person is already infected. Do you realize what chance you're taking?"

Linna sighed. "What chance do we have now?"

Rory opened his arms and she threw herself into them. "I love you," she whispered. "I couldn't let that horrible wolf have you for dinner."

"And I love you, woman," he murmured between kisses, "though you're as daft as a June snow flurry."

"You'll help me then? We'll have to start right away. Every hour counts if we're to inoculate the Shawnee before anyone else gets the sickness."

"Aye, I will," Rory agreed. "But God help us, woman, we'll need a miracle if we're to pull this off."

Rory was the first to be inoculated. Using a steel knife blade, cleansed in a white-hot flame, Linna nicked the skin of his forearm and pressed some of the pus from an infected pox into the incision. One by one the Shawnee people stepped forward to receive the magic. Melassa followed Rory, and the shaman offered his arm next. Only two families refused to be inoculated, and Iron Shirt banished them from the village.

All night Linna worked, heating the knife blade again and again, until her hands were blistered and her eyes swollen from the smoke. Rory stood beside her, speaking to the Indians in their language, soothing frightened children, and lending her his unfaltering strength.

Aatu, the Shawnee already suffering from smallpox, tossed and turned on his bed of pain. There was nothing Linna could do for him except pray and caution his bride-to-be to keep the man warm.

In early morning Linna went to the river and washed away the sweat of the long night. She was too weary to eat more than a few mouthfuls of fish and corn cake, falling onto the sleeping mat like one already dead. For twelve hours she slept with Rory keeping watch beside her. Both knew that there was nothing more to do but wait.

Days passed. Aatu remained critical, but clung to life. The Shawnee waited and watched. Linna had warned them that the black demon would test their courage.

On the sixth day, a child became feverish, quickly followed by others with the same symptom. Men and women complained of headache and thirst, and some people developed smallpox pustules.

"The witch has deceived us," an old woman cried. "Burn her!"

"When the first Shawnee dies," Iron Shirt reminded her.

Rory ran a fever; his eyesight became blurry and he was plagued with a devilish headache.

Linna cared for him, bringing him fresh water and rubbing his forehead.

"It is only the demon," she told Melassa. "My magic is strong. The sickness will pass."

On the fourteenth day, Aatu sat up and called for food. No more of the Shawnee had fallen sick for three days, and Rory's fever was nearly gone.

On the twentieth day, Iron Shirt called a meeting of the high council. Rory and Linna filed anxiously into the lodge to hear the verdict of the elders. To Linna's delight, a weak but obviously recovering Aatu was carried in to witness the decision.

This time, Melassa sat beside Linna. There was only a short discussion before Iron Shirt stood up and silenced the people. He motioned to the shaman, then sat down beside his wife.

Atchmoloh Calumet folded his arms and waited dramatically until even the shifting of feet and bodies stopped. "My people," the shaman said softly. "It is clear to me that Shaakhan speaks to this woman. Her magic is true. We have seen the shadow of the black demon, and he has fled before the power of the Irish witch. What say you?"

Melassa stood and waited to be recognized. "The white woman has kept her promise," she said. "Mishkwe-Tusca must go free."

"Yes! Yes!" came the cries of agreement. "Mishkwe-Tusca must go free."

The shaman turned to Rory. "You may return to your own land," he said. "But come no more to the country of the Shawnee, for we do not forget that you took up arms against your own blood."

Rory stood, placing his fist against his heart in a sign of respect. "I hear and obey, mighty Atchmoloh Calumet. I will take my wife and leave this place at first light."

"No!" The Raven leaped up to stand beside the shaman. "Mishkwe-Tusca can go," he cried, "but the witch must stay. She is too powerful to let go. If she knows this magic, what more does she conceal? With the aid of such a powerful witch, we will be invincible!"

"*Hoo!*" shouted Iron Shirt. "The Raven speaks wisdom. This witch may have the power to turn aside English bullets or to make our warriors invisible as the wind."

A great shout rose above Melassa's protests. Rory caught Linna's arm and lunged toward the entranceway, but they were immediately surrounded.

"You have heard the word of your chief," the shaman intoned. "We promised to give Mishkwe-Tusca his life in exchange for the magic. We promised nothing else. The witch remains!"

"I will not go without my wife!" Rory exclaimed.

"You will go, or you will die," Iron Shirt threatened. "Choose, Mishkwe-Tusca!"

"Go," Linna urged. "For Colin . . ."

"I'll be back," Rory promised in Gaelic as the warriors dragged him from the council lodge. "On the soul of my dead daughter, I swear . . . I'll come for you."

Chapter 25

December 1755

The red and gold and orange autumn leaves, more brilliant than Linna had ever seen, fell from the trees and dried to dull, lifeless brown, crumbling and blowing away, becoming part of the dark Ohio soil. The mild October weather gave way to the chill of November and then the first driving snows of December.

In all these weeks there had been no sign from Rory; he had disappeared as completely as though he had vanished from the earth. Still, Linna's faith in him did not falter. Rory had promised he would return for her, and she knew that if he lived, he would come.

According to Siike, the Shawnee warriors had carried Rory across the river by canoe, given him a bow and a quiver of arrows, a knife, and a pouch containing flint and steel for making fire. Two scouts had followed him through the woods for three days to be certain that Rory was traveling southeast, away from the Shawnee village.

The Raven had taunted Linna with the fact that her husband had deserted her. "He cares nothing for you,"

Uingaokuee had said as he led Linna from the council house. "You belong to me now. You will teach me your witch magic."

"No man can own a witch," she had retorted hotly.

"We will see," The Raven had muttered. "We will see."

Linna's place in the wigwam of Siike and Uingaokuee was that of a slave. Although he already had two wives, Siike and an older woman, H'kah-hih, and three children, it was obvious to Linna that he planned to add her to his seraglio.

The Raven's second wife, H'kah-hih, had her own wigwam next to Siike's. This second wife rarely spoke to Linna or even acknowledged her existence. H'kah-hih's two little girls seemed frightened of the white witch who had suddenly appeared in their father's wigwam. If H'kah-hih did say something, it was in rapid Shawnee and Linna was unable to understand her.

Siike adopted the role of cool, uninvolved supervisor. It was Siike who instructed Linna in her chores: skinning rabbits and other wild game, cleaning fish, scraping hides, and gathering wood. Siike's former friendliness was gone. She knew The Raven wanted Linna for a third wife, and Siike had no intention of making the white woman's place in the family a comfortable one. While never cruel, Siike made sure that Linna received the last scraping of the family cook pot and the toughest bit of overdone meat. The Indian woman had taken away the beautiful dress of soft doeskin and given Linna a shapeless, torn, and stained garment in its place.

"A slave should not be dressed in such finery," Siike had insisted, when she returned the white dress to Melassa. "She should know her place."

But Melassa had only smiled. She had made it clear from the first that she thought kindly of the white witch. Linna might be a slave in the household of Melassa's son, but Melassa had given the unspoken command that no physical harm should come to her.

The jealousy of the women and the ill treatment did not concern Linna; she had suffered worse as a child in her stepfather's house. Even the distasteful task of tanning hides using the brains of animals didn't trouble her. Her main concern was Uingaokuee.

It seemed to Linna as though The Raven's eyes never left her from first light of dawn until the fire burned low at night. He did not touch her, but he often followed when Linna and Siike went to gather wood, and once Linna caught him spying on her when she bathed at the bend in the river. Uingaokuee's constant watching wore away at her nerves; she knew he did it to frighten her, but it was difficult to pretend she didn't notice.

On nights when the weather was clear, Linna was forced to sleep outside under the stars. Ankles and wrists trussed together as though she were a sheep for slaughter, she was tied securely to a post outside the wigwam. A flea-ridden blanket served as her only covering. Often, village dogs would creep close to her in the night, and she welcomed their body warmth despite the smell and the continual scratching.

If it rained or snowed, Siike grudgingly allowed Linna a place near the entranceway of the wigwam. The heat of the fire was pleasant, but trying to sleep in the wigwam within yards of Uingaokuee was almost impossible. The fact that he did not speak a word to Linna or acknowledge her presence in any way did not lessen the menace she felt.

The Raven did not make love to Siike while Linna

was in the wigwam. Some nights he would leave the
hut and go to his second wife. Whenever that happened,
Linna knew that Siike would blame her for it the next
day and would be particularly ill-tempered, finding the
nastiest jobs for Linna to do.

This morning, Linna decided, would be one of those
days. Siike had untied Linna's ropes without speaking
to her, motioned toward the waterskin, then shoved
her toward the door flap. "Water," Siike ordered
sharply. Without watching to see if Linna obeyed, the
Indian woman picked up her baby and began to nurse
him.

Linna shivered as she stepped out into the frosty
December morning. The village was quiet; only a few
dogs stirred and the low murmur of voices came from
the nearby wigwams. Linna walked quickly between
the huts, knowing that there were corn cakes and a
little venison left from the evening meal. If she hurried
back with the water, she could snatch a bite of breakfast
before The Raven returned to the wigwam.

"Stop!"

Linna kept walking, ignoring the deep masculine
voice.

"Wait, witch." Uingaokuee took a few steps in her
direction. "Come here."

"Siike sent me for water," Linna replied stubbornly.

"Siike will carry your water if you come to my
bed," The Raven said. "I will make you first wife,
witch woman."

Linna's eyes flashed a warning. "Take me to your
mat and you will never know a man's pleasures again."

Uingaokuee laughed and came closer. "Wife or
slave, it is the same. You will spread your legs for
me, and you will cry out with the joy of a warrior's
thrusts."

"Touch me and I will curse you with the curse of fire and peat," she dared. "Fire will not warm you, and you will die with a coward's dust in your mouth. The women will laugh at your memory—they will remember you not as a Uingaokuee, The Raven, but as amotshiikus, the turkey-buzzard."

"You try my patience, witch! If you are not careful, I will sell you to the Huron."

Flinging a Gaelic oath at him, Linna turned and walked swiftly toward the river. If Rory didn't come soon, she might be forced to try to escape by herself. She didn't know how long she could tolerate The Raven's bullying without doing something stupid.

As she passed the first canoe, drawn up on the bank, Linna noticed a large hole in the bow. Someone had deliberately damaged the boat; the broken pieces of birchbark lay on the sand. Strange—a canoe was valuable; no Shawnee would dare to vandalize another's property in such a way.

Slipping off her moccasins, Linna waded out into the river. The water was icy cold, but she splashed it on her face and arms. A few yards downstream, another woman was washing her hair. The winter weather never seemed to bother the Indians; young and old, they bathed and swam in the river as long as it was free of ice.

Just as Linna was about to turn back toward the shore, she noticed an empty canoe floating down the river. She paused and stared at it. The canoe was coming downstream, but the village canoes were all drawn up on the bank, and there wasn't another village upstream for miles. Instinctively, she glanced at the other woman to see if she had seen the boat.

Seeing that the Indian squaw's attention was focused elsewhere, Linna waded out a little farther, gasping as the cold water soaked her dress to mid-thigh.

Suddenly, Uingaokuee shouted from the bank behind her, and a man flung aside a deerskin and sat up in the canoe.

"Linna!" Rory swung a paddle over the side and drove it into the water with all his strength. The birchbark canoe shot through the current toward her.

The Raven's war cry split the morning air as Linna dove into the water and began to swim. The cold numbed her body and the deerskin dress weighed her down like lead, but the distance between her and the canoe grew smaller with every stroke. Rory dropped the paddle into the boat and reached out to grab Linna. The little canoe tipped dangerously in the fast water as their hands met and Rory dragged her over the side.

"Get down!" he warned.

Shrieking with fury, Uingaokuee plunged into the river. Behind him, armed men and women were running from the wigwams toward the beach. A musket roared.

Half frozen, Linna crouched in the bottom of the canoe. Rory raised his musket and leveled it at Uingaokuee's chest. The Indian was waist-deep in the river, so close that Linna could see the whites of his eyes.

"Don't shoot!" she cried. "He's unarmed!"

Cursing, Rory dropped the musket and picked up the paddle. A rain of arrows fell around them. Another shot pierced the birchbark inches away from Linna. Rory leaned forward and began to paddle furiously. Caught in the swift current, the little boat leaped ahead like a living thing. In seconds, they were out of range of the bows and around the next bend.

Linna looked back to see the Shawnee braves turning over their canoes and howling with fury. One canoe was in midstream and sinking with two men aboard.

"How—" Linna cried.

Rory grinned back at her. "Sarah! She crept into the village last night and chopped holes in all the canoes."

Linna stared at her husband in disbelief. "You mean—"

"Later, woman," he chided. "Pick up that other paddle and use it. We aren't out of this hornet's nest yet!"

About two miles from the village, a sandbar stretched out into the river on the eastern side. As Linna and Rory brought the canoe downriver, two figures walked out on the sandbar and waved.

"Donal and Sarah," Linna managed to say. She was so cold that she was certain the dress was freezing on her. Her teeth were chattering and her bare feet and fingers were numb.

Donal caught the bow of the canoe and held it while Rory got out and helped Linna onto the sandbar. Sarah rushed forward and threw her arms around Linna.

"You are safe?" the Indian girl asked. Both she and Donal were warmly dressed in leggings and deerskin capes with robes of wolfskin.

Linna nodded, too cold to talk.

"Good," Sarah looked meaningfully at Donal. "We must go," she warned.

Donal hugged his brother and then Linna. "Good luck," he said. "First one to Connemara gets a hundred acres of bottomland," he dared.

Rory caught his hand and squeezed it. "Done," he agreed. "But if I beat you there?"

"Then I'll till it for you," Donal promised.

Rory scooped Linna up in his arms and carried her toward the woods as the canoe shot off down the river with Donal and Sarah. Just inside the trees, Rory bent and picked up two packs. He carried Linna and the packs about a half mile, then stopped and eased her to the ground.

"I've dry clothes in here for you," he said, "and some Huron moccasins like mine. With luck, the Shawnee will follow the river looking for us."

Linna sat on the ground and watched dully as Rory found the clothing. She made no objections as he pulled the soaking deerskin dress off over her head, dried her body with a fur, and dressed her much as Sarah had been dressed.

"Are you all right?" he demanded.

"J-just c-cold," she chattered. Her eyelids felt as though they weighed ten pounds. She knew that she should be afraid of the Shawnee, that she should be overjoyed to see Rory again, but it all seemed too much trouble. She just wanted to lie down and sleep.

"You've got to walk," Rory insisted. "It will warm your body."

"How d-did you know I-I would come to the river?" she asked. She still wasn't certain it wasn't a dream.

"We've been watching for three days. We know you always carried the morning water. I had to get you out before the river froze. We just got lucky when you came down to the river without Siike." Rory frowned. "Why wouldn't you let me kill Uingaokuee?"

"He's not important," she said. "He can't hurt us now."

"He can if he catches us."

"Will they catch us?"

"Not if I can help it. Sarah and Donal are acting as decoys. Uingaokuee's people will be chasing a white man and woman in a canoe. If Sarah and Donal are seen by any Indian along the river, the Shawnee will assume it's us." Rory tugged Linna to her feet. "Let's go. We've got to put distance between us and the river before dark."

"But isn't your plan putting Sarah and Donal in as much danger as we would be?"

"I hope not. It was their idea, and I couldn't come up with a better one. Sarah says there is a Delaware camp downriver. If they can reach it, they should be safe from the Shawnee. The Delaware are as fierce as any tribe, but they consider themselves peacemakers. They don't take kindly to other folks bringing their personal arguments into their villages."

Linna forced one foot ahead of the other. Gradually, feeling returned to her toes and she stopped shivering. She was hard-pressed to keep up with Rory's loping gait. She wondered how much time had passed since they had left the Shawnee village—it seemed like hours, but she knew it couldn't be very long. The sun was still low in the sky.

"We've got to keep going," Rory urged in Gaelic. "If you tire, tell me and I'll carry you."

Linna murmured assent, but she had no intentions of letting Rory carry her. They were headed home, toward New Connemara and Colin. Rory had risked his life to rescue her, and she wouldn't let him down now.

Sometime before dusk, Rory led the way down a gully and into a fast-rushing, rocky stream. They waded for nearly a quarter of a mile in water that grew ever deeper, and then at last, when Linna thought she could go no more, a wide pool and a waterfall appeared before them. To her surprise, Rory continued on through the pool and ducked low, vanishing under the waterfall. Taking a deep breath, Linna followed.

Behind the waterfall was a narrow fissure through

the solid rock. Hesitantly, feeling her way along the damp granite, Linna walked about ten feet and entered a large, dimly lit cave. She looked up at the ceiling and saw a hole no larger than a man's fist. Sunshine poured through it, spilling across the cave floor like a ribbon of spun gold.

"Take off your wet moccasins and leggings," Rory urged. "Use those furs to dry yourself. I'll have a fire going in no time." He crouched before a pile of kindling and took flint and steel from a skin bag.

Linna obeyed quickly. The thought of a warm fire after being so cold and wet was heavenly. As her eyes became accustomed to the semidarkness, Linna saw that the cave was well provisioned. A hindquarter of venison hung from a tree branch wedged in a crack in the ceiling, and a pile of furs formed a sleeping platform in one corner of the room. "How did you know about this place?" she asked.

Rory blew on the tinder and the small spark leaped into a flame. "Tumme Uoote told Sarah about it. We found it together and stocked it. I thought if I could get you away from the village, it would be safer to lie low here for a week or so." He grinned. "Of course, if we do, Donal wins the bet."

"None of the Shawnee knows about the cave?"

Rory stood and stripped off his own wet leggings and moccasins. "I hope to hell they don't," he admitted with a wry grin. "The best part is that there's always mist over the waterfall. We can have a fire here day and night without the smoke giving us away." He put out his arms. "Come here, woman, and give me a kiss. I've worked hard enough for it."

With a cry of delight, Linna threw herself against him. Their lips met and she hugged him tightly. "Rory, Rory," she murmured. "I thought you—"

"Hush," he said. "This is not the time for talking."
With one easy motion, he swept her up in his arms.
"You're a lot of trouble for a Connemara girl," he
said huskily. Quickly, he carried her across the cave
to the bed of furs and laid her down on a thick bearskin.
"I'm cold," he admitted. "Can you warm me?"

Linna laughed and opened her arms to him. "I can
try," she promised between kisses, "I can try."

Connemara Plantation
January 7, 1756

As the sloop nosed the edge of the plantation dock,
Rory leaped onto the wooden planks and pulled Linna
after him. Before the captain could loop the first rope
around a piling, Linna and Rory were running up the
snow-covered hill toward the manor house amid the
shouts of Ty and the excited servants.

Rory and Linna had almost reached the front door
when it was flung open and Sarah, Judith, and Donal
came out to meet them. Sarah was carrying a chubby,
dark-haired toddler.

"Colin!" Linna cried. Then all else faded as a laughing Sarah thrust the baby into her arms. Tears of joy
filled Linna's eyes as she rocked her little son against
her and murmured his name over and over.

Later, in the warm kitchen, when Rory had held the
baby and Linna had been kissed and hugged by all the
family, she was content to curl up in the high-backed
settle with Colin in her arms and the cat Brigand at
her feet. She listened to all that had happened at Connemara in their absence. And for a while, it seemed
as though everyone talked at once, but it didn't matter.
Linna let the tide of family chatter wash over her as

she planted gentle kisses on the soft places of Colin's neck and dark curls.

"Sarah is my wife," Donal declared proudly. "We were wed in Virginia by a priest."

"He knew better than to bring her here if they were living in sin," Judith added with a dry smile. It was obvious to Linna that relations between her mother-in-law and Sarah had improved tremendously since she had last seen them together.

"Married?" Rory echoed in disbelief. "You, little brother?"

"Aye, married. She's a rare woman, my Sarah," Donal said, pulling his plump wife against him and kissing her cheek soundly. "We mean to live at Sherwood if it suits you." Donal grinned. "Near my new bottomland."

"It suits me fine," Rory answered. "I always meant Sherwood to be a wedding gift for you."

"I'm going to live there with them," Judith stated flatly. "You and Linna will have to manage as best you can. Sarah is even more ignorant than Linna of managing a manor—if such a thing is possible."

Linna's head snapped up and she stared at Judith. "You're leaving Connemara?" she stammered. "For good?"

"I asked her to come," Sarah said softly. "There is much to learn if I am to become an Englishwoman. I am good with herbs and growing things, but . . ." She shrugged. "I do not want my new husband to be ashamed of me. We need Mistress Desmond more than you. I hope you will not be angry with me, Linna."

"No . . . no," Linna assured her. "We . . . we will . . ."

"Mother will be close enough for you to ride over

and ask her advice when you need it,'' Rory suggested smoothly.

"You must bring Colin to visit every day," Judith said, holding out her arms for the boy. "He is like my own child."

Reluctantly, Linna stood the baby on his feet and held his hands as he toddled unsteadily toward his grandmother, cooing loudly. "I will," Linna promised. It was clear that Colin, at least, had found a chink in Judith's armor. It could be that he would be the bridge between her and her sharp-tongued mother-in-law.

"Mother shipped a record crop of tobacco while we were gone," Donal continued. "Prices are supposed to be up in London, but . . ." Donal got to his feet, eyes twinkling. "I've saved the best news for last. Wait here."

Linna began to nod sleepily before the fire as they waited for Donal to come back. It felt so good to just sit here safe and warm after the long, dangerous journey on foot from the Ohio country. Even Judith's crisp voice was soothing. Colin was clutching the fringe on his father's deerskin leggings and swaying back and forth. As the baby jabbered happily, Linna could catch glimpses of pearly white teeth.

"I think it's about time I got Linna up to bed," Rory suggested. "We didn't stop to sleep last night. There'll be time for talk tomorrow." He passed Colin to Sarah and gathered Linna up in his arms. "Ready for bed, sweetheart?"

Rory had reached the bottom of the staircase when Donal came out of the great room with a packet of papers.

"You'll want to see this," Donal said. "It came in

October with the tobacco fleet. It's from Linna's father in Ireland.''

"From Sir Edmond?'' Linna was instantly awake. "Put me down.''

Rory lowered her gently, supporting her with his arm around her shoulder. "Let me see,'' he said to Donal.

Donal grinned. "He sent back the dowry, Rory—all of it. Mother didn't know if you were alive or dead, so she opened it. He sent gold coin.'' Donal fumbled through the envelopes and produced a wrinkled letter. "This is addressed to you, Linna. I'm afraid Mother opened it, too.''

Linna sunk down on the step, unfolded the paper, and began to skim over the contents in the dim hall light.

. . . I fail to understand your husband's reluctance to accept the dowry. Rory Desmond contracted to marry my daughter, and so he has.

. . . since the tragic death of your brother, Thomas, in early summer. He stepped on a nail at school, and the minor injury turned to lockjaw.

My own health is not good and my only remaining legal heir, Mary Aislinn, has entered a religious house against my will. I am determined that Mount Beatty and my estates pass intact to my own blood rather than the Catholic Church or the Crown. Therefore, I have taken legal steps to formally adopt you and to name any male children born to you and a lawful husband as my sole heirs. If you produce no male issue, the estate will pass to nephews of Lady

Maeve and their issue.

It is my fervent wish that you and your husband return to Ireland to take up your rightful position. I can assure you that Rory Desmond will be safe from prosecution.

> Warm regards,

> Your father,
> Edmond Beatty

Linna dropped the letter into her lap and stared at Rory. "Sir Edmond says that he is adopting me as his legal daughter, and that our oldest male child will become his heir." She twisted her hands together. "Can it be a joke?"

Donal laughed. "If it is a joke, it's a fine one. His gold coin is solid enough, and Mother has delivered the legal papers to her solicitor in Annapolis. It is all very legal, and so—might I add—are you, little sister. Or should I say Lady Mary Aislinn?"

"Linna will do fine."

"Come, woman," Rory said. "Rich heiress or not, it's to bed with you. You're the color of new cream. We'll sort all this out in the morning."

"But Sir Edmond wants us to return to Ireland!" Linna said. "He'd make you an Irish lord."

Rory lowered his head and gazed steadily into her eyes. "Do you want to go back?"

"No, never." A smile tilted the corners of her lips. "I'd be a fool to leave the promised land—wouldn't I?"

"You'd give up the chance to go home?" Donal asked his brother.

"I am home," Rory replied simply.

Linna's arms tightened around his neck as he carried

her up the wide stairs to their bedchamber. "You may regret it in the years to come," she whispered teasingly, "when our son wants to run off into the wilderness and play Indian."

"Hush, woman," he reprimanded. "You talk too much." He silenced her willing lips with a kiss.

The crackling fire on the hearth cast a warm glow across the room as Rory carried Linna to the poster bed and laid her down gently. Linna sighed and snuggled against the feather pillows. "Am I truly forgiven," she asked, "for deceiving you and—"

Rory's deep laugh echoed in the room. "This is another of your tricks, isn't it? Soon you will have me apologizing again, you'll begin to weep, and I'll be forced to kiss your tears away." He stripped the shirt off over his head and leaned over her. His voice dropped to a husky brogue. "Would ye be havin' sleep this night, me darlin', or nay?"

Linna opened her arms. "Do I have a choice?" Their lips met again and the playful kiss flared into open passion.

"God, woman," he groaned, tugging at his breeches. "You'll be the death of me." He slid in beside her and pulled a thick quilt over them.

Linna snuggled against him, savoring the utter joy of his embrace. "I love you," she whispered simply.

"Show me."

"It may take a while."

"No matter, woman . . . we've got a lifetime."

"Truly?"

"Aye."

"Then let's not waste a minute of it."

Neither heard the rising song of the wind or the soft tap of snowflakes against the windowpanes.

JUDITH E. FRENCH

JUDITH E. FRENCH and her husband of nearly thirty years make their home on a small farm in Kent County, Delaware. They are the proud parents of four children, and the grandparents of four grandchildren. Coincidentally, one of their daughters is also a published romance author. Judith has been writing professionally since 1959 and is known locally for her collection of authentic folk tales and ghost stories. She and her husband are presently restoring an 18th-century farmhouse that has been in the author's family since 1743. Judith E. French's other interests include caring for her dairy goats and Siamese cats, collecting Indian artifacts and antiques, and participating as a member of Romance Writers of America. She is also the author of four previous Avon Romances, *Tender Fortune*, *By Love Alone*, *Starfire*, and *Bold Surrender*.